Charles Francis Horne

The Sacred Books of the East

Volume 6

Charles Francis Horne

The Sacred Books of the East
Volume 6

ISBN/EAN: 9783337364168

Printed in Europe, USA, Canada, Australia, Japan

Cover: Foto ©Andreas Hilbeck / pixelio.de

More available books at **www.hansebooks.com**

THE SACRED BOOKS AND EARLY
LITERATURE OF THE EAST

─────────────

VOLUME VI

─────────────

MEDIEVAL ARABIC, MOORISH,
AND TURKISH

─────────────

In Translations by

E. J. W. GIBB of the Royal Asiatic Society; STANLEY LANE-POOLE, Litt.D., Professor of Arabic, Trinity College, Dublin; ARMINIUS VAMBERY, LL.D., Professor of Oriental Languages, University of Budapest; THOMAS CHENERY, M.A., Former Professor of Arabic at Oxford University; ERNEST RENAN, Former Professor of Hebrew, College of France; CLAUD FIELD, M.A.; and other authorities.

With brief Bibliographies by
PROF. CHARLES C. TORREY, LL.D., and PROF. EDWARD H. JOHNS, Ph.D.

─────────────

With an Historical Survey and Descriptions by
PROF. CHARLES F. HORNE, PH.D.

PARKE, AUSTIN, AND LIPSCOMB, INC.
NEW YORK   LONDON

═══════════════

"Let there be light." —GENESIS 1, 3.

*"There never was a false god, nor was there ever really a false religion, unless you call a child a false man.""*MAX MÜLLER.

8

CONTENTS OF VOLUME VI

LITERATURES DESCENDED FROM THE ARABIC

10

The Most Renowned Piece of Pure Literature in Arabic.

ILLUSTRATIONS IN VOLUME VI

SACRED BOOKS AND EARLY LITERATURE

OF

THE MEDIEVAL ARABS, MOORS, AND TURKS

INTRODUCTION
HOW THE TEACHING OF MOHAMMED SPREAD INTO MANY LANDS AND CREATED MANY LITERATURES

THE wide-spread Arabic empire and religion originated with Mohammed and was founded on his book, the Koran. That tremendously important work, with the primitive Arabic literature of even earlier date, formed the theme of our preceding volume. We have now to trace the Arabic literature and thought which, with the expanding of the Mohammedan empire, spread over a large part of the Eastern world. Geographically that empire reached from its Arabian center eastward through Babylonia and Persia into India, westward through all North Africa into Spain, southward through Egypt into the wilds of Central Africa, and northward through Asia Minor to all the Turkish possessions. Through much of this vast region, Arabic became the common speech, and books were written in its tongue. Even in our own day, Arabic continues as the language of a considerable part of Turkey in Asia, of Egypt, and of all North Africa.

We can scarcely, however, regard as a unit all the varying Mohammedan literatures of these many lands. The Persians, for example, retained their own language and wrote in it a literature of Mohammedan religious spirit, so important that we shall devote to it a later separate volume. Our present task, therefore, will confine itself to tracing through the Middle Ages the more strictly Arabian development. This includes first, the spread of literature and thought among the Arabs themselves, or among those people who completely adopted the Arabic faith and speech. Second, it includes the literature of the Moors, or semi-Arabic peoples,

14

of North Africa and Spain. And third, it leads us to the Turks, the last Mohammedan conquerors, who took up and carried on Arabic tradition, though in a language and spirit more Tartar than Arabian.

For the purely Arabic development, that is for the literature and thought that sprang directly from Mohammed's teaching, we turn first to the "Sunan," or traditions about Mohammed. After the prophet's death in A.D. 632, and while his followers were spreading his teachings by force of arms, they talked much of the doings and sayings of their adored master. Then, long after his own writings had been gathered in the official form of the Koran, a similar collection was made of what might be termed his unofficial teaching, that is of all his remembered words, the ideas which he had not proclaimed as inspired by God, but had given forth in ordinary conversation between man and man. The details of his life were also treasured. Thus sprang up the "Sunan," from which we may learn as much of Mohammed the man, and of the daily life and thought of his people, as from the Koran we learn of Mohammed the poet and of the poetic spirit of Arabia.

For a long time the Arabs developed no other religious literature than this. Of the third leader of their new faith, the Caliph Omar, there is a well-known legend which may be untrue in fact but is intensely true to the fanatic spirit of the Caliph and his followers. It says that when Omar's armies conquered Egypt the scholars of Alexandria entreated him to protect the books of their great library, the largest in the world. Instead, Omar ordered the thousands of manuscripts to be used to feed the fires of the public baths; and he based the destruction upon this verdict: "If these books disagree with the Koran they are evil; if they agree they are unnecessary."

15

The Arabic literary spirit was thus compelled to cling to its old pre-Mohammedan form. That is, it expressed itself only in brief personal poems, in skilfully phrased epigrams, satiric couplets, or "rubaiyat," called forth by a sudden occasion. A collection of the best known of these poems, gathered from successive ages of gay and dashing singers, is given at the close of our Arabic section.

Gradually, however, a change came over the victorious Arab race. The warriors lost their intense religious inspiration. They fought among themselves for place and power. The enormous wealth which they had conquered, with its resulting temptations to luxury and ease and empty vanity, weakened them, lured them from both the high moral strength which they had really attained, and from the fanatic frenzy of faith which had been their pride. They removed the capital of their empire from the holy cities of Arabia, first to Damascus and then to Bagdad, the wonderful dream-city of splendor which they built upon the banks of the ancient Tigris river.

Under these gorgeous Caliphs of Bagdad, such as Haroun al Raschid of "Arabian Nights'" fame, a civilization developed which Mohammed would never have recognized as his own, which he would indeed have been the first to repudiate. Unrestrained power bred a callous indifference to the sufferings of its victims, and even a barbarous delight in inflicting torture. The tyranny of the ruling classes bred a corresponding falsity in their helpless but supple servitors. Truth, the chief virtue in Mohammed's teaching, became unknown in human intercourse, except as a poetic ideal. From their priest-king down, through all the ranks of society, men talked much of the virtues, while surrendering themselves almost wholly to the passions. One might of course speak cynically of mankind's having found this somewhat true in every age, but seldom has the tragic contrast between the ideal and the actual been brought into such sharp and visible form as in the medieval world of Bagdad.

From this fertile though unhealthy soil a new literature sprang up, typical of the time and place. Here were centered the wealth and leisure and most of what survived of the culture of ancient Asia and Africa. So wit and learning journeyed there as well. At first the new literature found voice mainly as history or biography, or as a rather crude form of these collections of anecdotes purporting to give the virtues and chief events in the lives of former caliphs. Among the writers of these semi-biographic tales, by far the most noted and most noteworthy is Masoudi (died A.D. 957). His huge work, the "Golden Meadows," fills many volumes, from which we give the most attractive anecdotes. While such tales must not be taken as genuine history, they teach us very clearly the spirit of their age.

After these loose histories, a more careful science developed. The real learning of the Arab scholars of the eleventh and twelfth centuries far outranked that of their European and Christian contemporaries. As yet the various fields of science were scarcely differentiated; the student took all knowledge for his province. The earliest Arab writer, who may perhaps be regarded as a genuine historian, in contrast to the previous romancers, was Al Biruni (973-1048), whose "Chronology" our volume quotes. But Al Biruni was far more than an historian; he was a leading scientist of his day and also a geographer, his work on "India" being almost as celebrated as his "Chronology." Of even greater fame in science than Al Biruni was Avicenna (980-1037), a sort of universal genius, known first as a physician. To his works on medicine he afterward added religious tracts, poems, works on philosophy, on logic, on physics, on mathematics, and on astronomy. He was also a statesman and a soldier, and he is said to have died of debauchery. He is famed as the most versatile and brilliant member of a versatile and brilliant race.

With the increasing freedom of scientific thought and speech which Avicenna typifies, there sprang up among the Eastern Mohammedans a new religious impulse. They began to examine more carefully the faith which they had before accepted blindly. To this age therefore we owe the writings of Al Ghazali (1049-1111), whom some of his own countrymen have regarded as second only to Mohammed as a teacher of their religion. Indeed, it was a common saying of his day that "If there were still prophets in the world Al Ghazali would be one."

Western scholars have, some of them, gone still further in their admiration of Al Ghazali, declaring him to have been one of the world's greatest thinkers, whom his Mohammedan contemporaries never sufficiently appreciated, and to whose high moral stature the Mohammedan world has not even yet grown up. Among his writings the most interesting and useful to modern readers is his "Rescuer from Error," a sort of spiritual autobiography, his account of his own growth in religious faith. This striking book our volume gives in full.

From Al Ghazali, or even from before his time, dates the great flow of commentaries on the Koran. These half-philosophical, half-fanatical discussions would have seemed irreligious to the earliest Mohammedan age. The Koran had been originally accepted as perfect, and therefore as completely clear. But now the analytic spirit of the Semite reasserted itself; and even as the Hebrews in their Biblical commentaries weighed every "and" and "but" and every carelessly made letter in their Holy Book, so now the Mohammedan "mullahs," or priests, began to draw deductions from their law, to interpret and so develop it. Among these commentators two are chiefly celebrated. Zamakhshari (1074-1143) was perhaps the most learned and the shrewdest, but his ideas have seemed to his coreligionists a little too radical, too independent of Mohammed, daring almost to question the divine inspiration of the prophet. Therefore the work of Zamakhshari's more submissive successor of a century later, Al Baidawi, has gradually superseded the older book as the favorite exposition of the Koran. The Western reader, however, will distinctly prefer the independence of Zamakhshari.

Into the lighter literature of the medieval Arabs we need not look too far. They had their wholly unreligious and fantastic romances such as the "Arabian Nights." This famous work, however, draws largely upon Persian sources. Indeed, as our later Persian volume will emphasize, most of the pure romance of later Arab literature is of Persian origin, and may best be studied in the Persian books. There is, however, an intermediate class of tale peculiarly Arabian. This is the mingling of romance with poetry and moral teachings, just as the earlier historians had mingled it with history. Most celebrated in this peculiar class of semi-religious, semi-poetic romances is the work presented in this volume, the "Assemblies" of Al Hariri (1054-1122). Just as Masoudi stands to his race for history, Al Biruni for geography, Avicenna for science, Al Ghazali for philosophy, and Zamakhshari and Al Baidawi for religious study, so does Al Hariri stand for literary skill, for brilliancy and humor. His "Assemblies" is the Arabs' chief purely literary achievement.

MOORISH LITERATURE

19

In the year 1258 Bagdad was stormed and conquered by a Tartar general. It is true that most of the ravaging Tartars finally adopted the religion of the conquered, and so the region continued to obey in religious matters a Mohammedan caliph; but the rule of the Arabs, which had been long undermined by Persian influences, ended definitely with the fall of Bagdad. From the time of that disaster we must look to other lands for the continuation of a semi-Arabic literature.

Chief of the secondary developments from the Arabian stock was the remarkable and justly celebrated civilization of the Moors in Spain. The fame of medieval Arabic scholarship was carried to its climax by these first Mohammedan invaders of Europe. In the first wild onrush of Arabian conquest most of Spain was captured in the year A.D. 712, captured by an army having leaders of pure Arab blood, but with followers mainly of the semi-Arabic, or Moorish, people of North Africa. In the year 756 this Moorish kingdom in Spain broke completely from the Arabian Caliph and set up a priest-king of its own, a caliph whose capital was at Cordova in Spain, and whose connection with the older Arab world was only one of race and religion and not of empire. Our Hebraic volume has already spoken of the remarkable Hebrew writers and philosophers who flourished within the shelter of this Cordova caliphate. The Arabs themselves were not less able than their Hebrew servitors.

Here then, under the sunny skies of Southern Spain, far, far indeed from the first centers of Semitic civilization, was the last brilliant blossoming of distinctively Semitic thought. We have in our previous volumes traced the growth of Semitic thought and of the Semitic religious progress from their earliest home by the Euphrates river, where the Babylonian and the desert Arab warred in unrecognized brotherhood of race. Now we are ready to glance briefly at them in Spain, the last strong kingdom they were to possess, and the last literature of note which the Semites, except as scattered members of other communities, were to give the world.

Among the Arabic writers of Spain the most noted is the scientist and philosopher, Averroes (1126-1198). To Mohammedans he is the religious thinker, who strove to harmonize their faith with the advancing science of a later day, and who opposed his practical, rational spirit to the mysticism of Al Ghazali. To the European world he is the celebrated commentator on that greatest of philosophers, Aristotle. As the voice of Aristotle, Averroes thus became the leading teacher and philosopher of his day; he is the link which connects our present thought and science with the first splendor of independent inquiry under the Greeks. The name of Aristotle, the chief scientific teacher of all the world, is thus united forever with that of the great Arab teacher, Averroes.

Moorish literature was also a shrine of poetry and romance, though most of these lighter writings have only been preserved to us through the Spanish tongue. Our own Washington Irving found in these Moorish tales an inspiration for his genius, and has turned many of them into English. Others will be found included in our volume.

TURKISH LITERATURE

Of the Turkish literature we need speak but briefly. The Turks were not Semites, but a Tartar or East Asiatic stock who, after wandering into Western Asia, accepted the Mohammedan faith about A.D. 1288. At the very moment when the vast Mohammedan empire was crumbling to pieces, assailed by pagan Tartar hordes and crusading

Christian armies from without, and withering from spiritual decadence within, the Turks took up the waning faith, and with the energy of new and younger converts carried it onward to the military conquests which built up the Turkish Empire.

This new empire soon included geographically most of the older Arab Empire; but the Turks brought to their new faith only the dubious glory of victory in war. They added little, either to its thought or to its literature. They were, in fact, a nation still semi-barbaric, strong in the natural virtues of faith and honesty and a rude kindliness, but wholly lacking in the subtlety and intellectual keenness which could have advanced Mohammedan thought.

Hence we shall find in their literature, at first, only childish tales, echoes of the childhood of the world, magic stories close akin to those of our own fairyland. Then comes a native poetry, not rising to remarkable heights in any one great poet, but full of a warm human love of romance and justice. Later we come to more thoughtful and elaborate writings, but these incline to deal with the practical world rather than with that of religion and speculative thought. So that we close our Turkish section with what is perhaps the most valuable piece of early Turkish literature, a work of travel, the celebrated autobiography of Sidi Ali Reis.

ARABIC LITERATURE

THE SUNAN
THE DEEDS AND SAYINGS OF MOHAMMED AS
PRESERVED BY
HIS FOLLOWERS

"The proof of a Mohammedan's sincerity is that he pays no heed to what is not his business."

—SUNAN OF ABU DA'UD.

"The sayings [of the Sunan] are very numerous and very detailed; but how far they are genuine it is not easy to determine."

—STANLEY LANE-POOLE.

"The first thing which God created was a pen, and he said to it, 'Write.'"

—THE SUNAN.

THE SUNAN

(INTRODUCTION)

THE Sunan, or "traditions," of Mohammed are now gathered in six books, though two of these are more specifically called the Sahihs, or "sincere books." These six works bear to Mohammedanism much the same relation as the Four Gospels do to Christianity. That is to say, they are the accounts of the prophet's life as handed down by his disciples. Of course to the Mohammedans the Sunan are not the main source of teaching. That is the Koran, which, as we have seen, is Mohammed's own book, dictated by the prophet himself. Moreover, the Sunan do not approach Mohammed with anything like the same accuracy and closeness with which the Gospels approach Jesus. The Sunan are slight and fragmentary traditions, gathered from every possible source at an interval of more than two centuries after their prophet's death. They have, however, been accepted as holy books or "canons" of the Mohammedan faith. Much of the Mohammedan religious law of to-day is founded on them; and they are taught in all the schools and made the basis of many a hair-splitting argument about right and wrong.

Unlike the Christian religion, that of Mohammed sprang immediately into world-wide power; hence no sooner was the prophet dead than every companion of the revered teacher, every listener who had ever heard him speak, narrated to eager audiences each remembered trifle. Naturally these became exaggerated in the telling. Moreover, when rival caliphs fought and slew one another, each claiming rightful heirship from the prophet, their followers would inevitably invent traditions to justify each leader's claim. Exaggeration, if not direct falsehood, soon became inextricably mixed with fact. When, later on, men tried to set their faith upon a firmer basis, they sought to sift these manifold traditions and decide which were worthy of belief.

The first man who set down these sifted traditions in a book was Al Bukhari. He traveled all over the Arab Empire to gather all the tales he could, and he continued elaborating on his book, the first Sahih, until his death in A.D. 870. Al Bukhari himself tells us that in his travels he gathered six hundred thousand tales about Mohammed. Of these he admitted to his Sahih, as being most trustworthy, a little over seven thousand. The second Sahih, written by a follower of Al Bukhari, was garnered from three hundred thousand tales.

Of slightly later date than these two works were the four Sunan, founded partly on the earlier books, but built upon a stricter critical analysis of what should be accepted, and written after an even wider gathering of all the legends of the empire. Hence the Sunan include the earlier books, and the entire collection is commonly spoken of by the later name. When, however, we speak of these Sunan as a "critical" selection from the million legends, the modern reader must not think of this as implying modern scientific criticism and analytical accuracy. Each tale was chiefly accepted on the ground that, in the series of men by whom it was said to have been handed down through the generations, all the men were known and all were of reputed trustworthiness.

That is to say, in an age already become notorious for its lack of veracity, a superficial confidence in individual veracity, extending back through many links for over two hundred years, was accepted as the ultimate proof of truth.

The most widely read and quoted of the Sunan is that of Abu Da'ud, who sums up his own work by declaring that only four of all the thousands of religious rules he has gathered need be remembered by each man for his own religious guidance. These four laws Abu Da'ud gives as follows: "Actions will be judged according to intentions. The proof of a Moslem's sincerity is that he pays no heed to that which is not his business. No man is a true believer unless he desires for his brother that which he desires for himself. That which is lawful is clear, and that which is unlawful likewise, but there are certain doubtful things between the two, from which it is well to abstain."

SELECTIONS FROM THE
SUNAN
OR, SAYINGS AND TRADITIONS OF MOHAMMED

When God created the creation he wrote a book, which is near him upon the sovran throne; and what is written in it is this: "Verily my compassion overcometh my wrath."

Say not, if people do good to us, we will do good to them, and if people oppress us, we will oppress them: but resolve that if people do good to you, you will do good to them, and if they oppress you, oppress them not again.

God saith: Whoso doth one good act, for him are ten rewards, and I also give more to whomsoever I will; and whoso doth ill, its retaliation is equal to it, or else I forgive him; and he who seeketh to approach me one cubit, I will seek to approach him two fathoms; and he who walketh toward me, I will run toward him; and he who cometh before me with the earth full of sins, but joineth no partner to me, I will come before him with an equal front of forgiveness.

There are seven people whom God will draw under his own shadow, on that day when there will be no other shadow: one a just king; another, who hath employed himself in devotion from his youth; the third, who fixeth his heart on the mosque till he return to it; the fourth, two men whose friendship is to please God, whether together or separate; the fifth, a man who remembereth God when he is alone, and weepeth; the sixth, a man who is tempted by a rich and beautiful woman, and saith, Verily I fear God; the seventh, a man who hath given alms and concealed it, so that his left hand knoweth not what his right hand doeth.

The most excellent of all actions is to befriend any one on God's account, and to be at enmity with whosoever is the enemy of God.

Verily ye are in an age in which if ye abandon one-tenth of what is ordered, ye will be ruined. After this a time will come when he who shall observe one-tenth of what is now ordered will be redeemed.

Concerning Prayer

Angels come among you both night and day; then those of the night ascend to heaven, and God asketh them how they left his creatures: they say, We left them at prayer, and we found them at prayer.

The rewards for the prayers which are performed by people assembled together are double of those which are said at home.

Ye must not say your prayers at the rising or the setting of the sun: so when a limb of the sun appeareth, leave your prayers until her whole orb is up: and when the sun beginneth to set, quit your prayers until the whole orb hath disappeared; for, verily she riseth between the two horns of the devil.

No neglect of duty is imputable during sleep; for neglect can only take place when one is awake: therefore, when any of you forget your prayers, say them when ye recollect.

When any one of you goeth to sleep, the devil tieth three knots upon his neck; and saith over every knot, "The night is long, sleep." Therefore, if a servant awake and remember God, it openeth one knot; and if he perform the ablution, it openeth another; and if he say prayers, it openeth the other; and he riseth in the morning in gladness and purity:

28

otherwise he riseth in a lethargic state.

When a Moslem performeth the ablution, it washeth from his face those faults which he may have cast his eyes upon; and when he washeth his hands, it removeth the faults they may have committed, and when he washeth his feet, it dispelleth the faults toward which they may have carried him: so that he will rise up in purity from the place of ablution.

Of Charity

When God created the earth it began to shake and tremble; then God created mountains, and put them upon the earth, and the land became firm and fixed; and the angels were astonished at the hardness of the hills, and said, "O God, is there anything of thy creation harder than hills?" and God said, "Yes, water is harder than the hills, because it breaketh them." Then the angel said, "O Lord, is there anything of thy creation harder than water?" He said, "Yes, wind overcometh water: it doth agitate it and put it in motion." They said, "O our Lord! is there anything of thy creation harder than wind?" He said, "Yes, the children of Adam giving alms: those who give with their right hand, and conceal from their left, overcome all."

The liberal man is near the pleasure of God and is near paradise, which he shall enter into, and is near the hearts of men as a friend, and he is distant from hell; but the niggard is far from God's pleasure and from paradise, and far from the hearts of men, and near the fire; and verily a liberal ignorant man is more beloved by God than a niggardly worshiper.

A man's giving in alms one piece of silver in his lifetime is better for him than giving one hundred when about to die.

29

Think not that any good act is contemptible, though it be but your brother's coming to you with an open countenance and good humor.

There is alms for a man's every joint, every day in which the sun riseth; doing justice between two people is alms; and assisting a man upon his beast, and with his baggage, is alms; and pure words, for which are rewards; and answering a questioner with mildness is alms, and every step which is made toward prayer is alms, and removing that which is an inconvenience to man, such as stones and thorns, is alms.

The people of the Prophet's house killed a goat, and the Prophet said, "What remaineth of it?" They said, "Nothing but the shoulder; for they have sent the whole to the poor and neighbors, except a shoulder which remaineth." The Prophet said, "Nay, it is the whole goat that remaineth except its shoulder: that remaineth which they have given away, the rewards of which will be eternal, and what remaineth in the house is fleeting."

Feed the hungry, visit the sick, and free the captive if he be unjustly bound.

Of Fasting

A keeper of fasts, who doth not abandon lying and slandering, God careth not about his leaving off eating and drinking.

Keep fast and eat also, stay awake at night and sleep also, because verily there is a duty on you to your body, not to labor overmuch, so that ye may not get ill and destroy yourselves; and verily there is a duty on you to your eyes, ye must sometimes sleep and give them rest; and verily there is a duty on you to your wife, and to your visitors and guests that come to see you; ye must talk to them; and nobody hath kept fast who fasted always; the fast of three days in every month is equal to constant fasting: then keep three days' fast in every month.

Of Reading the Koran

The state of a Moslem who readeth the Koran is like the orange fruit, whose smell and taste are pleasant; and that of a Moslem who doth not read the Koran is like a date which hath no smell, but a sweet taste; and the condition of any hypocrite who doth not read the Koran is like the colocynth which hath no smell, but a bitter taste; and the hypocrite who readeth the Koran is like the sweet bazil, whose smell is sweet, but taste bitter.

Read the Koran constantly; I sware by him in the hands of whose might is my life, verily the Koran runneth away faster than a camel which is not tied by the leg.

Of Labor and Profit

Verily the best things which ye eat are those which ye earn yourselves or which your children earn.

Verily it is better for one of you to take a rope and bring a bundle of wood upon his back and sell it, in which case God guardeth his honor, than to beg of people, whether they give him or not; if they do not give him, his reputation suffereth and he returneth disappointed; and if they give him, it is worse than that, for it layeth him under obligations.

A man came to the Prophet, begging of him something, and the Prophet said, "Have you nothing at home?" He said, "Yes, there is a large carpet, with one part of which I cover

31

myself, and spread the other, and there is a wooden cup in which I drink water." Then the Prophet said, "Bring me the carpet and the cup." And the man brought them, and the Prophet took them in his hand, and said, "Who will buy them?" A man said, "I will take them at one silver piece." He said, "Who will give more?" This he repeated twice or thrice. Another man said, "I will take them for two pieces of silver." Then the Prophet gave the carpet and cup to that man, and took the two pieces of silver, and gave them to the helper, and said, "Buy food with one of these pieces, and give it to your family, that they may make it their sustenance for a few days; and buy a hatchet with the other piece and bring it to me." And the man brought it; and the Prophet put a handle to it with his own hands, and then said, "Go, cut wood, and sell it, and let me not see you for fifteen days." Then the man went cutting wood, and selling it; and he came to the Prophet, when verily he had got ten pieces of silver, and he bought a garment with part of it, and food with part. Then the Prophet said, "This cutting and selling of wood, and making your livelihood by it, is better for you than coming on the day of resurrection with black marks on your face."

Acts of begging are scratches and wounds by which a man woundeth his own face; then he who wisheth to guard his face from scratches and wounds must not beg, unless that a man asketh from his prince, or in an affair in which there is no remedy.

The Prophet hath cursed ten persons on account of wine: one, the first extractor of the juice of the grape for others; the second, for himself; the third, the drinker of it; the fourth, the bearer of it; the fifth, the person to whom it is brought; the sixth, the waiter; the seventh, the seller of it; the eighth, the eater of its price; the ninth, the buyer of it; the tenth, that person who hath purchased it for another.

Merchants shall be raised up liars on the day of resurrection, except he who abstaineth from that which is unlawful, and doth not swear falsely, but speaketh true in the price of his goods.

The taker of interest and the giver of it, and the writer of its papers and the witness to it, are equal in crime.

The holder of a monopoly is a sinner and offender.

The bringers of grain to the city to sell at a cheap rate gain immense advantage by it, and he who keepeth back grain in order to sell at a high rate is cursed.

He who desireth that God should redeem him from the sorrows and difficulties of the day of resurrection must delay in calling on poor debtors, or forgive the debt in part or whole.

A martyr shall be pardoned every fault but debt.

Whosoever has a thing with which to discharge a debt, and refuseth to do it, it is right to dishonor and punish him.

A bier was brought to the Prophet, to say prayers over it. He said, "Hath he left any debts?" They said, "Yes." He said, "Hath he left anything to discharge them?" They said, "No." The Prophet said, "Say ye prayers over him; I shall not."

Give the laborer his wage before his perspiration be dry.

Of Fighting for the Faith

We came out with the Prophet, with a part of the army, and a man passed by a cavern in which were water and verdure, and he said in his heart, "I shall stay here, and retire from the world." Then he asked the Prophet's

33

permission to live in the cavern; but he said, "Verily I have not been sent on the Jewish religion, nor the Christian, to quit the delights of society; but I have been sent on the religion inclining to truth, and that which is easy, wherein is no difficulty or austerity. I swear by God, in whose hand is my life, that marching about morning and evening to fight for religion is better than the world and everything that is in it: and verily the standing of one of you in the line of battle is better than supererogatory prayers performed in your house for sixty years."

When the Prophet sent an army out to fight, he would say, March in the name of God and by his aid and on the religion of the Messenger of God. Kill not the old man who can not fight, nor young children nor women; and steal not the spoils of war, but put your spoils together; and quarrel not among yourselves, but be good to one another, for God loveth the doer of good.

Of Judgments

The first judgment that God will pass on man at the day of resurrection will be for murder.

Whosoever throweth himself from the top of a mountain and killeth himself is in hell fire forever; and whosoever killeth himself with iron, his iron shall be in his hand, and he will stab his belly with it in hell fire everlastingly.

No judge must decide between two persons whilst he is angry.

There is no judge who hath decided between men, whether just or unjust, but will come to God's court on the day of resurrection held by the neck by an angel; and the angel will raise his head toward the heavens and wait for God's orders; and if God ordereth to throw him into hell,

34

the angel will do it from a height of forty years' journey.

Verily there will come on a just judge at the day of resurrection such fear and horror, that he will wish, Would to God that I had not decided between two persons in a trial for a single date.

Of Women and Slaves

The world and all things in it are valuable, but the most valuable thing in the world is a virtuous woman.

I have not left any calamity more hurtful to man than woman.

A Moslem can not obtain (after righteousness) anything better than a well-disposed, beautiful wife: such a wife as, when ordered by her husband to do anything, obeyeth; and if her husband look at her, is happy; and if her husband swear by her to do a thing, she doth it to make his oath true; and if he be absent from her, she wisheth him well in her own person by guarding herself from inchastity, and taketh care of his property.

Verily the best of women are those who are content with little.

Admonish your wives with kindness; for women were created out of a crooked rib of Adam, therefore if ye wish to straighten it, ye will break it; and if ye let it alone, it will be always crooked.

Every woman who dieth, and her husband is pleased with her, shall enter into paradise.

That which is lawful but disliked by God is divorce.

A woman may be married by four qualifications: one, on

account of her money; another, on account of the nobility of her pedigree; another, on account of her beauty; a fourth, on account of her faith; therefore look out for religious women, but if ye do it from any other consideration, may your hands be rubbed in dirt.

A widow shall not be married until she be consulted; nor shall a virgin be married until her consent be asked, whose consent is by her silence.

When the Prophet was informed that the people of Persia had made the daughter of Chosroes their queen, he said, The tribe that constitutes a woman its ruler will not find redemption.

Do not prevent your women from coming to the mosque; but their homes are better for them.

O assembly of women, give alms, although it be of your gold and silver ornaments; for verily ye are mostly of hell on the day of resurrection.

When ye return from a journey and enter your town at night, go not to your houses, so that your wives may have time to comb their disheveled hair.

God has ordained that your brothers should be your slaves: therefore him whom God hath ordained to be the slave of his brother, his brother must give him of the food which he eateth himself, and of the clothes wherewith he clotheth himself, and not order him to do anything beyond his power, and if he doth order such a work, he must himself assist him in doing it.

He who beateth his slave without fault, or slappeth him in the face, his atonement for this is freeing him.

A man who behaveth ill to his slave will not enter into

paradise.

Forgive thy servant seventy times a day.

Of Dumb Animals

Fear God in respect of animals: ride them when they are fit to be ridden, and get off when they are tired.

A man came before the Prophet with a carpet, and said, "O Prophet! I passed through a wood, and heard the voices of the young of birds; and I took and put them into my carpet; and their mother came fluttering round my head, and I uncovered the young, and the mother fell down upon them, then I wrapped them up in my carpet; and there are the young which I have." Then the Prophet said, "Put them down." And when he did so, their mother joined them: and the Prophet said, "Do you wonder at the affection of the mother toward her young? I swear by him who hath sent me, verily God is more loving to his servants than the mother to these young birds. Return them to the place from which ye took them, and let their mother be with them."

Verily there are rewards for our doing good to dumb animals, and giving them water to drink. An adulteress was forgiven who passed by a dog at a well; for the dog was holding out his tongue from thirst, which was near killing him; and the woman took off her hoot, and tied it to the end of her garment, and drew water for the dog, and gave him to drink; and she was forgiven for that act.

Of Hospitality

When a man cometh into his house and remembereth God and repeateth his name at eating his meals, the devil saith to his followers, "Here is no place for you to stay in to-night, nor is there any supper for you." And when a man cometh into his house without remembering God's name, the devil saith to his followers, "You have got a place to spend the night in."

Whosoever believeth in God and the day of resurrection must respect his guest, and the time of being kind to him is one day and one night, and the period of entertaining him is three days, and after that, if he doth it longer, he benefiteth him more. It is not right for a guest to stay in the house of the host so long as to inconvenience him.

I heard this, that God is pure, and loveth purity; and God is liberal, and loveth liberality; God is munificent, and loveth munificence: then keep the courts of your house clean, and do not be like Jews who do not clean the courts of their houses.

Of Government

Government is a trust from God, and verily government will be at the day of resurrection a cause of inquiry, unless he who hath taken it be worthy of it and have acted justly and done good.

Verily a king is God's shadow upon the earth; and every one oppressed turneth to him: then when the king doeth justice, for him are rewards and gratitude from his subjects: but, if the king oppresseth, on him is his sin, and for the oppressed resignation.

That is the best of men who disliketh power. Beware! ye are all guardians; and ye will be asked about your subjects: then the leader is the guardian of the subject, and he will be asked respecting the subject; and a man is a shepherd to his own family, and will be asked how they behaved, and his conduct to them; and a wife is guardian to her husband's

38

house and children, and will be interrogated about them; and a slave is a shepherd to his master's property, and will be asked about it, whether he took good care of it or not.

There is no prince who oppresseth the subject and dieth, but God forbiddeth paradise to him.

If a negro slave is appointed to rule over you, hear him, and obey him, though his head should be like a dried grape.

There is no obedience due to sinful commands, nor to any other than what is lawful.

O Prophet of God, if we have princes over us, wanting our rights, and withholding our rights from us, then what do you order us? He said, "Ye must hear them and obey their orders: it is on them to be just and good, and on you to be obedient and submissive."

He is not strong or powerful who throws people down, but he is strong who withholds himself from anger.

When one of you getteth angry, he must sit down, and if his anger goeth away from sitting, so much the better; if not, let him lie down.

Of Vanities and Sundry Matters

The angels are not with the company with which is a dog, nor with the company with which is a bell.

A bell is the devil's musical instrument.

The angels do not enter a house in which is a dog, nor that in which there are pictures.

Every painter is in hell fire; and God will appoint a person at the day of resurrection for every picture he shall have drawn, to punish him, and they will punish him in hell.

39

Then if you must make pictures, make them of trees and things without souls.

Whosoever shall tell a dream, not having dreamed, shall be put to the trouble at the day of resurrection of joining two barleycorns; and he can by no means do it; and he will be punished. And whosoever listeneth to others' conversation, who dislike to be heard by him, and avoid him, boiling lead will be poured into his ears at the day of resurrection. And whosoever draweth a picture shall be punished by ordering him to breathe a spirit into it, and this he can never do, and so he will be punished as long as God wills.

O servants of God, use medicine: because God hath not created a pain without a remedy for it, to be the means of curing it, except age; for that is a pain without a remedy.

He who is not loving to God's creatures and to his own children, God will not be loving to him.

The truest words spoken by any poet are those of Lebid, who said, "Know that everything is vanity except God."

Verily he who believeth fighteth with his sword and tongue: I swear by God, verily abuse of infidels in verse is worse to them than arrows.

Meekness and shame are two branches of faith, and vain talking and embellishing are two branches of hypocrisy.

The calamity of knowledge is forgetfulness, and to lose knowledge is this, to speak of it to the unworthy.

Who pursueth the road to knowledge, God will direct him to the road of paradise; and verily the angels spread their arms to receive him who seeketh after knowledge; and everything in heaven and earth will ask grace for him; and verily the superiority of a learned man over a mere worshiper is like that of the full moon over all the stars.

Hearing is not like seeing: verily God acquainted Moses of his tribe's worshiping a calf, but he did not throw down the tables; but when Moses went to his tribe, and saw with his eyes the calf they had made, he threw down the tables and broke them.

Be not extravagant in praising me, as the Christians are in praising Jesus, Mary's Son, by calling him God, and the Son of God; I am only the Lord's servant; then call me the servant of God, and his messenger.

It was asked, "O Messenger of God, what relation is most worthy of doing good to?" He said, "Your mother"; this he repeated thrice: "and after her your father, and after him your other relations by propinquity."

God's pleasure is in a father's pleasure, and God's displeasure is a father's displeasure.

Verily one of you is a mirror to his brother: Then if he see a vice in his brother he must tell him to get rid of it.

The best person near God is the best among his friends; and the best of neighbors near God is the best person in his own neighborhood.

Deliberation in undertaking is pleasing to God, and haste is pleasing to the devil.

The heart of the old is always young in two things: in love for the world, and length of hope.

Of Death

Wish not for death any one of you; either a doer of good

41

works, for peradventure he may increase them by an increase of life; or an offender, for perhaps he may obtain the forgiveness of God by repentance.

When the soul is taken from the body, the eyes follow it, and look toward it: on this account the eyes remain open.

When a believer is nearly dead, angels of mercy come, clothed in white silk garments, and say to the soul of the dying man, "Come out, O thou who art satisfied with God, and with whom he is satisfied; come out to rest, which is with God, and the sustenance of God's mercy and compassion, and to the Lord, who is not angry." Then the soul cometh out like the smell of the best musk, so that verily it is handed from one angel to another, till they bring it to the doors of the celestial regions. Then the angels say, "What a wonderful, pleasant smell this is which is come to you from the earth!" Then they bring it to the souls of the faithful, and they are very happy at its coming; more than ye are at the coming of one of your family after a long journey. And the souls of the faithful ask it, "What hath such a one done, and such a one? how are they?" and they mention the names of their friends who are left in the world. And some of them say, "Let it alone; do not ask it, because it was grieved in the world, and came from thence aggrieved; ask it when it is at rest." Then the soul saith when it is at ease, "Verily such a one about whom ye ask is dead." And as they do not see him among themselves, they say to one another, "Surely he was carried to his mother, which is hell fire."

And verily when an infidel is near death, angels of punishment come to him, clothed in sackcloth, and say to his soul, "Come out, thou discontented, and with whom God is displeased; come to God's punishments." Then it cometh out with a disagreeable smell, worse than the worst

42

stench of a dead body, until they bring it upon the earth, and they say, "What an extraordinarily bad smell this is"; till they bring it to the souls of the infidels.

A bier was passing, and the Prophet stood up for it; and we stood with him and said, "O Prophet! verily this bier is of a Jewish woman; we must not respect it." Then the Prophet said, "Verily death is dreadful: therefore when ye see a bier, stand up."

Do not abuse or speak ill of the dead, because they have arrived at what they sent before them; they have received the rewards of their actions; if the reward is good, you must not mention them as sinful; and if it is bad, perhaps they may be forgiven, but if not, your mentioning their badness is of no use.

Sit not upon graves, nor say your prayers fronting them.

Whoso consoleth one in misfortune, for him is a reward equal to that of the sufferer.

Whoso comforteth a woman who has lost her child will be covered with a garment in paradise.

The Prophet passed by graves in Medina, and turned his face toward them, and said, "Peace be to you, O people of the graves. God forgive us and you! Ye have passed on before us, and we are following you."

Of the State after Death

To whomsoever God giveth wealth, and he doth not perform the charity due from it, his wealth will be made into the shape of a serpent on the day of resurrection, which shall not have any hair upon its head, and this is a sign of its poison and long life, and it hath two black spots upon its eyes, and it will be twisted round his neck like a chain on the day of resurrection; then the serpent will seize the man's jaw-bones, and will say, "I am thy wealth, the charity for which thou didst not give, and I am thy treasure, from which thou didst not separate any alms."

The Prophet asked us, "Did any one of you dream?" We said, "No." He said, "But I did. Two men came to me and took hold of my hands, and carried me to a pure land: and behold, there was a man sitting and another standing: the first had an iron hook in his hand, and was hooking the other in the lip, and split it to the back of the neck, and then did the same with the other lip. While this was doing the first healed, and the man kept on from one lip to the other. I said, 'What is this?' They said, 'Move on,' and we did so till we reached a man sleeping on his back, and another standing at his head with a stone in his hand, with which he was breaking the other's head, and afterward rolled the stone about and then followed it, and had not yet returned, when the man's head was healed and well. Then he broke it again, and I said, 'What is this?' They said, 'Walk on'; and we walked, till we came to a hole like an oven, with its top narrow and its bottom wide, and fire was burning under it, and there were naked men and women in it; and when the fire burned high the people mounted also, and when the fire subsided they subsided also. Then I said, 'What is this?' They said, 'Move on'; and we went on till we came to a river of blood, with a man standing in the middle of it, and another man on the bank, with stones in his hands: and when the man in the river attempted to come out, the other threw stones in his face, and made him return. And I said, 'What is this'? They said, 'Advance'; and we moved forward, till we arrived at a green garden, in which was a large tree, and an old man and children sitting on the roots of it, and near it was a man lighting a fire. Then I was carried upon the tree, and put into a house which was in the middle of it —a better house I have never seen: and there were old men, young men, women, and children. After that they brought me out of the house and carried me to the top of the tree, and put me into a better house, where were old men and young men. And I said to my two conductors, 'Verily ye have shown me a great many things to-night, then inform me of what I have seen.' They said, 'Yes: as to the man whom you saw with split lips, he was a liar, and will be treated in that way till the day of resurrection; and the person you saw getting his head broken is a man whom God taught the Koran, and he did not repeat it in the night, nor practise what is in it by day, and he will be treated as you saw till the day of resurrection; and the people you saw in the oven are adulterers; and those you saw in the river are receivers of usury; and the old man you saw under the tree is Abraham; and the children around them are the children of men: and the person who was lighting the fire was Malik, the keeper of hell; and the first house you entered was for the common believers; and as to the second house, it is for the martyrs: and we who conducted you are one of us Gabriel, and the other Michael; then raise up your head'; and I did so, and saw above it as it were a cloud: and they said, 'That is your dwelling.' I said, 'Call it here, that I may enter it'; and they said, 'Verily your life remaineth, but when you have completed it, you will come into your house.'"

When God created paradise, he said to Gabriel, "Go and look at it"; then Gabriel went and looked at it and at the things which God had prepared for the people of it. After that Gabriel came and said, "O my Lord! I swear by thy glory no one will hear a description of paradise but will be ambitious of entering it." After that God surrounded paradise with distress and troubles, and said, "O Gabriel, go and look at paradise." And he went and looked, and then returned and said, "O my Lord, I fear that verily no one will enter it." And when God created hell fire he said to Gabriel, "Go and take a look at it." And he went and looked at it, and returned and said, "O my Lord, I swear by thy glory that no one who shall hear a description of hell fire will wish to enter it." Then God surrounded it with sins, desires, and vices; after that he said to Gabriel, "Go and look at hell fire," and he went and looked at it, and said, "O my Lord, I swear by thy glory I am afraid that every one will enter hell, because sins are so sweet that there is none but will incline to them."

If ye knew what I know of the condition of the resurrection and futurity, verily ye would weep much and laugh little.

Then I said, "O messenger of God! shall we perish while the virtuous are among us?" He said, Yes, when the wickedness shall be excessive, verily there will be tribes of my sects that will consider the wearing of silks and drinking liquor lawful, and will listen to the lute: and there will be men with magnificent houses, and their milch-animals will come to them in the evening, full of milk, and a man will come begging a little and they will say, Come to-morrow. Then God will quickly send a punishment upon them, and will change others into the shape of monkeys and swine, unto the day of resurrection.

Verily among the signs of the resurrection will be the taking away of knowledge from among men; and their being in great ignorance and much wickedness and much drinking of liquor, and diminution of men, and there being many women; to such a degree that there will be fifty women to one man, and he will work for a livelihood for the women.

46

How can I be happy, when Israfil hath put the trumpet to his mouth to blow it, leaning his ear toward the true God for orders, and hath already knit his brow, waiting in expectation of orders to blow it?

Of Destiny

The hearts of men are at the disposal of God like unto one heart, and he turneth them about in any way that he pleaseth. O Director of hearts, turn our hearts to obey thee.

The first thing which God created was a pen, and he said to it, "Write." It said, "What shall I write?" And God said, "Write down the quantity of every separate thing to be created." And it wrote all that was and all that will be to eternity.

There is not one among you whose sitting-place is not written by God, whether in the fire or in paradise. The companions said, "O Prophet! since God hath appointed our place, may we confide in this and abandon our religious and moral duty?" He said, "No, because the happy will do good works, and those who are of the miserable will do bad works."

The Prophet of God said that Adam and Moses (in the world of spirits) maintained a debate before God, and Adam got the better of Moses; who said, "Thou art that Adam whom God created by the power of his hands, and breathed into thee from his own spirit, and made the angels bow before thee, and gave thee an habitation in his own paradise: after that thou threwest man upon the earth, from the fault which thou committedst." Adam said, "Thou art that Moses whom God elected for his prophecy, and to converse with, and he gave to thee twelve tables, in which are explained everything, and God made thee his confidant, and the bearer of his secrets: then how long was the Bible written before I was created?" Moses said, "Forty years." Then Adam said, "Didst thou see in the Bible that Adam disobeyed God?" He said, "Yes." Adam said, "Dost thou then reproach me on a matter which God wrote in the Bible forty years before creating me?"

Ayesha relates that the Prophet said to her, "Do you know, O Ayesha! the excellence of this night?" (the fifteenth of Ramadan). I said, "What is it, O Prophet?" He said, "One thing in this night is, that all the children of Adam to be born in the year are written down; and also those who are to die in it, and all the actions of the children of Adam are carried up to heaven in this night; and their allowances are sent down." Then I said, "O Prophet, do none enter Paradise except by God's mercy?" He said, "No, none enter except by God's favor": this he said thrice. I said, "You, also, O Prophet! will you not enter into paradise, excepting by God's compassion?" Then the Prophet put his hand on his head, and said, "I shall not enter, except God cover me with his mercy": this he said thrice.

A man asked the Prophet what was the mark whereby a man might know the reality of his faith. He said, "If thou derive pleasure from the good which thou hast done, and be grieved for the evil which thou hast committed, thou art a true believer." The man said, "What doth a fault really consist in?" He said, "When anything pricketh thy conscience, forsake it."

I am no more than man: when I order you anything with respect to religion, receive it; and when I order you about the affairs of the world, then I am nothing more than man.

48

ARABIC LITERATURE

EARLY HISTORY AND SCIENCE

"O Thou who diest not, have mercy on him who dies."
THE GOLDEN MEADOWS OF MASOUDI.

ARABIC LITERATURE

―――――――――

EARLY HISTORY AND SCIENCE

(INTRODUCTION)

AMONG the early chronicles of the Arabs, as we have already stated, by far the most celebrated is the many-volumed work of Masoudi, called, the "Book of Golden Meadows." It is a collection of interesting and sometimes scandalous anecdotes about anything and everything in the past, but chiefly about the earlier caliphs. These, with true Eastern subtlety, Masoudi criticises where criticism will be safe, in order that he may praise with a convincing air where he thinks praise will be especially pleasing to the powerful of his own day. In other words, the author is an accomplished courtier as well as a witty and entertaining writer. His book begins, as do all Arab books, with the formula, "In the name of the most merciful God," followed by the usual preface praising Mohammed and the author's own work, and explaining its origin. Then follow, chronologically arranged, the anecdotes of which we quote some that refer to the best-known caliphs.

Masoudi himself was of the genuine Arab blood, a man of prominence descended from one of the comrades of Mohammed. He was born at Bagdad, but was, like many of his countrymen, a wanderer. After visiting all lands, he finally selected Egypt as his dwelling-place, and there died, probably in A.D. 957. Al Bukhari and other earlier travelers

51

had collected all the tales of the Prophet, so Masoudi devoted himself to gathering other legends. From the vast bulk of these he made a thirty-volume historical work, most of which has disappeared. He then selected from this the material for a briefer work, and then, by a third process of distillation, gathered the best of his anecdotes into the "Golden Meadows."

Of the more careful historians and genuine scientists who followed, Avicenna, from whose philosophical work we give an extract here, must assuredly be ranked the first.

EARLY HISTORY AND SCIENCE

────────────

THE BOOK OF GOLDEN MEADOWS AND OF MINES OF PRECIOUS STONES

IN THE NAME OF THE MOST MERCIFUL GOD, PITIFUL AND HELPFUL:

Let us praise God, whose works we should study, and celebrate and glorify. May God grant his blessing and his peace to Mohammed, chief of the prophets, and to all his holy posterity.

THE CALIPHATE OF ABU BEKR, THE TRUTHFUL

Abu Bekr surpassed all the Mohammedans in his austerity, his frugality, and the simplicity of his life and outward appearance. During his rule he wore but a single linen garment and a cloak. In this simple dress he gave audience to the chiefs of the noblest Arab tribes and to the kings of Yemen. The latter appeared before him dressed in richest robes, covered with gold embroideries and wearing splendid crowns. But at sight of the Caliph, shamed by his mingling of pious humility and earnest gravity, they followed his example and renounced their gorgeous attire.

THE CALIPHATE OF AL MANSUR, THE BUILDER OF BAGDAD

Al Mansur, the third Caliph of the house of Abbas, succeeded his brother Es-Saffah ("'the blood-shedder") A.D. 754. He was a prince of great prudence, integrity, and discretion; but these good qualities were sullied by his extraordinary covetousness and occasional cruelty. He patronized poets and learned men, and was endowed with a

53

remarkable memory. It is said that he could remember a poem after having only once heard it. He also had a slave who could commit to memory anything that he had heard twice, and a slave-girl who could do the same with what she had heard three times.

One day there came to him a poet bringing a congratulatory ode, and Al Mansur said to him: "If it appears that anybody knows it by heart, or that any one composed it—that is to say, that it was brought here by some other person before thee—will give thee no recompense for it; but if no one knows it, we will give thee the weight in money of that upon which it is written."

So the poet repeated his poem, and the Caliph at once committed it to memory, although it contained a thousand lines. Then he said to the poet: "Listen to it from me," and he recited it perfectly. Then he added: "And this slave, too, knows it by heart." This was the case, as he had heard it twice, once from the poet and once from the Caliph. Then the Caliph said: "And this slave-girl, who is concealed by the curtain, she also recollects it." So she repeated every letter of it, and the poet went away unrewarded.

Another poet, El Asmaïy, was among the intimate friends and table-companions of the Caliph. He composed some very difficult verses, and scratched them upon a fragment of a marble pillar, which he wrapped in a cloak and placed on the back of a camel. Then he disguised himself like a foreign Arab, and fastened on a face-cloth, so that nothing was visible but his eyes, and came to the Caliph and said: "Verily I have lauded the Commander of the Faithful in a 'Kasidah'" (ode).

Then said Al Mansur: "O brother of the Arabs! if the poem has been brought by any one beside thee, we will give thee no recompense for it; otherwise we will bestow on thee

54

the weight in money of that upon which it is written." So El Asmaïy recited the Kasidah, which, as it was extraordinarily intricate and difficult, the Caliph could not commit to memory. He looked toward the slave and the girl, but they had neither of them learned it. So he cried: "O brother of the Arabs! bring hither that whereon it is written, that we may give thee its weight."

Then said the seeming Arab: "O my Lord! of a truth I could find no paper to write it upon; but I had amongst the things left me at my father's death a piece of a marble column which had been thrown aside as useless, so I scratched the Kasidah upon that."

Then the Caliph had no help for it but to give him its weight in gold, and this nearly exhausted his treasury. The poet took it and departed.

When he had gone away, the Caliph said: "It forces itself upon my mind that this is El Asmaïy." So he commanded him to be brought back, and lo! it was El Asmaïy, who said: "O Commander of the Faithful! verily the poets are poor and are fathers of families, and thou dost debar them from receiving anything by the power of thy memory and the memories of this slave and this slave-girl. But wert thou to bestow upon them what thou couldst easily spare, they might with it support their families, and it could not injure thee."

One day the poet Thalibi recited an ode in the presence of Al Mansur, hoping for a reward. When he had finished, the Caliph said to him: "Will you have three hundred dinars from my treasury, or hear three wise sayings from my lips?" "Oh," said the poet, anxious to curry favor with his master, "durable wisdom is better than transitory treasure." "Very well," said the Caliph, "the first word of wisdom is: When your garment is worn, don't sew on a new patch, for it looks badly." "Alas! alas!" wailed the poet, "there go a hundred dinars at one blow." The Caliph smiled, and continued: "The second piece of advice is: When you anoint your beard, don't anoint the bottom of it, lest you soil your clothes." "Ah!" sighed the poet, "there go the second hundred." Again the Caliph smiled, and continued: "The third piece of advice—-" "O Caliph," cried the poet in an agony: "keep the third piece of advice to yourself and let me have the last hundred dinars." Then the Caliph laughed outright and ordered five hundred dinars to be paid him from the treasury.

Al Mansur and Abu Muslim

Abu Muslim was one of the chief generals of Es-Saffah, Al Mansur's brother and predecessor. On his accession Al Mansur became jealous of Abu Muslim's great power and influence, but sent him notwithstanding to put down a revolt raised by Abd Allah, the son of Ali. After several battles, Abd Allah fled and took refuge in Bassorah, the whole of his camp and treasure falling into the hands of Abu Muslim. Al Mansur sent Yaktin bin Musa to take charge of the treasure. On appearing before Abu Muslim, Yaktin said to him: "Peace be to thee, Emir!" "A murrain on thee, son of a prostitute!" answered the general. "They can use me to shed my blood, but not to guard a treasure." "My lord," answered the messenger, "what has put such thoughts into your head?" "Has not thy master," answered Abu Muslim, "sent thee to confiscate all the treasure which has come into my possession?" "May my wife be divorced forever," said the Caliph's agent, "if he has not sent me simply and solely to congratulate you upon your victory and success!" On these words Abu Muslim embraced him and made him sit by his side. Notwithstanding this, however, when he had bidden him farewell, he said to his officers: "By Allah! I know this man will divorce his wife, simply out of fidelity to his master."

When he had resolved to revolt against Al Mansur, Abu Muslim left Mesopotamia, and set out for Khorassan; while on his part Al Mansur left Anbar, and encamped near the city of Rumiyeh. From thence he sent the following message to Abu Muslim: "I wish to consult you on matters which can not be confided to a letter; come hither, and I shall not detain you long." Abu Muslim read the letter, but would not go. Al Mansur then sent to him Djerir, son of Yezid, the most accomplished diplomatist of his time, who had already made the acquaintance of Abu Muslim in Khorassan.

When Djerir came into Abu Muslim's presence, he addressed him as follows: "My lord, you have fought hitherto faithfully for the Abbassides (Al Mansur's family); why should you now turn against them? No information has reached the Caliph which should inspire you with any sort of fear; you have really, in my belief, no reason to pursue this line of conduct." Abu Muslim was on the point of promising to return with him, when one of his intimates pressed him not to do so. "My friend," the chief answered him, "I can resist the suggestions of the devil, but not those of a man like this." And in fact Djerir did not cease his persuasions till he had induced him to proceed to the Caliph.

Abu Muslim had consulted astrologers, who told him that he was to destroy a dynasty, create a dynasty,[1] and be slain in the land of Rum (Asia Minor). Al Mansur was then at Rumaiyat al-Madain, a place founded by one of the Persian kings, and Abu Muslim never suspected that he should meet with his death there, as he fancied that it was Asia Minor which was meant by the oracle.

On entering into Al Mansur's presence, he met with a

57

most favorable reception, and was then told to retire to his tent; but the Caliph only waited a favorable opportunity to take him unawares. Abu Muslim then rode a number of times to visit Al Mansur, whose manner appeared less cordial than before. At last he went to the palace one day, and, being informed that the Caliph was making his ablutions previously to his prayers, sat down in an antechamber. In the meanwhile Al Mansur had posted some persons behind a curtain near to the sofa where Abu Muslim was sitting, with the orders not to appear till the Caliph clapped his hands. On this signal they were to strike off Abu Muslim's head.

Al Mansur then took his seat on the throne, and Abu Muslim, being introduced, made his salutation, which the Caliph returned. Al Mansur then permitted him to sit, and, having commenced the conversation, proceeded to level sundry reproaches against him. "Thou hast done this," said he, "and thou hast done that." "Why does my lord speak so to me," replied Abu Muslim, "after all my efforts and services?" "Son of a prostitute!" exclaimed Al Mansur, "thou owest thy success to our own good fortune. Had a negress slave been in thy place, she would have done as much as thou! Was it not thou who soughtest to obtain in marriage my aunt, Aasiya, pretending indeed that thou wast a descendant of Salit, the son of Abd Allah Ibn Abbas? Thou hast undertaken, infamous wretch! to mount where thou canst not reach."

On this Abu Muslim seized him by the hand, which he kissed and pressed, offering excuses for his conduct; but Al Mansur shouted: "May God not spare me if I spare thee!" He then clapped his hands, on which the assassins rushed out upon Abu Muslim and cut him to pieces with their swords, Al Mansur exclaiming all the time: "God cut your hands off, rascals! Strike!" On receiving the first blow Abu Muslim said: "Commander of the Faithful, spare me that I may be useful against thy enemies." The Caliph replied: "May God never spare me if I do! Where have I a greater enemy than thee?"

When Abu Muslim was slain, his body was rolled up in a carpet, and soon after Al Mansur's general, Jafar Ibn Hanzala, entered. "What think you of Abu Muslim?" the Caliph said to him. "Commander of the Faithful," answered the other, "if you have ever the misfortune to pull a single hair out of his head, there is no resource for you but to kill him, and to kill him, and to kill him again." "God has given thee understanding," replied Al Mansur: "here he is in the carpet." On seeing him dead, Hanzala said: "Commander of the Faithful, count this as the first day of your reign." Al Mansur then recited this verse: "He threw away his staff of travel, and found repose after a long journey." After this he turned toward the persons present, and recited these lines over the prostrate body:

"Thou didst pretend that our debt to thee could never be paid! Receive now thy account in full, O Abu Mujrim.[2] Drink of that draught which thou didst so often serve to others a draught more bitter to the throat than gall."

THE DEATH OF ABU MUSTEM.

The Favorite Counsellor of the Caliph Al Mansur, slain for presuming to imitate the Caliph.

Al Mansur and Ibn al Mukaffa

Ibn al Mukaffa, the translator of the book "Kalilah and Dimnah" from Pehlevi into Arabic, was one of the most learned men during the reign of Al Mansur, but suspected of Zendikism, or free-thinking. Al Mansur is reported to have said: "I never found a book on Zendikism which did not owe its origin to Ibn al Mukaffa." The latter used to be a thorn in the side of Sofyan, the governor of Basra. As Sofyan had a large nose, Ibn al Mukaffa used to say to him when he visited him: "How are you both?" meaning him and his nose. Sofyan once said: "I had never reason to repent keeping silence." And Ibn al Mukaffa replied: "Dumbness becomes you; why should you repent of it?"

These gibes rankled in Sofyan's mind, and ere long he had an opportunity of glutting his vengeance on Ibn al Mukaffa.

Abdallah, the uncle of Al Mansur, had revolted against his nephew, and aspired to the Caliphate; but being defeated by Abu Muslim, who had been sent against him at the head of an army, he took to flight, and dreading the vengeance of Al Mansur, lay concealed at the house of his brothers, Sulaiman and Isa. These two then interceded for him with the Caliph, who consented to forgive what had passed; and it was decided that a letter of pardon should be granted by Al Mansur.

On coming to Basra the two brothers told Ibn al Mukaffa, who was secretary to Isa, to draw up the letter of pardon, and to word it in the strongest terms, so as to leave no pretext to Al Mansur for making an attempt against Abdallah's life. Ibn al Mukaffa obeyed their directions, and drew up the letter in the most binding terms, inserting in it, among others, the following clause: "And if at any time the Commander of the Faithful act perfidiously toward his uncle, Abdallah Ibn Ali, his wives shall be divorced from him, his horses shall be confiscated for the service of God in war, his slaves shall become free, and the Moslems loosed from their allegiance to him." The other conditions of the deed were expressed in a manner equally strict. Al Mansur, having read the paper, was highly displeased, and asked who wrote it. On being informed that it was Ibn al Mukaffa, his brother's secretary, he sent a letter to Sofyan, the governor of Basra, ordering him to put Ibn al Mukaffa to death. Sofyan was already filled with rancor against Ibn al Mukaffa, for the reasons mentioned above. He summoned him, and, when he appeared, reminded him of his gibes. "Emir!" exclaimed Ibn al Mukaffa, "I implore you in the name of God to spare my life." "May my mother be disgraced," replied Sofyan, "if I do not kill thee in a manner such as none was ever killed in before." On this he ordered an oven to be heated, and the limbs of Ibn al Mukaffa to be cut off, joint by joint; these he cast into the oven before his eyes, and he then threw him in bodily, and closed the oven on him, saying; "It is not a crime in me to punish you thus, for you are a Zindik (free-thinker) who corrupted the people."

Sulaiman and Isa, having made inquiries about their secretary, were informed that he had gone into the palace of Sofyan in good health and that he had not come out. They therefore cited Sofyan before Al Mansur, and brought him with them in chains. Witnesses were produced, who declared that they saw Ibn al Mukaffa enter Sofyan's palace, and that he never came out after, and Al Mansur promised to examine into the matter. He then said to them: "Suppose that I put Sofyan to death in retaliation for the death of Ibn al Mukaffa, and that Ibn al Mukaffa himself then came forth from that door" (pointing to one which was behind him) "and spoke to you—what should I do to you in that case? I should put you to death in retaliation for the death of Sofyan." On this the witnesses retraced their evidence, and

Isa and Sulaiman ceased to speak of their secretary, knowing that he had been killed by order of Al Mansur, who, disregarding his promise, cast Abdallah Ibn Ali into prison.

Terrible as was the wrath of Al Mansur when roused, there were not wanting on occasion those among his subjects who had the courage to rebuke him. Once the Caliph was addressing an audience at Damascus, and said: "O ye people! it is incumbent on you to give praise to the Most High that he has sent me to reign over you. For verily since I began to reign over you, he has taken away the plague which had come amongst you." But a certain Arab cried out to him: "Of a truth Allah is too merciful to give us both thee and the plague at one time!" On another occasion the theologian Malik Ibn Anas relates the following: "One day the Caliph Mansur sent for me and my friend Ibn Taous, against whom he was known to entertain a grudge. When we entered the presence-chamber, we beheld the executioner with his sword drawn and the leather carpet spread, on which it was customary to behead criminals. The Caliph signed to us to seat ourselves, and when we had done so he remained a long time with his head bent in meditation. He then raised it, and turning to Ibn Taous, said: 'Recite me a saying of the Prophet, on whom be peace.'

"Ibn Taous replied: 'The Prophet of God has said, "The worst punished criminals in the day of judgment will be those to whom God has entrusted authority and who have abused it."' The Caliph was silent, and there was a pause. I trembled, and drew my garments close round me, lest any of the blood of Ibn Taous, whom I expected to see instantly executed, should spurt upon them.

"Then the Caliph said to Ibn Taous: 'Hand me that ink-pot.' But he never stirred. 'Why don't you hand it?' asked the Caliph. 'Because,' he said, 'I fear you may write some wrong order, and I do not wish to share the responsibility.' 'Get up and go,' the Caliph growled. 'Precisely what we were desiring,' answered Ibn Taous, of whose courage and coolness I from that day formed a high opinion."

Another bold rebuker of Al Mansur was the saint and mystic, Amr Ibn Obaid, of whom it was said that he had been "educated by the angels and brought up by the prophets." Before Al Mansur's elevation to the Caliphate, Amr Ibn Obaid had been his companion and intimate friend. When Mansur came to the throne Amr went one day into his presence, and was told by him to draw near and sit down. The Caliph then asked to hear an exhortation from him. Amr addressed him an admonition, in which he said, among other things: "The power which thou now wieldest, had it remained in the hands of thy predecessors, would never have come to thee. Be warned, then, of that night which shall give birth to a day never more to be followed by another night." When Amr rose to depart, Al Mansur said: "We have ordered ten thousand pieces of silver to be given thee." "I stand not in need thereof," replied Amr. "By Allah, thou shalt take it!" exclaimed the Caliph. "By Allah, I shall not take it!" answered the other.

On this Al Mansur's son, Al Mahdi, who happened to be present, said to Amr: "The Commander of the Faithful swears that a thing shall be done, and yet thou art bold enough to swear that it shall not." "Who is this youth?" said Amr, turning to Al Mansur. "He is the declared successor to the Caliphate, my son, Al Mahdi," replied Mansur. "Thou hast clothed him in raiment," said Amr, "which is not the raiment of the righteous, and thou hast given him a name[3] which he deserveth not, and thou hast smoothed for him a path wherein the more profit the less heed."

Al Mansur then asked him if there was anything he

wished, and Amr made answer: "Send not for me, but wait till I come to thee." "In that case," said Mansur, "thou wilt never meet me." "That," replied Amr, "is precisely what I desire." He then withdrew, and Al Mansur looked after him and said: "All of you walk with stealthy steps; all of you are in pursuit of prey—all except Amr Ibn Obaid!"

How Al Mansur Was Tricked

It has before been mentioned that Al Mansur, disregarding the promise of pardon he had made to his uncle, Abdallah Ibn Ali, who had revolted against him, cast him into prison, where he remained a long time. When the Caliph set out on the pilgrimage to Mecca, he committed Abdallah to the care of Isa Ibn Musa, with private orders to put him to death. Isa, not wishing to kill Abdallah, contented himself with concealing him, sending a message to the Caliph to say that he had been put to death. This rumor spread about, and the Alides, the partisans of Abdallah, petitioned Al Mansur on the subject. The Caliph declared that he had been committed to the care of Isa. The Alides then went to Isa, and hearing from him that Abdallah had been put to death, came again with complaints to Al Mansur. The latter feigned to be in a rage, and exclaimed: "Since Isa has killed my uncle without my authorizing him to do so, he shall perish in his turn." The Caliph secretly desired that Isa should have perpetrated this murder, so that he might have a reasonable pretext for killing him, and thus ridding himself of two enemies at once.

He accordingly sent for Isa, and said, "Is it true that you have killed my uncle?" "Yes," replied Isa; "you yourself ordered me to do so." "I never gave such an order!" cried the Caliph. "My lord, here is the letter you sent me." "I never

65

wrote it," said Mansur. Isa, seeing the mood the Caliph was in, and fearing for his own life, confessed at last that the prisoner had been spared, and was in safe-keeping. The Caliph then ordered him to hand Abdallah over to the keeping of Abou 'l Azhar, which was accordingly done, and Abdallah remained in prison till his death was decided on.

When Abou 'l Azhar came to execute the sentence, he found Abdallah with one of his female slaves. He strangled him first, but when he was proceeding to strangle the slave also, she cried out: "Servant of God, I pray thee for another kind of death." "It was the only time," Abou 'l Azhar said, "that I felt pity in carrying out a death-sentence. I turned away my eyes while I gave the order to kill her. She was strangled and placed by the side of her master. I then had the house demolished, and they remained buried in the ruins."

Al Mansur visited Medina, and said to his chamberlain, Ar-Rabi, on entering the city: "Find me some learned and intelligent person who can point out to me the chief mansions of the place: it is now so long since I saw the dwellings of my family." An intelligent youth was discovered by Ar-Rabi, and presented to the Caliph. During their excursion the guide did not make any observations unless asked by Al Mansur to do so, but he then proceeded with great precision and eloquence to furnish every requisite information.

Al Mansur was so highly pleased with him that he ordered him a considerable sum of money, but the payment was delayed so long that the youth found himself under the necessity of asking for it. On being asked again to accompany Al Mansur, he fulfilled his object in the following ingenious manner: As they passed by the house which belonged to Aatika, the granddaughter of Abu

Sofyan, the young man said, "This, O Commander of the Faithful, is the house of that Aatika to whom Ibn Muhammad al Ansari alluded in these lines:

"'Dwelling of Aatika! mansion which I avoid through dread of foes! although my heart be fixed on thee, I turn away and fly thee; but yet unconsciously I turn toward thee again.'"

These words caused Al Mansur to reflect; and he said to himself that the youth here must have some reason for giving information, contrary to his habit, without being asked for it. He therefore turned over the leaves of the poem from which the verses were taken, passage by passage, till he came to the following line:

"We see that you do what you promise, but there are persons with deceitful tongues who promise but never perform."

He immediately asked his chamberlain if he had given the youth what had been awarded him, and was informed by him that a particular circumstance, which he mentioned, had caused delay in the payment. The Caliph then ordered Ar-Rabi to give him immediately the double of what had been promised. The youth had most ingeniously hinted the circumstance, and Al Mansur showed great penetration in perceiving it.

Death of Al Mansur

Al Mansur was in the habit of saying: "I was born in the month of Z'ul hajja, circumcised in it, attained the Caliphate in it, and I think I shall die in the same month." And so it befell. Fadl, son of Rabi, relates the following: "I accompanied Al Mansur in the journey during which he died. When we had arrived at one of the stages of the march he sent for me. I found him seated in his pavilion, with his face turned toward the wall. He said to me: 'Have I not told you to prevent people coming into this room and writing doleful sentences upon the wall?' 'What do you mean, Prince?' I asked. 'Don't you see what is written on the wall?'

"' "Abu Jafar,[4] thou art about to die; thy years are fulfilled: the will of God must be done.

"' "Abu Jafar, can any astrologer bind the decrees of God, or art thou entirely blind?"

"'Truly, Prince,' I replied, 'I can see no inscription on this wall: its surface is smooth and quite white.' 'Swear it, by God!' he said. I did so. 'It is, then,' he replied, 'a warning given me to prepare for my approaching demise. Let us hasten to reach the sacred territory, that I may place myself under the protection of God, and ask pardon for that wherein I have exceeded.'

"We continued our journey, during which the Caliph suffered great pain. When we arrived at the well of Maimun, I told him the name of the place, and that we had reached the sacred territory. He said, 'God be praised!' and died the same day."

THE CALIPHATE OF AL MAHDI

Al Mahdi, the third Caliph of the Abbasside dynasty, succeeded his father, Abu Jafar al Mansur, A.D. 774. He was as prodigal as his father was avaricious, and rapidly squandered his vast inheritance. Al Mansur had appointed as his instructor, before he succeeded to the throne, Sharki Ibn Kotami, who was learned in all the lore and traditions of the Arabs. One evening Al Mahdi asked his preceptor to divert him with some amusing anecdote. "I obey, Prince. May God protect you," answered Sharki. "They relate that a certain King of Hirah had two courtiers whom he loved equally with himself. They never quitted his society night or day, in the palace or on a journey. He took no decision without consulting them, and his wishes coincided with theirs. Thus they lived together a long time; but one evening the King, having drunk to excess, drew his sword from the sheath, and, rushing upon his two friends, killed them; then he fell into a drunken slumber.

"The next morning, when told of what he had done, he cast himself upon the earth, biting it in his fury, weeping for his friends, and bewailing the loss of them. He fasted for some days, and swore that for the rest of his life he would abstain from the beverage which had deprived him of reason. Then he had them buried, and erected a shrine over their remains, to which he gave the title, 'El-Ghareiain' (The Two Effigies). He commanded, in addition, that no persons should pass this monument without prostrating themselves.

"Now, like the laws of the Medes and Persians, every custom set up by a King of Hirah could not be changed, but became a hard-and-fast tradition, handed on from generation to generation. The command, therefore, of the King was rigidly obeyed: his subjects, of low and high degree, never passed before the double tomb without prostrating themselves. This usage gradually acquired the binding force of a religious rite. The King had ordered that any one who refused to conform to it should be punished with death after expressing two wishes, which would be granted, no matter what they were.

"One day a fuller passed, bearing on his back a bundle of clothes and a mallet. The guardians of the mausoleum ordered him to kneel down. He refused. They threatened him with death. He persisted in his refusal. They brought him before the King, whom they informed of the matter. 'Why did you refuse to bow down?' asked the King. 'I did bow down,' answered the man; 'they are lying.' 'No; you are the liar!' said the King. 'Express two wishes; they shall be granted, and then you will die.' 'Nothing, then, can save me from death after those men have accused me?' asked the fuller. 'Nothing.' 'Very well,' replied the fuller, 'here is my wish: I wish to strike the King on the head with this mallet.' 'Fool!' answered the King. 'It were better worth your while to let me enrich those whom you leave behind you.' 'No,' said the fuller; 'I only wish to strike the King on the back of his head.'

"The King then addressed his ministers: 'What do you think,' he said to them, 'of the wish of this madman?' 'Your Majesty,' they answered, 'you yourself have instituted this law: your Majesty knows better than any one that the violation of law is a shame, a calamity, a crime which involves damnation. Besides, after having violated one law, you will violate a second, then a third; your successors will do the same, and all our laws will be profaned.' The King replied: 'Get this man to ask anything he likes; provided he lets me off, I am ready to grant all his requests, even to the half of my kingdom.'

"They laid these proposals before the fuller, but in vain; he declared that he had no other wish but to strike the King. The latter, seeing that the man was thoroughly resolved, convoked a public assembly. The fuller was introduced. He took his mallet and struck the King on the back of the head so violent a blow that he fell from his throne and lay stretched on the ground unconscious. Subsequently he lay ill with fever for six months, and was so severely injured that he could only drink a drop at a time. At last he got well, recovered the use of his tongue and could eat and drink. He asked for news of the fuller. On being told that he

70

was in prison, he summoned him and said: 'There is still a wish remaining to you: express it, so that I may order your death according to law.'

"'Since it is absolutely necessary that I must die,' replied the fuller, 'I wish to strike you another blow on the head.' At these words the King was seized with dismay and exclaimed that it was all over with him. At last he said to the fuller: 'Wretch! renounce a claim which is profitless to you. What advantage have you reaped from your first wish? Ask for something else, and whatever it is, I will grant it.' 'No, said the man, 'I only demand my right—the right to strike you once more.'

"The King again consulted his ministers, who answered that the best thing for him was to resign himself to death, in obedience to the law. 'But,' said the King, 'if he strikes me again, I shall never be able to drink any more; I know what I have already suffered.' 'We can not help that, your Majesty,' answered the ministers.

"Finding himself in this extremity, the King said to the fuller: 'Answer, fellow! that day when you were brought hither by the guardians of the mausoleum, did not I hear you declare that you had prostrated yourself and that they had slandered you?' 'Yes, I did say so,' answered the fuller, 'but you would not believe me.' The King jumped from his seat, embraced the fuller, and exclaimed: 'I swear that you are more truthful than these rascals, and that they have lied at your expense. I give you their place, and authorize you to inflict upon them the punishment they have deserved.'"

Al Mahdi laughed heartily on hearing this story, complimented the narrator, and rewarded him generously.

The following anecdotes are related by Faika, the daughter of Abd Allah: "We were one day with the Caliph

71

Al Mahdi, who had just returned from Anbar, to which he had made a pleasure excursion, when Ar-Kabi, the chamberlain, came in, holding a piece of leather on which some words were written in charcoal, and to which was attached a seal composed of clay mixed with ashes and bearing the impression of the Caliph's signet-ring. 'Commander of the Faithful,' said Ar-Kabi, 'I never saw anything more extraordinary than this document; I received it from an Arab of the desert who was crying out: "This is the Commander of the Faithful's letter! Show me where to find the man who is called Ar-Rabi, for it is to him that he told me to deliver it!"'

"Al Mahdi took the letter and laughed; he then said: 'It is true: this is my writing and this is my seal. Shall I relate how it happened?' To this we replied: 'If it please the Commander of the Faithful.' Then he said: 'I went out to hunt yesterday evening when the shower was over. The next morning a thick mist overwhelmed us, and I lost sight of my companions; I then suffered such cold, hunger, and thirst as God only knows, and I lost my way besides. At that moment came to my mind a form of prayer which my father, Al Mansur, had taught me, saying that his father, Muhammad, had learned it from his grandfather, Ali, who had been taught it by his father, Abd Allah, the son of Abbas. It was this: "In the name of God," and "By the might of God! We have no power or force but in God! I fly to God for protection! I confide in God: God sufficeth me! He protected, sufficeth, directeth, and healeth, from fire and flood, from the fall of house, and from evil death!"

"'When I had uttered these words, God raised up a light before me, and I went toward it, and lo! I found this very Arab of the desert in his tent, with a fire which he had been just lighting up. "Arab of the desert," said I, "hast thou withal to treat a guest?" "Dismount!" said he. Then I dismounted, and he said to his wife: "Bring here that barley"; and she brought it. "Grind it," said he; and she began to grind it. I then said to him: "Give me a drink of water"; and he brought me a skin in which was a little milk mixed with water, and I drank thereof a drink such as I had never drunk before, it was so sweet! and he gave me one of his saddle-cloths, and I laid my head on it, and never did I sleep a sounder sleep.

"'On awaking, I saw him seize on a poor miserable sheep and kill it, when his wife said to him: "Beware, wretched man! thou hast slain thyself and thy children; our nourishment came from this sheep, and yet thou hast killed it! What then have we to live upon?" On this I said: "Do not mind. Bring the sheep here"; and I opened it with the knife I wore in my boot, and I took out the liver, and having split it open, I placed it upon the fire and I ate thereof. I then said to him: "Dost thou want anything? I shall give thee a written order for it." On this he brought me that piece of leather, and I wrote on it with a bit of burnt wood which I picked up at his feet that very note. I then set this seal on it, and told him to go and ask for one Ar-Rabi, to whom he was to give it.' This note contained an order for five hundred thousand dirhems, and Al Mahdi exclaimed on hearing it: 'By Allah! I meant only fifty thousand, but since five hundred thousand are written in it, I shall not diminish the sum one single dirhem; and were there no more in the treasury, he should have it. So give him beasts of burden, and let him take it away.'

"In a very short time that Arab had numerous flocks of camels and sheep, and his dwelling became a halting-place for those who were going on the pilgrimage, and it received the name of the 'Dwelling of the host of Al Mahdi, the Commander of the Faithful.'"

On another occasion it is recorded that Al Mahdi went out hunting, and his horse ran away with him until he came to the hut of an Arab. And the Caliph cried: "O Arab! hast thou wherewith to feed a guest? "The Arab replied, "Yes," and produced for him a barley loaf, which Al Mahdi ate; then he brought some wine in a bottle, and gave him to drink. And when Al Mahdi had drunk it, he said "O brother of the Arabs, dost thou know who I am?" "No, by Allah," he replied. "I am one of the personal attendants of the Commander of the Faithful," said Al Mahdi. "May Allah prosper thee in thy situation!" returned the Arab. Then he poured out a second glass, and when Al Mahdi had drunk it, he cried: "O Arab, dost thou know who I am?"

He answered: "Thou hast stated that thou art one of the personal attendants of the Commander of the Faithful." "No," said Al Mahdi, "but I am one of the chief officers of the Commander of the Faithful." "May thy country be enlarged and thy wishes fulfilled!" exclaimed the Arab. Then he poured out a third glass for him, and when Al Mahdi had drained it, he said: "O Arab! dost thou know who I am? "The man replied: "Thou hast made me believe thou art one of the chief officers of the Commander of the Faithful." "Not so," said Al Mahdi, "but I am the Commander of the Faithful himself."

Then the Arab took the bottle and put it away and said: "By Allah! wert thou to drink the fourth, thou wouldst declare thyself to be Mohammed the Prophet of God!"

Then Al Mahdi laughed till he could laugh no more. And lo! the horsemen surrounded them, and the Princes and nobles dismounted before him, and the heart of the Arab stood still. But Al Mahdi said to him: "Fear not! thou hast done no wrong." And he ordered a robe and a sum of money to be given him.

Al Mahdi and His Vizier Yakub ibn Daud

When Al Mahdi's father, Al Mansur, died, he left in the treasury nine hundred million and sixty thousand dirhems ($112,507,500), and Abu Obaid Allah, the first Vizier of Al Mahdi, advised the Caliph to be moderate in his expenses and to spare the public money. When Abu Obaid Allah was deposed, his successor, Yakub ibn Daud, flattered the inclinations of the Caliph, and encouraged him to spend money, enjoy all sorts of pleasures, drink wine, and listen to music. By this means he succeeded in obtaining the entire administration of the State. One of the poets of the time composed an ode containing the following lines:

"Family of Abbas! your Caliphate is ruined! If you seek for the Vicar of God, you will find him with a wine-flask on one side and a lute on the other."

Abu Haritha, the guardian of the treasure-chambers, seeing that they had become empty, waited on Al Mahdi with the keys, and said: "Since you have spent all your treasures, what is the use of my keeping these keys? Give orders that they be taken from me." Al Mahdi replied: "Keep them still, for money will be coming in to you." He then dispatched messengers to all quarters in order to press the payment of the revenues, and in a very short time these sums arrived. They were so abundant that Abu Haritha had enough to do in receiving them and verifying the amount. During three days he did not appear before Al Mahdi, who at length said: "What is he about, that silly Bedouin Arab?" Being informed of the cause which kept him away, he sent for him and said: "What prevented your coming to see us?" "The arrival of cash," replied the other. "How foolish it was in you," said Al Mahdi, "to suppose that money would not come in to us!" "Commander of the Faithful," replied Abu Haritha, "if some unforeseen event happened which could not be surmounted without the aid of money, we should not have time to wait till you sent to have the cash brought in."

It is related that Al Mahdi made the pilgrimage one year, and passed by a milestone on which he saw something written. He stopped to see what it was, and read the following line:

"O Mahdi! you would be truly excellent if you had not taken for a favorite Yakub, the son of Daud."

He then said to a person who was with him: "Write underneath that: 'It shall still be so, in spite of the fellow who wrote that—bad luck attend him!' "On his return from the pilgrimage, he stopped at the same milestone, because the verse had probably made an impression on his mind; and such, in fact, appears to have been the case, for very soon after he let his vengeance fall on Yakub. Rumors unfavorable to this minister had greatly multiplied. His enemies had discovered a point by which he might be attacked, and they reminded the Caliph of his having seconded Ibn Abd Allah the Alide[5] in the revolt against Al Mansur.

One of Yakub's servants informed Al Mahdi that he had heard his master say: "The Caliph has built a pleasure-house, and spent on it fifty millions of dirhems ($6,250,000) out of the public money." The fact was that Al Mahdi had just founded the town of Isabad.

Another time Al Mahdi was about to execute some project when Yakub said to him: "Commander of the Faithful, that is mere profusion." To this Al Mahdi answered: "Evil betide you! does not profusion befit persons of a noble race?"

At last Yakub got so tired of the post which he filled that

he requested of Al Mahdi permission to give it up, but that favor he could not obtain. Al Mahdi then wished to try if he was still inclined toward the party of the Alides, and sent for him, after taking his seat in a salon of which all the furniture was red. He himself had on red clothes, and behind him stood a young female slave dressed in red; before him was a garden filled with roses of all sorts. "Tell me, Yakub," said he, "what do you think of this salon of ours?" The other replied: "It is the very perfection of beauty. May God permit the Commander of the Faithful to enjoy it long!" "Well," said Al Mahdi, "all that it contains is yours, with this girl to crown your happiness, and, moreover, a sum of one hundred thousand dirhems" ($12,500). Yakub invoked God's blessing on the Caliph, who then said to him: "I have something to ask of you." On this, Yakub stood up from his seat, and exclaimed: "Commander of the Faithful, such words can only proceed from anger. May God protect me from your wrath." Al Mahdi replied: "I wish you to promise to do what I ask." Yakub answered: "I hear, and shall obey." "Swear by Allah," said the Caliph. He swore. "Swear again by Allah." He swore. "Swear again by Allah." He swore for the third time, and the Caliph then said to him: "Lay your hand on my head and swear again." Yakub did so.

Al Mahdi, having thus obtained from him the firmest promise that could be made, said: "There is an Alide, and I wish you to deliver me from the uneasiness which he causes me, and thus set my mind at rest. Here he is; I give him up to you." He then delivered the Alide over to him, and bestowed on him the girl, with all the furniture that was in the salon and the money. When the Alide was alone with him, he said: "Yakub, beware lest you have my blood to answer for before God. I am descended from Fatima, the daughter of Mohammed, on whom God's blessings and favors always repose." To this Yakub replied: "Tell me, sir, if there be good in you." The Alide answered: "If you do good to me, I shall be grateful and pray for your happiness." "Receive the money," said Yakub, "and take whatever road you like." "Such a road," said the Alide, naming it, "is the safest." "Depart with my good wishes," said Yakub.

The girl heard all this conversation, and told a servant of hers to go and relate it to Al Mahdi, and to say in her name: "Such is the conduct of one whom in giving me to him you preferred to yourself; such is the return he makes you for your kindness." Al Mahdi immediately had the road watched, so that the Alide was taken prisoner. He then sent for Yakub, and said to him: "What has become of that man?" Yakub replied: "I have delivered you from the uneasiness he gave you." "Is he dead?" "He is." "Swear by Allah." "I swear by Allah." "Lay your hand upon my head." Yakub did so, and swore by his head. Al Mahdi then said to an attendant: "Boy, bring out to us those who are in that room." The boy opened the door, and there the Alide was seen with the very money which Yakub had given him.

Yakub was so much astounded that he was unable to utter a word. "Your life," said Al Mahdi, "is justly forfeited, and it is in my power to shed your blood, but I will not. Shut him up in the *matbak*."[6]

He had him confined in that dungeon, and gave orders that no one should ever speak to him or to any other about him. Yakub remained there during the rest of Al Mahdi's reign (over two years), and during the reign of Musa-al-Hadi, the son of Al Mahdi, and during five years and seven months of the reign of Haroun al Rashid.

Al Mahdi and the Poet Abu'l Atahiyah

Some historians relate that the poet Abu'l Atahiyah had

conceived a passion for Otbah, the slave of Khayzuran, the chief wife of the Caliph. This young girl complained to her mistress of the gossip to which this affair gave rise. One day Al Mahdi found her seated near her mistress in tears. He questioned her, and having discovered the cause of her grief, sent for Abu'l Atahiyah. When the poet came and stood before him, Al Mahdi said to him: "You are the author of this verse concerning Otbah: 'May God judge between me and my mistress, since she shows me nothing but disdain and reproach!'" He then continued: "What kindness has Otbah ever shown you that you have the right to complain of her disdainfulness?"

"Sire," answered Abu'l Atahiyah, "I am not the author of that verse, but of these:
"'O my camel, carry me rapidly; be not beguiled by
what thou deemest repose—
Carry me to a Prince to whom God has given the gift
of working miracles;
A Prince who, when the wind rises, says, "O wind,
hast thou partaken of my benefits?"
Two crowns adorn his brow the crown of beauty and
the diadem of humility.'"
Al Mahdi sat silent for some time, looking at the ground, which he tapped with his staff; then he lifted his head and continued: "You have also said:
"'What does my mistress think upon when she
displays her charms and allurements?
There is among the slaves of Princes a young girl
who conceals beneath her veil Beauty itself.'
"How do you know what she conceals beneath her veil?" the Caliph asked. Abu'l Atahiyah replied in the same flattering style:
"Royalty has come to do him obeisance, and trailing
her robe majestically,

She only is fit for him, as he for her."

But as the Caliph continued to ply him with questions Abu'l Atahiyah became embarrassed in his answers, and was condemned to expiate his temerity by a flogging. He had just undergone his punishment when Otbah met him in this piteous plight. The poet reproached her thus: "Praise be to thee, Otbah! It is because of thee that the Caliph has shed the blood of a man already dying of love." Tears started to Otbah's eyes; she ran sobbing to her mistress, Khayzuran, and there met the Caliph. He asked why she wept, and hearing she had seen the poet after his flagellation, consoled her; then he caused a sum of fifty thousand dirhems to be given to the former.

Abu'l Atahiyah distributed them to all those whom he met in the palace. Al Mahdi, being informed of his generosity, asked him why he had thus disposed of the money he had just received from the Caliph. The poet answered: "I did not wish to profit by what my love had won." Al Mahdi sent him fifty thousand more dirhems, making him swear not to employ them in fresh benefactions.

Another historian relates that Abu'l Atahiyah, on a certain New Year's Day, presented Al Mahdi with a Chinese vase containing perfumes. On the vase were engraved these verses:

"My soul is attached to one of the good things of this
world; the accomplishment of its desires
depends on God and Al Mahdi, his Vicar.
I despair of obtaining my object, but thy contempt of
the world and all which it contains reanimates
my hope."

The Caliph thought of giving him Otbah, when she said to him. "Prince of the believers! would you, in spite of my privileges, my rights, and my services, bestow me upon a pottery merchant—a man who makes money out of his poetry?" Al Mahdi then sent a message to the poet: "As to Otbah, you will never obtain her, but I have ordered the vase you sent to be filled with money."

Soon afterward Otbah, passing by, found the poet disputing with the clerks of the treasury, and maintaining that by "money" the Caliph meant gold dinars, while they alleged that he only intended silver dirhems. "If you really loved Otbah," she said to him, "you would not think of the difference between gold and silver."

Death of Al Mahdi

Tabari, the historian, describes the death of Al Mahdi as taking place in the following tragic manner: Among his wives there were two for whom he seems to have entertained an equal degree of affection; but as one of them seemed to the other to have the preference in his heart, the latter, whose name was Hassanna, conceived a bitter jealousy against her rival, and determined to be avenged on her. In order to accomplish her purpose, she prepared a dish of confectionery, in which she mixed a malignant poison, and sent it as an offering to her rival.

As the damsel who was dispatched upon the errand happened to pass beneath one of the balconies of the palace, Al Mahdi, who was watching the sunset, saw her. The confectionery, which was uncovered, attracting his notice, he asked the messenger whither she was bound. She having informed him, he took and ate heartily of it, saying: "Hassanna will, I am sure, be better pleased that I should partake of her sweets than any one else." In a few hours he was a corpse.

THE CALIPH HAROUN AL RASHID

81

Haroun al Rashid became Caliph in the year A.D. 786, and he ranks among the Caliphs who have been most distinguished by eloquence, learning, and generosity. During the whole of his reign he performed the pilgrimage to Mecca or carried on war with the unbelievers nearly every year. His daily prayers exceeded the number fixed by the law,[7] and he used to perform the pilgrimage on foot, an act which no previous Caliph had done. When he went on pilgrimage he took with him a hundred learned men and their sons, and when he did not perform it himself he sent three hundred substitutes, whom he appareled richly, and whose expenses he defrayed with generosity.

His conduct generally resembled that of the Caliph Mansur, but he did not imitate the parsimony of the latter. He always repaid services done to him, and that without much delay. He was fond of poetry and poets, and patronized literary and learned men. Religious controversies were hateful to him. Eulogy he relished highly, especially eulogy by gifted poets, whom he richly rewarded.

The historian Asmai relates the following anecdote: One day the Caliph gave a feast in a magnificently decorated hall. During the feast he sent for the poet Abu'l Atahiyah, and commanded him to depict in verse the gorgeous scene.

The poet began: "Live, O Caliph, in the fulfilment of all thy desire, in the shelter of thy lofty palace!"

"Very good!" exclaimed Rashid. "Let us hear the rest."

The poet continued: "Each morn and eve be all thy servitors swift to execute thy behests!"

"Excellent!" said the Caliph. "Go on!"

The poet replied: "But when the death-rattle chokes thy breath thou wilt learn, alas! that all thy delights were a shadow."

Rashid burst into tears. Fadhl, the son of Yahya (Haroun's Vizier), seeing this, said to the poet: "The Caliph sent for you to divert him, and you have plunged him into melancholy." "Let him be," said Rashid; "he saw us in a state of blindness, and tried to open our eyes."

This Prince treated learned men with great regard. Abou Moawia, one of the most learned men of his time, related that when he was sitting one day at food with the Caliph, the latter poured water on his hands after the meal, and said to him: "Abou Moawia, do you know who has just washed your hands?" He answered: "No." Rashid informed him that it was himself. Abou Moawia replied: "Prince, you doubtless act in this manner in order to do homage to learning." "You speak truth," answered Rashid.

Ibrahim Mouseli relates the following story: "Rashid one day summoned all his musicians. I and Meskin of Medina were among the performers. Rashid had partaken freely of wine, and wished to hear performed an air which had suddenly occurred to his mind. The officer stationed before the curtain which concealed the Caliph told Ibn Jami to sing this piece. The latter obeyed, but did not succeed in pleasing the Caliph. Each of the singers present attempted it, but were no more successful than Ibn Jami. Then the officer, addressing Meskin, said: 'The Commander of the Faithful orders you to sing this air if you can do it properly.'

"Meskin commenced at once to sing, to the great surprise of the audience, who could not understand how a musician like him had the courage to attempt, before us, an air which none of us had been able to render to the satisfaction of the Caliph. As soon as he had finished I heard Rashid raise his voice and ask to hear it a second time. Meskin recommenced with a skill and spirit which won him everybody's applause.

The Caliph congratulated and praised him to the skies; then he had the curtain behind which he had been sitting drawn aside.

"'Prince of the believers,' then said Meskin to him, 'a strange story attaches to this piece'; and at the invitation of the Caliph he narrated it in these words: 'I was formerly a slave of a member of the family of Zobeir, and carried on the trade of a tailor. My master claimed from me a tax of two dirhems daily, after paying which I was free to do what I liked. I was passionately fond of singing. One day a descendant of Ali, for whom I had just completed a tunic, paid me two dirhems for it, kept me to eat with him, and made me drink generously. As I left him I met a negress carrying her pitcher on her shoulder, and singing the song you have just heard. I was so delighted at it that, forgetting everything else, I said to her: "By the Prophet, I adjure thee to teach me that air." "By the Prophet," she answered, "I will not teach it unless you pay me two dirhems."

"'Then, Prince of believers, I took out the two dirhems, with which I had intended to pay my daily tax, and gave them to the negress. She, setting her pitcher down, sat on the ground and, keeping time with her fingers on the pitcher, sang the piece, and repeated it till it was well impressed on my memory.

"'I then proceeded to my master. As soon as he saw me he demanded his two dirhems, and I related my adventure to him. "Scoundrel!" he said. "Have I not warned you that I will take no excuse, even if a farthing is missing?" Saying this, he laid me on the ground and, with the utmost vigor of his arm, gave me fifty strokes of a rod, and, as an additional disgrace, caused my head and chin to be shaved. Verily, O Prince, I passed a melancholy night. The severe punishment I had undergone made me forget the piece I had learned, and this was the saddest of all. In the morning, wrapping my head in a cloak, I hid my large tailor's scissors in my sleeve, and directed my steps to the spot where I had met the negress. I waited there in perplexity, not knowing her name nor her abode. All at once I saw her coming; the sight of her dispersed all my cares. I approached her, and she said to me: "By the Lord of the Kaaba, you have forgotten the song!" "Yes, I have," I answered. I told her how my head and chin had been shaved, and offered her a reward if she would sing her song again. "By the Prophet," she answered, "I will not for less than two dirhems."

"'I took out my scissors and ran and pawned them for two dirhems, which I gave her. She put down her pitcher, and began to sing as she had done the evening before; but as soon as she began, I said: "Give me back the two dirhems; I don't need your song." "By Allah," she said, "you shall not see them again; don't think it." Then she added: "I am certain that the four dirhems you have spent will be worth to you four thousand dinars from the hand of the Caliph." Then she resumed her song, accompanying herself, as before, on her pitcher, and did not cease repeating it till I had got it by heart.

"'We separated. I returned to my master, but in a state of great apprehension. When he saw me he demanded his daily due, while I stammered out excuses. "Beast!" he shouted, "was not yesterday's lesson enough for you?" "I wish to speak to you frankly and without falsehood," I answered. "Yesterday's and to-day's dirhems went in payment for a song"; and I began to sing it to him. "What!" he exclaimed, "you have known an air like that for two days and told me nothing of it? May my wife be divorced if it is not true that I would have let you go yesterday if you had sung it to me! Your head and chin have been shaved—I can not help that —but I let you off your tax till your hair grows again.'"

"Hearing this recital, Rashid laughed heartily, and said to the musician: 'I don't know which is better, your song or your story; I will see in my turn that the forecast of the negress is verified.' So Meskin went out from the Caliph's presence richer by four thousand dinars."

The Barmecides, Viziers of Haroun al Rashid

On attaining the Caliphate, Rashid conferred the Viziership on Yahya, son of Khaled, son of Barmek. Yahya had served him as secretary before his accession to the throne, and this was the foundation of the magnificence of the family of the Barmecides, whose commencement and whose tragic fall we are about to narrate.

The family of the Barmecides had originally been Zoroastrians in religion, but from the time of their embracing Islam they continued to be good Mussulmen. They were the crown and ornament of their age. Their generosity passed into a proverb; adherents thronged to their court from every side, and multitudes centered their hopes on them. Fortune showered upon them a prodigality of favors. Yahya and his sons were like brilliant stars, vast oceans, impetuous torrents, beneficent showers. Every kind of talent and learning was represented in their court, and men of worth received a hearty welcome there. The world was revived under their administration, and the empire reached its culminating point of splendor. They were a refuge for the afflicted and a haven for the distressed. The poet Abou-Nowas said of them:

"Since the world has lost you, O sons of Barmek, we no longer see the ways crowded with travelers at sunrise and sunset."

We have an example of the generosity of the Barmecides in

86

the following story, related by Salih bin Muhran, one of the intimate attendants of Haroun al Rashid:

"One day Haroun sent for me, and when I arrived in his presence I saw that he was vexed and perplexed, and full of thought, and very much enraged. When I stood still awhile he lifted up his head, and said: 'Go this moment to Mansur Bin Ziyad, and before night thou must have from him ten thousand thousand dirhems, and, if not, cut off his head and bring it to me; and if thou fail in this, I swear by the soul of Mahdi I will command thy head to be severed from thy body.' I said: 'May the life of the Commander of the Faithful be prolonged! If he gives a part to-day, and sends somewhat more to-morrow on the condition that he gives me a pledge for the payment of the whole--' He replied: 'No! If he does not give thee to-day ten thousand thousand dirhems in coined money, bring me his head. What concern hast thou in this matter?' When he said this I knew he was aiming at the life of Mansur, and I went out from him in great perplexity and distress, saying, 'O Lord, what has come to me? It will be needful to slay Mansur, and he is one of the most worthy and best-known men of Bagdad, and has a numerous following.'

"At length I went to the house of Mansur, and, taking him on one side, told him the whole story as it had happened, and what my commands were. When he heard he wept aloud, and fell at my feet, saying: 'In truth the Commander of the Faithful seeks my life; for his courtiers and many others know there is no such sum in my house. Nor could I in my whole life bring together so much; how, then, can I do it in one day? But do thou show me one favor, for God's sake-. take me to my house, that I may bid farewell to my children and followers and clansmen, and ask forgiveness of my offenses from my companions and acquaintances.'

"I took him to his house, as he desired, and when his family and chief friends heard what had happened there was an outcry among them. They wept and bewailed so that jinns and men, and wild beasts and birds, were sorrowful for them, and my heart burned to see them. At last he brought out what money and valuables he had, amounting to two million dirhems, and gave it to me, saying: 'In days past, before Haroun al Rashid was Caliph, I often vexed Yahya the Barmecide, and during this present reign also he suffered much annoyance and persecution from me. But on a certain occasion he treated me with kindness, and put my hand in his, and I knew that he had forgiven my fault, and that there was no feeling of revenge remaining in his heart; and afterward he did me many kindnesses with the Caliph. If thou wilt deal kindly with me—his house is at the head of the way—take me there. It may be his heart will be touched for me; for all the members of his house are men of liberality, and they desire that even their enemy and ill-wisher may take refuge with them, that they may help him in his distress and misery.'

"I said: 'Thou speakest truly, and it will be a delight to myself to take thee there. Come, let us go. By Allah the Most High, it must needs be they will cause thee to rejoice.' When we arrived at the house of Yahya, he had just finished the afternoon prayer, and was repeating the *Tesbih*.[8] When he saw Mansur, and he had explained to him his distress and misery, Yahya came up to me and inquired of me the state of the case, which I revealed to him. He comforted Mansur, and bade him keep up his heart; 'For,' said he, 'I will not be wanting in doing all that is in my power to help thee.' At the same time he called his treasurer, and said to him: 'Bring me all that is in the treasury.' The treasurer brought all that he had of coined money and jewels, and the amount was two hundred thousand dirhems.

"Then he wrote a letter to his eldest son, Fadhl, bidding him send what money he had, for that an unfortunate man was waiting for it. When Fadhl had read the note, he immediately sent two hundred thousand dirhems. Then he wrote a note to Jafar, his younger son, bidding him send immediately all the money he had. He also sent three hundred thousand dirhems. Then he said to me: 'Take this money to the Commander of the Faithful, and represent to him that I will send to-morrow three million dirhems more into his treasury.' I replied: 'This is not in my orders. To-day, by the hour of evening prayer, I must be in the presence of the Caliph with the gold or the head.'

"When Yahya heard this he sent for his slave Otbah, and bade her go to Fatima, the sister of the Commander of the Faithful, and to explain the case to her. When Otbah had told Fatima how the matter stood, that lady, who was a woman of much generosity, took off a collar set with jewels which she had received from the Caliph, of which the value was estimated at two hundred thousand dinars of gold, and sent it to Yahya, asking besides a thousand pardons that she could do no more.

"When at last the ten million of dirhems was raised, Yahya delivered it all to porters, and sent it by me to the Caliph. It was near the setting of the sun when I brought the money to Haroun al Rashid. When he saw me, he cried: 'Hast thou brought Mansur?' I told him all that had passed, whereupon he bade me send the money to the treasury and go for Yahya. When I had placed the money in the treasury, I went to Yahya and told him that the Caliph had accepted the money, and wished to see him. He broke out into exclamations of gladness when he heard this, and, calling for Mansur, he said: 'Take courage, for thou art saved from destruction. The Commander of the Faithful has just asked for me, and I will so contrive as to render him again favorably disposed toward thee.'

"Then Mansur's soul again returned to his body, and he thanked Yahya fervently. When Yahya arrived in the presence of the Caliph and saw his face averted, he was afraid; for he thought: 'Perchance he will reprove me for my want of respect in releasing Mansur.' So, after some time, he prayed for pardon of his offense, and conciliated the Caliph. Afterward he said: 'Wilt thou tell me what was the crime of which Mansur was guilty?' The Caliph replied: 'His crime was his enmity against you and his evil-speaking concerning you. For this reason I have long wished to strike off his head. To-day I was so incensed that I commanded either that he should pay this money or that his head should be cut off. But thou hast done as the generous always do.' Yahya said: 'May the life of the Commander of the Faithful be long! For if the Commander of the Faithful had said, "The wealth of Yahya and his sons is of my gift, and this necklace, too, of my sister's is a gift of mine. What has any one to do in this matter? Go and cut off Mansur's head," what could he have done and what could I have done?'

"This speech pleased Haroun al Rashid, but he blamed Yahya because he had asked for his sister's necklace, and sent it to the treasury to meet the demand on Mansur. He also blamed his sister for giving away the necklace. She replied: 'It would have been shame if I had not answered the request of one who was in the place of a father to me.' This reply pleased the Caliph, and he restored to Fatima the jeweled collar, and Yahya and Mansur were again glad at heart."

The Fall of the Barmecides

Haroun al Rashid had such an extraordinary affection to Jafar the Barmecide that he could not bear to be one hour apart from him. Rashid loved his own sister Abbasah also with an extreme affection, and could not bear to be long absent from her. She was a woman of extraordinary beauty, and exceeded all in science and knowledge. Zobeidah, who was the chief favorite of the Caliph, and all her dependents were opposed to Abbasah.

One day Rashid said to Jafar: "Thou knowest how great is my affection to thee, and also how greatly I love my sister Abbasah, and that I can not live without the company of either of you. I have thought of an expedient whereby you may both accompany me in the same assembly—that a marriage take place between you. That will legalize your meeting and authorize your beholding one another. But all this is on condition that you never meet except I am a third in the party."

When Jafar heard this, the world on all sides grew black with darkness to his eyes. Distressed and confounded, he fell at the feet of Rashid, and said: "Commander of the Faithful, wilt thou slay me? From the time of Adam to our day no servant has been admitted to such confidence as that he should marry with the family of his lords and benefactors; or if any one hath treacherously imagined such a thing, very shortly he hath been reduced to nothingness, and all men have counted him a bread-and-salt traitor. And what sin hath thy slave committed, O Commander of the Faithful, that thou shouldest seek after his blood? Is this the reward of all my services and devotion? And, besides, how should I, the son of a Persian *Guebre* (fire-worshiper), be allied to the family of Hashem and the nephews of the Prophet—may the mercy of God be upon him and his family!—and by what right can I aspire to such a distinction? If my father and mother heard of this, they would mourn for me, and my enemies would rejoice."

91

Some days passed, and he neither ate nor drank, but all was of no avail. He could not oppose the decrees of heaven and the ordainment of God by remedy or contrivance. Unable to help himself, he submitted and consented to a marriage on the terms before mentioned. When Yahya, the father of Jafar and Fadhl, and his other brothers heard of this, they were full of sorrow, and looked for the reversal of their fortune and the downfall of their power.

These forebodings were soon justified. The cruel commands of Rashid to his favorite and his sister were disregarded, and Abbasah became a mother. The birth of the child, concealed for a time, was revealed to Rashid by a revengeful slave-girl whom Abbasah had struck. The Caliph was intensely wroth, but concealed his indignation for a time, though betraying it at unguarded moments.

Ahmed Bin Muhammad Wasil, who was one of his confidential attendants, relates as follows: "One day I was standing before Rashid in his private apartment when no one besides was there. Perfumes were burning, and the place was filled with sweet odors. Haroun al Rashid lay down to rest, and wrapped his head in the skirt of his garment to keep his eyes cool, when Jafar the Barmecide came in and told his business to the Caliph, receiving in return a gracious answer, and retiring. In those days the story of Abbasah and her union with Jafar was talked of currently among the people.

"When Jafar was gone Rashid lifted his head out of his skirt, and from his mouth came these words: 'O God, do thou so favor Jafar the Barmecide that he may kill me, or make me quickly powerful over him that I may cut off his head from his body; for with anger and jealousy against him I am near to destruction.' These words he spoke to himself, but they reached my ears, and I trembled within and without, and I said to myself: 'If the Commander of the Faithful knows that I have heard this, he will not leave me alive.'

"Suddenly Haroun al Rashid lifted up his head from its covering, and said to me: 'Hast thou heard that which I said to myself just now?' I said: 'I have not heard it.' The Commander of the Faithful said: 'There is no one but thyself here, and so truly as the censer is in thy hand, thou hast heard all. If thou care for thy life, keep this secret concealed; and if not, I will strike off thy head.' I replied: 'May the life of the Commander of the Faithful be long! I have not heard any of these words.' And with this the Caliph was satisfied."

It was not long after this that the blow fell on the Barmecides. On his return from one of his pilgrimages to Mecca, Rashid came by water from Hira to Anbar, on the River Euphrates. Here he invited the three brothers Fadhl, Jafar, and Mousa, to his presence, and, having caressed them with extraordinary cordiality, dismissed them once more to their quarters, with rich *khelats*, the customary robe of honor. The Caliph withdrew to his apartments, and betook himself to his usual indulgence in wine. In a little time he sent one of his domestics to inquire if Jafar was employed in the same way. Finding that such was not the case, Rashid sent his attendant again to Jafar, urging him by the life of his master to imitate his example without further delay, for that his wine seemed deprived of all its zest until he knew that his faithful Jafar partook of the same enjoyment.

Jafar felt, however, unaccountably alarmed and averse to such a gratification, and, reluctantly withdrawing to his chamber, called for the wine. It happened that he was attended by a favorite blind minstrel named Abou Zaccar, to whom, after a few goblets, he could not forbear from communicating his apprehensions. The minstrel treated them as merely imaginary, urged his master to banish them from his thoughts, and to resume his usual cheerfulness. But Jafar declared that he found it impossible to dispel the uneasiness which seemed to haunt him. About the hour of evening prayer another messenger arrived from Rashid with a present of nuts and sweetmeats for Jafar, as a relish to his wine, from his own table.

When midnight came, Rashid called for Mesrour, his favorite domestic, and directed him to bring Jafar and strike off his head. Mesrour proceeded accordingly, and entering Jafar's apartment while Abou Zaccar was singing some Arabic verses, stood suddenly at the head of Jafar, who started involuntarily at his appearance. Mesrour told him that he was summoned to attend the Caliph. Jafar entreated that he might be permitted to withdraw for a moment, to speak to the women of his family. This last indulgence was withheld, Mesrour observing that any instructions which he had to communicate might as well be delivered where he was. This he was accordingly obliged to do, after which he accompanied Mesrour to his tent, on entering which the latter immediately drew his sword. Jafar asked that the Caliph's instructions might be explained to him, and when he heard them, cautioned Mesrour to beware how he carried into execution an order which had evidently been given under the influence of wine, lest, when their sovereign should be restored to himself, it might be followed by unavailing repentance and remorse. He further adjured Mesrour by the memory of their past friendship that he would return to the Caliph's presence, and require his final commands.

Mesrour yielded to these entreaties, and appeared before Rashid, whom he found expecting his return. "Is this the head of Jafar?" demanded the Caliph. "Jafar is at the door, my lord," replied Mesrour, with some trepidation. "I wanted not Jafar," said the Caliph sternly; "I wanted his head." This sealed the fate of the unhappy favorite. Mesrour immediately withdrew, decapitated Jafar in the antechamber, and returned with his head, which he laid at the Caliph's feet. He was then directed by Rashid to keep that head by him till he should receive further orders.

In the meantime he was enjoined to proceed without delay and apprehend Yahya, his three sons, Fadhl, Muhammad, and Mousa, and his brother Muhammad. These commands were immediately carried into execution. The head of Jafar was dispatched the next day, to be suspended to a gibbet on the bridge of Bagdad, after which the Caliph continued his journey to Rakkah.

Stripped of all their wealth and honors, Yahya, his three sons, and his brother Muhammad, languished in confinement, until the former perished in prison. At first they were allowed some liberty, but subsequently they experienced alternatives of rigor and relaxation, according to the reports which reached Rashid concerning them. He then confiscated the property of every member of the family. It is said that Mesrour was sent by him to the prison, and that he told the jailor to bring Fadhl before him. When he was brought out, Mesrour addressed him thus: "The Commander of the Faithful sends me to say that he ordered thee to make a true statement of thy property, and that thou didst pretend to do so; but he is assured that thou hast still great wealth in reserve, and his orders to me are that, if thou dost not inform me where the money is, I am to give thee two hundred strokes of a whip. I should therefore advise thee not to prefer thy riches to thyself."

On this Fadhl looked up at him and said: "By Allah, I made no false statements; and were the choice offered to me of being sent out of the world or of receiving a single stroke of a whip, I should prefer the former alternative—*that* the Commander of the Faithful well knoweth, and thou also knowest full well that we maintained our reputation at the expense of our wealth. How, then, could we now shield our wealth at the expense of our bodies? If thou hast really got any orders, let them be executed."

On this Mesrour produced some whips, which he brought with him rolled up in a napkin, and ordered his servants to inflict on Al Fadhl two hundred stripes. They struck him with all their force, using no moderation in their blows, so that they nearly killed him. There was in that place a man skilled in treating wounds, who was called in to attend Al Fadhl. When he saw him he observed that fifty strokes had been inflicted on him; and when the others declared that two hundred had been given, he asserted that his back bore the traces of fifty, and not more. He then told Al Fadhl that he must lie down on his back on a reed-mat, so that they might tread on his breast. Al Fadhl shuddered at the proposal, but, having at length given his consent, they placed him on his back. The operator then trod on him, after which he took him by the arms and dragged him along the mat, by which means a great quantity of flesh was torn off the back. He then proceeded to dress the wounds, and continued his services regularly, till one day, when, on examining them, he immediately prostrated himself in thanksgiving to God. They asked him what was the matter, and he replied that the patient was saved, because new flesh was forming. He then said: "Did I not say that he had received fifty strokes? Well, by Allah! one thousand strokes could not have left worse marks; but I merely said so that he might take courage, and thus aid my efforts to cure him."

Al Fadhl, on his recovery, borrowed ten thousand dirhems from a friend, and sent them to the doctor, who returned them. Thinking that he had offered too little, he borrowed ten thousand more; but the man refused them, and said: "I can not accept a fee for curing the greatest among the generous. Were it even twenty thousand dinars, I should refuse them." When this was told to Al Fadhl, he declared that such an act of generosity surpassed all that he himself had done during the whole course of his life.

When Rashid had overthrown the family of the Barmecides, he endeavored to obliterate even their very name. He forbade the poets to compose elegies on their fall, and commanded that those who did so should be punished. One day one of the soldiers of the guard, passing near some ruined and abandoned buildings, perceived a man standing upright with a paper in his hand. It contained a lament for the ruin of the Barmecides, which he was reciting with tears.

The soldier arrested him, and conducted him to the palace of Rashid. He related the whole matter to the Caliph, who caused the accused to be brought before him. When he was convinced by the man's own confession of the truth of the accusation, he said to him: "Did you not know that I have forbidden the utterance of any lament for the family of the Barmecides? Assuredly I will treat thee according to thy deserts." "Prince," the accused answered, "if thou wilt allow, I will relate my history. Afterward deal with me as thou pleasest."

Rashid having allowed him to speak, he went on: "I was one of the petty officials in the court of Yahya. One day he said to me: 'I must dine at your house.' 'My lord,' I said to him, 'I am far too mean for such an honor, and my house is not fit to receive you.' 'No,' replied Yahya, 'I must come to you.' 'In that case,' I said, 'will you allow me some time to make the proper arrangements and put my house in order? —and afterward do as you like.'

"He then wished to know how much time I wanted. At first I asked for a year. This appeared to him too much; I therefore asked for some months. He consented, and I immediately began to prepare everything necessary for his reception. When all the preparations were complete I sent to inform Yahya, who said he would come on the morrow. On the next day, accordingly, he came, with his two sons Jafar and Fadhl and a few of his most intimate friends. Scarcely had he dismounted than he addressed me by name, and said: 'Make haste and get me something to eat, for I am hungry.' Fadhl told me that his father was especially fond of roast fowl; accordingly I brought some, and when Yahya had eaten he rose and began to walk about the house, and asked me to show him all over it. 'My lord,' I said, 'you have just been over it: there is no more.' 'Certainly there is more,' he replied.

"It was in vain that I assured him, in the name of God, that that was all I had: he had a mason sent for, and told him to make a hole in the wall. The mason began to do so. I said to Yahya: 'My Lord, is it permissible to make a hole into one's neighbor's house when God has commanded us to respect our neighbors' rights?' 'Never mind,' said he. And when the mason had made a sufficiently wide entrance, he went through, with his sons.

"I followed them, and we came into a delicious garden, well planted and watered by fountains. In this garden were pavilions and halls adorned with all kinds of marbles and tapestry; on all sides were numbers of beautiful slaves of both sexes. Yahya then said to me: This house and all that you see is yours.' I hastened to kiss his hands and to pray God to bless him, and then I learned that from the very day he had told me that he was coming to my house he had bought the ground adjacent to it, and caused a beautiful mansion to be constructed, furnished, and adorned, without my knowing anything of it. I saw indeed that building was going on, but I thought it was some work being carried on by one of my neighbors.

"Yahya then, addressing his son Jafar, said to him: 'Well, here is a house, with attendants, but how is he to keep it up?' 'I will make over to him such and such a farm, with its revenues,' answered Jafar, 'and sign a contract with him to that effect.' 'Very good,' said Yahya, turning to his other son, Fadhl; 'but till he receives those revenues, how is he to meet current expenses?' 'I will give him ten thousand pieces of gold,' answered Fadhl, 'and have them conveyed to his house.' 'Be quick, then,' said Yahya, 'and fulfil your promises without delay.' This they both did, so that I found myself rich of a sudden and living a life of ease. Thus, O Commander of the Faithful, I have never failed on all fitting occasions to rehearse their praises and to pray for them, in order to discharge my debt of gratitude, but never shall I be able to do so completely. If thou choosest, slay me for doing that."

Rashid was moved at this recital, and let him go. He also gave a general permission to the poets to bewail the tragic end of the Barmecides. A pathetic anecdote relating to their fall is recorded by Muhammad, son of Abdur Bahman the Hashimite.

"Having gone to visit my mother on the day of the Feast of Sacrifice, I found her talking with an old woman of venerable appearance, but meanly clad. My mother asked if I knew her, and I answered, 'No.' She replied: 'It is Abbadab, the mother of Jafar Bin Yahya.' I turned to her and saluted her with respect. After some time I said to her: 'Madam, what is the strangest thing you have seen?' 'My friend,' she replied, 'there was once a time when this same festival saw me escorted by four hundred slaves, and still I thought that my son was not sufficiently grateful to me. To-day the feast has returned, and all I wish for is two sheepskins—one to lie down on and one to cover me.'

"I gave her," adds the narrator, "five hundred dirhems, and she nearly died of joy. She did not cease her visits till the day death separated us."

After the destruction of this family, the affairs of Rashid fell into irretrievable confusion. Treason, revolt, and rebellion assailed him in different parts of the empire. He himself became a prey to disease, and was tortured by unavailing remorse. If any one blamed the Barmecides in his

100

presence he would say: "Cease to blame them or fill the void." So great was the disaffection aroused by his treatment of them that he removed the seat of government from Bagdad to Rakkah, on the Euphrates.

Yahya, the father of Jafar and Fadhl, died in prison, A.D. 805. On his body was found a paper containing these words: "The accuser has gone on before to the tribunal, and the accused shall follow soon. The Cadi will be that just Judge who never errs and who needs no witnesses." This, being reported to Rashid, deepened his gloom, which began to wear the appearance of madness. One morning his physician, finding him greatly discomposed, inquired the reason. Rashid replied: "I will describe to thee what presented itself to my imagination. Methought I saw an arm suddenly extend itself from beneath my pillow, holding in the palm of the hand a quantity of red earth, while a voice addressed me in the following words: 'Haroun, behold this handful of earth; it is that in which they are about to bury thee.' I demanded to know where I was about to find my grave, and the voice replied: 'At Tus.' The arm disappeared and I awoke."

Shortly after this Rashid, though suffering from the disease which was to end his life, set out to put down a rebellion in Transoxiana. When one of the captured rebel leaders was brought into his presence, he ordered him to be cut to pieces limb by limb on the spot.

When the execution was over Rashid fell into a swoon, and, on recovering himself, asked his physician if he did not recollect the dream which had occurred to him at Rakkah, for they were now in the neighborhood of Tus. He also desired his chamberlain Mesrour to bring him a sample of the native earth of the country. When Mesrour returned with his naked arm extended, Rashid immediately exclaimed:

101

"Behold the arm and the earth, precisely as they appeared in my dream!"

The Caliph died at midnight the following Saturday, March 23, A.D. 809.

THE CALIPH AL MAMOUN

When Haroun al Rashid died he left the empire to his sons Emin and Mamoun, giving the former Irak and Syria, and the latter Khorassan and Persia. Emin had the title of Caliph, to which Mamoun was to succeed. War broke out between the brothers; Emin fled from Bagdad, but was captured and slain, and his head sent to Mamoun in Khorassan, who wept at the sight of it. He had, however, previously, when his general Tahir sent to him requesting to know what to do with Emin in case he caught him, sent to the general a shirt with no opening in it for the head. By this Tahir knew that he wished Emin to be put to death, and acted accordingly.

The Caliph, however, bore a grudge against Tahir for the death of his brother, as was shown by the following circumstance: Tahir went one day to ask some favor from Al Mamoun; the latter granted it, and then wept till his eyes were bathed in tears. "Commander of the Faithful," said Tahir, "why do you weep? May God never cause you to shed a tear! The universe obeys you, and you have obtained your utmost wishes." "I weep not," replied the Caliph, "from any humiliation which may have befallen me, neither do I weep from grief, but my mind is never free from cares."

These words gave great uneasiness to Tahir, and, on retiring, he said to Husain, the eunuch who waited at the door of the Caliph's private apartment: "I wish you to ask the Commander of the Faithful why he wept on seeing me." On reaching home Tahir sent Husain one hundred thousand dirhems. Some time afterward, when Al Mamoun was alone and in a good humor, Husain said to him: "Why did you weep when Tahir came to see you?" "What is that to you?" replied the Prince. "It made me sad to see you weep," answered the eunuch. "I shall tell you the reason," the Caliph said; "but if you ever allow it to pass your lips, I shall have your head taken off." "O my master," the eunuch replied, "did I ever disclose any of your secrets?" "I was thinking of my brother Emin," said the Caliph, "and of the misfortune which befell him, so that I was nearly choked with weeping; but Tahir shall not escape me! I shall make him feel what he will not like."

Husain related this to Tahir, who immediately rode off to the Vizier Abi Khalid, and said to him: "I am not parsimonious in my gratitude, and a service rendered to me is never lost; contrive to have me removed away from Al Mamoun." "I shall," replied Abi Khalid. "Come to me to-morrow morning." He then rode off to Al Mamoun, and said: "I was not able to sleep last night." "Why so?" asked the Caliph. "Because you have entrusted Ghassan with the government of Khorassan, and his friends are very few, and I fear that ruin awaits him." "And whom do you think a proper person for it?" said Al Mamoun. "Tahir," replied Abi Khalid. "He is ambitious," observed the Caliph. "I will answer for his conduct," said the other.

Al Mamoun then sent for Tahir, and named him governor of Khorassan on the spot; he made him also a present of an eunuch, to whom he had just given orders to poison his new master if he remarked anything suspicious in his conduct. When Tahir was solidly established in his government he ceased mentioning Al Mamoun's name in the public prayers as the reigning Caliph. A dispatch was immediately sent off by express to inform Al Mamoun of the circumstance, and the next morning Tahir was found dead

103

in his bed. It is said that the eunuch administered the poison to him in some sauce.

Al Mamoun placed his two sons under the tuition of Al Farra, so that they might be instructed in grammar. One day Al Farra rose to leave the house, and the two young princes hastened to bring his shoes. They struggled between themselves for the honor of offering them to him, and they finally agreed that each of them should present him with one slipper. As Al Mamoun had secret agents who informed him of everything that passed, he learned what had taken place, and caused Al Farra to be brought before him.

When he entered, the Caliph said to him: "Who is the most honored of men?" Al Farra answered: "I know not any one more honored than the Commander of the Faithful." "Nay," replied Al Mamoun, "it is he who arose to go out, and the two designated successors of the Commander of the Faithful contended for the honor of presenting him his slippers, and at length agreed that each of them should offer him one."

Al Farra answered: "Commander of the Faithful, I should have prevented them from doing so had I not been apprehensive of discouraging their minds in the pursuit of that excellence to which they ardently aspire. We know by tradition that Ibn Abbas held the stirrups of Hasan and Husain, when they were getting on horseback after paying him a visit. One of those who were present said to him: 'How is it that you hold the stirrups of these striplings, you who are their elder?' To which he replied: 'Ignorant man! No one can appreciate the merit of people of merit except a man of merit.'"

Al Mamoun then said to him: "Had you prevented them, I should have declared you in fault. That which they have done is no debasement of their dignity; on the contrary, it

104

exalts their merit. No man, though great in rank, can be dispensed from three obligations: he must respect his sovereign, venerate his father, and honor his preceptor. As a reward for their conduct, I bestow upon them twenty thousand dinars ($50,000), and on you for the good education you give them, ten thousand dirhems" ($2,500).

When Al Mamoun was still in Khorassan, a revolt was raised against him in Bagdad by his uncle, Ibrahim, the son of Mahdi. This prince had great talent as a singer, and was a skilful performer on musical instruments. Being of a dark complexion, which he inherited from his mother, Shikla, who was a negress, and of a large frame of body, he received the name of At-Tinnin (the Dragon). He was proclaimed Caliph at Bagdad during the absence of Al Mamoun. The cause which led the people to renounce Al Mamoun and choose Ibrahim was that the former had chosen as his successor one of the descendants of Ali, and in doing so had ordered the public to cease wearing black, which was the distinctive color of the Abbassides, the reigning family, and to put on green, the color of the family of Ali and their partizans.

On Mamoun's entry into Bagdad, Ibrahim fled disguised as a woman. He was, however, detected and arrested by one of the negro police. When he was before Al Mamoun, who addressed him in ironic terms, he replied: "Prince of the believers, my crime gives you the right of retaliation, but 'forgiveness is near neighbor to piety.'[9] God has placed you above all those who are generous, as he has placed me above all criminals in the magnitude of my crime. If you punish me you will be just; if you pardon me you will be great." "Then I pardon you," said Mamoun, and prostrated himself in prayer.

He commanded, however, that Ibrahim should continue

to wear the *burqa*, or long female veil in which he had fled, so that people might see in what disguise he had been arrested; he ordered also that he should be exposed to view in the palace courtyard; then he committed him to police supervision, and finally, after some days of detention, set him free.

The following anecdote was related by Ibrahim regarding the time when he was in hiding with a price set on his head: "I went out one day at the hour of noon without knowing whither I was going. I found myself in a narrow street, which ended in a *cul-de-sac*, and noticed a negro standing in front of the door of a house. I went straight to him, and asked if he could afford me shelter for a short time. He consented, and bade me enter. The hall was adorned with mats and leather cushions. Then he left me alone, closed the door, and departed. A suspicion flashed across my mind; this man knew that a price was set on my head, and had gone to denounce me.

"While I was revolving these gloomy thoughts, he returned with a servant bearing a tray loaded with victuals. 'May my life be a sacrifice for you,' he said. 'I am a barber, and therefore I have not touched any of these things with my hand; do me the honor to partake of them.' Hunger pressed me; I rose and obeyed. 'What about some wine?' he asked. 'I do not detest it,' I replied. He brought some, and then said again: 'May my life be your ransom! Will you allow me to sit near you and drink to your health?' I consented. After having emptied three cups, he opened a cupboard and took out a lute. 'Sir,' he said, 'it does not behoove a man of my low degree to beg you to sing, but your kindness prompts me to do so; if you deign to consent it will be a great honor for your slave.'

"'How do you know that I am a good singer?' I asked

106

him. 'By Allah!' he answered, with an air of astonishment, 'your reputation is too great for me not to know it: you are Ibrahim, the son of Mahdi, and a reward of a hundred thousand dirhems is promised by Al Mamoun to the man who will find you.' At these words I took the lute, and was about to commence, when he added: 'Sir, would you be so kind as first to sing the piece which I shall choose?' When I consented he chose three airs in which I had no rival. Then I said to him: 'You know me, I admit; but where did you learn to know these three airs?' 'I have been,' he answered, 'in the service of Ishak, son of Ibrahim Mausili,[10] and I have often heard him speak of the great singers and the airs in which they excelled; but who could have guessed that I would hear you myself and in my own house?'

"I sang to him accordingly, and remained some time in his company, charmed with his agreeable manners. At nightfall I took leave of him. I had brought with me a purse full of gold pieces; I offered it to him, promising him a greater reward some day. This is strange,' he said; 'it is rather I who should offer you all I possess, and implore you to do me the honor to accept it. Only respect has restrained me from doing so.' He refused, accordingly, to receive anything from me; but he went out with me and put me on the road to the place whither I wished to go. Then he went off, and I have never seen him since."

Al Mamoun and Ibrahim, the Son of Mahdi

One day ten inhabitants of Basra were denounced to Al Mamoun as heretics who held the doctrine of Manes (Manichæans) and the two principles of light and darkness. He ordered them to be brought into his presence. A parasite, who saw them being taken, said to himself: "Here are folk who are going off for a jollification." He slipped in among them, and accompanied them without perceiving who they were till they reached the boat in which their guards made them embark. "Doubtless this is a pleasure party!" he exclaimed, and went on board with them. Soon, however, the guards brought chains and fettered the whole band, including the parasite, who said to himself: "My greediness has ended by making me a prisoner." Then he addressed the seniors of the band: "Pardon me," he said; "may I ask who you are?" "Tell us, rather, who *you* are," they answered, "and whether we may reckon you among our brothers." "God knows I scarcely know you," he replied. "As for me, to tell the truth, I am a professional parasite. When I left my home this morning I happened to fall in with you. Struck with your agreeable appearance and good manners, I said to myself: 'Here are some well-to-do people going to enjoy themselves.' Consequently I joined your company, and took my place beside you as though I were one of you. When we reached the boat, which was provided with carpets and cushions, and I saw all these bags and well-filled baskets, I thought: 'They are going for an outing in some park or pleasure-ground; this is a lucky day for me.'

"I was still congratulating myself when the guards came and fettered you, and me with you. I now feel quite bewildered; tell me, therefore, what it is all about." These words amused the prisoners, and made them smile. They replied: "Now that you are on the list of the suspected, and are chained, know that we are Manichæans who have been denounced to Mamoun, and are being taken to him. He will ask us who we are, will question us concerning our belief, and will exhort us to repent and to abjure our religion, proposing various tests to us; he will, for example, show us an image of Manes, commanding us to spit upon it and to renounce him; he will command us to sacrifice a pheasant. Whoever will do so will save his life; whoever refuses will be put to death. When you are called and put to the test you will say who you are and what your belief is, according as you feel prompted. But did you not say you were a parasite? Now, such people have an ample store of anecdotes and stories; shorten our journey, then, by recounting some."

As soon as they arrived at Bagdad the prisoners were conducted into the presence of Mamoun. He called each in turn as his name was on the list; he asked each concerning his sect, and urged them to renounce Manes, showing them his image, and commanding them to spit on it. As they refused, he had them handed over one by one to the executioner.

At last the parasite's turn came. But as the ten prisoners had been done with and the list was exhausted, Mamoun asked the guards who he was. "Truly, we know nothing about him," they answered. "We found him among them and brought him hither." "Who are you?" the Caliph asked him. "Prince of the believers," he said, "may my wife be divorced if I understand what they are talking about! I am only a poor parasite." And he told him his whole story from beginning to end.

The Caliph was much amused, and ordered the image of Manes to be presented to him; the parasite cursed and renounced the heretic heartily. Al Mamoun, however, was about to punish him for his temerity and impudence, when Ibrahim, the son of Mahdi, who was present, said: "Sire, let this man off, and I will relate to you a kind of Bohemian adventure, of which I was the hero." The Caliph assented, and Ibrahim continued:

"Prince of the believers, I had gone out one day, and was roving at random through the streets of Bagdad, when I came to the porch of a lofty mansion, whence issued a delicious odor of spices and dressed meats, by which I was strongly attracted. I addressed a passer-by, and asked to whom the house belonged. 'To a linen-merchant,' he answered. 'What is his name?' I asked. 'Such a one, son of such a one,' was his reply. I lifted my eyes to the house. Through the lattice-work which covered one of the windows I saw appear such a beautiful hand and wrist as I had never seen before. The charm of this apparition made me forget the enticing odors, and I stood there troubled and perplexed. Finally, I asked the man, who had remained standing near, if the master of the house ever gave entertainments. 'Yes, I think he is giving one to-day,' he answered; 'but his guests are merchants, staid and sober people like himself.'

"We were thus engaged in talk when two persons of well-to-do appearance came down the street toward us. 'There are his two guests,' the man said to me. 'What are their names and their fathers' names?' I asked. He informed me, and I accosted them immediately, saying: 'May my life be your sacrifice; your host is waiting impatiently for you.' I escorted them to the door as if I belonged to the house; they went in, and I followed. The master of the house perceived me, and, supposing that I had been brought by his friends, received me graciously, and placed me in the seat of honor. Then the meal was brought; it was well served, and we did honor to the dishes, whose savor excelled their odor. When the food had been removed and we had washed our hands, our host led us into another hall richly adorned. He redoubled his politeness toward me, and specially addressed his conversation to me. The two guests believed me to be an intimate friend of his, while the host treated me in this fashion because he believed I had been brought by his two friends.

"We had already emptied several cups when a young female slave came forward, as graceful as a willow-branch, and saluted us without timidity. She was offered a cushion to sit upon, and a lute was brought to her, which she tuned with a skill which struck me. She then sang an air in a most enchanting fashion; so great was the skill and art with which she sang that I could not suppress a feeling of jealousy. 'Young girl,' I said to her, 'you have still a good deal to learn.' These words irritated her; she threw down the lute, and exclaimed to the host: 'Since when do you admit to your intimacy such vexatious guests?'

"I repented of my remark when I saw the others look at me askance. 'Is there a lute here?' I asked. 'Yes,' was the reply. They brought me one, which I tuned to my liking, and then sang. I had hardly finished when the young slave cast herself at my feet, and, embracing them, said: 'Sir, pardon me in the name of heaven; I have never heard that air sung so exquisitely.' Her master and those present followed her example in praising me; cheerfulness was restored, and the cups circulated rapidly. I sang again, and the enthusiasm of my hearers was roused to such a pitch that I thought they would take leave of their senses. I waited awhile to let them recover themselves; then, taking my lute again, I sang for the third time. 'By Allah!' cried the slave, 'that is what deserves to be called singing!'

"The others, however, were beginning to feel the effects of the wine; the master of the house, who had a stronger head than his guests, entrusted them to the care of his own servants and of theirs, and had them conveyed home. I remained alone with him. After we had emptied some more cups, he said to me: 'Truly, sir, I consider the past days of my life, in which I did not know you, wasted. Kindly inform me who you are.' He pressed me so much that at last I told him my name. Immediately he rose, kissed my hand, and said: 'I should have been surprised, sir, had any one of a rank inferior to your own possessed such skill. To think one of

111

the royal house was with me all the time, and I knew it not!' Being pressed by him to tell my story and what had attracted me to his house, I told him how I had stopped when I smelt the odor of the food, and described the hand and wrist I had seen at the window.

"He straightway called one of his female slaves and said: 'Go and tell So-and-so to come down.' He had all the slaves in succession brought before me. After having examined their hands, I said: 'No! the possessor of the hand I saw is not among them.' 'By Allah!' said my host, 'there are only my mother and my sister left! I will send for them.' Such generosity and kindness of heart surprised me. I said to him: 'May my life be your sacrifice! Before calling your mother, call your sister; it is probably she of whom I am in search.' 'Very well,' he said, and sent for her.

"As soon as I set eyes on her hand and wrist I cried: 'It is she, my dear host, it is she!' Without losing a moment, he ordered his servants to bring together ten respectable elderly men from the neighborhood. They came; he then sent for a sum of twenty thousand dirhems in two bags, and, addressing the ten men, said: 'I take you to witness that I give my sister here in marriage to Ibrahim, son of Mahdi, and that I bestow upon her a dowry of twenty thousand dirhems.' His sister and I both gave our agreement to the marriage, after which I gave one of the bags of money to my young wife, and distributed the other among the witnesses, saying: 'Excuse me, but this is all I have by me at present.' They accepted my present and retired.

"My host then proposed to prepare in his own house an apartment for us. Such generosity and kindness made me feel quite embarrassed. I said that I only desired a litter to convey my wife. He readily agreed, and sent along with it so magnificent a trousseau that it entirely fills one of my houses."

Mamoun was astonished at the generosity of the merchant. He granted his freedom and a rich present to the parasite, and ordered Ibrahim to present his father-in-law at court. The latter became one of the most intimate courtiers and companions of the Caliph.

The Death of Al Mamoun

During Al Mamoun's last campaign against the Greek Emperor he arrived at the River Qushairah, and encamped on its banks. Charmed by the clearness and purity of its waters, and by the beauty and fertility of the surrounding country, he had a kind of arbor constructed by the banks of the stream, intending to rest there some days. So clear was the water that the inscription on a coin lying at the bottom could be clearly read; but it was so cold that it was impossible for any one to bathe in it.

All at once a fish, about a fathom in length and flashing like an ingot of silver, appeared in the water. The Caliph promised a reward to any one who would capture it; an attendant went down, caught the fish and regained the shore, but as he approached the spot where Al Mamoun was sitting, the fish slipped from his grasp, fell into the water, and sank like a stone to the bottom. Some of the water was splashed on the Caliph's neck, chest, and arms, and wetted his clothes. The attendant went down again, recaptured the fish, and placed it, wriggling, in a napkin before the Caliph. Just as he had ordered it to be fried, Al Mamoun felt a sudden shiver, and could not move from the place. In vain he was covered with rugs and skins; he trembled like a leaf, and exclaimed: "I am cold! I am cold!" He was carried into his tent, covered with clothes, and a fire was lit, but he continued to complain of cold. When the fish had been cooked it was brought to him, but he could neither taste nor touch it, so great was his suffering.

As he grew rapidly worse, his brother Mutasim questioned Bakhteshou and Ibn Masouyieh, his physicians, on his condition, and whether they could do him any good. Ibn Masouyieh took one of the patient's hands and Bakhteshou the other, and felt his pulse together; the irregular pulsations heralded his dissolution. Just then Al Mamoun awoke out of his stupor; he opened his eyes, and caused some of the natives of the place to be sent for, and questioned them regarding the stream and the locality. When asked regarding the meaning of the name "Qushairah" they replied that it signified "Stretch out thy feet" (i.e., "die"). Al Mamoun then inquired the Arabic name of the country, and was told "Rakkah." Now, the horoscope drawn at the moment of his birth announced that he would die in a place of that name; therefore he had always avoided residing in the city of Rakkah, fearing to die there. When he heard the answer given by these people, he felt sure that this was the place predicted by his horoscope. Feeling himself becoming worse, he commanded that he should be carried outside his tent in order to survey his camp and his army once more. It was now night-time. As his gaze wandered over the long lines of the camp and the lights twinkling into the distance, he cried: "O thou whose reign will never end, have mercy on him whose reign is now ending." He was then carried back to his bed. Mutasim, seeing that he was sinking, commanded some one to whisper in his ear the confession of the Mohammedan faith ("There is no God but God, and Mohammed is the Apostle of God"). As the attendant was about to speak, in order that Al Mamoun might repeat the words after him, Ibn Masouyieh said to him: "Do not speak, for truly he could not now distinguish between God and Manes." The dying man opened his eyes—

114

they seemed extraordinarily large, and shone with a wonderful luster; his hands clutched at the doctor; he tried to speak to him, but could not; then his eyes turned toward heaven and filled with tears; finally his tongue was loosened, and he spoke: "O thou who diest not, have mercy on him who dies," and he expired immediately. His body was carried to Tarsus and buried there.

ON MEDICINE
(BY AVICENNA)

Medicine considers the human body as to the means by which it is cured and by which it is driven away from health. The knowledge of anything, since all things have causes, is not acquired or complete unless it is known by its causes. Therefore in medicine we ought to know the causes of sickness and health. And because health and sickness and their causes are sometimes manifest, and sometimes hidden and not to be comprehended except by the study of symptoms, we must also study the symptoms of health and disease. Now it is established in the sciences that no knowledge is acquired save through the study of its causes and beginnings, if it has had causes and beginnings; nor completed except by knowledge of its accidents and accompanying essentials. Of these causes there are four kinds: material, efficient, formal, and final.

Material causes, on which health and sickness depend, are —the affected member, which is the immediate subject, and the humors; and in these are the elements. And these two are subjects that, according to their mixing together, alter. In the composition and alteration of the substance which is thus composed, a certain unity is attained.

Efficient causes are the causes changing and preserving the conditions of the human body; as airs, and what are united with them; and evacuation and retention; and districts and cities, and habitable places, and what are united with them; and changes in age and diversities in it, and in races and arts and manners, and bodily and animate movings and restings, and sleepings and wakings on account of them; and in things which befall the human body when they touch it, and are either in accordance or at

116

variance with nature.

Formal causes are physical constitutions, and combinations and virtues which result from them.

Pinal causes are operations. And in the science of operations lies the science of virtues, as we have set forth. These are the subjects of the doctrine of medicine; whence one inquires concerning the disease and curing of the human body. One ought to attain perfection in this research; namely, how health may be preserved and sickness cured. And the causes of this kind are rules in eating and drinking, and the choice of air, and the measure of exercise and rest; and doctoring with medicines and doctoring with the hands. All this with physicians is according to three species: the well, the sick, and the medium of whom we have spoken.

THE EXISTING MONUMENTS
OR "CHRONOLOGY" OF AL BIRUNI

IN THE NAME OF GOD, THE COMPASSIONATE, THE MERCIFUL

Praise be to God who is high above all things, and blessings be on Mohammed, the elected, the best of all created beings, and on his family, the guides of righteousness and truth.

One of the exquisite plans in God's management of the affairs of his creation, one of the glorious benefits which he has bestowed upon the entirety of his creatures, is that categorical decree of his, not to leave in his world any period without a just guide, whom he constitutes as a protector for his creatures, with whom to take refuge in unfortunate and sorrowful cases and accidents, and upon whom to devolve their affairs, when they seem indissolubly perplexed, so that the order of the world should rest upon—and its existence be supported by—his genius. And this decree (that the affairs of mankind should be governed by a prophet) has been settled upon them as a religious duty, and has been linked together with the obedience toward God, and the obedience toward his prophet, through which alone a reward in future life may be obtained—in accordance with the word of him, who is truth and justice—and his word is judgment and decree, "O ye believers, obey God, and obey the prophets, and those among yourselves who are invested with the command."

ERA OF THE CREATION.—The first and most famous of the beginnings of antiquity is the fact of the creation of mankind. But among those who have a book of divine revelation, such as the Jews, Christians, Magians, and their various sects, there exists such a difference of opinion as to the nature of this fact, and as to the question how to date from it, the like of which is not allowable for eras. Everything, the knowledge of which is connected with creation and with the history of bygone generations, is mixed up with falsifications and myths, because it belongs to a far remote age; because a long interval separates us therefrom, and because the student is incapable of keeping it in memory, and of fixing it (so as to preserve it from confusion). God says: "Have they not got the stories about those who were before them gone but God knows them." (Surah ix, 71.) Therefore it is becoming not to admit any account of a similar subject, if it is not attested by a book, the correctness of which is relied upon, or by a tradition, for which the conditions of authenticity, according to the prevalent opinion, furnish grounds of proof.

If we now first consider this era, we find a considerable divergence of opinion regarding it among these nations. For the Persians and Magians think that the duration of the world is 12,000 years, corresponding to the number of signs in the zodiac and of the months; and that Zoroaster, the founder of their law, thought that of those there had passed, till the time of his appearance, 3,000 years, intercalated with the day-quarters, for he himself had made their computation, and had taken into account that defect, which had accrued to them on account of the day-quarters, till the time when they were intercalated and made to agree with real time. From his appearance to the beginning of the Aera Alexandri, they count 258 years; therefore they count from the beginning of the world to Alexander 3,258 years. However, if we compute the years from the creation of Gayomarth, whom they hold to be the first man, and sum up the years of the reign of each of his successors—for the rule of Iran remained with his descendants without interruption—this number is, for the time till Alexander, the sum total of 3,354 years. So the specification of the single items of the addition does not agree with the sum total.

A section of the Persians is of the opinion that those past 3,000 years which we have mentioned are to be counted from the creation of Gayomarth; because, before that, already six thousand years had elapsed—a time during which the celestial globe stood motionless, the natures (of created beings) did not interchange, the elements did not mix—during which there was no growth, and no decay, and the earth was not cultivated. Thereupon, when the celestial globe was set a-going, the first man came into existence on the equator, so that part of him in longitudinal direction was on the north, and part south of the line. The animals were reproduced, and mankind commenced to reproduce their own species and to multiply; the atoms of the elements mixed, so as to give rise to growth and decay; the earth was cultivated, and the world was arranged in conformity with fixed forms.

The Jews and Christians differ widely on this subject; for, according to the doctrine of the Jews, the time between Adam and Alexander is 3,448 years, whilst, according to the Christian doctrine it is 5,180 years. The Christians reproach the Jews with having diminished the number of years with the view of making the appearance of Jesus fall into the fourth millennium in the middle of the seven millennia, which are, according to their view, the time of the duration of the world, so as not to coincide with that time at which, as the prophets after Moses had prophesied, the birth of Jesus from a pure virgin at the end of time, was to take place.

ERA OF THE DELUGE.—The next following era is the era of

the great deluge, in which everything perished at the time of Noah. Here, too, there is such a difference of opinions, and such a confusion, that you have no chance of deciding as to the correctness of the matter, and do not even feel inclined to investigate thoroughly its historical truth. The reason is, in the first instance, the difference regarding the period between the Aera Adami and the Deluge, which we have mentioned already; and secondly, that difference, which we shall have to mention, regarding the period between the Deluge and the Aera Alexandri. For the Jews derive from the Torah, and the following books, for this latter period 1,792 years, whilst the Christians derive from *their* Torah for the same period 2,938 years.

The Persians, and the great mass of the Magians, deny the Deluge altogether; they believe that the rule of the world has remained with them without any interruption ever since Gayomarth Gilshah, who was, according to them, the first man. In denying the Deluge, the Indians, Chinese, and the various nations of the East, concur with them. Some, however, of the Persians admit the fact of the Deluge, but they describe it in a different way from what it is described in the books of the prophets. They say, a partial deluge occurred in Syria and the West at the time of Tahmurath, but it did not extend over the whole of the then civilized world, and only a few nations were drowned in it; it did not extend beyond the peak of Hulwan, and did not reach the empires of the East. Further, they relate, that the inhabitants of the West, when they were warned by their sages, constructed buildings of the kind of the two pyramids that have been built in Egypt, saying: "If the disaster comes from heaven, we shall go into them; if it comes from the earth, we shall ascend above them." People are of opinion that the traces of the water of the Deluge, and the efforts of the waves, are still visible on these two pyramids half-way up,

121

above which the water did not rise. Another report says, that Joseph had made them a magazine where he deposited the bread and victuals for the years of drought.

It is related that Tahmurath on receiving the warning of the Deluge—231 years before the Deluge—ordered his people to select a place of good air and soil in his realm. Now they did not find a place that answered better to this description than Ispahan. Thereupon, he ordered all scientific books to be preserved for posterity and to be buried in a part of that place least exposed to obnoxious influences. In favor of this report we may state that in our time in Jay, the city of Ispahan, there have been discovered hills, which, on being excavated, disclosed houses, filled with many loads of that tree-bark with which arrows and shields are covered, and which is called Tuz, bearing inscriptions, of which no one was able to say what they are and what they mean.

These discrepancies in their reports inspire doubts in the student, and make him inclined to believe what is related in some books, that Gayomarth was not the first man, but that he was Gomer ben Yaphet ben Noah, that he was a prince to whom a long life was given, that he settled on the Mount Dumbawand, where he founded an empire, and that finally his power became very great, whilst mankind was still living in elementary conditions, similar to those at the time of creation and of the first stage of the development of the world. Then he, and some of his children, took control of the guidance of the world. Toward the end of his life, he became tyrannical, and called himself Adam, saying: "If anybody calls me by another name than this, I shall cut off his head."

ARABIC LITERATURE

PHILOSOPHY AND RELIGION

AL GHAZALI'S "RESCUER FROM ERROR"

"If all the other books of Islam were destroyed, the loss would be small if but Al Ghazali's work were preserved."

MOHAMMEDAN PROVERB.

"The variety of doctrines and sects which divide men are like a deep ocean strewed with shipwrecks, from which very few escape."

AL GHAZALI IN "THE RESCUER FROM ERROR."

"Al Ghazali is the greatest, certainly the most sympathetic, figure in the history of Islam."

PROF. D. B. MACDONALD

PHILOSOPHY AND RELIGION

(INTRODUCTION)

WHEN we move with Al Ghazali or Zamakhshari through the deeply searching paths of Arab philosophy, we feel that we are following the guidance of men whom modern thought has in no way outgrown. They lacked much of our scientific knowledge, but none of our reasoning powers. Al Ghazali has sounded all philosophy's profundities of thought, and Zamakhshari has soared to theology's highest peak of adoration.

Al Ghazali (1049-1111), as we have already said, is often ranked next to Mohammed as a teacher and uplifter of his Arab brethren. He was a native of Khorassan, named Abu Hamid Mohammed. Arab custom, however, seldom designates a noted man by his birth-name. He is most often honored with the distinctive prefix "Al," which means "The," much as we use the word as a superlative. Thus just as Holy Writ speaks of The Nazarine, so Al Ghazali probably means "The Man of Ghazali," the village of his birth, though the name may also be derived from his father's trade in *gazzel* (thread), and so may mean "The Thread Merchant." As a youth Al Ghazali studied much and traveled widely; and his wanderings led, as did those of most men in his day, to Bagdad. Here he became famed as the foremost philosophic teacher of the age. But his own philosophy did not satisfy him. Withdrawing from his official position on the ground of ill-health, he wandered over the world for eleven years, seeking true wisdom. He felt at last that he had found it in the ecstasy of religious faith; and then, resuming his public teaching, he led an earnest reform in

125

Mohammedanism, bringing his people to look more deeply and nobly upon their faith. So convincing were his appeals and explanations that his people called him "The Decisive Argument for the Faith."

Al Ghazali's own search for truth is told in his remarkable little book here given in full, "The Rescuer from Error," in which the Rescuer is Mohammed with his Koran. Al Ghazali wrote many other works, religious and philosophical, but none which have so profoundly touched modern readers as this simple, earnest account of himself. It is a "confession" worthy to rank with the "Confessions of Saint Augustine," or any greatest work of its own type. Al Ghazali soon afterward withdrew from public life, hoping to teach men more by his books than by spoken words, and he died in seclusion in his native home.

Great as was the influence of Al Ghazali, he was scarcely a typical Mohammedan teacher. He was, as his book will show, an independent thinker who reached his firm religious faith only after seeking through all systems of philosophy. He had tasted of the emptiness of materialism, and had faced the black shadows of despair. Of far other type was Zamakhshari, the most renowned of commentators on the Koran. He seems never to have doubted the divinity of the holy book. He spent years in studying it, and while he used keen intelligence in weighing its every word, and even shocked his narrower coreligionists by the freedom of his criticism, yet it was always criticism based on the assumption that of course the Koran was right, and that the only danger lay in that men might blunder in interpreting its meaning. He therefore called his celebrated commentary the "Kashshaf," or "Discoverer of Truth."

We give here the noted opening of this work. The main attack upon the author by the orthodox Mohammedans of a

126

later age was because the commentary began with the words, "Praise be to God who created the Koran," whereas the orthodox regarded the book as always existent with God, so that instead of "created" they would have had the writer say that God "revealed" the Koran.

Zamakhshari (1070-1143) was born and died in Khiva in Turkestan. He was, however, another of the many youths eager for knowledge who took advantage of the wide-spread dominion of the Arab caliphs to travel far through the East. He journeyed indeed through such hardships that he lost a leg, frozen in a snowstorm; and he dwelt so long in Mecca, the holy city, that he was called the "neighbor of God." It was from such earnest men as Zamakhshari and Al Ghazali, the "neighbor of God" and the "Decisive Argument," that the Mohammedan religion learned its final form, and the reader will be ignoring the real and manifest energy and intellect of these great men if he dismisses their religion lightly as a teaching easily to be disproved or childishly defective.

PHILOSOPHY AND RELIGION

THE RESCUER FROM ERROR

IN THE NAME OF THE MOST MERCIFUL GOD

Quoth the Imam Ghazali:

Glory be to God, whose praise should precede every writing and every speech! May the blessings of God rest on Mohammed, his Prophet and his Apostle, on his family and companions, by whose guidance error is escaped!

You have asked me, O brother in the faith, to expound the aim and the mysteries of religious sciences, the boundaries and depths of theological doctrines. You wish to know my experiences while disentangling truth lost in the medley of sects and divergencies of thought, and how I have dared to climb from the low levels of traditional belief to the topmost summit of assurance. You desire to learn what I have borrowed, first of all from scholastic theology; and secondly from the method of the Ta'limites, who, in seeking truth, rest upon the authority of a leader; and why, thirdly, I have been led to reject philosophic systems; and finally, what I have accepted of the doctrine of the Sufis, and the sum total of truth which I have gathered in studying every variety of opinion. You ask me why, after resigning at Bagdad a teaching post which attracted a number of hearers, I have, long afterward, accepted a similar one at Nishapur. Convinced as I am of the sincerity which prompts your inquiries, I proceed to answer them, invoking the help and protection of God.

Know then, my brothers (may God direct you in the right way), that the diversity in beliefs and religions, and the variety of doctrines and sects which divide men, are like a deep ocean strewn with shipwrecks, from which very few escape safe and sound. Each sect, it is true, believes itself in possession of the truth and of salvation, "each party," as the Koran saith, "rejoices in its own creed"; but as the chief of the apostles, whose word is always truthful, has told us, "My people will be divided into more than seventy sects, of whom only one will be saved." This prediction, like all others of the Prophet, must be fulfilled.

From the period of adolescence, that is to say, previous to reaching my twentieth year to the present time when I have passed my fiftieth, I have ventured into this vast ocean; I have fearlessly sounded its depths, and like a resolute diver, I have penetrated its darkness and dared its dangers and abysses. I have interrogated the beliefs of each sect and scrutinized the mysteries of each doctrine, in order to disentangle truth from error and orthodoxy from heresy. I have never met one who maintained the hidden meaning of the Koran without investigating the nature of his belief, nor a partizan of its exterior sense without inquiring into the results of his doctrine. There is no philosopher whose system I have not fathomed, nor theologian the intricacies of whose doctrine I have not followed out.

Sufism has no secrets into which I have not penetrated; the devout adorer of Deity has revealed to me the aim of his austerities; the atheist has not been able to conceal from me the real reason of his unbelief. The thirst for knowledge was innate in me from an early age; it was like a second nature implanted by God, without any will on my part. No sooner had I emerged from boyhood than I had already broken the

129

fetters of tradition and freed myself from hereditary beliefs.

Having noticed how easily the children of Christians become Christians, and the children of Moslems embrace Islam, and remembering also the traditional saying ascribed to the Prophet, "Every child has in him the germ of Islam, then his parents make him Jew, Christian, or Zoroastrian," I was moved by a keen desire to learn what was this innate disposition in the child, the nature of the accidental beliefs imposed on him by the authority of his parents and his masters, and finally the unreasoned convictions which he derives from their instructions.

Struck with the contradictions which I encountered in endeavoring to disentangle the truth and falsehood of these opinions, I was led to make the following reflection: "The search after truth being the aim which I propose to myself, I ought in the first place to ascertain what are the bases of certitude." In the next place I recognized that certitude is the clear and complete knowledge of things, such knowledge as leaves no room for doubt nor possibility of error and conjecture, so that there remains no room in the mind for error to find an entrance. In such a case it is necessary that the mind, fortified against all possibility of going astray, should embrace such a strong conviction that, if, for example, any one possessing the power of changing a stone into gold, or a stick into a serpent, should seek to shake the bases of this certitude, it would remain firm and immovable. Suppose, for instance, a man should come and say to me, who am firmly convinced that ten is more than three, "No; on the contrary, three is more than ten, and, to prove it, I change this rod into a serpent," and supposing that he actually did so, I should remain none the less convinced of the falsity of his assertion, and although his miracle might arouse my astonishment, it would not instil any doubt into my belief.

I then understood that all forms of knowledge which do not unite these conditions (imperviousness to doubt, etc.) do not deserve any confidence, because they are not beyond the reach of doubt, and what is not impregnable to doubt can not constitute certitude.

The Subterfuges of the Sophists

I then examined what knowledge I possessed, and discovered that in none of it, with the exception of sense-perceptions and necessary principles, did I enjoy that degree of certitude which I have just described. I then sadly reflected as follows: "We can not hope to find truth except in matters which carry their evidence in themselves—that is to say, in sense-perceptions and necessary principles; we must therefore establish these on a firm basis. Is my absolute confidence in sense-perceptions and on the infallibility of necessary principles analogous to the confidence which I formerly possessed in matters believed on the authority of others? Is it only analogous to the reliance most people place on their organs of vision, or is it rigorously true without admixture of illusion or doubt?"

I then set myself earnestly to examine the notions we derive from the evidence of the senses and from sight in order to see if they could be called in question. The result of a careful examination was that my confidence in them was shaken. Our sight, for instance, perhaps the best practised of all our senses, observes a shadow, and finding it apparently stationary pronounces it devoid of movement. Observation and experience, however, show subsequently that a shadow moves not suddenly, it is true, but gradually and imperceptibly, so that it is never really motionless.

Again, the eye sees a star and believes it as large as a piece of gold, but mathematical calculations prove, on the contrary, that it is larger than the earth. These notions, and all others which the senses declare true, are subsequently contradicted and convicted of falsity in an irrefragable manner by the verdict of reason.

Then I reflected in myself: "Since I can not trust to the evidence of my senses, I must rely only on intellectual notions based on fundamental principles, such as the following axioms: 'Ten is more than three. Affirmation and negation can not coexist together. A thing can not both be created and also existent from eternity, living and annihilated simultaneously, at once necessary and impossible.'" To this the notions I derived from my senses made the following objections: "Who can guarantee you that you can trust to the evidence of reason more than to that of the senses? You believed in our testimony till it was contradicted by the verdict of reason, otherwise you would have continued to believe it to this day. Well, perhaps, there is above reason another judge who, if he appeared, would convict reason of falsehood, just as reason has confuted us. And if such a third arbiter is not yet apparent, it does not follow that he does not exist."

To this argument I remained some time without reply; a reflection drawn from the phenomena of sleep deepened my doubt. "Do you not see," I reflected, "that while asleep you assume your dreams to be indisputably real? Once awake, you recognize them for what they are—baseless chimeras. Who can assure you, then, of the reliability of notions which, when awake, you derive from the senses and from reason? In relation to your present state they may be real; but it is possible also that you may enter upon another state of being which will bear the same relation to your present state as this does to your condition when asleep. In that new sphere you will recognize that the conclusions of reason are only chimeras."

132

This possible condition is, perhaps, that which the Sufis call "ecstasy" (*hal*), that is to say, according to them, a state in which, absorbed in themselves and in the suspension of sense-perceptions, they have visions beyond the reach of intellect. Perhaps also Death is that state, according to that saying of the prince of prophets: "Men are asleep; when they die, they wake." Our present life in relation to the future is perhaps only a dream, and man, once dead, will see things in direct opposition to those now before his eyes; he will then understand that word of the Koran, "To-day we have removed the veil from thine eyes and thy sight is keen."

Such thoughts as these threatened to shake my reason, and I sought to find an escape from them. But how? In order to disentangle the knot of this difficulty, a proof was necessary. Now a proof must be based on primary assumptions, and it was precisely these of which I was in doubt. This unhappy state lasted about two months, during which I was, not, it is true, explicitly or by profession, but morally and essentially, a thorough-going skeptic.

God at last deigned to heal me of this mental malady; my mind recovered sanity and equilibrium, the primary assumptions of reason recovered with me all their stringency and force. I owed my deliverance, not to a concatenation of proofs and arguments, but to the light which God caused to penetrate into my heart—the light which illuminates the threshold of all knowledge. To suppose that certitude can be only based upon formal arguments is to limit the boundless mercy of God. Some one asked the Prophet the explanation of this passage in the Divine Book: "God opens to Islam the heart of him whom he chooses to direct." "That is spoken," replied the Prophet, "of the light which God sheds in the heart." "And how can man recognize that light?" he was asked. "By his detachment from this world of illusion and by a secret drawing toward

133

the eternal world," the Prophet replied.

On another occasion he said: "God has created his creatures in darkness, and then has shed upon them his light." It is by the help of this light that the search for truth must be carried on. As by his mercy this light descends from time to time among men, we must ceaselessly be on the watch for it. This is also corroborated by another saying of the Apostle: "God sends upon you, at certain times, breathings of his grace; be prepared for them."

My object in this account is to make others understand with what earnestness we should search for truth, since it leads to results we never dreamed of. Primary assumptions have not got to be sought for, since they are always present to our minds; if we engage in such a search, we only find them persistently elude our grasp. But those who push their investigation beyond ordinary limits are safe from the suspicion of negligence in pursuing what is within their reach.

The Different Kinds of Seekers after Truth

When God in the abundance of his mercy had healed me of this malady, I ascertained that those who are engaged in the search for truth may be divided into three groups.

I. Scholastic theologians, who profess to follow theory and speculation.

II. The philosophers, who profess to rely upon formal logic.

III. The Sufis, who call themselves the elect of God and possessors of intuition and knowledge of the truth by means of ecstasy.

"The truth," I said to myself, "must be found among these three classes of men who devote themselves to the search for it. If it escapes them, one must give up all hope of attaining it. Having once surrendered blind belief, it is impossible to return to it, for the essence of such belief is to be unconscious of itself. As soon as this unconsciousness ceases it is shattered like a glass whose fragments can not be again reunited except by being cast again into the furnace and refashioned." Determined to follow these paths and to search out these systems to the bottom, I proceeded with my investigations in the following order: Scholastic theology; philosophical systems; and, finally Sufism.

The Aim of Scholastic Theology and Its Results

Commencing with theological science, I carefully studied and meditated upon it. I read the writings of the authorities in this department and myself composed several treatises. I recognized that this science, while sufficing its own requirements, could not assist me in arriving at the desired goal. In short, its object is to preserve the purity of orthodox beliefs from all heretical innovation. God, by means of his apostle, has revealed to his creatures a belief which is true as regards their temporal and eternal interests; the chief articles of it are laid down in the Koran and in the traditions. Subsequently, Satan suggested to innovators principles contrary to those of orthodoxy; they listened greedily to his suggestions, and the purity of the faith was menaced. God then raised up a school of theologians and inspired them with the desire to defend orthodoxy by means of a system of proofs adapted to unveil the devices of the heretics and to foil the attacks which they made on the doctrines established by tradition.

Such is the origin of scholastic theology. Many of its

adepts, worthy of their high calling, valiantly defended the orthodox faith by proving the reality of prophecy and the falsity of heretical innovations. But, in order to do so, they had to rely upon a certain number of premises, which they accepted in common with their adversaries, and which authority and universal consent or simply the Koran and the traditions obliged them to accept. Their principal effort was to expose the self-contradictions of their opponents and to confute them by means of the premises which they had professed to accept. Now a method of argumentation like this has little value for one who only admits self-evident truths. Scholastic theology could not consequently satisfy me nor heal the malady from which I suffered.

It is true that in its later development theology was not content to defend dogma; it betook itself to the study of first principles, of substances, accidents and the laws which govern them; but through want of a thoroughly scientific basis, it could not advance far in its researches, nor succeed in dispelling entirely the overhanging obscurity which springs from diversities of belief.

I do not, however, deny that it has had a more satisfactory result for others; on the contrary, I admit that it has; but it is by introducing the principle of authority in matters which are not self-evident. Moreover, my object is to explain my own mental attitude and not to dispute with those who have found healing for themselves. Remedies vary according to the nature of the disease; those which benefit some may injure others.

PHILOSOPHY.—How far it is open to censure or not—On what points its adherents may be considered believers or unbelievers, orthodox or heretical—What they have borrowed from the true doctrine to render their chimerical theories acceptable—Why the minds of men swerve from the truth—What criteria are available wherewith to separate the pure gold from the alloy in their systems.

I proceeded from the study of scholastic theology to that of philosophy. It was plain to me that, in order to discover where the professors of any branch of knowledge have erred, one must make a profound study of that science; must equal, nay surpass, those who know most of it, so as to penetrate into secrets of it unknown to them. Only by this method can they be completely answered, and of this method I can find no trace in the theologians of Islam. In theological writings devoted to the refutation of philosophy I have only found a tangled mass of phrases full of contradictions and mistakes, and incapable of deceiving, I will not say a critical mind, but even the common crowd. Convinced that to dream of refuting a doctrine before having thoroughly comprehended it was like shooting at an object in the dark, I devoted myself zealously to the study of philosophy; but in books only and without the aid of a teacher. I gave up to this work all the leisure remaining from teaching and from composing works on law. There were then attending my lectures three hundred of the students of Bagdad. With the help of God, these studies, carried on in secret, so to speak, put me in a condition to thoroughly comprehend philosophical systems within a space of two years. I then spent about a year in meditating on these systems after having thoroughly understood them. I turned them over and over in my mind till they were thoroughly clear of all obscurity. In this manner I acquired a complete knowledge of all their subterfuges and subtleties, of what was truth and what was illusion in them.

I now proceed to give a *résumé* of these doctrines. I ascertained that they were divided into different varieties, and that their adherents might be ranged under diverse heads. All, in spite of their diversity, are marked with the

137

stamp of infidelity and irreligion, although there is a considerable difference between the ancient and modern, between the first and last of these philosophers, according as they have missed or approximated to the truth in a greater or less degree.

Concerning the Philosophical Sects and the Stigma of Infidelity Which Attaches to Them All

The philosophical systems, in spite of their number and variety, may be reduced to three: (1) the Materialists; (2) the Naturalists; (3) the Theists.

(1) *The Materialists.* They reject an intelligent and omnipotent Creator and disposer of the universe. In their view the world exists from all eternity and had no author. The animal comes from semen and semen from the animal; so it had always been and will always be; those who maintain this doctrine are atheists.

(2) *The Naturalists.* These devote themselves to the study of nature and of the marvelous phenomena of the animal and vegetable world. Having carefully analyzed animal organs with the help of anatomy, struck with the wonders of God's work and with the wisdom therein revealed, they are forced to admit the existence of a wise Creator who knows the end and purpose of everything. And certainly no one can study anatomy and the wonderful mechanism of living things without being obliged to confess the profound wisdom of him who has framed the bodies of animals and especially of man. But carried away by their natural researches they believed that the existence of a being absolutely depended upon the proper equilibrium of its organism. According to them, as the latter perishes and is destroyed, so is the thinking faculty which is bound up with it; and as they assert that the restoration of a thing once destroyed to

138

existence is unthinkable, they deny the immortality of the soul. Consequently they deny heaven, hell, resurrection, and judgment. Acknowledging neither a recompense for good deeds nor a punishment for evil ones, they fling off all authority and plunge into sensual pleasures with the avidity of brutes. These also ought to be called atheists, for the true faith depends not only on the acknowledgment of God, but of his Apostle and of the day of judgment. And although they acknowledge God and his attributes, they deny a judgment to come.

(3) Next come the *Theists*. Among them should be reckoned Socrates, who was the teacher of Plato as Plato was of Aristotle. This latter drew up for his disciples the rules of logic, organized the sciences, elucidated what was formerly obscure, and expounded what had not been understood. This school refuted the systems of the two others, *i.e.*, the Materialists and Naturalists; but in exposing their mistaken and perverse beliefs, they made use of arguments which they should not. "God suffices to protect the faithful in war" (Koran, xxxiii. 25).

Aristotle also contended with success against the theories of Plato, Socrates, and the theists who had preceded him, and separated himself entirely from them; but he could not eliminate from his doctrine the stains of infidelity and heresy which disfigure the teaching of his predecessors. We should therefore consider them all as unbelievers, as well as the so-called Mussulman philosophers, such as Ibn Sina (Avicenna) and Farabi, who have adopted their systems.

Let us, however, acknowledge that among Mussulman philosophers none has better interpreted the doctrine of Aristotle than the latter. What others have handed down as his teaching is full of error, confusion, and obscurity adapted to disconcert the reader. The unintelligible can

139

neither be accepted nor rejected. The philosophy of Aristotle, all serious knowledge of which we owe to the translation of these two learned men, may be divided into three portions: the first contains matter justly chargeable with impiety, the second is tainted with heresy, and the third we are obliged to reject absolutely. We proceed to details:

Divisions of the Philosophic Sciences

These sciences, in relation to the aim we have set before us, may be divided into six sections: (1) Mathematics; (2) Logic; (3) Physics; (4) Metaphysics; (5) Politics; (6) Moral Philosophy.

(1) *Mathematics*. Mathematics comprises the knowledge of calculation, geometry, and cosmography: it has no connection with the religious sciences, and proves nothing for or against religion; it rests on a foundation of proofs which, once known and understood, can not be refuted. Mathematics tend, however, to produce two bad results.

The first is this: Whoever studies this science admires the subtlety and clearness of its proofs. His confidence in philosophy increases, and he thinks that all its departments are capable of the same clearness and solidity of proof as mathematics. But when he hears people speak of the unbelief and impiety of mathematicians, of their professed disregard for the Divine Law, which is notorious, it is true that, out of regard for authority, he echoes these accusations, but he says to himself at the same time that, if there was truth in religion, it would not have escaped those who have displayed so much keenness of intellect in the study of mathematics.

Next, when he becomes aware of the unbelief and rejection of religion on the part of these learned men, he concludes that to reject religion is reasonable. How many of such men gone astray I have met whose sole argument was that just mentioned. And supposing one puts to them the following objection: "It does not follow that a man who excels in one branch of knowledge excels in all others, nor that he should be equally versed in jurisprudence, theology, and medicine. It is possible to be entirely ignorant of metaphysics, and yet to be an excellent grammarian. There are past masters in every science who are entirely ignorant of other branches of knowledge. The arguments of the ancient philosophers are rigidly demonstrative in mathematics and only conjectural in religious questions. In order to ascertain this one must proceed to a thorough examination of the matter." Supposing, I say, one makes the above objection to these "apes of unbelief," they find it distasteful. Falling a prey to their passions, to a besotted vanity, and the wish to pass for learned men, they persist in maintaining the pre-eminence of mathematicians in all branches of knowledge. This is a serious evil, and for this reason those who study mathematics should be checked from going too far in their researches. For though far removed as it may be from the things of religion, this study, serving as it does as an introduction to the philosophic systems, casts over religion its malign influence. It is rarely that a man devotes himself to it without robbing himself of his faith and casting off the restraints of religion.

The second evil comes from the sincere but ignorant Mussulman who thinks the best way to defend religion is by rejecting all the exact sciences. Accusing their professors of being astray, he rejects their theories of the eclipses of the sun and moon, and condemns them in the name of religion. These accusations are carried far and wide, they reach the ears of the philosopher who knows that these theories rest on infallible proofs; far from losing confidence in them, he

141

believes, on the contrary, that Islam has ignorance and the denial of scientific proofs for its basis, and his devotion to philosophy increases with his hatred to religion.

It is therefore a great injury to religion to suppose that the defense of Islam involves the condemnation of the exact sciences. The religious law contains nothing which approves them or condemns them, and in their turn they make no attack on religion. The words of the Prophet, "The sun and the moon are two signs of the power of God; they are not eclipsed for the birth or the death of any one; when you see these signs take refuge in prayer and invoke the name of God"—these words, I say, do not in any way condemn the astronomical calculations which define the orbits of these two bodies, their conjunction and opposition according to particular laws. But as for the so-called tradition, "When God reveals himself in anything, he abases himself thereto," it is unauthentic, and not found in any trustworthy collection of the traditions.

Such is the bearing and the possible danger of mathematics.

(2) *Logic.* This science, in the same manner, contains nothing for or against religion. Its object is the study of different kinds of proofs and syllogisms, the conditions which should hold between the premises of a proposition, the way to combine them, the rules of a good definition, and the art of formulating it. For knowledge consists of conceptions which spring from a definition or of convictions which arise from proofs. There is therefore nothing censurable in this science, and it is laid under contribution by theologians as well as by philosophers. The only difference is that the latter use a particular set of technical formulæ and that they push their divisions and subdivisions further.

142

It may be asked, What, then, this has to do with the grave questions of religion, and on what ground opposition should be offered to the methods of logic? The objector, it will be said, can only inspire the logician with an unfavorable opinion of the intelligence and faith of his adversary, since the latter's faith seems to be based upon such objections. But, it must be admitted, logic *is* liable to abuse. Logicians demand in reasoning certain conditions which lead to absolute certainty, but when they touch on religious questions they can no longer postulate these conditions, and ought therefore to relax their habitual rigor. It happens, accordingly, that a student who is enamored of the evidential methods of logic, hearing his teachers accused of irreligion, believes that this irreligion reposes on proofs as strong as those of logic, and immediately, without attempting the study of metaphysics, shares their mistake. This is a serious disadvantage arising from the study of logic.

(3) *Physics.* The object of this science is the study of the bodies which compose the universe: the sky and the stars, and, here below, simple elements such as air, earth, water, fire, and compound bodies—animals, plants, and minerals; the reasons of their changes, developments, and intermixture. By the nature of its researches it is closely connected with the study of medicine, the object of which is the human body, its principal and secondary organs, and the law which governs their changes. Religion having no fault to find with medical science, can not justly do so with physical, except on some special, matters which we have mentioned in the work entitled, "The Destruction of the Philosophers." Besides these primary questions, there are some subordinate ones depending on them, on which physical science is open to objection. But all physical science rests, as we believe, on the following principle: Nature is

entirely subject to God; incapable of acting by itself, it is an instrument in the hand of the Creator; sun, moon, stars, and elements are subject to God and can produce nothing of themselves. In a word, nothing in nature can act spontaneously and apart from God.

(4) *Metaphysics.* This is the fruitful breeding-ground of the errors of philosophers. Here they can no longer satisfy the laws of rigorous argumentation such as logic demands, and this is what explains the disputes which arise between them in the study of metaphysics. The system most closely akin to the system of the Mohammedan doctors is that of Aristotle as expounded to us by Farabi and Avicenna. The sum total of their errors can be reduced to twenty propositions: three of them are irreligious, and the other seventeen heretical. It was in order to combat their system that we wrote the work, "Destruction of the Philosophers." The three propositions in which they are opposed to all the doctrines of Islam are the following:

(*a*) Bodies do not rise again; spirits alone will be rewarded or punished; future punishments will be therefore spiritual and not physical. They are right in admitting spiritual punishments, for there will be such; but they are wrong in rejecting physical punishments, and contradicting in this manner the assertions of the Divine Law.

(*b*) "God takes cognizance of universals, not of specials." This is manifestly irreligious. The Koran asserts truly, "Not an atom's weight in heaven or earth can escape his knowledge" (x. 62).

(*c*) They maintain that the universe exists from all eternity and will never end.

None of these propositions has ever been admitted by Moslems.

144

Besides this, they deny that God has attributes, and maintain that he knows by his essence only and not by means of any attribute accessory to his essence. In this point they approach the doctrine of the Mutazilites, doctrines which we are not obliged to condemn as irreligious. On the contrary, in our work entitled, "Criteria of the Differences Which Divide Islam from Atheism," we have proved the wrongness of those who accuse of irreligion everything which is opposed to their way of looking at things.

(5) *Political Science.* The professors of this confine themselves to drawing up the rules which regulate temporal matters and the royal power. They have borrowed their theories on this point from the books which God has revealed to his prophets and from the sentences of ancient sages, gathered by tradition.

(6) *Moral Philosophy.* The professors of this occupy themselves with defining the attributes and qualities of the soul, grouping them according to genus and species, and pointing out the way to moderate and control them. They have borrowed this system from the Sufis. These devout men, who are always engaged in invoking the name of God, in combating concupiscence and following the way of God by renouncing the pleasures of this world, have received, while in a state of ecstasy, revelations regarding the qualities of the soul, its defects and its evil inclinations. These revelations they have published, and the philosophers making use of them have introduced them into their own systems in order to embellish and give currency to their falsehoods. In the times of the philosophers, as at every other period, there existed some of these fervent mystics. God does not deprive this world of them, for they are its sustainers, and they draw down to it the blessings of heaven according to the tradition: "It is by them that you obtain rain; it is by them that you receive your subsistence."

Such were "the Companions of the Cave," who lived in ancient times, as related by the Koran (xviii.). Now this mixture of moral and philosophic doctrine with the words of the Prophet and those of the Sufis gives rise to two dangers, one for the upholder of those doctrines, the other for their opponent.

The danger for their opponent is serious. A narrow-minded man, finding in their writings moral philosophy mixed with unsupported theories, believes that he ought to entirely reject them and to condemn those who profess them. Having only heard them from their mouth he does not hesitate in his ignorance to declare them false because those who teach them are in error. It is as if some one was to reject the profession of faith made by Christians, "There is only one God and Jesus is his prophet," simply because it proceeds from Christians and without inquiring whether it is the profession of this creed or the denial of Mohammed's prophetic mission which makes Christians infidels. Now, if they are only infidels because of their rejection of our Prophet, we are not entitled to reject those of their doctrines which do not wear the stamp of infidelity. In a word, truth does not cease to be true because it is found among them. Such, however, is the tendency of weak minds: they judge the truth according to its professors instead of judging its professors by the standard of the truth. But a liberal spirit will take as its guide this maxim of the prince of believers, Ali the son of Abu Talib: "Do not seek for the truth by means of men; find first the truth and then you will recognize those who follow it." This is the procedure followed by a wise man. Once in possession of the truth he examines the basis of various doctrines which come before him, and when he has found them true, he accepts them without troubling himself whether the person who teaches them is sincere or a deceiver. Much rather, remembering

146

how gold is buried in the bowels of the earth, he endeavors to disengage the truth from the mass of errors in which it is engulfed. The skilled coin-assayer plunges without hesitation his hand into the purse of the coiner of false money, and relying on experience, separates good coins from bad. It is the ignorant rustic, and not the experienced assayer, who will ask why we should have anything to do with a false coiner. The unskilled swimmer must be kept away from the seashore, not the expert in diving. The child, not the charmer, must be forbidden to handle serpents.

As a matter of fact, men have such a good opinion of themselves, of their mental superiority and intellectual depth; they believe themselves so skilled in discerning the true from the false, the path of safety from those of error, that they should be forbidden as much as possible the perusal of philosophic writings, for though they sometimes escape the danger just pointed out, they can not avoid that which we are about to indicate.

Some of the maxims found in my works regarding the mysteries of religion have met with objectors of an inferior rank in science, whose intellectual penetration is insufficient to fathom such depths. They assert that these maxims are borrowed from the ancient philosophers, whereas the truth is that they are the fruit of my own meditations, but as the proverb says, "Sandal follows the impress of sandal."[11] Some of them are found in our books of religious law, but the greater part are derived from the writings of the Sufis.

But even if they were borrowed exclusively from the doctrines of the philosophers, is it right to reject an opinion when it is reasonable in itself, supported by solid proofs, and contradicting neither the Koran nor the traditions? If we adopt this method and reject every truth which has chanced to have been proclaimed by an impostor, how

147

many truths we should have to reject! How many verses of the Koran and traditions of the prophets and Sufi discourses and maxims of sages we must close our ears to because the author of the "Treatise of the Brothers of Purity" has inserted them in his writings in order to further his cause, and in order to lead minds gradually astray in the paths of error! The consequence of this procedure would be that impostors would snatch truths out of our hands in order to embellish their own works. The wise man, at least, should not make common cause with the bigot blinded by ignorance.

Honey does not become impure because it may happen to have been placed in the glass which the surgeon uses for cupping purposes. The impurity of blood is due, not to its contact with this glass, but to a peculiarity inherent in its own nature; this peculiarity, not existing in honey, can not be communicated to it by its being placed in the cupping-glass; it is therefore wrong to regard it as impure. Such is, however, the whimsical way of looking at things found in nearly all men. Every word proceeding from an authority which they approve is accepted by them, even were it false; every word proceeding from one whom they suspect is rejected, even were it true. In every case they judge of the truth according to its professors and not of men according to the truth which they profess, a *ne plus ultra* of error. Such is the peril in which philosophy involves its opponents.

The second danger threatens those who accept the opinions of the philosophers. When, for instance, we read the "Treatise of the Brothers of Purity," and other works of the same kind, we find in them sentences spoken by the Prophet and quotations from the Sufis. We approve these works; we give them our confidence; and we finish by accepting the errors which they contain, because of the good opinion of them with which they have inspired us at the outset. Thus, by insensible degrees, we are led astray. In view of this danger the reading of philosophic writings so full of vain and delusive utopias should be forbidden, just as the slippery banks of a river are forbidden to one who knows not how to swim. The perusal of these false teachings must be prevented just as one prevents children from touching serpents. A snake-charmer himself will abstain from touching snakes in the presence of his young child, because he knows that the child, believing himself as clever as his father, will not fail to imitate him; and in order to lend more weight to his prohibition the charmer will not touch a serpent under the eyes of his son.

Such should be the conduct of a learned man who is also wise. But the snake-charmer, after having taken the serpent and separated the venom from the antidote, having put the latter on one side and destroyed the venom, ought not to withhold the antidote from those who need it. In the same way the skilled coin-assayer, after having put his hand in the bag of the false coiner, taken out the good coins and thrown away the bad ones, ought not to refuse the good to those who need and ask for it. Such should be the conduct of the learned man. If the patient feels a certain dislike of the antidote because he knows that it is taken from a snake whose body is the receptacle of poison, he should be disabused of this fallacy.

If a beggar hesitates to take a piece of gold which he knows comes from the purse of a false coiner, he should be told that his hesitation is a pure mistake which would deprive him of the advantage which he seeks. It should be proved to him that the contact of the good coins with the bad does not injure the former and does not improve the latter. In the same way the contact of truth with falsehood does not change truth into falsehood, any more than it changes falsehood into truth.

Thus much, then, we have to say regarding the inconveniences and dangers which spring from the study of philosophy.

Sufism

When I had finished my examination of these doctrines I applied myself to the study of Sufism. I saw that in order to understand it thoroughly one must combine theory with practise. The aim which the Sufis set before them is as follows: To free the soul from the tyrannical yoke of the passions, to deliver it from its wrong inclinations and evil instincts, in order that in the purified heart there should only remain room for God and for the invocation of his holy name.

As it was more easy to learn their doctrine than to practise it, I studied first of all those of their books which contain it: "The Nourishment of Hearts," by Abu Talib of Mecca, the works of Hareth el Muhasibi, and the fragments which still remain of Junaid, Shibli, Abu Yezid Bustami, and other leaders (whose souls may God sanctify). I acquired a thorough knowledge of their researches, and I learned all that was possible to learn of their methods by study and oral teaching. It became clear to me that the last stage could not be reached by mere instruction, but only by transport, ecstasy, and the transformation of the moral being.

To define health and satiety, to penetrate their causes and conditions, is quite another thing from being well and satisfied. To define drunkenness, to know that it is caused by vapors which rise from the stomach and cloud the seat of intelligence, is quite a different thing to being drunk. The drunken man has no idea of the nature of drunkenness, just because he is drunk and not in a condition to understand anything, while the doctor, not being under the influence of

150

drunkenness, knows its character and laws. Or if the doctor fall ill, he has a theoretical knowledge of the health of which he is deprived.

In the same way there is a considerable difference between knowing renouncement, comprehending its conditions and causes, and practising renouncement and detachment from the things of this world. I saw that Sufism consists in experiences rather than in definitions, and that what I was lacking belonged to the domain, not of instruction, but of ecstasy and initiation.

The researches to which I had devoted myself, the path which I had traversed in studying religious and speculative branches of knowledge, had given me a firm faith in three things—God, Inspiration, and the Last Judgment. These three fundamental articles of belief were confirmed in me, not merely by definite arguments, but by a chain of causes, circumstances, and proofs which it is impossible to recount. I saw that one can only hope for salvation by devotion and the conquest of one's passions, a procedure which presupposes renouncement and detachment from this world of falsehood in order to turn toward eternity and meditation on God. Finally, I saw that the only condition of success was to sacrifice honors and riches and to sever the ties and attachments of worldly life.

Coming seriously to consider my state, I found myself bound down on all sides by these trammels. Examining my actions, the most fair-seeming of which were my lecturing and professorial occupations, I found to my surprise that I was engrossed in several studies of little value, and profitless as regards my salvation. I probed the motives of my teaching and found that, in place of being sincerely consecrated to God, it was only actuated by a vain desire of honor and reputation. I perceived that I was on the edge of

151

an abyss, and that without an immediate conversion I should be doomed to eternal fire. In these reflections I spent a long time. Still a prey to uncertainty, one day I decided to leave Bagdad and to give up everything; the next day I gave up my resolution. I advanced one step and immediately relapsed. In the morning I was sincerely resolved only to occupy myself with the future life; in the evening a crowd of carnal thoughts assailed and dispersed my resolutions. On the one side the world kept me bound to my post in the chains of covetousness, on the other side the voice of religion cried to me, "Up! Up! Thy life is nearing its end, and thou hast a long journey to make. All thy pretended knowledge is naught but falsehood and fantasy. If thou dost not think now of thy salvation, when wilt thou think of it? If thou dost not break thy chains to-day, when wilt thou break them?" Then my resolve was strengthened, I wished to give up all and flee; but the Tempter, returning to the attack, said, "You are suffering from a transitory feeling; don't give way to it, for it will soon pass. If you obey it, if you give up this fine position, this honorable post exempt from trouble and rivalry, this seat of authority safe from attack, you will regret it later on without being able to recover it."

Thus I remained, torn asunder by the opposite forces of earthly passions and religious aspirations, for about six months from the month Rajab of the year A.D. 1096. At the close of them my will yielded and I gave myself up to destiny. God caused an impediment to chain my tongue and prevented me from lecturing. Vainly I desired, in the interest of my pupils, to go on with my teaching, but my mouth became dumb. The silence to which I was condemned cast me into a violent despair; my stomach became weak; I lost all appetite; I could neither swallow a morsel of bread nor drink a drop of water.

The enfeeblement of my physical powers was such that the doctors, despairing of saving me, said, "The mischief is in the heart, and has communicated itself to the whole organism; there is no hope unless the cause of his grievous sadness be arrested."

Finally, conscious of my weakness and the prostration of my soul, I took refuge in God as a man at the end of himself and without resources. "He who hears the wretched when they cry" (Koran, xxvii. 63) deigned to hear me; He made easy to me the sacrifice of honors, wealth, and family. I gave out publicly that I intended to make the pilgrimage to Mecca, while I secretly resolved to go to Syria, not wishing that the Caliph (may God magnify him) or my friends should know my intention of settling in that country. I made all kinds of clever excuses for leaving Bagdad with the fixed intention of not returning thither. The Imams of Irak criticized me with one accord. Not one of them could admit that this sacrifice had a religious motive, because they considered my position as the highest attainable in the religious community. "Behold how far their knowledge goes!" (Koran, liii. 31). All kinds of explanations of my conduct were forthcoming. Those who were outside the limits of Irak attributed it to the fear with which the Government inspired me. Those who were on the spot and saw how the authorities wished to detain me, their displeasure at my resolution and my refusal of their request, said to themselves, "It is a calamity which one can only impute to a fate which has befallen the Faithful and Learning!"

At last I left Bagdad, giving up all my fortune. Only, as lands and property in Irak can afford an endowment for pious purposes, I obtained a legal authorization to preserve as much as was necessary for my support and that of my children; for there is surely nothing more lawful in the

153

world than that a learned man should provide sufficient to support his family. I then betook myself to Syria, where I remained for two years, which I devoted to retirement, meditation, and devout exercises. I only thought of self-improvement and discipline and of purification of the heart by prayer in going through the forms of devotion which the Sufis had taught me. I used to live a solitary life in the Mosque of Damascus, and was in the habit of spending my days on the minaret after closing the door behind me.

From thence I proceeded to Jerusalem, and every day secluded myself in the Sanctuary of the Rock.[12] After that I felt a desire to accomplish the pilgrimage, and to receive a full effusion of grace by visiting Mecca, Medina, and the tomb of the Prophet. After visiting the shrine of the Friend of God (Abraham), I went to the Hedjaz. Finally, the longings of my heart and the prayers of my children brought me back to my country, although I was so firmly resolved at first never to revisit it. At any rate I meant, if I did return, to live there solitary and in religious meditation; but events, family cares, and vicissitudes of life changed my resolutions and troubled my meditative calm. However irregular the intervals which I could give to devotional ecstasy, my confidence in it did not diminish; and the more I was diverted by hindrances, the more steadfastly I returned to it.

Ten years passed in this manner. During my successive periods of meditation there were revealed to me things impossible to recount. All that I shall say for the edification of the reader is this: I learned from a sure source that the Sufis are the true pioneers on the path of God; that there is nothing more beautiful than their life, nor more praiseworthy than their rule of conduct, nor purer than their morality. The intelligence of thinkers, the wisdom of philosophers, the knowledge of the most learned doctors of

154

the law would in vain combine their efforts in order to modify or improve their doctrine and morals; it would be impossible. With the Sufis, repose and movement, exterior or interior, are illumined with the light which proceeds from the Central Radiance of Inspiration. And what other light could shine on the face of the earth? In a word, what can one criticize in them? To purge the heart of all that does not belong to God is the first step in their cathartic method. The drawing up of the heart by prayer is the key-stone of it, as the cry "Allahu Akbar" (God is great) is the key-stone of prayer, and the last stage is the being lost in God. I say the last stage, with reference to what may be reached by an effort of will; but, to tell the truth, it is only the first stage in the life of contemplation, the vestibule by which the initiated enter.

From the time that they set out on this path, revelations commence for them. They come to see in the waking state angels and souls of prophets; they hear their voices and wise counsels. By means of this contemplation of heavenly forms and images they rise by degrees to heights which human language can not reach, which one can not even indicate without falling into great and inevitable errors. The degree of proximity to Deity which they attain is regarded by some as intermixture of being (haloul), by others as identification (ittihad), by others as intimate union (wasl). But all these expressions are wrong, as we have explained in our work entitled, "The Chief Aim." Those who have reached that stage should confine themselves to repeating the verse—

What I experience I shall not try to say;
Call me happy, but ask me no more.

In short, he who does not arrive at the intuition of these truths by means of ecstasy, knows only the *name* of inspiration. The miracles wrought by the saints are, in fact, merely the earliest forms of prophetic manifestation. Such was the state of the Apostle of God, when, before receiving his commission, he retired to Mount Hira to give himself up to such intensity of prayer and meditation that the Arabs said: "Mohammed is become enamored of God."

This state, then, can be revealed to the initiated in ecstasy, and to him who is incapable of ecstasy, by obedience and attention, on condition that he frequents the society of Sufis till he arrives, so to speak, at an imitative initiation. Such is the faith which one can obtain by remaining among them, and intercourse with them is never painful.

But even when we are deprived of the advantage of their society, we can comprehend the possibility of this state (revelation by means of ecstasy) by a chain of manifest proofs. We have explained this in the treatise entitled "Marvels of the Heart," which forms part of our work, "The Revival of the Religious Sciences." The certitude derived from proofs is called "knowledge"; passing into the state we describe is called "transport"; believing the experience of others and oral transmission is "faith." Such are the three degrees of knowledge, as it is written, "The Lord will raise to different ranks those among you who have believed and those who have received knowledge from him" (Koran, lviii. 12).

But behind those who believe comes a crowd of ignorant people who deny the reality of Sufism, hear discourses on it with incredulous irony, and treat as charlatans those who profess it. To this ignorant crowd the verse applies: "There

156

are those among them who come to listen to thee, and when they leave thee, ask of those who have received knowledge, 'What has he just said?' These are they whose hearts God has sealed up with blindness and who only follow their passions." Among the number of convictions which I owe to the practise of the Sufi rule is the knowledge of the true nature of inspiration. This knowledge is of such great importance that I proceed to expound it in detail.

The Reality of Inspiration: Its Importance for the Human Race

The substance of man at the moment of its creation is a simple monad, devoid of knowledge of the worlds subject to the Creator, worlds whose infinite number is only known to him, as the Koran says: "Only thy Lord knoweth the number of his armies."

Man arrives at this knowledge by the aid of his perceptions; each of his senses is given him that he may comprehend the world of created things, and by the term "world" we understand the different species of creatures. The first sense revealed to man is touch, by means of which he perceives a certain group of qualities—heat, cold, moist, dry. The sense of touch does not perceive colors and forms, which are for it as though they did not exist. Next comes the sense of sight, which makes him acquainted with colors and forms; that is to say, with that which occupies the highest rank in the world of sensation. The sense of hearing succeeds, and then the senses of smell and taste.

When the human being can elevate himself above the world of sense, toward the age of seven, he receives the faculty of discrimination; he enters then upon a new phase of existence and can experience, thanks to this faculty, impressions, superior to those of the senses, which do not occur in the sphere of sensation.

157

He then passes to another phase and receives reason, by which he discerns things necessary, possible, and impossible; in a word, all the notions which he could not combine in the former stages of his existence. But beyond reason and at a higher level by a new faculty of vision is bestowed upon him, by which he perceives invisible things, the secrets of the future and other concepts as inaccessible to reason as the concepts of reason are inaccessible to mere discrimination and what is perceived by discrimination to the senses. Just as the man possessed only of discrimination rejects and denies the notions acquired by reason, so do certain rationalists reject and deny the notion of inspiration. It is a proof of their profound ignorance; for, instead of argument, they merely deny inspiration as a sphere unknown and possessing no real existence. In the same way, a man blind from birth, who knows neither by experience nor by information what colors and forms are, neither knows nor understands them when some one speaks of them to him for the first time.

God, wishing to render intelligible to men the idea of inspiration, has given them a kind of glimpse of it in sleep. In fact, man perceives while asleep the things of the invisible world either clearly manifest or under the veil of allegory to be subsequently lifted by divination. If, however, one was to say to a person who had never himself experienced these dreams that, in a state of lethargy resembling death and during the complete suspension of sight, hearing, and all the senses, a man can see the things of the invisible world, this person would exclaim, and seek to prove the impossibility of these visions by some such argument as the following: "The sensitive faculties are the causes of perception. Now, if one can perceive certain things when one is in full possession of these faculties, how much more is their perception impossible when these faculties are suspended."

The falsity of such an argument is shown by evidence and experience. For in the same way as reason constitutes a particular phase of existence in which intellectual concepts are perceived which are hidden from the senses, similarly, inspiration is a special state in which the inner eye discovers, revealed by a celestial light, mysteries out of the reach of reason. The doubts which are raised regarding inspiration relate (1) to its possibility, (2) to its real and actual existence, (3) to its manifestation in this or that person.

To prove the possibility of inspiration is to prove that it belongs to a category of branches of knowledge which can not be attained by reason. It is the same with medical science and astronomy. He who studies them is obliged to recognize that they are derived solely from the revelation and special grace of God. Some astronomical phenomena only occur once in a thousand years; how then can we know them by experience?

We may say the same of inspiration, which is one of the branches of intuitional knowledge. Further, the perception of things which are beyond the attainment of reason is only one of the features peculiar to inspiration, which possesses a great number of others. The characteristic which we have mentioned is only, as it were, a drop of water in the ocean, and we have mentioned it because people experience what is analogous to it in dreams and in the sciences of medicine and astronomy. These branches of knowledge belong to the domain of prophetic miracles, and reason can not attain to them.

As to the other characteristics of inspiration, they are only revealed to adepts in Sufism and in a state of ecstatic transport. The little that we know of the nature of

159

inspiration we owe to the kind of likeness to it which we find in sleep; without that we should be incapable of comprehending it, and consequently of believing in it, for conviction results from comprehension. The process of initiation into Sufism exhibits this likeness to inspiration from the first. There is in it a kind of ecstasy proportioned to the condition of the person initiated, and a degree of certitude and conviction which can not be attained by reason. This single fact is sufficient to make us believe in inspiration.

We now come to deal with doubts relative to the inspiration of a particular prophet. We shall not arrive at certitude on this point except by ascertaining, either by ocular evidence or by reliable tradition, the facts relating to that prophet. When we have ascertained the real nature of inspiration and proceed to the serious study of the Koran and the traditions, we shall then know certainly that Mohammed is the greatest of prophets. After that we should fortify our conviction by verifying the truth of his preaching and the salutary effect which it has upon the soul. We should verify in experience the truth of sentences such as the following: "He who makes his conduct accord with his knowledge receives from God more knowledge"; or this, "God delivers to the oppressor him who favors injustice"; or again, "Whosoever when rising in the morning has only one anxiety (to please God), God will preserve him from all anxiety in this world and the next."

When we have verified these sayings in experience thousands of times, we shall be in possession of a certitude on which doubt can obtain no hold. Such is the path we must traverse in order to realize the truth of inspiration. It is not a question of finding out whether a rod has been changed into a serpent, or whether the moon has been split in two.[13] If we regard miracles in isolation, without their

160

countless attendant circumstances, we shall be liable to confound them with magic and falsehood, or to regard them as a means of leading men astray, as it is written, "God misleads and directs as he chooses" (Koran, xxxv. 9); we shall find ourselves involved in all the difficulties which the question of miracles raises. If, for instance, we believe that eloquence of style is a proof of inspiration, it is possible that an eloquent style composed with this object may inspire us with a false belief in the inspiration of him who wields it. The supernatural should be only one of the constituents which go to form our belief, without our placing too much reliance on this or that detail. We should rather resemble a person who, learning a fact from a group of people, can not point to this or that particular man as his informant, and who, not distinguishing between them, can not explain precisely how his conviction regarding the fact has been formed.

Such are the characteristics of scientific certitude. As to the transport which permits men to see the truth and, so to speak, to handle it, it is only known to the Sufis. What I have just said regarding the true nature of inspiration is sufficient for the aim which I have proposed to myself. I may return to the subject later, if necessary.

I pass now to the causes of the decay of faith and show the means of bringing back those who have erred and of preserving them from the dangers which threaten them. To those who doubt because they are tinctured with the doctrine of the Ta'limites, my treatise entitled, "The Just Balance," affords a sufficient guide; therefore it is unnecessary to return to the subject here.

As to the vain theories of the Ibahat, I have grouped them in seven classes, and explained them in the work entitled, "Alchemy of Happiness." For those whose faith has been

161

undermined by philosophy, so far that they deny the reality of inspiration, we have proved the truth and necessity of it, seeking our proofs in the hidden properties of medicines and of the heavenly bodies. It is for them that we have written this treatise, and the reason for our seeking for proofs in the sciences of medicine and of astronomy is because these sciences belong to the domain of philosophy. All those branches of knowledge which our opponents boast of—astronomy, medicine, physics, and divination—provide us with arguments in favor of the Prophet.

As to those who, professing a lip-faith in the Prophet, adulterate religion with philosophy, they really deny inspiration, since in their view the Prophet is only a sage whom a superior destiny has appointed as guide to men, and this view belies the true nature of inspiration. To believe in the Prophet is to admit that there is above intelligence a sphere in which are revealed to the inner vision truths beyond the grasp of intelligence, just as things seen are not apprehended by the sense of hearing, nor things understood by that of touch. If our opponent denies the existence of such a higher region, we can prove to him, not only its possibility, but its actuality. If, on the contrary, he admits its existence, he recognizes at the same time that there are in that sphere things which reason can not grasp; nay, which reason rejects as false and absurd. Suppose, for instance, that the fact of dreams occurring in sleep were not so common and notorious as it is, our wise men would not fail to repudiate the assertion that the secrets of the invisible world can be revealed while the senses are, so to speak, suspended.

Again, if it were to be said to one of them, "Is it possible that there is in the world a thing as small as a grain, which being carried into a city can destroy it and afterward destroy itself so that nothing remains either of the city or of itself?"

"Certainly," he would exclaim, "it is impossible and ridiculous." Such, however, is the effect of fire, which would certainly be disputed by one who had not witnessed it with his own eyes. Now, the refusal to believe in the mysteries of the other life is of the same kind.

As to the fourth cause of the spread of unbelief—the decay of faith owing to the bad example set by learned men—there are three ways of checking it.

(1) One can answer thus: "The learned man whom you accuse of disobeying the divine law knows that he disobeys, as you do when you drink wine or exact usury or allow yourself in evil-speaking, lying, and slander. You know your sin and yield to it, not through ignorance, but because you are mastered by concupiscence. The same is the case with the learned man. How many believe in doctors who do not abstain from fruit and cold water when strictly forbidden them by a doctor! That does not prove that those things are not dangerous, or that their faith in the doctor was not solidly established. Similar errors on the part of learned men are to be imputed solely to their weakness."

(2) Or again, one may say to a simple and ignorant man: "The learned man reckons upon his knowledge as a viaticum for the next life. He believes that his knowledge will save him and plead in his favor, and that his intellectual superiority will entitle him to indulgence; lastly, that if his knowledge increases his responsibility, it may also entitle him to a higher degree of consideration. All that is possible; and even if the learned man has neglected practise, he can at any rate produce proofs of his knowledge. But you, poor, witless one, if, like him, you neglect practise, destitute as you are of knowledge, you will perish without anything to plead in your favor."

(3) Or one may answer, and this reason is the true one:

"The truly learned man only sins through carelessness, and does not remain in a state of impenitence. For real knowledge shows sin to be a deadly poison, and the other world to be superior to this. Convinced of this truth, man ought not to exchange the precious for the vile. But the knowledge of which we speak is not derived from sources accessible to human diligence, and that is why progress in mere worldly knowledge renders the sinner more hardened in his revolt against God."

True knowledge, on the contrary, inspires in him who is initiate in it more fear and more reverence, and raises a barrier of defense between him and sin. He may slip and stumble, it is true, as is inevitable with one encompassed by human infirmity, but these slips and stumbles will not weaken his faith. The true Moslem succumbs occasionally to temptation, but he repents and will not persevere obstinately in the path of error.

I pray God the Omnipotent to place us in the ranks of his chosen, among the number of those whom he directs in the path of safety, in whom he inspires fervor lest they forget him; whom he cleanses from all defilement, that nothing may remain in them except himself; yea, of those whom he indwells completely, that they may adore none beside him.

END OF THE RESCUES FROM ERROR

THE DISCOVERER OF TRUTH

ZAMAKHSHARI'S COMMENTARY ON THE KORAN

IN THE NAME OF THE MOST MERCIFUL GOD, KIND AND PITYING

Praise to God, who has sent from heaven the Koran, in the form of an address of which the words are coherent and arranged in order, and who has sent it in continuous chapters according to the demands of necessity; who has willed that it should begin by expressing the praise due to God, and end by recounting his power and protection; who has included in it two kinds of revelations, the one obscure, the other perfectly clear; who has divided the Koran into Suras, and the Suras into verses, and has distinguished the different parts by divisions and conclusions: qualifications which apply only to that which has been created, and produced without a model, and could only be the attributes of things which have had a beginning and recognize an author of whom they are the work. Praise to him who has reserved to himself alone the privilege of priority and eternity, and who has given to everything save himself the characteristic of having been created.

Praise to him who has created the Koran, the sense of which is a light to guide the spirit, the demonstrations of which are clear; like an inspiration which blazons forth its proof and authentic title; like a lecture written in the Arabic language, and free from all faults, which is the key to open the treasures of all spiritual and temporal blessings, and which confirms and witnesses the truth of all the Holy Books which have preceded it; like a miracle which, alone among all miracles, has existed during all the passage of the centuries, and a book which, alone among all books, will be repeated in every language and in every place.

By this book, he has shut the mouths of the most nobly born Arabs, in that they are challenged to produce something to be compared with it, he has rendered mute the most eloquent orators in that he has defied them to imitate it. Amongst those who possess the greatest command of the language in all its purity, no one has the enterprise to compose anything which equals it, or even approaches it. No one of those who are distinguished for their eloquence has dared to compete with him in a single chapter equal to the shortest Sura included in the Koran. Yet the orators of the land are more numerous than the pebbles of the Batha valley and more plentiful than the grains of sand in the desert of Dahna. The blood of patriotism has not boiled in their veins, and zeal for the honor of their cause has not moved them to the undertaking, although they are known to be naturally inclined to disputes and quarrels, and ready to embrace with ardor and without moderation every opportunity for rivalry and hostility; although when roused to fight for the defense of their reputation, they are quick to face the gravest dangers, and will plunge themselves into every excess to obtain the object of their desires. If any one opposes their title to glory or prevails against them, they oppose him in great numbers; if any one in their hearing boasts of a glorious deed, they respond with a multitude of glorious deeds.

God has employed against them two kinds of weapons, first the written law, then the sword; but they have not challenged him to combat nor attempted to cope with the sword, although the drawn sword is no more than a trifling weapon, fitted only for badinage, if the strength of authentic truth is not joined to the victorious point. Certainly, if they have in no way put up even a semblance of resistance to the truth which has been presented to them, it is simply because they know well that the sea, released from its boundaries, would envelop and overflow any mere well made by human hands; and the sun, by the brightness of its fire, eclipses the light of all the stars.

May the favors of God shine on the most worthy of those who have received revelations, on the friend of God, Abu'l-Kasem Mohammed, son of Abd-Allah, son of Abd-Almotalleb, son of Haschem, whose standard is raised amongst the descendants of Lowaiy; who has been fortified by constant protection and assisted by wisdom, whose visage radiates glory, and who shines with all the signs of nobility; on the illustrious Prophet whose name has been inscribed in the Law and the Gospel! May blessings fall also upon his sainted descendants, on those successors to his authority who have with him the ties which are born of marriage!

It is well known that, in the profundities of science and the principles of the arts, there is little difference between the learned of different classes. Those who practise the various arts are equal, or nearly equal. If one professor outdistances another, it is only by a few steps; and if one artist outstrips another, it is only by a short distance. But where one sees a true difference among the classes, where they make every effort to surpass each other, where there is true emulation and rivalry, there one finds real inferiors and superiors, of the sort that there is among those who pursue the same career from incomprehensible distances, distances so great that one alone balances a thousand others. There are, in the sciences as in the arts, the beauties of certain delicate points; there are subtle thoughts which arouse the wisdom of reflective spirits, profound, hidden secrets covered with veils which very few men, even among those of the most distinguished talent, can lift, secrets which can only be discovered and brought to light by those who among men of merit are like the pearl placed in the center of the necklace, and like the stone which is set in the gold of the ring. Ordinary men have not the eyes to create such excellences, and are as though chained to their seats by a servile desire to imitate, and can not even flatter themselves that any one will trim the hair from their foreheads[14] and give them freedom.

Of all the sciences, that which abounds in the most difficulties, which demands the greatest effort in spirit, which offers the largest number of problems capable of fatiguing the strongest intellect, I mean those extraordinary subtleties from which it is difficult to extricate oneself, which are locked as if in vaults, whose thread is cut and difficult to regain—that science is the interpreting of the Koran. It is a science for which, as has been said by Djahed in his work entitled, "Composition of the Koran," no savants are fitted, and to which they devote their lives without hope of complete success.

I have often noticed that my confrères in religion, men who hold the foremost rank among the disciples of the true faith and law, men exceptionally proficient in the knowledge of the language of the Arabs and in the fundamental dogmas of religion, have been enthusiastic in expressing their satisfaction and admiration every time that, consulted by them for the interpretation of some passage of the Koran, I have explained their difficulty and disclosed to them the truth which was hidden from them. They expressed a keen desire for me to write a work treating on the subject in all its phases. At last they joined in begging me to dictate to them a commentary which should unveil all the mysteries of the Holy Book, and help them to understand the different explanations and opinions. I excused myself from doing as they desired, but they continually renewed their pleading; and, to conquer my resistance, they employed the mediation of the chief religious men, and the most learned among those who professed doctrines of justice and unity. I realized that it was obligatory upon me to defer to their desires, so that I came to consider such a work as a personal duty and task; but that which finally brought me to consent was that I saw our age to be in a state of decay, and the men of our time to be degenerating. I realized that far from being able to raise themselves to worthy heights in the two sciences of thought and exposition, they were not even capable of attaining to those weaker means which serve as instruments in the interpretation of the Koran. I therefore resolved to write this book that it might be for them The Discoverer of Truth.

GOLDEN NECKLACES
OR
THE MAXIMS OF ZAMAKHSHAHI

I

When you go to the mosque, walk with reverence; and when you pray, fill your heart with humility. Think of the power of the glorious King, and do not forget what is written concerning the temptations of the devil. Consider before what all-powerful sovereign you kneel, and what deceitful enemy you have to combat. Verily, no one can maintain himself on a firm foundation in this difficult world, except it be the man who is loyal to noble principles and fortified by his profession of faith; the faithful who sighs in fear of chastisement, contrite, repentant, eager in the pursuit of reward, who spurs his horse into the arena of obedience, and disciplines his spirit in the practise of submission.

II

Did I say to you that our country is destined to mourning? That will become true when an unjust sovereign rules. Tyranny is heavier than the horse's hoofs, more destructive than the unchained torrents, more deadly than the poisoned winds of Yemen, more devastating than the plague. Tyranny prevents prayers rising to heaven and prevents the blessings of heaven from falling upon the earth. Flee far from the abode of this menace, even if you are one of the highest nobles of the land, the most illustrious because of your wealth and your children. Fear lest the birds of ruin fatten on the land, and earthquakes or lightnings destroy its inhabitants.

III

Do not pride yourself on the nobility of your birth, for that belongs to your father; join to your hereditary virtues those which you have acquired recently. By this union you will be truly noble. Do not feel elated over the nobility of your father, if you can not draw pride from that which is in yourself; for the glory of your ancestors is vain if you have not a personal glory. There is the same difference between the fame of your ancestors and your own fame that there is between your food of yesterday and of to-day; for the feast that has passed can not calm the hunger of to-day, and still less can it provide for the days which follow.

ARABIC LITERATURE

THE "ASSEMBLIES" OF AL HARIRI

"The richness of the style is even more wonderful than the delicate web of the stories."

CLEMENT HUART.

"I composed fifty assemblies, comprising the serious in language and the lively, the delicate and the dignified, the brilliancies of eloquence and its pearls, the beauties of scholarship and its rarities."

AL HARIRI.

THE "ASSEMBLIES" OF AL HARIRI

(INTRODUCTION)

THE work of Al Hariri may well stand as our best example of typical Arab prose. With regard to religious writing, a few thoughtful Mohammedans, as we have seen, might travel, and seek new light, and meditate profoundly; but the great mass of the people were merely blindly fanatic. Mohammed was the prophet of God, and any one who failed to shout this with the rest of the world, was to be killed. Popular interest went but little further. But when you turned to the art of stringing words together, every true Arab was immediately attentive. There was an Arab proverb that God had given genius, or true creative ability, to three things, the brain of the Frank, the hand of the Chinaman, and the tongue of the Arab.

To our own more sober literary sense the clever twists of phrase and sound in which these people took such pride, seem but the outer garment of thought, more apt to confuse than to reveal its deeper meaning. Yet what the Arabs admire, they admire; and they find it to perfection in Al Hariri's "Assemblies." No mere translation can convey its intricacies of sound and sense. Only such an artistic word-juggler as Al Hariri himself could convey the impression of the original. And Al Hariri himself labored long on each brief "Assembly," polishing and repolishing, before he submitted each tale to the judgment of his keenly critical listeners.

The name "Assemblies" he gave to his work because each tale pictures an assembly of people. The form is highly artificial, for, while the author represents himself as accidentally stumbling upon each assembly, yet each proves ultimately to consist of a gathering of people listening with admiration to the brilliant words and clever rascalities of the same old beggar, Abu Zayd. The trick played by Abu Zayd is usually slight, the chief interest from the Arab view-point depending on the beggar's witty words and especially upon his supposedly extemporaneous verse.

Neither should the reader pass unnoticed the moral side of Hariri's work. He quite definitely thinks of himself as a teacher, and studies to make each "Assembly" a worthy guide to righteousness. His "Assemblies" number fifty in all, but the earlier ones are generally accepted as the best, the eleventh and twelfth being particularly noted for their excellence, after which the collection seems slightly to decline.

Of course Al Hariri was by no means alone in composing this sort of tale. Similar "Assemblies" had preceded his; many more were to follow. In short we touch here upon the "popular literature" of the Arabs, the collection of short stories which were to blossom into the "Arabian Nights"— though in the later tales of this character we find less of verse and more of story, in short less of the Arab and more of the increasing Persian influence.

THE "ASSEMBLIES" OF AL HARIRI

PREFACE

IN THE NAME OF GOD THE MERCIFUL, MOST MERCIFUL

Thus saith the excellent, the incomparable, Abu Mohammed al Kasim ibn 'Ali ibn Mohammed ibn 'Othman Al Hariri of Basrah (God cool his resting-place).

O God, we praise thee for what perspicuity thou hast taught, and what enunciation thou hast inspired; as we praise thee for what bounty thou hast enlarged, what mercy thou hast diffused: And we take refuge with thee from the vehemence of fluency and the immoderation of talkativeness, as we take refuge with thee from the vice of inarticulateness and the shame of hesitation. And by thee we seek to be kept from temptation through the flattery of the praiser and the connivance of the favor, as we seek to be kept from exposure to the defaming of the slanderer and the betrayal of the informer. And we ask pardon of thee if our desires carry us into the region of ambiguities, as we ask pardon if our steps advance to the domain of errors. And we ask of thee succor which shall lead us aright, and a heart turning with justice, and a tongue adorned with truth, and a speech strengthened with demonstration, and accuracy that shall keep us from mistake, and resolution that shall conquer caprice, and perception by which we may estimate duly: And that thou wilt help us by thy guidance to conceive, and enable us by thy assistance to express; that thou wilt

175

guard us from error in narration, and turn us from unseemliness in jesting; that we may be secure from slanders of the tongue; that we may be free from the ill of tinseled speech; that we walk not in the road of sin, nor stand in the place of repentance; that we be not pursued by suit or censure, nor need to flee from hastiness to excuse. O God, fulfil to us this wish; give us to attain to this desire: put us not forth of thy large shadow, make us not a morsel for the devourer. For now we stretch forth to thee the hand of entreaty; we are thorough in humiliation to thee and abasement. And we call down thy abundant grace and thy bounty that is over all, with humbleness of seeking and with the venture of hope. Also approaching thee through the merits of Mohammed, lord of men, the intercessor whose intercession shall be received at the congregation of judgment. By whom thou hast set the seal to the prophets, and whose degree thou hast exalted to the highest heaven; whom thou hast described in thy clear-speaking Book, and hast said (and thou art the most truthful of sayers): "It is the word of a noble envoy, of him who is mighty in the presence of the Lord of the throne, having authority, obeyed, yea, faithful." O God, send thy blessing on him and his house who guide aright, and his companions who built up the faith; and make us followers of his guidance and theirs, and profit us all by the loving of him and them: for thou art Almighty, and one meet to answer prayer.

And now: In a meeting devoted to that learning whose breeze has stilled in this age, whose lights are nigh gone out, there ran a mention of the Assemblies which had been invented by Badi'az Zeman, the sage of Hamadan (God show him mercy); in which he had referred the composition to Abu'l Fath of Alexandria and the relation of 'Isa, son of Hisham. And both these are persons obscure, not known; vague, not to be recognized. Then suggested to me one

176

whose suggestion is as a decree, and obedience to whom is as a prize, that I should compose Assemblies, following in them the method of Badi' (although the lame steed attains not to outrun like the stout one). Then I reminded him of what is said concerning him who joins even two words, or strings together one or two verses: and deprecated this position in which the understanding is bewildered, and the fancy misses aim, and the depth of the intelligence is probed, and a man's real value is made manifest: and in which one is forced to be as a wood-gatherer by night, or as he who musters footmen and horsemen together: considering, too, that the voluble man is seldom secure or pardoned if he trips. But when he consented not to forbearance, and freed me not from his demand, I assented to his invitation with the assenting of the obedient, and displayed in according with him all my endeavor; and composed, in spite of what I suffered from frozen genius, and dimmed intelligence, and failing judgment, and afflicting cares, fifty Assemblies, comprising what is serious in language and lively, what is delicate in expression and dignified; the brilliancies of eloquence and its pearls, and beauties of scholarship and its rarities: besides what I have adorned them with of verses of the Koran and goodly metonymies, and studded them with of Arab proverbs, and scholarly elegancies, and grammatical riddles, and decisions dependent on the meaning of words, and original addresses, and ornate orations, and tear-moving exhortations, and amusing jests: all of which I have indited as by the tongue of Abu Zayd of Seruj, while I have attributed the relating of them to Al Harith, son of Hammam, of Basra. And whenever I change the pasture I have no purpose but to inspirit the reader, and to increase the number of those who shall seek my book. And of the poetry of others I have introduced nothing but two single verses, on which I have based the fabric of the Assembly of Holwan; and two others, in a couplet, which I have inserted

177

at the conclusion of the Assembly of Kerej. And, as for the rest, my own mind is the father of its virginity, the author of its sweet and its bitter. Yet I acknowledge withal that Badi' (God show him mercy) is a mighty passer of goals, a worker of wonders; and that he who essays after him to the composition of an Assembly, even though he be gifted with the eloquence of Kodameh, does but scoop up of his overflow, and travels that path only by his guidance. And excellently said one:

If before it mourned, I had mourned my love for Su'da, then should I have healed my soul, nor had afterward to repent.

But it mourned before me, and its mourning excited mine, and I said, "The superiority is to the one that is first."

Now I hope I shall not be, in respect of the playful style that I display, and the source that I repair to, like the beast that scratched up its death with its hoof, or he who cut off his nose with his own hand; so as to be joined to those who are "most of all losers in their works, whose course on earth has been in vain, while they count that they have done fair deeds." Since I know that although he who is intelligent and liberal will connive at me, and he who is friendly and partial may defend me, I can hardly escape from the simpleton who is ignorant, or the spiteful man who feigns ignorance; who will detract from me on account of this composition, and will give out that it is among the things forbidden of the law. But yet, whoever scans matters with the eye of intelligence, and makes good his insight into principles, will rank these Assemblies in the order of useful writings, and class them with the fables that relate to brutes and lifeless objects. Now none was ever heard of whose hearing shrank from such tales, or who held as sinful those who related them at ordinary times. Moreover, since deeds depend on intentions, and in these lies the effectiveness of religious obligations, what fault is there in one who

178

composes stories for instruction, not for display, and whose purpose in them is the education and not the fablings? Nay, is he not in the position of one who assents to doctrine, and "guides to the right path"?

Yet am I content if I may carry my caprice, and then be quit of it, without any debt against me or to me.

And of God I seek to be helped in what I purpose, and to be kept from that which makes defective, and to be led to that which leads aright. For there is no refuge but to him, and no seeking of succor but in him, and no prospering but from him, and no sanctuary but he. On him I rely, and to him I have recourse.

THE FIRST ASSEMBLY
(CALLED "OF SAN'A")[15]

Al Harith, son of Hammam, related: When I mounted the hump of exile, and misery removed me from my fellows, the shocks of the time cast me to San'a of Yemen. And I entered it with wallets empty, manifest in my need; I had not a meal; I found not in my sack a mouthful. Then began I to traverse its ways like one crazed, and to roam in its depths as roams the thirsting bird. And wherever ranged my glances, wherever ran my goings at morn or even, I sought some generous man before whom I might fray the tissue of my countenance, to whom I might be open concerning my need; or one well bred, whose aspect might dispel my pain, whose anecdote might relieve my thirsting. Until the close of my circuit brought me, and the overture of courtesy guided me, to a wide place of concourse, in which was a throng and a wailing. Then I entered the thicket of the crowd to explore what was drawing forth tears. And I saw in the middle of the ring a person slender of make; upon him was the equipment of pilgrimage, and he had the voice of lamentation. And he was studding cadences with the jewels of his wording, and striking hearings with the reproofs of his admonition. And now the medley of the crowds had surrounded him, as the halo surrounds the moon, or the shell the fruit. So I crept toward him, that I might catch of his profitable sayings, and gather up of his gems. And I heard him say, as he coursed along in his career, and the throat of his improvisation made utterance:

O thou reckless in petulance, trailing the garment of vanity! O thou headstrong in follies, turning aside to idle tales! How long wilt thou persevere in thine error, and eat sweetly of the pasture of thy wrong? How far wilt thou be

180

extreme in thy pride, and not abstain from thy wantonness? Thou provokest by thy rebellion the Master of thy forelock; in the foulness of thy behaving thou goest boldly against the Knower of thy secret. Thou hidest thyself from thy neighbor, but thou art in the sight of thy Watcher; thou concealest from thy slave, but no hidden thing is hidden from thy Ruler. Thinkest thou that thy state will profit thee when thy departure draweth near? or that thy wealth will deliver thee when thy deeds destroy thee? or that thy repentance will suffice for thee when thy foot slippeth? or that thy kindred will lean to thee in the day that thy judgment-place gathereth thee? How is it thou hast not walked in the high-road of guidance, and hastened the treatment of thy disease, and blunted the edge of thine iniquity, and restrained thyself—thy chief enemy? Is not death thy doom? What then is thy preparation? Is not gray hair thy warning? What then is thy excuse? And in the grave's niche thy sleeping-place? What dost thou say? And to God thy going? and who shall be thy defender? Oft hath the time awakened thee, but thou hast set thyself to slumber; and admonition hath drawn thee, but thou hast strained against it; and warnings have been manifest to thee, but thou hast made thyself blind; and truth hath been established to thee, but thou hast disputed it; and death hath bid thee remember, but thou hast sought to forget; and it hath been in thy power to impart of good, but thou hast not imparted. Thou preferrest money which thou mayest hoard before piety which thou mayest keep in mind: thou choosest a castle thou mayest rear rather than bounty thou mayest confer. Thou inclinest from the guide from whom thou mightest get guidance, to the pelf thou mayest gain as a gift; thou lettest the love of the raiment thou covetest overcome the recompense thou mightest earn. The rubies of gifts cling to thy heart more than the seasons of prayer; and the heightening of dowries is preferred with thee to

181

continuance in almsgivings. The dishes of many meats are more desired to thee than the leaves of doctrines; the jesting of comrades is more cheerful to thee than the reading of the Koran. Thou commandest to righteousness, but violatest its sanctuary; thou forbiddest from deceit, but refrainest not thyself: thou turnest men from oppression, and then thou drawest near to it; thou fearest mankind, but God is more worthy that thou shouldest fear him. Then he recited:

Woe to him who seeks the world, and turns to it his
    careering:
And recovers not from his greediness for it, and the excess
    of his love.
Oh, if he were wise, but a drop of what he seeks would
    content him.

Then he laid his dust, and let his spittle subside; and put his bottle on his arm, and his staff under his armpit. And when the company gazed on his uprising, and saw that he equipped himself to move away from the midst, each of them put his hand into his bosom, and filled for him a bucket from his stream: and said, "Use this for thy spending, or divide it among thy friends." And he received it with half-closed eyes, and turned away from them, giving thanks; and began to take leave of whoever would escort him, that his road might be hidden from them; and to dismiss whoever would follow him, that his dwelling might be unknown. Said Al Harith, son of Hammam: Now I went after him, concealing from him my person; and followed on his track from where he could not see me; until he came to a cave, and slipped into it suddenly. So I waited for him till he put off his sandals and washed his feet, and then I ran in upon him; and found him sitting opposite an attendant, at some white bread and a roast kid, and over against them was a jar of date-wine. And I said to him, "Sirrah, was that thy story, and is this thy reality? "But he puffed the puff of heat and went near to burst with rage; and ceased not to stare at me till I thought he would leap upon me. But when his fire was allayed, and his flame hid itself, he recited:

I don the black robe to seek my meal, and I fix my hook in
     the hardest prey:
And of my preaching I make a noose, and steal with it
     against the chaser and the chased.
Fortune has forced me to make way even to the lion of the
     thicket by the subtlety of my beguiling.
Yet do I not fear its change, nor does my loin quiver at it:
Nor does a covetous mind lead me to water at any well
     that will soil my honor.
Now if Fortune were just in its decree it would not
     empower the worthless with authority.

Then he said to me, "Come and eat; or, if thou wilt, rise and tell." But I turned to his attendant, and said, "I conjure thee, by him through whom harm is deprecated, that thou tell me who is this." He said, "This is Abu Zayd, of Seruj, the light of foreigners, the crown of the learned." Then I turned back to whence I came, and was extreme in wonder at what I saw.

THE SECOND ASSEMBLY
(CALLED "OF HOLWAN")[16]

Al Harith, son of Hammam, related: Ever since my amulets were doffed and my turbans were donned, I was eager to visit learning's seat and to jade to it the camels of seeking, that through it I might cleave to what would be my ornament among men, my rain-cloud in thirst. And through the excess of my longing to kindle at it, and my desire to robe myself in its raiment, I discussed with every one, great and small, and sought my draught both of the rain-flood and the dew, and solaced myself with hope and desire. Now when I descended at Holwan, and had already tried the brethren, and tested their values, and proved what

183

was worthless or fine, I found there Abu Zayd of Seruj, shifting among the varieties of pedigree, beating about in various courses of gain-getting; for at one time he claimed to be of the race of Sasan, and at another he made himself kin to the princes of Ghassan; and now he sallied forth in the vesture of poets; and anon he put on the pride of nobles. And yet with all this diversifying of his condition, and this display of contradiction, he is adorned with grace and information, and courtesy and knowledge, and astonishing eloquence, and obedient improvisation, and excelling accomplishments, and a foot that mounts the hills of the sciences. Now, through his goodly attainments he is associated with in spite of his faults; and through the largeness of his information there is a fondness for the sight of him; and through the blandishment of his fair-speaking men are loath to oppose him; and through the sweetness of his address he is helped to his desire. Then I clung to his skirts for the sake of his peculiar accomplishments, and valued highly his affection by reason of his precious qualities.

With him I wiped away my cares, and beheld my fortune
       displayed to me, open of face, gleaming with light.
I looked upon his nearness to me as kinship, his abiding
       as wealth, his aspect as a full draught, his life as
       rain.

Thus we remained a long season; he produced for me daily some pleasantness, and drove some doubt from my heart, until the hand of want mixed for him the cup of parting, and the lack of a meal urged him to abandon Irak; and the failures of supply cast him into desert regions, and the waving of the banner of distress ranged him in the line of travelers; and he sharpened for departure the edge of determination, and journeyed away, drawing my heart with his leading cord.

After he was gone none pleased me who kept by me, none

184

filled me with affection by urging me to intimacy.
Since he strayed away none has appeared to me his like in
    excellence; no friend has gotten the equal of his
    qualities.

So he was hidden from me a season: I knew not his lair; I found none to tell of him; but when I had returned from my wandering to the place where my branch had sprouted, I was once present in the town library, which is the council-hall of scholars, the meeting-place of residents and strangers: Then there entered one with a thick beard and a squalid aspect, and he saluted those who sat, and took seat in the last rows of the people. Then began he to produce what was in his wallet, and to astonish those present by the sagacity of his judgment. And he said to the man who was next him, "What is the book into which thou lookest?" He said, "The poems of Abu 'Obadeh; him of whose excellence men bear witness." He said, "In what thou hast seen hast thou hit on any fine thing which thou admirest?" He said, "Yes; the line,

As though she smiled from strung pearls or hailstones, or
    camomile-flowers.

For it is original in the use of similitude which it contains." He said to him, "Here is a wonder! here is a lack of taste, Sir, thou hast taken for fat what is only swollen; thou hast blown on that which is no fuel: where art thou in comparison with the rare verse which unites the similitudes of the teeth?

My life a ransom for those teeth whose beauty charms,
    and which a purity adorns sufficing thee for all
    other.
She parts her lips from fresh pearls, and from hail-stones,
    and from camomile-flowers, and from the palm-
    shoot, and from bubbles.

Then each one approved the couplet and admired it, and bade him repeat it and dictate it. And he was asked, "Whose is this verse, and is its author living or dead?" He said, "By Allah, right is most worthy to be followed, and truth is most fitting to be listened to: Know, friends, that it is his who talks with you to-day." Said Al Harith: Now it was as though the company doubted of his fathering, and were unwilling to give credit to his claim. And he perceived what had fallen into their thoughts, and was aware of their inward unbelief; and was afraid that blame might chance to him, or ill-fame reach him; so he quoted from the Koran, "Some suspicions are a sin." Then he said, "O ye reciters of verse, physicians of sickly phrase!—Truly the purity of the gem is shown by the testing, and the hand of truth rends the cloak of doubt.—Now it was said aforetime that by trial is a man honored or contemned. So come! I now expose my hidden store to the proving, I offer my saddle-bag for comparison." Then hastened one who was there and said: "I know a verse such that there is no weaving on its beam, such that no genius can supply one after its image. Now, if thou wish to draw our hearts to thee, compose after this style:

She rained pearls from the daffodil, and watered the rose,
and bit upon the 'unnab with hail-stone.

And it was but the glance of an eye, or less, before he recited rarely:

I asked her when she met me to put off her crimson veil,
and to endow my hearing with the sweetest of
tidings:
And she removed the ruddy light which covered the
brightness of her moon, and she dropped pearls
from a perfumed ring.

Then all present were astonished at his readiness, and acknowledged his honesty. And when he perceived that they approved his diction, and were hastening into the path of honoring him, he looked down the twinkling of an eye; then he said, "Here are two other verses for you"; and recited:

> She came on the day when departure afflicted, in black
>   robes, biting her fingers like one regretful,
>   confounded:
> And night lowered on her morn, and a branch supported
>   them both, and she bit into crystal with pearls.

Then did the company set high his value, and deem that
his steady rain was a plenteous one; and they made pleasant
their converse with him, and gave him goodly clothing.
Said the teller of this story: Now when I saw the blazing of
his firebrand, and the gleam of his unveiled brightness, I
fixed a long look to guess at him, and made my eye to stray
over his countenance. And lo! he was our Shaykh of Seruj;
but now his dark night was moon-lit. Then I congratulated
myself on his coming thither, and hastened to kiss his hand:
and said to him, "What has changed thy appearance, so that
I could not recognize thee? what has made thy beard gray,
so that I knew not thy countenance?" And he indited and
said:

> The stroke of calamities makes us hoary, and fortune to
>   men is a changer.
> If it yields to-day to any, to-morrow it overcomes him.
> Trust not the gleam of its lightning, for it is a deceitful
>   gleam.
> But be patient if it hounds calamities against thee, and
>   drives them on.
> For there is no disgrace on the pure gold when it is
>   turned about in the fire.

Then he rose and departed from his place, and carried
away our hearts with him.

THE THIRD ASSEMBLY
(CALLED "OF KAYLAH")[17]

Al Harith, son of Hammam, related: I was set with some

187

comrades in a company wherein he that made appeal was never bootless, and the rubbing of the fire-shafts never failed, and the flame of contention never blazed. And while we were catching from each other the cues of recitations, and betaking ourselves to novelties of anecdote, behold there stood by us one on whom was a worn garment, and in whose walk was a limp. And he said, O ye best of treasures, joys of your kindred: Health to you this morning; may ye enjoy your morning draught. Look on one who was erewhile master of guest-room and largess, wealth and bounty, land and villages, dishes and feasting. But the frowning of calamities ceased not from him, and the warrings of sorrows, and the fire-flakes of the malice of the envious, and the succession of dark befallings, until the court was empty, and the yard was bare, and the fountain sank, and the dwelling was desolate, and the hall was void, and the chamber stone-strewed. And fortune shifted so that the household wailed; and the stalls were vacant, so that the rival had compassion; and the cattle and the goods they perished, so that the envious and malignant pitied. And to such a pass did we come, through assailing fortune and prostrating need, that we were shod with soreness, and fed on choking, and filled our bellies with ache, and wrapped our entrails upon hunger, and anointed our eyes with watching, and made pits our home, and deemed thorns a smooth bed, and came to forget our saddles, and thought destroying death to be sweet, and the ordained day to be tardy. And now is there any one generous to heal, bountiful to bestow? For by him who made me to spring from Kaylah, surely I am now a brother of penury, I have not a night's victual.

Said Al Harith, son of Hammam: Now I pitied his distresses, and inclined to the eliciting of his rhymes. So I drew forth for him a denar, and said to him, to prove him,

"If thou praise it in verse it is thine, full surely." And he betook himself to recite on the spot, borrowing nothing:

How noble is that yellow one, whose yellowness is pure,
Which traverses the regions, and whose journeying is
        afar.
Told abroad are its fame and repute:
Its lines are set as the secret sign of wealth;
Its march is coupled with the success of endeavors;
Its bright look is loved by mankind;
As though its ore had been molten of their hearts.
By its aid whoever has gotten it in his purse assails
        boldly,
Though kindred be perished, or tardy to help.
Oh charming are its purity and brightness;
Charming are its sufficiency and help.
How many a ruler is there whose rule has been perfected
        by it!
How many a sumptuous one is there whose grief, but for
        it, would be endless!
How many a host of cares has one charge of it put to
        flight!
How many a full moon has a sum of it brought down!
How many a one burning with rage, whose coal is
        flaming,
Has it been secretly whispered to, and then his anger has
        softened.
How many a prisoner, whom his kin had yielded,
Has it delivered, so that his gladness has been unmingled,
Now by the Truth of the Lord whose creation brought it
        forth,
Were it not for his fear, I should say its power is supreme.

Then he stretched forth his hand after his recitation, and said, "The honorable man performs what he promises, and the rain-cloud pours if it has thundered." So I threw him the denar, and said, "Take it; no grudging goes with it." And he put it in his mouth and said, "God bless it." Then he girt up his skirts for departure, after that he had paid his thanks. But there arose in me, through his pleasantry, a giddiness of desire which made me ready to incur indebtedness. So I bared another denar, and said, "Does it suit thee to blame this, and then gather it?" And he recited impromptu, and sang with speed:

Ruin on it for a deceiver and insincere,
The yellow one with two faces like a hypocrite!
It shows forth with two qualities to the eye of him that
      looks on it,
The adornment of the loved one, the color of the lover.
Affection for it, think they who judge truly,
Tempts men to commit that which shall anger their
      Maker.
But for it no thief's right hand were cut off;
Nor would tyranny be displayed by the impious;
Nor would the niggard shrink from the night-farer;
Nor would the delayed claimant mourn the delay of him
      that withholds;
Nor would men call to God from the envious who casts at
      them.
Moreover, the worst quality that it possesses
Is that it helps thee not in straits,
Save by fleeing from thee like a runaway slave.
Well done he who casts it away from a hill-top,
And who, when it whispers to him with the whispering
      of a lover,
Says to it in the words of the truth-speaking, the
      veracious,
"I have no mind for intimacy with thee—begone!"

Then said I to him, "How abundant is thy shower!" He said, "Agreement binds strongest." So I tossed him the second denar and said, "Consecrate them both with the Twice-read Chapter." He cast it into his mouth and joined it with its twin, and turned away blessing his morning's walk, praising the assembly and its bounty. Said Al Harith, son of Hammam: Now my heart whispered me that he was Abu Zayd, and that his going lame was for a trick; so I called him back and said to him, "Thou art recognized by thy eloquence, so straighten thy walk." He said, "If thou be the son of Hammam, be thou greeted with honor and live long among the honorable." I said, "I am Harith; but what is thy condition amid all thy fortunes." He said, "I change between two conditions, distress and ease; and I veer with two winds, the tempest and the breeze." I said, "And how hast thou pretended lameness? the like of thee plays not buffoon." Then his cheerfulness, which had shone forth, waned; but he recited as he moved away:

I have feigned to be lame, not from love of lameness, but
    that I may knock at the gate of relief.
For my cord is thrown on my neck, and I go as one who
    ranges freely.
Now if men blame me I say, "Excuse me: sure there is no
    guilt on the lame."

THE FOURTH ASSEMBLY
(CALLED "OF DAMIETTA")[18]

Al Harith, son of Hammam, related: I journeyed to Damietta in a year of much coming and going, and in those days was I glanced after for my affluence, desired in friendship: I trained the bordered robes of wealth and looked upon the features of joy. And I was traveling with companions who had broken the staff of dissension, who were suckled on the milk-flows of concord, so that they showed like the teeth of a comb in uniformity, and like one soul in agreement of desires; but we coursed on withal apace, and not one of us but had saddled a fleet she-camel; and if we alighted at a station or went aside to a spring, we

191

snatched the halt and lengthened not the staying.

Now it happened that we were urging our camels on a night youthful in prime, raven-locked of complexion; and we journeyed until the night-season had put off its prime, and the morning had wiped away the dye of the dark; but when we wearied of the march and inclined to drowsiness, we came upon a ground with dew-moistened hillocks, and a faint east breeze: and we chose it as a resting-place for the white camels, an abode for the night-halt. Now when the caravan had descended there, and the groan and the roar of the beasts were still, I heard a loud-voiced man say to his talk-fellow in the camp, "What is the rule of thy conduct with thy people and neighbors?" The other answered, I am duteous to my neighbor though he wrong me; and give my fellowship even to the violent; and bear with a partner though he disorder my affairs; and love my friend even though he drench me with a tepid draught; and prefer my well-wisher above my brother; and fulfil to my comrade even though he requite me not with a tenth; and think little of much if it be of my guest; and whelm my companion with my kindness; and put my talk-fellow in the place of my prince; and hold my intimate to be as my chief; and commit my gifts to my acquaintance; and confer my comforts on my associate; and soften my speech to him that hates me; and continue to ask after him that disregards me; and am pleased with but the crumbs of my due; and am content with but the least portion of my reward; and complain not of wrong even when I am wronged; and revenge not, even though a viper sting me.

Then said his companion to him, Alas! my boy, only he who clings should be clung to; only he who is valuable should be prized. As for me I give only to him who will requite; I distinguish not the insolent by my regard; nor will I be of pure affection to one who refuses me fair-dealing;

192

nor treat as a brother one who would undo my tethering-rope; nor aid one who would baulk my hopes; nor care for one who would cut my cords; nor be courteous to him who ignores my value; nor give my leading rope to one who breaks my covenant; nor be free of my love to my adversaries; nor lay aside my menace to the hostile; nor plant my benefits on the land of my enemies; nor be willing to impart to him who rejoices at my ills; nor show my regard to him who will exult at my death; nor favor with my gifts any but my friends; nor call to the curing of my sickness any but those who love me; nor confer my friendship on him who will not stop my breach; nor make my purpose sincere to him who wishes my decease; nor be earnest in prayer for him who will not fill my wallet; nor pour out my praise on him who empties my jar. For who has adjudged that I should be lavish and thou shouldest hoard, that I should be soft and thou rough, that I should melt and thou freeze, that I should blaze and thou smolder? No, by Allah, but let us balance in speech as coin, and match in deed as sandals, that each to each we may be safe from fraud and free from hatred. For else, why should I give thee full water and thou stint me? why should I hear with thee and thou contemn me? why should I gain for thee and thou wound me? why should I advance to thee and thou repel me? For how should fair-dealing be attracted by injury? how can the sun rise clear with cloud? And when did love follow docilely after wrong? and what man of honor consents to a state of abasement? For excellently said thy father:

> Whoso attaches his affection to me, I repay him as one
>   who builds on his foundation:
> And I mete to a friend as he metes to me, according to the
>   fulness of his meting or its defect.
> I make him not a loser! for the worst of men is he whose
>   to-day falls short of his yesterday.

Whoever seeks fruit of me gets only the fruit of his own
planting.
I seek not to defraud, but I will not come off with the
bargain of one who is weak in his reason.
I hold not truth binding on me toward a man who holds
it not binding on himself.
There may be some one insincere in love who fancies that
I am true in my friendship for him, while he is
false;
And knows not in his ignorance that I pay my creditor
his debt after its kind.
Sunder, with the sundering of hate, from one who would
make thee a fool, and hold him as one entombed in
his grave.
And toward him in whose intercourse there is aught
doubtful put on the garb of one who shrinks from
his intimacy.
And hope not for affection from any who sees that thou
art in want of his money.
Said Al Harith, son of Hammam: Now, when I had
gathered what passed between them, I longed to know them
in person. And when the sun shone forth, and robed the
sky with light, I went forth before the camels had risen, and
with an earliness beyond the earliness of the crow, and
began to follow the direction of that night-voice, and to
examine the faces with a searching glance: until I caught
sight of Abu Zayd and his son talking together, and upon
them were two worn mantles. Then I knew that they were
my two talkers of the night, the authors of my recitation. So
I approached them as one enamored of their refinement,
pitying their shabbiness; and offered them a removal to my
lodging, and the disposal of my much and my little; and
began to tell abroad their worth among the travelers, and to
shake for them the fruited branches; until they were
whelmed with gifts, and taken as friends. Now we were in a

194

night-camp, whence we could discern the build of the villages, and spy the fires of hospitality. And when Abu Zayd saw that his purse was full, and his distress removed, he said to me, "Truly my body is dirty, and my filth has caked: Wilt thou permit me to go to a village, and bathe, and fulfil this urgent need?" I said, "If thou wilt; but quick! return!" He said, "Thou shalt find me appear again to thee, quicker than the glancing of thine eye." Then he coursed away, as courses the good steed in the training-ground, and said to his son, "Haste! haste!" And we imagined not that he was deceiving, or seeking to escape. So we stayed and watched for him as men watch for the new moons of feasts, and made search for him by spies and scouts, until the sunlight was weak with age, and the wasted bank of the day had nigh crumbled in. Then, when the term of waiting had been prolonged, and the sun showed in faded garb, I said to my companions, "We have gone to the extreme in delay, and have been long in the setting forth; so that we have lost time, and it is plain that the man was lying. Now, therefore, prepare for the journey, and turn not aside to the greenness of dung-heaps." Then I rose to equip my camel and lade for the departure; and found that Abu Zayd had written on the pack-saddle:

Oh thou, who wast to me an arm and a helper, above all
    mankind!
Reckon not that I have left thee through impatience or
    ingratitude:
For since I was born I have been of those who "when they
    have eaten separate."

Said Al Harith: Then I made the company read the words of the Koran that were on the pack-saddle, so that he who had blamed him might excuse him. And they admired his witticism, but commanded themselves from his mischief. Then we set forth, nor could we learn whose company he had gotten in our place.

THE FIFTH ASSEMBLY
(CALLED "OF KUFA")[19]

Al Harith, son of Hammam, related: I was conversing at
Kufa, in a night whose complexion was of a two-fold hue,
whose moon was as an amulet of silver, with companions
who had been nourished on the milk of eloquence, who
might draw the train of oblivion over Sahban. Each was a
man to remember from, and not to guard against; each was
one whom his friend would incline to, and not avoid. And
the night talk fascinated us until the moon had set, and the
watching overcame us. Now when night's unmingled dark
had spread its awning, and there was naught but nodding
among us, we heard from the gate the faint sound of a
wayfarer, rousing the dogs; then followed the knock of one
bidding to open. We said, "Who is it that comes in the dark
night?" Then the traveler answered:
O people of the mansion, be ye guarded from ill!
Meet not harm as long as ye live!
Lo! the night which glooms has driven
To your abode one disheveled, dust-laden,
A brother of journeying, that has been lengthened,
     extended,
Till he has become bent and yellow
Like the new moon of the horizon when it smiles.
And now he approaches your courtyard, begging boldly,
And repairs to you before all people else,
To seek from you food and a lodging.
Ye have in him a guest contented, ingenuous,
One pleased with all, whether sweet or bitter,
One who will withdraw from you, publishing your
     bounty.
Said Al Harith, son of Hammam: Now when we were
caught by the sweetness of his utterance, and knew what
was behind his lightning, we hastened to open the gate, and

196

met him with welcome; and said to the boy "Quick, quick! bring what is ready!" Then said our guest, "Now, by him who has set me down at your abode, I will not roll my tongue over your food, unless ye pledge me that ye will not make me a burden, that ye will not, for my sake, task yourselves with a meal. For sometimes a morsel aches the eater, and forbids him his repasts. And the worst of guests is he who imposes trouble and annoys his host, and especially with a harm that affects the body and tends to sickness. For, by that proverb, which is widely current, 'The best Slippers are those that are clearly seen,' is only meant that supper-time should be hastened, and eating by night, which dims the sight, avoided. Unless, by Allah, the fire of hunger kindle and stand in the way of sleep." Said Al Harith: Now it was as though he had got sight of our desire, and so had shot with the bow of our conviction. Accordingly we gratified him by agreeing to the condition, and commended him for his easy temper. And when the boy brought what was to be had, and lighted the candle in the midst of us, I looked close at him, and lo! it was Abu Zayd. So I said to my company, "Joy to you of the guest who has come! Nay, but the spoil is lightly won! For if the moon of Sirius has gone down, truly the moon of poetry has risen: Or if the full moon of the Lion has waned, the full moon of eloquence shines forth." Then ran through them the wine-glow of joy, and sleep flew away from their eye-corners. And they refused the rest which they had purposed, and returned to the spreading out of pleasantry, after they had folded it. But Abu Zayd kept intent upon plying his hands; however, when what was before him might be removed, I said to him, "Present us with one of the rare stories from thy night talkings, or some wonder from among the wonders of thy journeys." He said, "Of wonders I have met with such as no seers have seen, no tellers have told. But among the most wondrous was that which I beheld to-night, a little before

my visit to you and my coming to your gate." Then we bade
him tell us of this new thing which he had seen in the field
of his night-faring. He said, Truly the hurlings of exile have
thrown me to this land: And I was in hunger and distress,
with a scrip like the heart of the mother of Moses. Now, as
soon as the dark had settled, I arose, in spite of all my
footsoreness, to seek a host or to gain a loaf. Then the driver
hunger, and Fate, which is by-named the Father of
Wonders, urged me on, till I stood at the door of a house,
and spoke, improvising:

Hail people of this dwelling,
May ye live in the ease of a plenteous life!
What have ye for a son of the road, one crushed to the
      sand,
Worn with journeys, stumbling in the night-dark night,
Aching in entrails, which enclose naught but hunger?
For two days he has not tasted the savor of a meal:
In your land there is no refuge for him.
And already the van of the drooping darkness has
      gloomed;
And through bewilderment he is in restlessness.
Now in this abode is there any one, sweet of spring,
Who will say to me, "Throw away thy staff and enter:
Rejoice in a cheerful welcome and a ready meal?"
Then came forth to me a lad in a tunic, and answered:
Now by the sanctity of the Shaykh who ordained
      hospitality,
And founded the House of Pilgrimage in the Mother of
      cities,
We have naught for the night-farer when he visits us
But conversation and a lodging in our hall.
For how should he entertain whom hinders from
      sleepfulness
Hunger which peels his bones when it assails him?
Now what thinkest thou of my tale? what thinkest thou?

I said, "What shall I do with an empty house, and a host the ally of penury? But tell me, youth, what is thy name, for thy understanding has charmed me." He said, "My name is Zayd, and my birth-place Fayd: and I came to this city yesterday with my mother's kindred of the Benu 'Abs." I said to him, "Show me further, so mayest thou live and be raised when thou fallest!" He said, "My mother Barrah told me (and she is like her name, 'pious') that she married in the year of the foray on Mawan a man of the nobles of Seruj and Ghassan; but when he was aware of her pregnancy (for he was a crafty bird, it is said) he made off from her by stealth, and away he has stayed, nor is it known whether he is alive and to be looked for, or whether he has been laid in the lonely tomb." Said Abu Zayd, "Now I knew by sure signs that he was my child; but the emptiness of my hand turned me from making known to him, so I parted from him with heart crushed and tears unsealed. And now, ye men of understanding, have ye heard aught more wondrous than this wonder?" We said, "No, by him who has knowledge of the Book." He said, "Record it among the wonders of chance; bid it abide forever in the hearts of scrolls; for nothing like it has been told abroad in the world." Then he bade bring the ink-flask, and its snake-like reeds, and we wrote the story elegantly as he worded it; after which we sought to draw from him his wish about receiving his boy. He said, "If my purse were heavy, then to take charge of my son would be light." We said, "If a *nisab* of money would suffice thee, we will collect it for thee at once." He said, "And how should a *nisab* not content me? would any but a madman despise such a sum?" Said the narrator, Then each of us undertook a share of it, and wrote for him an order for it. Whereupon he gave thanks for the kindness, and exhausted the plenteousness of praise; until we thought his speech long, or our merit little. And then he spread out such a bright mantle of talk as might shame the stuffs of

199

Yemen, until the dawn appeared and the light-bearing morn went forth. So we spent a night of which the mixed hues had departed, until its hind-locks grew gray in the dawn; and whose lucky stars were sovereign until its branch budded into light. But when the limb of the sun peeped forth, he leaped up as leaps the gazelle, and said, "Rise up, that we may take hold on the gifts and draw payment of the checks: for the clefts of my heart are widening through yearning after my child." So I went with him, hand in hand, to make easy his success. But as soon as he had secured the coin in his purse the marks of his joy flashed forth, and he said, "Be thou rewarded for the steps of thy feet! be God my substitute toward thee!" I said, "I wish to follow thee that I may behold thy noble child, and speak with him that he may answer eloquently." Then looked he at me as looks the deceiver on the deceived, and laughed till his eyeballs gushed with tears; and he recited:

O thou who didst fancy the mirage to be water when I
      quoted to thee what I quoted!
I thought not that my guile would be hidden, or that it
      would be doubtful what I meant.
By Allah, I have no Barrah for a spouse; I have no son
      from whom to take a by-name.
Nothing is mine but divers kinds of magic, in which I am
      original and copy no one:
They are such as Al Asma'i tells not of in what he has
      told; such as Al Komayt never wove.
These I use when I will to reach whatever my hand
      would pluck:
And were I to abandon them, changed would be my state,
      nor should I gain what I now gain.
So allow my excuse; nay, pardon me, if I have done
      wrong or crime.

Then he took leave of me and passed away, and set coals of the *ghada* in my breast.

THE SIXTH ASSEMBLY
(CALLED "OF MERAGHAH," OR "THE DIVERSIFIED")[20]

Al Harith, son of Hammam, related: I was present in the Court of Supervision at Meraghah when the talk ran of eloquence. Then agreed all who were there of the knights of the pen, and the lords of genius, that there remained no one who could select his diction, or use himself freely in it as he willed: and that since the men of old were gone, there was none now left who could originate a brilliant method, or open a virgin style. And that even one marvelous among the writers of this age, and holding in his grasp the cords of eloquence, is but a dependent on the ancients, even though he possess the fluency of Sahban Wa'il. Now there was in the assembly an elderly man, sitting on the outskirts, in the places of the attendants: and as often as the company overran in their career, and scattered fruit, good and bad, from their store, the side-glance of his eye and the up-turning of his nose showed that he was one silent to spring, one crouching who would extend his stride: that he was a twanger of the bow who shapes his arrows, one who sits in wait desiring the conflict. But when the quivers were empty, and quiet returned; when the storms had fallen, and the disputer was stayed, he turned to the company and said, Ye have uttered a grievous thing; ye have wandered much from the way: for ye have magnified moldering bones; ye have been excessive in your leaning to those who are gone; ye have contemned your generation, among whom ye were born, and with whom your friendships are established. Have ye forgotten, ye skilful in testing, ye sages of loosing and binding, how much new springs have given forth; how the colt has surpassed the full-grown steed; in refined expressions, and delightful metaphors, and ornate addresses, and admired cadences? And, if any one here will look diligently, is there in the ancients aught but ideas

201

whose paths are worn, whose ranges are restricted; which have been handed down from them through the priority of their birth, not from any superiority in him who draws first at the well over him who comes after? Now truly know I one who, when he composes, colors richly; and when he expresses, embellishes; and when he is lengthy, finds golden thoughts; and when he is brief, baffles his imitator; and when he improvises, astonishes; and when he creates, cuts the envious.

Then said to him the President of the Court, the Eye of those Eyes: "Who is it that strikes on this rock, that is the hero of these qualities?" He said, "It is the adversary of this thy skirmish, the partner of thy disputation: Now, if thou wilt, rein a good steed, call forth one who will answer, so shalt thou see a wonder." He said to him, "Stranger, the chough in our land is not taken for an eagle, and with us it is easy to discern between silver and shingle. Rare is he who exposes himself to the conflict, and then escapes the mortal hurt; or who stirs up the dust of trial, and then catches not the mote of contempt. So offer not thy honor to shame, turn not from the counsel of the counselor." He answered, "Each man knows best the mark of his arrow, and be sure the night shall disclose its morn."

Then whispered the company as to how his well should be fathomed, and his proving undertaken. Said one of them, "Leave him to my share, that I may pelt him with the stone of my story; for it is the tightest of knots, the touchstone of testing." Then they invested him with the command in this business as the Rebels invested Abu Na'ameh. Whereupon he turned to the elder and said, Know that I am attached to this Governor and maintain my condition by ornamental eloquence. Now, in my country, I could rely for the straightening of my crookedness on the sufficiency of my means, coupled with the smallness of my family. But when

202

my back was weighted, and my thin rain failed, I repaired to him from my home with hope, and besought him to restore my comeliness and my competence. And he looked pleasantly on my coming, and was gracious, and served me morn and even. But when I sought permission from him to depart to my abode, on the shoulder of cheerfulness, he said, "I have determined that I will not provide thee with supplies, I will bring together for thee no scattered means, unless, before thy departure, thou compose an address, setting in it an exposition of thy state; such, that the letters of one of every two words shall all have dots, while the letters of the other shall not be pointed at all." And now have I waited for my eloquence a twelvemonth, but it has returned me not a word; and I have roused my wit for a year, but only my sluggishness has increased. And I have sought aid among the gathering of the scribes, but each of them has frowned and drawn back. Now, if thou hast disclosed thy character with accuracy, *Come with a sign if thou be of the truthful.*

Then answered the elder, "Thou hast put a good steed to the pace; thou hast sought water at a full stream; thou hast given the bow to him who fashioned it; thou hast lodged in the house him who built it." And he thought a while till he had let his flow of wit collect, his milch-camel fill her udder: and then he said: Wool thy ink-flask, and take thy implements and write:

"Generosity (may God establish the host of thy successes) adorns; but meanness (may fortune cast down the eyelid of thy enviers) dishonors; the noble rewards, but the base disappoints; the princely entertains, but the niggard frights away; the liberal nourishes, but the churl pains; giving relieves, but deferring torments; blessing protects, and praise purifies; the honorable repays, for repudiation abases; the rejection of him who should be respected is error; a denial to

203

the sons of hope is outrage; and none is miserly but the fool, and none is foolish but the miser; and none hoards but the wretched; for the pious clenches not his palms.

"But thy promise ceases not to fulfil; thy sentiments cease not to relieve; nor thy clemency to indulge; nor thy new moon to illumine; nor thy bounty to enrich; nor thy enemies to praise thee; nor thy blade to destroy; nor thy princeship to build up; nor thy suitor to gain; nor thy praiser to win; nor thy kindness to succor; nor thy heaven to rain; nor thy milk-flow to abound; nor thy refusal to be rare. Now he who hopes in thee is an old man like a shadow, one to whom nothing remains. He seeks thee with a persuasion whose eagerness leaps onward; he praises thee in choice phrases, which merit their dowries. His demand is a light one, his claims are clear; his praise is striven for, his blame is shunned. And behind him is a household whom misery has touched, whom wrong has stripped, whom squalor involves. And he is ever in tears that come at call, and trouble that melts him, and care that is as a guest, and growing sadness: on account of hope that has disappointed him, and loss that has made him hoary, and the enemy that has fixed tooth in him, and the quiet that is gone. And yet his love has not swerved, that there should be anger at him; nor is his wood rotten, that he should be lopped away; nor has his breast spit foulness that he should be shaken off; nor has his intercourse been froward that he should be hated. Now thy honor admits not the rejection of his claim, so whiten his hope by the lightening of his distress: then will he publish thy praise throughout the world. So mayest thou live to avert misfortune, and to bestow wealth; to heal grief and to care for the aged: attended by affluence and fresh joyousness; as long as the hall of the rich is visited, or the delusion of the selfish is feared. And so Peace."

Now when he had ceased from the dictation of his

address, and showed forth his prowess in the strife of
eloquence, the company gratified him both by word and
deed, and made large to him their courtesy and their
bounty. Then was he asked from what tribe was his origin,
and in what valley was his lair; and he answered:

Ghassan is my noble kindred, and Seruj my ancient land:
There my home was like the sun in splendor and mighty
    rank;
And my dwelling was as paradise in sweetness and
    pleasantness and worth.
Oh, excellent were the life I led there and the plenteous
    delights,
In the day that I drew my broidered robe in its meadow,
    sharp of purpose,
I walked proudly in the mantle of youth and looked upon
    goodly pleasures;
Fearing not the visitations of time and its evil haps.
Now if grief could kill, surely I should perish from my
    abiding griefs;
Or if past life could be redeemed my good heart's blood
    should redeem it.
For death is better for a man than to live the life of a beast.
When the ring of subjection leads him to mighty trouble
    and outrage,
And he sees lions whom the paws of assailing hyenas
    seize.
But the fault is in the time: but for its ill luck character
    would not miss its place:
If the time were upright, then would the conditions of
    men be upright in it.

After this his story reached the Governor, who filled his
mouth with pearls, and bade him join himself to his
followers, and preside over his court of public writing. But
the gifts sufficed him, and unwillingness restrained him
from office. Said the narrator: Now I had recognized the
wood of his tree before the ripening of his fruit: And I had
nigh roused the people to the loftiness of his worth before
that his full moon shone forth. But he hinted to me by a
twinkle of his eyelid that I should not bare his sword from
its sheath. And when he was going forth, full of purse, and

parting from us, having gotten victory, I escorted him, performing the duty of respect, and chiding him for his refusal of office. But he turned away with a smile and recited with a chant:

> Sure to traverse the lands in poverty is dearer to me than rank:
> For in rulers there is caprice and fault-finding, oh what fault-finding!
> There is none of them who completes his good work, or who builds up where has laid foundation.
> So let not the glare of the mirage beguile thee; undertake not that which is doubtful:
> For how many a dreamer has his dream made joyful; but fear has come upon him when he waked.

THE SEVENTH ASSEMBLY
(CALLED "OF BARAK'ID")[21]

Al Harith, son of Hammam, related: I had determined on journeying from Barak'id; but now I noted the signs of the coming feast, and I disliked to set forth from the city until I had witnessed there the day of adornment. So when it came on with its rites, bounden or of free will, and brought up its horsemen and footmen, I followed the tradition in new apparel, and went forth with the people to keep festival. Now when the congregation of the prayer-court was gathered and ranged, and the crowding took men's breath, there appeared an old man in a pair of cloaks, and his eyes were closed: and he bore on his arm what was like a horse-bag, and had for a guide an old woman like a goblin. Then he stopped, as stops one tottering to sink, and greeted with the greeting of him whose voice is feeble. And when he had made an end of his salutation he circled his five fingers in his wallet, and brought forth scraps of paper that had been written on with colors of dyes in the season of leisure, and

207

gave them to his old beldame, bidding her to detect each simple one. So whenever she perceived of any that his hand was moist in bounty, she cast one of the papers before him. Said Al Harith: Now cursed fate allotted to me a scrap whereon was written:

Sure I have become crushed with pains and fears;
Tried by the proud one, the crafty, the assailer,
By the traitor among my brethren, who hates me for my
    need,
By jading from those who work to undo my toils.
How oft do I burn through spites and penury and
    wandering;
How oft do I tramp in shabby garb, thought of by none.
Oh, would that fortune when it wronged me had slain
    my babes!
For were not my cubs torments to me and ills,
I would not have addressed my hopes to kin or lord:
Nor would I draw my skirts along the track of abasement.
For my garret would be more seemly for me, and my rags
    more honorable.
Now is there a generous man who will see that the
    lightening of my loads must be by a denar;
Or will quench the heat of my anxiety by a shirt and
    trousers?

Said Al Harith, son of Hammam: Now when I had looked on the garb of the verses, I longed for a knowledge of him who wove it, the broiderer of its pattern. And my thought whispered to me that the way to him was through the old woman, and advised me that a fee to an informer is lawful. So I watched her, and she was wending through the rows, row by row, begging a dole of the hands, hand by hand. But not at all did the trouble prosper her; no purse shed aught upon her palm. Wherefore when her soliciting was baffled, and her circuit wearied her, she commended herself to God with the "Return," and addressed herself to collect the scraps of paper. But the devil made her forget the scrap that I held, and she turned not aside to my spot: but went back to the old man weeping at the denial, complaining of the oppression of the time. And he said, "In God's hands I am, to God I commit my case; there is no strength or power but by God," then he recited:

There remains not any pure, not any sincere; not a
        spring, not a helper:
But of baseness there is one level; not any is trusty, not
        any of worth.

Then said he to her, "Cheer thy soul and promise it good; collect the papers and count them." She said, "Truly I counted them when I asked them back, and I found that one of them the hand of loss had seized." He said, "Perdition on thee, wretch; shall we be hindered, alas, both of the prey and the net, both of the brand and the wick? Surely this is a new handful to the load." Then did the old woman hasten back, retracing her path to seek her scroll; and when she drew near to me I put with the paper a dirhem and a mite, and said to her, "If thou hast a fondness for the polished, the engraved (and I pointed to the dirhem), show me the secret, the obscure; but if thou willest not to explain, take then the mite and begone." Then she inclined to the getting of that whole full moon, the bright-faced, the large. So she said, "Quit contention and ask what thou wilt." Whereupon I asked her of the old man and his country, of the poem, and of him who wove its mantle. She said, "Truly, the old man is of the people of Seruj, and he it was who broidered that woven poem." Then she snatched the dirhem with the snatch of a hawk, and shot away as shoots the darting arrow. But it troubled my heart that perchance it was Abu Zayd who was indicated, and my grief kindled at his mishap with his eyes. And I should have preferred to have gone suddenly on him and talked to him, that I might test the quality of my discernment upon him. But I was unable to come to him save by treading on the necks of the congregation, a thing forbidden in the law; and, moreover, I was unwilling that people should be annoyed by me, or that blame should arrive to me. So I cleaved to my place, but made his form the fetter of my sight, until the sermon was ended, and to leap to him was lawful. Then I went briskly to him and examined him in spite of the closing of his eyelids. And, lo! my shrewdness was as the shrewdness of Ibn 'Abbas, and my discernment as the discernment of Iyas. So at once I made myself known, and presented him with one of my tunics, and bade him to my bread. And he was joyful at my bounty and recognition, and acceded to the call to my loaves; and he set forth, and my hand was his leading cord, my shadow his conductor; and the old woman was the third prop of the pot; yes, by the Watcher from whom no secret is hidden! Now, when he had taken seat in my nest, and I had set before him what hasty meal was in my power, he said, "Harith, is there with us a third?" I said, "There is none but the old woman." He said, "From her no secret is withheld." Then he opened his eyes and stared round with the twin balls, and, lo! the two lights of his face kindled like the Farkadan. And I was joyful at the safety of his sight, but marveled at the strangeness of his ways. Nor did quiet possess me, nor did patience fit with me, until I asked him, "What led thee to feign blindness; thou, with thy journeying in desolate places, and thy traversing of wildernesses, and thy pushing into far lands?" But he made show as if his mouth were full, and kept as though busied with his meal, until, when he had fulfilled his need, he sharpened his look upon me and recited:

Since Time (and he is the father of mankind) makes
      himself blind to the right in his purposes and aims,
I too have assumed blindness, so as to be called a brother
      of it. What wonder that one should match himself
      with his father!

Then said he to me, "Rise, and go to the closet, and fetch me alkali that may clear the eye, and clean the hand, and soften the skin, and perfume the breath, and brace the gums, and strengthen the stomach: and let it be clean of box, fragrant of odor, new of pounding, delicate of powdering; so that one touching it shall count it to be eye-paint, and one smelling it shall fancy it to be camphor. And join with it a toothpick choice in material, delightful in use, goodly in shape, that invites to the repast: and let it have the slimness of a lover, and the polish of a sword, and the sharpness of the lance of war, and the pliancy of a green bough." Said Al Harith: Then I rose to do what he bade that I might rid him of the trace of his food; and thought not that he purposed to deceive by sending me into the closet; nor suspected that he was mocking of his messenger when he called for the alkali and toothpick. But when I returned with what was asked for, in less than the drawing of a breath, I found that the hall was empty, and that the old man and woman had sped away. Then was I extreme in anger at his deceit, and I pressed on his track in search of him; but he was as one who is sunk in the sea, or has been borne aloft to the clouds of heaven.

THE EIGHTH ASSEMBLY
(CALLED "OF MA'AKRAH")[22]

Al Harith, son of Hammam, related: Among the wonders of time, I saw that two suitors came before the Kadi of Ma'arrat an No'man. From the one of them the two excellencies of life had departed, while the other was as a bough of the ben tree. And the old man said: God strengthen the judge, as by him he strengthens whoever seeks judgment. Behold I had a slave girl, elegant of shape, smooth of cheek, patient to labor; at one time she ambled like a good steed, at another she slept quietly in her bed:

even in July thou wouldst feel her touch to be cool. She had understanding and discretion, sharpness and wit, a hand with fingers, but a mouth without teeth: yet did she pique as with tongue of snake, and saunter in training robe; and she was displayed in blackness and whiteness; and she drank, but not from cisterns. She was now truth-telling, now beguiling; now hiding, now peeping forth; yet fitted for employment, obedient in poverty and in wealth: if thou didst spurn she showed affection, but if thou didst put her from thee, she remained quietly apart. Generally would she serve thee, and be courteous to thee, though sometimes she might be froward to thee and pain thee, and trouble thee. Now this youth asked her service of me for a purpose of his own, and I made her his servant, without reward, on the condition that he should enjoy the use of her, but not burden her with more than she could bear. But he forced on her too hard a work, and exacted of her long labor; then returned her to me broken in health, offering a compensation which I accept not.

Then said the youth: Sure the old man is more truthful than the Kata: but as for my hurting her it fell out by mistake. And now have I pledged to him in payment of his damage, a slave[23] of mine, of equal birth as regards either kin, tracing his lineage to Al Kayn, free from stain and disgrace, whose place was the apple of his master's eye. He showed forth kindness, and called up admiration; he nourished mankind, and set guard on his tongue. If he was placed in power he was generous, if he marked aught for his own he was noble with it; if he was supplied he gave of his supply, and when he was asked for more he added. He stayed not in the house, and rarely visited his wives, save two by two. He was generous with his possession, he was lofty in his bounty; he kept with his spouse although she was not of his own clay; and there was pleasure in his comeliness, although he was not desired for his effeminacy.

Then said to them the Kadi, "Now either explain or depart." Then pressed forward the lad, and said:

He lent me a needle to darn my rags, which use has worn
    and blackened;
And its eye broke in my hand by chance, as I drew the
    thread through it.
But the old man would not forgive me the paying for it
    when he saw that it was spoiled;
But said, "Give me a needle like it, or a price, after thou
    hast mended it."
And he keeps my *kohl*-pencil by him as a pledge: oh, the
    shame that he has gotten by so doing:
For my eye is dry through giving him this pledge; my
    hand fails to ransom its anointer.
Now by this statement fathom the depth of my misery
    and pity one unused to bear it.

Then turned the Kadi to the old man, and said "Come, speak without glozing." and he said:

I swear by the holy place of sacrifice, and the devout
    whom the slope of Mina brings together;
If the time had been my helper, thou wouldst not have
    seen me taking in pledge the pencil which he has
    pledged to me.
Nor would I bring myself to seek a substitute for a needle
    that he had spoiled; no, nor the price of it.
But the bow of calamities shoots at me with deadly
    arrows from here and there:
And to know my condition is to know his; misery, and
    distress, and exile, and sickness.
Fortune has put us on a level: I am his like in misery, and
    he is as I.
He can not ransom his pencil now that it lies pledged in
    my hand:

213

And, through the narrowness of my own means, it is not
    within my bounds to forgive him for his offending.
Now this is my tale and his: so look upon us, and judge
    between us, and pity us.

Now when the Kadi had learned their stories, and was
aware of their penury and their distinction, he took out for
them a denar from under his prayer-cushion, and said,
"With this end and decide your contention." But the old
man caught it before the youth, and claimed the whole of it
in earnest, not in jest, saying to the youth, "Half is mine as
my share of the bounty, and thy share is mine, in payment
for my needle: nor do I swerve from justice, so come and
take thy pencil." Now there fell on the youth, at the words
of the old man, a sadness at which the heart of the Kadi
grew sullen, stirring its sorrow for the lost denar. Yet did he
cheer the concern of the youth and his anguish by a few
dirhems which he doled to him. Then he said to the two,
"Avoid transactions, and put away disputes, and come not
before me with wranglings, for I have no purse of fine-
money for you." And they rose to go out from him,
rejoicing at his gift, fluent in his praise. But as for the Kadi,
his ill-humor subsided not after his stone had dripped; his
sad look cleared not away after his rock had oozed. But
when he recovered from his fit he turned to his attendants,
and said, "My perception is imbued with the thought, and
my guess announces to me, that these are practisers of craft,
not suitors in a claim: but what is the way to fathom them,
and to draw forth their secret?" Then said to him the
Knowing One of his assemblage, the Light of his following:
"Surely the discovery of what they hide must be through
themselves." So he bade an attendant follow them and bring
them back; and when they stood before him he said to them,
"Tell me truly your camel's age: so shall ye be secure from
the consequence of your deceit." Then did the lad shrink
back and ask for pardon; but the old man stepped forward

and said:

I am the Seruji and this is my son; and the cub at the
proving is like the lion.

Now never has his hand nor mine done wrong in matter
of needle or pencil:

But only fortune, the harming, the hostile, has brought
us to this, that we came forth to beg

Of each one whose palm is moist, whose spring is sweet;
of each whose palm is close, whose hand is fettered;

By every art, and with every aim: by earnest, if it prosper,
and if not, by jest.

That we may draw forth a drop for our thirsty lot, and
consume our life in wretched victual.

And afterward Death is on the watch for us: if he fall not
on us to-day he will fall to-morrow.

Then said the Kadi to him, "Oh rare! how admirable are
the breathings of thy mouth; well done! should I say of
thee, were it not for the guile that is in thee. Now know
that I am of those that warn thee, and will beware of thee.
So act not again deceitfully with judges, but fear the might
of those who bear rule. For not every minister will excuse,
and not at every season will speech be listened to." Then the
old man promised to follow his counsel, and to abstain from
disguising his character. And he departed from the Kadi's
presence, while the guile beamed from his forehead. Said Al
Harith, son of Hammam: Now I never saw aught more
wonderful than these things in the changes of my journeys,
nor read aught like them in the records of books.

THE NINTH ASSEMBLY,
(CALLED "OF ALEXANDRIA")[24]

Al Harith, son of Hammam, related: The liveliness of
youth and the desire of gain sped me on until I had
traversed all that is between Farghanah and Ghanah. And I

dived into depths to gather fruits, and plunged into perils to reach my needs. Now I had caught from the lips of the learned, and understood from the commandments of the wise, that it behooves the well-bred, the sagacious, when he enters a strange city, to conciliate its Kadi and possess himself of his favor: that his back may be strengthened in litigation, that he may be secure in a strange land from the wrong of the powerful. So I took this doctrine as my guide and made it the leading-cord to my advantages. And I entered not a city, I went not into a lair, but I mingled myself with its judge as water is mingled with wine, and strengthened myself by his patronage as bodies are strengthened by souls. Now while I was in presence of the judge of Alexandria one cold evening, and he had brought out the alms-money to divide it among the needy, behold there entered an ill-looking old man whom a young matron dragged along. And she said: God strengthen the Kadi and through him make concord to be lasting: know that I am a woman of stock the most noble, of root the most pure, of mother's and father's kin the most honorable: my character is moderation, my disposition is contentment; my nature is to be a goodly help-meet; between me and my neighbors is a wide difference. Now whenever there wooed me any who had built up honor or were lords of wealth my father silenced and chid them and misliked their suit and their gift: making plea that he had covenanted with God Most High that he would not ally himself save with the master of a handicraft. Then did Providence destine for my calamity and pain that this deceiver should present himself in my father's hall; and swear among his people that he fulfilled his condition: asserting that long time he had strung pearl to pearl and sold them for great price. Then was my father deceived by the gilding of his falsehood, and married me to him before proving his condition. And when he had drawn me forth from my covert, and carried me away from my

216

people, and removed me to his habitation, and brought me under his bond, I found him slothful, a sluggard; I discovered him to be a lie-a-bed, a slumberer. Now I had come to him with apparel and goodly show, with furniture and affluence. But he ceased not to sell it in a losing market and to squander the price in greedy feeding, until he had altogether destroyed whatever was mine, and spent my property on his need. So when he had made to me to forget the taste of rest and left my house cleaner than my hand's palm, I said to him, "Sir, know that there is no concealment after distress, no perfume after the wedding. Rise up then to gain something by thy trade, to gather the fruit of thy skill." But he declared that his trade had been struck with slackness through the violence that was abroad in the earth. Also I have a boy by him, thin as a toothpick: neither of us gets a fill by him, and through hunger our weeping to him ceases not. So I have brought him to thee and set him before thee, that thou mayest test the substance of his assertion, and decide between us as God shall show thee.

Then turned the Kadi to him and said: "Thou hast heard thy wife's story; now testify of thyself: else will I discover thy deceit and bid thy imprisonment." But he looked down as looks the serpent; then girt up his garment for a long strife, and said:

Hear my story, for it is a wonder; there is laughter in its
    tale, and there is wailing.
I am a man on whose qualities there is no blame, neither
    is there suspicion on his glory.
Seruj is my home where I was born, and my stock is
    Ghassan when I trace my lineage:
And study is my business; to dive deep in learning is my
    pursuit; and, oh! how excellent a seeking.
And my capital is the magic of speech, out of which are
    molded both verse and prose.

I dive into the deep of eloquence, and from it I choose the
     pearls and select them:
I cull of speech the ripe fruit and the new; while another
     gathers but firing of the wood:
I take the phrase of silver, and when I have molded it men
     say that it is gold.
Now formerly I drew forth wealth by the learning I had
     gotten; I milked by it:
And my foot's sole in its dignity mounted to ranges above
     which were no higher steps.
Oft were the presents brought in pomp to my dwelling,
     but I accepted not every one who gave.
But to-day learning is the chattel of slackest sale in the
     market of him on whom hope depends.
The honor of its sons is not respected; neither are
     relationship and alliance with them regarded.
It is as though they were corpses in their courtyards, from
     whose stench men withdraw and turn aside.
Now my heart is confounded through my trial by the
     times; strange is their changing.
The stretch of my arm is straitened through the straitness
     of my hand's means; cares and grief assail me.
And my fortune, the blameworthy, has led me to the
     paths of that which honor deems base.
For I sold until there remained to me not a mat nor
     household goods to which I might turn.
So I indebted myself until I had burdened my neck by the
     carrying of a debt such that ruin had been lighter.
Then five days I wrapped my entrails upon hunger; but
     when the hunger scorched me,
I could see no goods except her outfit, in the selling of
     which I might go about and bestir myself.
So I went about with it; but my soul was loathing, and
     my eye tearful, and my heart saddened.
But when I made free with it, I passed not the bound of

her consent, that her wrath should rise against me.
And if what angers her be her fancying that it was my
 fingers that should make gain by stringing;
Or that when I purposed to woo her I tinseled my speech
 that my need might prosper:
I swear by him to whose Ka'beh the companies journey
 when the fleet camels speed them onward,
That deceit toward chaste ladies is not of my nature, nor
 are glozing and lying my badge.
Since I was reared naught has attached to my hand save
 the swiftly moving reeds and the books:
For it is my wit that strings necklaces, not my hand; what
 is strung is my poetry, and not chaplets.
And this is the craft I meant as that by which I gathered
 and gained.
So give ear to my explaining, as thou hast given ear to
 her; and show respect to neither, but judge as is
 due.

Now when he had completed the structure of his story
and perfected his recitation, the Kadi turned to the young
woman, being heart-struck at the verses, and said, now that
it is settled among all judges and those who bear authority
that the race of the generous is perished, and that the times
incline to the niggardly. Now I imagine that thy husband is
truthful in his speech, free from blame. For lo! he has
acknowledged the debt to thee, and spoken the clear truth;
he has given proof that he can string verses, and it is plain
that he is bared to the bone. Now to vex him who shows
excuse is baseness, to imprison the destitute is a sin: to
conceal poverty is self-denial, to await relief with patience is
devotion. So return to thy chamber and pardon the master
of thy virginity: refrain from thy sharpness of tongue and
submit to the will of thy Lord. Then in the almsgiving he
assigned them a portion, and of the dirhems he gave them a
pinch; and said to them, "Beguile yourselves with this drop,

moisten yourselves with this driblet: and endure against the fraud and the trouble of the time, for 'it may be that God will bring victory or some ordinance from himself.'" Then they arose to go, and on the old man was the joy of one loosed from the bond, and the exulting of one who is in affluence after need.

Said the narrator: Now I knew that he was Abu Zayd in the hour that his son peeped forth and his spouse reviled him: and I went near to declare his versatility and the fruiting of his divers branches. But then I was afraid that the Kadi would hit on his falsehood and the lacking of his tongue, and not see fit, when he knew him, to train him to his bounty. So I forebore from speech with the forbearing of one who doubts, and I folded up mention of him as the roll is folded over the writing: save that when he had departed and had come whither he was to come, I said, "If there were one who would set out on his track, he might bring us the kernel of his story, and what tissues he is spreading forth." Then the Kadi sent one of his trusty ones after him and bade him to spy out of his tidings. But he delayed not to return bounding in, and to come back loudly laughing. Said the Kadi to him, "Well, Abu Maryam!" He said, "I have seen a wonder; I have heard what gives me a thrill." Said the Kadi to him, "What hast thou seen, and what is it thou hast learned?" He said, "Since the old man went forth he has not ceased to clap with his hands and to caper with his feet and to sing with the full of his cheeks:

I was near falling into trouble through an impudent jade;
And should have gone to prison but for the Kadi of
    Alexandria."

Then the Kadi laughed till his hat fell off, and his composure was lost: but when he returned to gravity and had followed excess by prayer for pardon, he said, "O God, by the sanctity of thy most honored servants, forbid that I

220

should imprison men of letters." Then said he to that trusty one, "Hither with him!" and he set forth earnest in the search; but returned after a while, telling that the man was gone. Then said the Kadi, "Know that if he had been here he should have had no cause to fear, for I would have imparted to him as he deserves; I would have shown him that *the latter state is better for him than the former.*" Said Al Harith, son of Hammam, Now, when I saw the leaning of the Kadi toward him, and that yet the fruit of the Kadi's notice was lost to him, there came on me the repentance of Al Farazdak when he put away Nawar, or of Al Kosa'i when the daylight appeared.

THE TENTH ASSEMBLY
(CALLED "OF RAHBAH")[25]

Al Harith, son of Hammam, related: The summoning of desire called me to Rahbah, the city of Malik, son of Towk, and I obeyed it, mounted on a fleet camel, and unsheathing an active purpose. Now when I had cast my anchors there, and fastened my ropes, and had gone forth from the bath after shaving my head, I saw a boy cast in the mold of comeliness, and clothed by beauty in the garb of perfection; and an old man was holding on to his sleeve, asserting that he had slain his son; but the boy denied knowledge of him and was horror-struck at his suspicion; and the contention between them scattered its sparks, and the crowding upon them was made up of good and bad. Now after their quarreling had been excessive, they agreed to refer to the Governor of the town; so they hastened to his court with the speed of Sulayk in his career; and when they were there the old man renewed his charge and claimed help. So the Governor made the boy speak, for the boy had already fascinated him by the graces of his bright brow, and cloven

221

his understanding by the disposition of his forelocks. And the boy said, "It is the lie of a great liar against one who is no blood-shedder, and the slander of a knave against one who is not an assassin." Then said the Governor to the old man, "If two just Moslems testify for thee, well; if not, demand of him the oath." Said the old man, "Surely he struck him down remote from men, and shed his blood when alone; and how can I have a witness, when on the spot there was no beholder? But empower me to dictate an oath that it may appear to thee whether he speaks true or lies." He said to him, "Thou hast authority for that; thou with thy vehement grief for thy slain son." Then said the old man to the boy: "Say, I swear by him who hath adorned foreheads with forelocks, and eyes with their black and white, and eyebrows with separation, and smiling teeth with regularity, and eyelids with languor, and noses with straightness, and cheeks with flame, and mouths with purity, and fingers with softness, and waists with slenderness, that I have not killed thy son by negligence, nor of wilfulness, nor made his head a sheath to my sword; if it be otherwise, may God strike my eyelid with soreness, and my cheek with freckles, and my forelocks with dropping, and my palm-shoot with greenness, and my rose with the ox-eye, and my musk with a foul steam, and my full moon with waning, and my silver with tarnishing, and my rays with the dark."

Then said the boy, "The scorching of affliction be my lot rather than to take such an oath! let me yield to vengeance rather than swear as no one has ever sworn!" But the old man would naught but make him swallow the oath which he had framed for him, and the draughts which he had bittered. And the dispute ceased not to blaze between them, and the road of concord to be rugged. Now the boy, while thus resisting, captivated the Governor by his motions, and made him covet that he should belong to him; until love subdued his heart and fixed in his breast; and the passion which enslaved him, and the desire which he had imagined tempted him to liberate the boy and then get possession of him, to free him from the noose of the old man, and then catch him himself. So he said to the old man, "Hast thou a mind for that which is more seemly in the stronger and nearer to god-fearing?" He said, "Whither art thou pointing that I should follow and not delay?" He said, "I think it well that thou cease from altercation and be content with a hundred denars, on condition that I take on myself part of it, and collect the rest as may be." Said the old man, "I refuse not; but let there be no failure to thy promise." Then the Governor paid him down twenty and assigned among his attendants the making up of fifty. But the robe of evening grew dim, and from this cause the rain of collection was cut short. Then he said, "Take what is ready and leave disputing; and on me be it to-morrow to accomplish that the rest be doled to thee and reach thee." Said the old man, "I will do this on the condition that I keep close to him to-night, that the pupil of my eye guard him, until when on the dawning of the morn he has made up what remains of the sum of reconciliation, shell may get clear of chick, and he may go guiltless as the wolf went guiltless of the blood of the son of Jacob." Then said to him the Governor, "I think that thou dost not impose what is immoderate or ask what is excessive."

Said Al Harith, son of Hammam: Now when I perceived that the pleadings of the old man were as the pleadings of Ibn Surayj, I knew him to be the Glory of the Serujis: and I delayed until the stars of the darkness glittered, and the knots of the crowd dispersed: and then I sought the Governor's courtyard; and lo! the old man guarding the youth. And I adjured him by God to say whether he was

223

Abu Zayd: he said, "Yes, by him who hath permitted the chase." I said, "Who is this boy, after whom the understanding darts?" He said, "In kin he is my chick, and in making gain my springe." I said, "Wilt thou not be satisfied with the graces of his make, and spare the Governor temptation by his forelock?" He said, "Were it not that his forehead put forth its ringlets, I should not have snatched the fifty." Then he said, "Pass the night near me that we may quench the fire of grief, and give enjoyment its turn after separation. For I have resolved to slip away at dawn, and to burn the Governor's heart with the flame of regret." Said Al Harith, Then I spent the night with him in conversation more pleasant than a garden of flowers, or a woodland of trees: until when the Wolf's Tail lighted the horizon, and the brightening of the daybreak came on in its time, he mounted the back of the highway, and left the Governor to taste burning torment. And he committed to me, in the hour of his departure a paper firmly closed, and said, "Hand it to the Governor when he has been bereft of composure, when he has convinced himself of our flight." But I broke the seal as one who would free himself from a letter of Mutelemmis, and behold there was written in it:

Tell the Governor whom I have left, after my departure,
        repenting, grieving, biting his hands,
That the old man has stolen his money and the young
        one his heart; and he is scorched in the flame of a
        double regret.
He was generous with his coin when love blinded his eye,
        and he has ended with losing either.
Calm thy grief, O afflicted, for it profits not to seek the
        traces after the substance is gone.
But if what has befallen thee is terrible to thee as the ill-
        fate of Al Hosayn is terrible to the Moslems;
Yet hast thou gotten in exchange for it understanding and
        caution; and the wise man, the prudent, wishes for

224

these.

So henceforth resist desires, and know that the chasing of
gazelles is not easy;

No, nor does every bird enter the springe, even though it
be surrounded by silver.

And how many a one who seeks to make a prey becomes
a prey himself, and meets with naught but the
shoes of Honayn!

Now consider well, and forecast not every thundercloud:
many a thundercloud may have in it the bolts of
death:

And cast down thine eye, that thou mayest rest from a
passion by which thou wouldest clothe thyself
with the garment of infamy and disgrace.

For the trouble of man is the following of the soul's
desire; and the seed of desire is the longing look of
the eye.

Said the narrator, But I tore the paper piecemeal, and
cared not whether he blamed or pardoned me.

THE ELEVENTH ASSEMBLY
(CALLED "OF SAWEH")[26]

Al Harith, son of Hammam, related: I was aware of
hardness of heart while I sojourned at Saweh. So I betook
myself to the Tradition handed down, that its cure is by
visiting the tombs. And when I had reached the mansion of
the dead, the storehouse of moldering remains, I saw an
assemblage over a grave that had been dug, and a corpse
that was being buried. So I drew aside to them, meditating
on the end of man, and calling to mind those of my people
who were gone. And when they had sepulchered the dead,
and the crying of Alas! was over, an old man stood forth on
high, from a hillock, leaning on a staff. And he had veiled
his face with his cloak, and disguised his form for craftiness.

225

And he said: *Let those who work, work for an end like this.* Now take thought, O yet negligent and gird yourselves, ye slothful, and look well, ye observers. How is it with you that the burying of your fellows grieves you not, and that the pouring in of the mold frightens you not; that ye heed not the visitations of misfortune; that ye prepare not for the going down to your graves; that ye are not moved to tears at the eye that weeps; that ye take not warning at the death-message when it is heard; that ye are not affrighted when an intimate is lost; that ye are not saddened when the mourning assembly is gathered? One of you follows home the dead man's bier, but his heart is set toward his house; and he is present at the burying of his kinsman, but his thought is of securing his portion. He leaves his loved friend with the worms, then retires alone with his pipes and lutes. Ye have sorrowed over your riches, if but a grain were notched away, yet have ye been forgetful of the cutting off of your friends: and ye have been cast down at the befalling of adversity, but have made little of the perishing of your kindred. Ye have laughed at a funeral as ye laughed not in the hour of dancing; ye have walked wantonly behind biers, as ye walked not in the day that ye grasped gifts. Ye have turned from the recital of the mourning women to the preparing of banquets; and from the anguish of the bereaved to daintiness in feastings. Ye care not for him who molders, and ye move not the thought of death in your mind. So that it is as if ye were joined to Death by clientship, or had gotten security from Time, or were confident of your own safety, or had made sure of a peace with the Destroyer of delights. No! it is an ill thing that ye imagine. Again, no! surely ye shall learn. Then he recited:

O thou who claimest understanding; how long, O
    brother of delusion, wilt thou marshal sin and
    blame, and err exceeding error?
Is not the shame plain to thee? doth not hoariness warn

thee? (and in its counsel there is no doubtfulness);
nor hath thy hearing become deaf.

Is not Death calling thee? doth he not make thee hear his
voice? dost thou not fear thy passing away, so as to
be wary and anxious?

How long wilt thou be bewildered in carelessness, and
walk proudly in vanity, and go eagerly to
diversion, as if death were not for all?

Till when will last thy swerving, and thy delaying to
mend habits that unite in thee vices whose every
sort shall be collected in thee?

If thou anger thy Master thou art not disquieted at it; but
if thy scheme be bootless thou burnest with
vexation.

If the graving of the yellow one gleam to thee thou art
joyful; but if the bier pass by thee thou feignest
grief, and there is no grief.

Thou resistest him who counseleth righteousness; thou
art hard in understanding; thou swervest aside:
but thou followest the guiding of him who
deceiveth, who lieth, who defameth.

Thou walkest in the desire of thy soul; thou schemest
after money; but thou forgettest the darkness of the
grave, and rememberest not what is there.

But if true happiness had looked upon thee, thy own look
would not have led thee amiss; nor wouldest thou
be saddened when the preaching wipeth away
griefs.

Thou shalt weep blood, not tears, when thou perceivest
that no company can protect thee in the Court of
Assembling; no kinsman of mother or father.

It is as though I could see thee when thou goest down to
the vault and divest deep; when thy kinsmen have
committed thee to a place narrower than a needle's
eye.

There is the body stretched out that the worms may
     devour it, until the coffin-wood is bored through
     and the bones molder.
And afterward there is no escape from that review of
     souls: since Sirat is prepared; its bridge is stretched
     over the fire to every one who cometh thither.
And how many a guide shall go astray! and how many a
     great one shall be vile! and how many a learned
     one shall slip and say, "The business surpasseth."
Therefore hasten, O simple one, to that by which the
     bitter is made sweet; for thy life is now near to
     decay and thou hast not withdrawn thyself from
     blame.
And rely not on fortune though it be soft, though it be
     gay: for so wilt thou be found like one deceived by
     a viper that spitteth venom.
And lower thyself from thy loftiness; for death is meeting
     thee and reaching at thy collar; and he is one who
     shrinketh not back when he hath purposed.
And avoid proud turning away of the cheek if fortune
     have prospered thee: bridle thy speech if it would
     run astray; for how happy is he who bridleth it!
And relieve the brother of sorrow, and believe him when
     he speaketh and mend thy ragged conduct; for he
     hath prospered who mendeth it.
And plume him whose plumage hath fallen in calamity
     great or small; and sorrow not at the loss, and be
     not covetous in amassing.
And resist thy base nature, and accustom thy hand to
     liberality, and listen not to blame for it, and keep
     thy hand from hoarding.
And make provision of good for thy soul, and leave that
     which will bring on ill, and prepare the ship for
     thy journey, and dread the deep of the sea.
Thus have I given my precepts, friends, and shown as one

who showeth clearly: and happy the man who walketh by my doctrines and maketh them his example.

Then he drew back his sleeve from an arm strong of sinew, on which he had fastened the splints of deceit not of fracture; presenting himself to beg in the garb of impudence: and by it he beguiled those people until his sleeve was brimmed and full; then he came down from the hillock merry at the gift. Said the narrator: But I pulled him from behind by the hem of his cloak; and he turned to me submissively, and faced me, saluting me: and lo! it was our old Abu Zayd, in his very self, and in all his deceit: and I said to him,

How many, Abu Zayd, will be the varieties of thy cunning to drive the prey to thy net? and wilt thou not care who censures?

And he answered without shame and without hesitation:

Look well, and leave thy blaming; for, tell me, hast thou ever known a time when a man would not win of the world when the game was in his hands?

Then I said to him: Away with thee, Old Shaykh of Hell, laden with infamy! For there is nothing like thee for the fairness of thy seeming and the foulness of thy purpose; except silvered dung or a whited sewer. Then we parted; and I went away to the right, and he went away to the left; and I set myself to the quarter of the south, and he set himself to the quarter of the north.

THE TWELFTH ASSEMBLY
(CALLED "OF DAMASCUS")[27]

Al Harith, son of Hammam, related: I journeyed from Irak

to the Ghutah; and then was I master of haltered steeds and envied wealth. Freedom of arm called me to diversion, fulness of store led me to pride. And when I had reached the place after toil of soul, after making lean my camel, I found it such as tongues describe it; and in it was whatever souls long for or eyes delight in. So I thanked the bounty of travel and ran a heat with pleasure: and began there to break the seals of desires and gather the clusters of delights, until some travelers were making ready for the journey to Irak, and I had so recovered from my drowning, that regret visited me in calling to mind my home and longing after my fold. Then I struck the tents of exile and saddled the steeds of return. And when the company had equipped themselves and agreement was completed, we shrank from setting forth without taking with us a guard. And we sought one from every tribe and used a thousand devices to obtain him. But to find him in the clans failed, so that we thought he was not among the living. And for the want of such a one the resolves of the travelers were bewildered, and they assembled at the gate of Jayrun to take counsel. And they ceased not tying and untying, and plaiting and twining, until suggestion was exhausted and the hoper despaired. But opposite them was a person whose demeanor was as the demeanor of the youthful, and his garb as the garb of monks, and in his hand was the rosary of women, and in his eyes the mark of giddiness from watchings. And he had fastened his gaze on the assemblage and sharpened his ear to steal a hearing. And when it was the time of their turning homeward and their secret was manifest to him, he said to them, "O people, let your care relieve itself, let your mind be tranquil; for I will guard you with that which shall put off your fear and show itself in accord with you." Said the narrator: Then we asked him to show us concerning his safe conduct, and promised him a higher wage for it than for an embassy. And he declared it to be some words which

230

he had been taught in a dream, whereby to guard himself from the malice of mankind. Then began one to steal a look at another, and to move his eyes between glances sideward and downward. So that it was plain to him that we thought meanly of his story, and conceived it to be futile. Whereupon he said, How is it that ye take my earnest for jest, and treat my gold as dross? Now, by Allah, oft have I gone through fearful tracts and entered among deadly dangers: and with this I have needed not the companying of a guard or to take with me a quiver. Besides, I will remove what gives you doubt, I will draw away the distrust that has come on you, in that I will consent with you in the desert and accompany you on the Semaweh. Then, if my promise has spoken you true, do ye renew my weal and prosper my fortune: but if my mouth has lied to you, then rend my skin and pour out my blood.

Said Al Harith, son of Hammam: Then we were inspired to believe his vision and take as true what he had related; so we ceased from disputing with him and cast lots for carrying him. And at his word we cut the loops of hindrance, and put away fear of harm or stay; and when the pack-saddles were fastened on and the setting forth was near, we sought to learn from him the magic words that we might make them a lasting safeguard. He said: "Let each of you repeat the Mother of the Koran as often as day or night comes on; then let him say with lowly tongue and humble voice: O God! O thou who givest life to the moldering dead! O thou who avertest harms! O thou who guardest from terrors! O thou generous in rewarding! O thou the refuge of suppliants! O thou the Lord of pardon and protection! Send thy blessing on Mohammed, the Seal of thy prophets, the Bringer of thy messages, and on the Lights of his kindred, the Keys of his victory; and give me refuge, O God, from the mischiefs of devils and the assaults of princes; from the vexing of the wrongers, and from suffering through the tyrannous; from the enmity of transgressors, and from the transgression of enemies; from the conquest of conquerors, from the spoiling of spoilers, from the crafts of the crafty, from the treacheries of the treacherous; and deliver me, O God, from the wrongfulness of neighbors and the neighborhood of the wrongful; and keep from me the hands of the harmful; bring me forth from the darkness of the oppressors; place me by thy mercy among thy servants who do aright. O God, keep me in my own land and in my journeying, in my exile and my coming homeward, in my foraging and my return from it, in my trafficking and my success from it, in my adventuring and my withdrawing from it. And guard me in myself and my property, in my honor and my goods, in my family and my means, in my household and my dwelling, in my strength and my fortune, in my riches and my death. Bring not on me reverse; make not the invader lord over me, but give me from thyself helping power. O God, watch over me with thy eye and thy aid, distinguish me by thy safeguard and thy bounty, befriend me with thy election and thy good, and consign me not to the keeping of any but thee. But grant to me health that weareth not away, and allot to me comfort that perisheth not; and free me from the terrors of misfortune, and shelter me with the coverings of thy boons; make not the talons of enemies to prevail against me, for thou art he that heareth prayer."

Then he looked down, and he turned not a glance, he answered not a word: so that we said, "A fear has confounded him or a stupor struck him dumb." Then he raised his head and drew his breath, and said, "I swear by the heaven with its constellations, and the earth with its plains, and the pouring flood, and the blazing sun, and the sounding sea, and the wind and the dust-storm, that this is

the most sure of charms, one that will best suffice you for
the wearers of the helmet. He who repeats it at the smiling
of the dawn has no alarm of danger to the red of eve; and he
who whispers it to the vanguard of the dark is safe the
night long from plunder."

Said the narrator: So we learned it till we knew it
thoroughly, and rehearsed it together that we might not
forget it. Then we set forth, urging the beasts by prayers,
not by the song of drivers; and guarding the loads by
words, not by warriors. And our companion frequented us
evening and morning, but required not of us our promises:
till when we spied the house-tops of 'Anah, he said to us,
"Now, your help, your help!" Then we set before him the
exposed and the hidden, and showed him the corded and
the sealed, and said to him, "Decide as thou wilt, for thou
wilt find among us none but will consent." But nothing
enlivened him but the light, the adorning; nothing was
comely in his eye but the coin. So of those he loaded on his
burden, and rose up with enough to repair his poverty.
Then he dodged us as dodges the cut-purse, and slipped
away from us as slips quicksilver. And his departure
saddened us, his shooting away astonished us: and we
ceased not to seek him in every assembly, and to ask news of
him from each that might mislead or guide. Until it was
said, "Since he entered 'Anah he has not quitted the tavern."
Then the foulness of this report set me on to test it, and to
walk in a path to which I belonged not. So I went by night
to the wine-hall in disguised habit; and there was the old
man in a gay-colored dress amid casks and wine-vats; and
about him were cup-bearers surpassing in beauty, and lights
that glittered, and the myrtle and the jasmine, and the pipe
and the lute. And at one time he bade broach the wine-
casks, and at another he called the lutes to give utterance;
and now he inhaled the perfumes, and now he courted the

gazelles. But when I had thus stumbled on his hypocrisy, and the differing of his to-day from his yesterday, I said to him, Woe to thee, accursed! hast thou forgotten the day at the Jayrun? But he laughed heartily, and then indited charmingly:

234

I cling to journeying, I cross deserts, I loathe pride that I
   may cull joy:
And I plunge into floods, and tame steeds that I may
   draw the trains of pleasure and delight.
And I throw away staidness, and sell my land, for the
   sipping of wine, for the quaffing of cups.
And were it not for longing after the drinking of wine my
   mouth would not utter its elegancies;
Nor would my craft have lured the travelers to the land of
   Irak, through my carrying of rosaries.
Now be not angry, nor cry aloud, nor chide, for my
   excuse is plain:
And wonder not at an old man who settles himself in a
   well-filled house by a wine-cask that is brimming.
For truly wine strengthens the bones and heals sickness
   and drives away grief.
And the purest of joy is when the grave man throws off
   the veils of shame and flings them aside:
And the sweetest of passion is when the love-crazed ceases
   from the concealing of his love, and shows it
   openly.
Then avow thy love and cool thy heart: or else the fire-
   staff of thy grief will rub a spark on it;
And heal thy wounds, and draw out thy cares by the
   daughter of the vine, her the desired:
And assign to thy evening draught a cup-bearer who will
   stir the torment of desire when she gazes;
And a singer who will raise such a voice that the
   mountains of iron shall thrill at it when she
   chants.
And rebel against the adviser who will not permit thee to
   approach a beauty when she consents.
And range in thy cunning even to perverseness; and care
   not what is said of thee, and catch what suits thee:
And leave thy father if he refuse thee, and spread thy nets

and hunt who comes by thee.

But be sincere with thy friend, and avoid the niggardly,
      and bestow kindness, and be constant in gifts;

And take refuge in repentance before thy departure; for
      whoso knocks at the door of the Merciful causes it
      to open.

Then I said to him, "O rare thy recitation, but fie on thy
misconduct! Now, by Allah, tell me from what thicket is thy
root, for thy puzzle vexes me." He said I love not to disclose
myself; yet I will intimate it:

I am the novelty of the time, the wonder of nations;

I am the wily one, who plays his wiles among Arabs and
      foreigners;

But not the less a brother of need, whom fortune vexes
      and wrongs,

And the father of children who lie out like meat on the
      tray:

Now the brother of want, who has a household, is not
      blamed if he be wily.

Said the narrator: Then I knew that it was Abu Zayd, the
man of ill-fame and disgrace, he that blackens the face of his
hoariness. And the greatness of his contumacy offended me,
and the foulness of the path of his resorting: so I said to him
with the tongue of indignation and the confidence of
acquaintance: "Is it not time, old man, that thou withdraw
from debauchery?" But he was angry, and growled, and his
countenance changed, and he thought a while: and then he
said, "It is a night for merriment, not for rebuke, an
occasion for drinking wine, not for contention; so leave
speaking thy thought until we meet to-morrow." Then I left
him, through fear of his drunken humor, not through
dependence on his promise; and I passed my night clothed
in the mourning of repentance, at having advanced the steps
of my foot to the daughter of the vine, not of grace. And I
made a vow to God Almighty that I would never again

enter the tavern of a liquor-seller, even that I might be endowed with the dominion of Bagdad; and that I would not look upon the vats of wine, even that the season of youth might be restored to me. Then we saddled the white camels in the last darkness of night, and left together Abu Zayd and Iblis.

—————————————————————

ARABIC LITERATURE

THE POETS OF ARABIA

"Mortal joys, however pure,
Soon their turbid source betray;
Mortal bliss, however sure,
Soon must totter and decay."

THE CALIPH RAHDI.

THE POETS OF ARABIA

(INTRODUCTION)

ARABIC poetry, as explained in introducing the "Assemblies" of Al Hariri, is based largely on harmonies of sound and striking turns of phrasing. Hence most of the poems are brief; and a poet's fame depended upon a few brilliant couplets rather than on any sustained melody or long-continued flight of noble thought. One distinguished philosophical poem of some length is the well-known "Lament of the Vizier Abu Ismael." This we give in full at the conclusion of this section; but mainly we must illustrate the finest flowering of Arabic verse by selecting specimens of characteristic brevity.

Many of the Arab caliphs inclined to the gaieties of life rather than to their religious duties, and kept many poets around them. Indeed some of the caliphs themselves were poets: The Caliph Walid composed music as well as verse; and was hailed by his immediate companions as a great artist. His neglect of religion, however, was so reckless as to rouse the resentment of his people, and he lost his throne and life.

Most noted of all the Arab poets was Mutanabbi (905-965). His fantastic imagery and extravagant refinements of language were held by his admirers to be the very perfection of literature. More than forty commentaries were written to explain the subtleties of his verse. Such, indeed, was the intensity of Mutanabbi's poetic ecstasy that he fancied himself a prophet and began to preach a new religion, until a term in prison persuaded him to cling to the accepted form of Mohammedanism. In one well-known passage ridiculed by the great French critic, Huart, Mutanabbi says of an advancing army that it was so vast

"The warriors marched hidden in their dust;
     They saw only with their ears."

The commentators explain, perhaps unnecessarily, that this means that the warriors' senses were confused by all the tumult, so that while they thought they saw, in reality they only heard the clamor of the marchers around them. In translation, Mutanabbi's verses lose all value. Deprived of their Arabic melody they seem mere bombast and absurdity. This, in fact, is the general charge which must be made against the later Arabic poetry. It too often degenerated into empty sound.

THE POETS OF ARABIA

THE SONG OF MAISUNA[28]

(WIFE OF THE CALIPH MOWIAH)

The russet suit of camel's hair,
  With spirits light, and eye serene,
Is dearer to my bosom far
  Than all the trappings of a queen.

The humble tent and murmuring breeze
  That whistles thro' its fluttering wall,
My unaspiring fancy please
  Better than towers and splendid halls.

Th' attendant colts that bounding fly
  And frolic by the litter's side,
Are dearer in Maisuna's eye
  Than gorgeous mules in all their pride.

The watch-dog's voice that bays whene'er
  A stranger seeks his master's cot,
Sounds sweeter in Maisuna's ear
  Than yonder trumpet's long-drawn note.

The rustic youth unspoilt by art,
  Son of my kindred, poor but free,
Will ever to Maisuna's heart
  Be dearer, pamper'd fool, than thee.

TO MY FATHER[29]

Must then my failings from the shaft
  Of anger ne'er escape?
And dost thou storm because I've quaff'd
  The water of the grape?

That I can thus from wine be driv'n
  Thou surely ne'er canst think—
Another reason thou hast giv'n
  Why I resolve to drink.

'Twas sweet the flowing cup to seize,
  'Tis sweet thy rage to see;
And first I drink myself to please;
  And next—to anger thee.

ON FATALISM[30]

(BY THE HOLY IMAN SHAFAY)
Not always wealth, not always force
  A splendid destiny commands;
The lordly vulture gnaws the corse
  That rots upon yon barren sands.

Nor want, nor weakness still conspires
  To bind us to a sordid state;
The fly that with a touch expires
  Sips honey from the royal plate.

TO THE CALIPH HAROUN AL RASHID[31]

(BY PRINCE IBRAHIM BEN ADHAM)
Religion's gems can ne'er adorn
The flimsy robe by pleasure worn;
Its feeble texture soon would tear,
And give those jewels to the air.

242

Thrice happy they who seek th' abode
Of peace and pleasure in their God!
Who spurn the world, its joys despise,
And grasp at bliss beyond the skies.

LINES TO HAROUN AND YAHIA[32]

(By the Musician, Isaac Al Mouseli)

Th' affrighted sun ere while he fled,
  And hid his radiant face in night;
A cheerless gloom the world o'erspread—
  But Haroun came and all was bright.

Again the sun shoots forth his rays,
  Nature is decked in beauty's robe—
For mighty Haroun's scepter sways,
  And Yahia's arm sustains the globe.

THE RUIN OF THE BARMECIDES[33]

No, Barmec Time hath never shown
  So sad a change of wayward fate;
Nor sorrowing mortals ever known
  A grief so true, a loss so great.

Spouse of the world! Thy soothing breast
  Did balm to every woe afford;
And now no more by thee caressed,
  The widowed world bewails her lord.

TO TAHER BEN HOSIEN[34]

A pair of right hands and a single dim eye
Must form not a man, but a monster, they cry:
Change a hand to an eye, good Taher, if you can,
And a monster perhaps may be chang'd to man.

THE SONG OF ABU AL SALAM.

"Think not that we will take the cup
From any hand but thine."

TO MY MISTRESS[35]

(By Abu Tammam Habib)

Ungenerous and mistaken maid,
   To scorn me thus because I'm poor!
Canst thou a liberal hand upbraid
   For dealing round some worthless ore?

To spare 's the wish of little souls,
   The great but gather to bestow;
Yon current down the mountain rolls,
   And stagnates in the swamp below.

TO A FEMALE CUP-BEARER[36]

(By Abu Al Salam)

Come, Leila, fill the goblet up,
   Beach round the rosy wine,

Think not that we will take the cup
   From any hand but thine.

A draught like this 'twere vain to seek,
   No grape can such supply;
It steals its tint from Leila's cheek,
   Its brightness from her eye.

MASHDUD ON THE MONKS OF KHABBET[37]

Tenants of yon hallowed fane!
   Let me your devotions share,
There increasing raptures reign —
None are ever sober there.

Crowded gardens, festive bowers
   Ne'er shall claim a thought of mine;
You can give in Khabbet's towers —
   Purer joys and brighter wine.

Though your pallid faces prove
   How you nightly vigils keep,
'Tis but that you ever love
   Flowing goblets more than sleep.

Though your eye-balls dim and sunk
   Stream in penitential guise,
'Tis but that the wine you've drunk
   Bubbles over from your eyes.

RAKEEK TO HIS FEMALE COMPANIONS

Though the peevish tongues upbraid,
   Though the brows of wisdom scowl,
Fair ones here on roses laid,
   Careless will we quaff the bowl.

Let the cup, with nectar crowned,
   Through the grove its beams display,

245

It can shed a luster round,
　　Brighter than the torch of day.

Let it pass from hand to hand,
　　Circling still with ceaseless flight,
Till the streaks of gray expand
　　O'er the fleeting robe of night.

As night flits, she does but cry,
　　"Seize the moments that remain"—
Thus our joys with yours shall vie,
　　Tenants of yon hallowed fane!

DIALOGUE BY RAIS

Rais

Maid of sorrow, tell us why
　　Sad and drooping hangs thy head?
Is it grief that bids thee sigh?
　　Is it sleep that flies thy bed?

Lady

Ah! I mourn no fancied wound,
　　Pangs too true this heart have wrung,
Since the snakes which curl around
　　Selim's brows my bosom stung.

Destined now to keener woes,
　　I must see the youth depart,
He must go, and as he goes
　　Bend at once my bursting heart.

Slumber may desert my bed,
　　'Tis not slumber's charms I seek—
'Tis the robe of beauty spread
　　O'er my Selim's rosy cheek.

TO A LADY WEEPING[38]

(By Ebn Alrumi)
When I beheld thy blue eyes shine
   Through the bright drop that pity drew,
I saw beneath those tears of thine
   A blue-ey'd violet bathed in dew.

The violet ever scents the gale,
   Its hues adorn the fairest wreath,
But sweetest through a dewy veil
   Its colors glow, its odors breathe.

And thus thy charms in brightness rise—
   When wit and pleasure round thee play,
When mirth sits smiling in thine eyes,
   Who but admires their sprightly ray?
But when through pity's flood they gleam,
Who but must love their softened beam?

ON A VALETUDINARIAN

(By Ebn Alrumi)
So careful is Isa, and anxious to last,
   So afraid of himself is he grown,
He swears through two nostrils the breath goes too fast,
   And he's trying to breathe through but one.

ON A MISER

(By Ebn Alrumi)
"Hang her, a thoughtless, wasteful fool,
   She scatters corn where'er she goes"—
Quoth Hassan, angry at his mule,
   That dropped a dinner to the crows.

TO CASSIM OBIO ALLAH[39]

(By Ali Ibn Ahmed)
Poor Cassim! thou art doomed to mourn
   By destiny's decree;
Whatever happens it must turn
   To misery for thee.

Two sons hadst thou, the one thy pride,
   The other was thy pest;
Ah, why did cruel death decide
   To snatch away the best?

No wonder thou shouldst droop with woe,
   Of such a child bereft;
But now thy tears must doubly flow,
   For, ah! the other's left.

A FRIEND'S BIRTHDAY[40]

When born, in tears we saw thee drowned,
While thine assembled friends around,
   With smiles their joy confessed;
So live, that at thy parting hour,
They may the flood of sorrow pour,
   And thou in smiles be dressed!

TO A CAT

(By Ibn Alalaf Alnaharwany)
Poor puss is gone! 'Tis fate's decree—
   Yet I must still her loss deplore,
For dearer than a child was she,
   And ne'er shall I behold her more.

With many a sad presaging tear
   This morn I saw her steal away,
While she went on without a fear
   Except that she should miss her prey.

248

I saw her to the dove-house climb,
  With cautious feet and slow she stept
Resolved to balance loss of time
  By eating faster than she crept.

Her subtle foes were on the watch,
  And marked her course, with fury fraught,
And while she hoped the birds to catch,
  An arrow's point the huntress caught.

In fancy she had got them all,
  And drunk their blood and sucked their breath;
Alas! she only got a fall,
  And only drank the draught of death.

Why, why was pigeons' flesh so nice,
  That thoughtless cats should love it thus?
Hadst thou but lived on rats and mice,
  Thou hadst been living still, poor puss.

Curst be the taste, howe'er refined,
  That prompts us for such joys to wish,
And curst the dainty where we find
  Destruction lurking in the dish.

FIRE

A Riddle

The loftiest cedars I can eat,
  Yet neither paunch nor mouth have I,
I storm whene'er you give me meat,
  Whene'er you give me drink I die.

TO A LADY BLUSHING[41]

(BY THE CALIPH RADHI BILLAH)

Leila, whene'er I gaze on thee
  My altered cheek turns pale,
While upon thine, sweet maid, I see
  A deep'ning blush prevail.

Leila, shall I the cause impart
  Why such a change takes place?
The crimson stream deserts my heart,
  To mantle on thy face.

ON THE VICISSITUDES OF LIFE

(BY THE CALIPH RADHI BILLAH)

Mortal joys, however pure,
  Soon their turbid source betray;
Mortal bliss, however sure,
  Soon must totter and decay.

Ye who now, with footsteps keen,
  Range through hope's delusive field,
Tell us what the smiling scene
  To your ardent grasp can yield?

Other youths have oft before
  Deemed their joys would never fade,
Till themselves were seen no more
  Swept into oblivion's shade.

Who, with health and pleasure gay,
  E'er his fragile state could know,
Were not age and pain to say
  Man is but the child of woe?

TO A DOVE

(BY SERAGE ALWARAK)

The dove to ease an aching breast,

In piteous murmurs vents her cares;
Like me she sorrows, for opprest,
　　Like me, a load of grief she bears.

Her plaints are heard in every wood,
　　While I would fain conceal my woes;
But vain's my wish, the briny flood,
　　The more I strive, the faster flows.

Sure, gentle bird, my drooping heart
　　Divides the pangs of love with thine,
And plaintive murm'rings are thy part,
　　And silent grief and tears are mine.

ON A THUNDER-STORM

(By Ibrahim ben Khiret Abou Isaac)

Bright smiled the morn, till o'er its head
The clouds in thicken'd foldings spread
　　　　A robe of sable hue;
Then, gathering round day's golden king,
They stretched their wide o'ershadowing wing,
　　　　And hid him from our view.

The rain his absent beams deplored,
And, soften'd into weeping, poured
　　　　Its tears in many a flood;
The lightning laughed with horrid glare;
The thunder growled, in rage; the air
　　　　In silent sorrow stood.

TO MY FAVORITE MISTRESS

(By Saif Addaulet, Sultan of Aleppo)

I saw their jealous eyeballs roll,
　　I saw them mark each glance of mine,
I saw thy terrors, and my soul

Shared ev'ry pang that tortured thine.

In vain to wean my constant heart,
　　Or quench my glowing flame, they strove;
Each deep-laid scheme, each envious art,
　　But waked my fears for her I love.

'Twas this compelled the stern decree,
　　That forced thee to those distant towers,
And left me naught but love for thee,
　　To cheer my solitary hours.

Yet let not Abla sink deprest,
　　Nor separation's pangs deplore;
We meet not—'tis to meet more blest;
　　We parted—'tis to part no more.

CRUCIFIXION OF EBN BAKIAH

(By Abu Hassan Alanbary)

Whate'er thy fate, in life and death,
　　hou'rt doomed above us still to rise,
Whilst at a distance far beneath
　　We view thee with admiring eyes.

The gazing crowds still round thee throng,
　　Still to thy well-known voice repair,
As when erewhile thy hallow'd tongue
　　Poured in the mosque the solemn prayer.

Still, generous Vizier, we survey
　　Thine arms extended o'er our head,
As lately, in the festive day,
　　When they were stretched thy gifts to shed.

Earth's narrow boundaries strove in vain
　　To limit thy aspiring mind,

252

And now we see thy dust disdain
  Within her breast to be confin'd.

The earth's too small for one so great,
  Another mansion thou shalt have—
The clouds shall be thy winding sheet,
  The spacious vault of heaven thy grave.

CAPRICES OF FORTUNE[42]

(By Shems Almaali Cabus)

Why should I blush that Fortune's frown
  Dooms me life's humble paths to tread?
To live unheeded, and unknown?
  To sink forgotten to the dead?

'Tis not the good, the wise, the brave,
  That surest shine, or highest rise;
The feather sports upon the wave,
  The pearl in ocean's cavern lies.

Each lesser star that studs the sphere
Sparkles with undiminish'd light;
Dark and eclipsed alone appear
  The lord of day, the queen of night.

ON LIFE

Like sheep, we're doomed to travel o'er
  The fated track to all assigned,
These follow those that went before,
  And leave the world to those behind.

As the flock seeks the pasturing shade,
  Man presses to the future day,
While death, amidst the tufted glade,
  Like the dun robber,[43] waits his prey.

EXTEMPORE VERSES[44]

(By EBN ALRAMACRAM)

Lowering as Barkaidy's face
  The wintry night came in,
Cold as the music of his bass,
  And lengthened as his chin.

Sleep from my aching eyes had fled,
  And kept as far apart,
As sense from Ebn Fahdi's head,
  Or virtue from his heart.

The dubious paths my footsteps balked,
  I slipp'd along the sod,
As if on Jaber's faith I'd walked,
  Or on his truth had trod.

At length the rising King of day
  Burst on the gloomy wood,
Like Carawash's eye, whose ray
  Dispenses every good.

ON THE DEATH OF A SON[45]

(By ALI BEN MOHAMMED ALTAHMANY)

Tyrant of man! Imperious Fate!
  I bow before thy dread decree,
Nor hope in this uncertain state
  To find a seat secure from thee.

Life is a dark, tumultuous stream,
  With many a care and sorrow foul,
Yet thoughtless mortals vainly deem
  That it can yield a limpid bowl.

Think not that stream will backward flow,

254

Or cease its destined course to keep;
As soon the blazing spark shall glow
  Beneath the surface of the deep.

Believe not Fate at thy command
  Will grant a meed she never gave;
As soon the airy tower shall stand,
  That's built upon a passing wave.

Life is a sleep of threescore years,
  Death bids us wake and hail the light,
And man, with all his hopes and fears,
  Is but a phantom of the night.

ON MODERATION IN OUR PLEASURES[46]

(By Abu Alcassim Ebn Tabataba)

How oft does passion's grasp destroy
  The pleasure that it strives to gain?
How soon the thoughtless course of joy
  Is doomed to terminate in pain?

When prudence would thy steps delay,
  She but restrains to make thee blest;
Whate'er from joy she lops away,
  But heightens and secures the rest.

Wouldst thou a trembling flame expand,
  That hastens in the lamp to die?
With careful touch, with sparing hand,
  The feeding stream of life supply.

But if thy flask profusely sheds
  A rushing torrent o'er the blaze,
Swift round the sinking flame it spreads,
  And kills the fire it fain would raise.

THE VALE OF BOZAA[47]

(By Ahmed ben Yusef Almenazy)

The intertwining boughs for thee
   Have wove, sweet dell, a verdant vest,
And thou in turn shalt give to me
   A verdant couch upon thy breast.

To shield me from day's fervid glare
   Thine oaks their fostering arms extend,
As anxious o'er her infant care
   I've seen a watchful mother bend.

A brighter cup, a sweeter draught,
   I gather from that rill of thine,
Than maddening drunkards ever quaff'd,
   Than all the treasures of the vine.

So smooth the pebbles on its shore,
   That not a maid can thither stray,
But counts her strings of jewels o'er,
   And thinks the pearls have slipped away.

TO ADVERSITY[48]

(By Abu Menbaa Carawash)

Hail, chastening friend Adversity! 'Tis thine
The mental ore to temper and refine,
To cast in virtue's mold the yielding heart,
And honor's polish to the mind impart.
Without thy wakening touch, thy plastic aid,
I'd lain the shapeless mass that nature made;
But formed, great artist, by thy magic hand,
I gleam a sword to conquer and command.

ON THE INCOMPATIBILITY OF PRIDE AND TRUE

256

GLORY[49]

(By Abu Alola)

Think not, Abdallah, pride and fame
  Can ever travel hand in hand;
With breast opposed, and adverse aim,
  On the same narrow path they stand.

Thus youth and age together meet,
  And life's divided moments share;
This can't advance till that retreat,
  What's here increased is lessened there.

And thus the falling shades of night
  Still struggle with the lucid ray,
And e'er they stretch their gloomy flight
  Must win the lengthened space from day.

THE DEATH OF NEDHAM ALMOLK

(By Shebal Addaulet)

Thy virtues famed through every land,
  Thy spotless life, in age and youth,
Prove thee a pearl, by nature's hand,
  Formed out of purity and truth.

Too long its beams of Orient light
  Upon a thankless world were shed;
Allah has now revenged the slight,
  And called it to its native bed.

TO A LADY

No, Abla, no—when Selim tells
Of many an unknown grace that dwells
    In Abla's face and mien,
When he describes the sense refined,
That lights thine eye and fills thy mind,

257

By thee alone unseen.

'Tis not that drunk with love he sees
Ideal charms, which only please
        Through passion's partial veil,
'Tis not that flattery's glozing tongue
Hath basely framed an idle song,
        But truth that breathed the tale.

Thine eyes unaided ne'er could trace
Each opening charm, each varied grace,
        That round thy person plays;
Some must remain concealed from thee,
For Selim's watchful eye to see,
        For Selim's tongue to praise.

One polished mirror can declare
That eye so bright, that face so fair,
        That cheek which shames the rose;
But how thy mantle waves behind,
How float thy tresses on the wind,
        Another only shows.

AN EPIGRAM[50]

Whoever has recourse to thee
    Can hope for health no more,
He's launched into perdition's sea,
    A sea without a shore.

Where'er admission thou canst gain,
    Where'er thy phiz can pierce,
At once the Doctor they retain,
    The mourners and the hearse.

ON A LITTLE MAN WITH A VERY LARGE BEARD

(By Isaac ben Khalif)

How can thy chin that burden bear?
  Is it all gravity to shock?
Is it to make the people stare?
  And be thyself a laughing stock?

When I behold thy little feet
  After thy beard obsequious run,
I always fancy that I meet
  Some father followed by his son.

A man like thee scarce e'er appeared—
  A beard like thine—where shall we find it?
Surely thou cherishest thy beard
  In hopes to hide thyself behind it.

THE LAMENT OF THE VIZIER ABU ISMAEL[51]

No kind supporting hand I meet,
But Fortitude shall stay my feet;
No borrowed splendors round me shine,
But Virtue's luster all is mine;
A Fame unsullied still I boast,
Obscured, concealed, but never lost—
The same bright orb that led the day
Pours from the West his mellowed ray.

Zaura, farewell! No more I see
Within thy walls, a home for me;
Deserted, spurned, aside I'm tossed,
As an old sword whose scabbard's lost:
Around thy walls I seek in vain
Some bosom that will soothe my pain—
No friend is near to breathe relief,
Or brother to partake my grief.
For many a melancholy day
Through desert vales I've wound my way;
The faithful beast, whose back I press,

In groans laments her lord's distress;
In every quivering of my spear
A sympathetic sigh I hear;
The camel bending with his load,
And struggling through the thorny road,
'Midst the fatigues that bear him down,
In Hassan's woes forgets his own;
Yet cruel friends my wand'rings chide,
My sufferings slight, my toils deride.

Once wealth, I own, engrossed each thought,
There was a moment when I sought
The glitt'ring stores Ambition claims
To feed the wants his fancy frames;
But now 'tis past—the changing day
Has snatched my high-built hopes away,
And bade this wish my labors close—
Give me not riches, but repose.
'Tis he—that mien my friend declares,
That stature, like the lance he bears;
I see that breast which ne'er contained
A thought by fear or folly stained,
Whose powers can every change obey,
In business grave, in trifles gay,
And, formed each varying taste to please,
Can mingle dignity with ease.

What, though with magic influence, sleep,
O'er every closing eyelid creep:
Though drunk with its oblivious wine
Our comrades on their bales recline,
My Selim's trance I sure can break—
Selim, 'tis I, 'tis I who speak.
Dangers on every side impend,
And sleep'st thou, careless of thy friend?

Thou sleep'st while every star on high,
Beholds me with a wakeful eye—
Thou changest, ere the changeful night
Hath streak'd her fleeting robe with white.

'Tis love that hurries me along—
I'm deaf to fear's repressive song—
The rocks of Idham I'll ascend,
Though adverse darts each path defend,
And hostile sabers glitter there,
To guard the tresses of the fair.

Come, Selim, let us pierce the grove,
While night befriends, to seek my love.
The clouds of fragrance as they rise
Shall mark the place where Abla lies.
Around her tent my jealous foes,
Like lions, spread their watchful rows;
Amidst their bands, her bow'r appears
Embosomed in a wood of spears—
A wood still nourished by the dews,
Which smiles, and softest looks diffuse.
Thrice happy youths! who midst yon shades
Sweet converse hold with Idham's maids,
What bliss, to view them gild the hours,
And brighten wit and fancy's powers,
While every foible they disclose
New transport gives, new graces shows.
'Tis theirs to raise with conscious art
The flames of love in every heart;
'Tis yours to raise with festive glee
The flames of hospitality:
Smit by their glances lovers lie,
And helpless sink and hopeless die;
While slain by you the stately steed

To crown the feast, is doomed to bleed,
To crown the feast, where copious flows
The sparkling juice that soothes your woes,
That lulls each care and heals each wound,
As the enliv'ning bowl goes round.
Amidst those vales my eager feet
Shall trace my Abla's dear retreat,
A gale of health may hover there,
To breathe some solace to my care.
I fear not love—I bless the dart
Sent in a glance to pierce the heart:
With willing breast the sword I hail
That wounds me through an half-closed veil:
Though lions howling round the shade,
My footsteps haunt, my walks invade,
No fears shall drive me from the grove,
If Abla listen to my love.

Ah, Selim! shall the spells of ease
Thy friendship chain, thine ardor freeze!
Wilt thou enchanted thus, decline
Each gen'rous thought, each bold design?
Then far from men some cell prepare;
Or build a mansion in the air—
But yield to us, ambition's tide,
Who fearless on its waves can ride;
Enough for thee if thou receive
The scattered spray the billows leave.

Contempt and want the wretch await
Who slumbers in an abject state—
'Midst rushing crowds, by toil and pain
The meed of Honor we must gain;
At Honor's call, the camel hastes
Through trackless wilds and dreary wastes,

Till in the glorious race she find
The fleetest coursers left behind:
By toils like these alone, he cries,
Th' adventurous youths to greatness rise;
If bloated indolence were fame,
And pompous ease our noblest aim,
The orb that regulates the day
Would ne'er from Aries' mansion stray.

I've bent at Fortune's shrine too long—
Too oft she heard my suppliant tongue—
Too oft has mocked my idle prayers,
While fools and knaves engrossed her cares,
Awake for them, asleep to me,
Heedless of worth she scorned each plea.
Ah! had her eyes more just surveyed
The diff'rent claims which each displayed,
Those eyes from partial fondness free
Had slept to them, and waked for me.
But, 'midst my sorrows and my toils,
Hope ever soothed my breast with smiles;
The hand removed each gathering ill,
And oped life's closing prospects still.
Yet spite of all her friendly art
The specious scene ne'er gained my heart;
I loved it not although the day
Met my approach, and cheered my way;
I loath it now the hours retreat,
And fly me with reverted feet.

My soul from every tarnish free
May boldly vaunt her purity,
But ah, how keen, however bright,
The saber glitter to the sight,
Its splendor's lost, its polish vain,

Till some bold hand the steel sustain.

Why have my days been stretched by fate,
To see the vile and vicious great—
While I, who led the race so long,
Am last and meanest of the throng?
Ah, why has death so long delayed
To wrap me in his friendly shade,
Left me to wander thus alone,
When all my heart held dear is gone!

But let me check these fretful sighs—
Well may the base above me rise,
When yonder planets as they run
Mount in the sky above the sun.
Resigned I bow to Fate's decree,
Nor hope his laws will change for me;
Each shifting scene, each varying hour,
But proves the ruthless tyrant's power.

But though with ills unnumbered curst,
We owe to faithless man the worst;
For man can smile with specious art,
And plant a dagger in the heart.
He only's fitted for the strife
Which fills the boist'rous paths of life,
Who, as he treads the crowded scenes,
Upon no kindred bosom leans.
Too long my foolish heart had deemed
Mankind as virtuous as they seemed;
The spell is broke, their faults are bare,
And now I see them as they are;
Truth from each tainted breast has flown,
And falsehood marks them all her own.
Incredulous I listen now
To every tongue, and every vow,

For still there yawns a gulf between
Those honeyed words, and what they mean;
With honest pride elate, I see
The sons of falsehood shrink from me,
As from the right line's even way
The biassed curves deflecting stray—
But what avails it to complain?
With souls like theirs reproof is vain;
If honor e'er such bosoms share
The saber's point must fix it there.

But why exhaust life's rapid bowl,
And suck the dregs with sorrow foul,
When long ere this my mouth has drained
Whatever zest the cup contained?
Why should we mount upon the wave,
And ocean's yawning horrows brave,
When we may swallow from the flask
Whate'er the wants of mortals ask?
Contentment's realms no fears invade,
No cares annoy, no sorrows shade,
There placed secure, in peace we rest,
Nor aught demand to make us blest.
While pleasure's gay fantastic bower,
The splendid pageant of an hour,
Like yonder meteor in the skies,
Flits with a breath no more to rise.

As through life's various walks we're led,
May prudence hover o'er our head!
May she our words, our actions guide,
Our faults correct, our secrets hide!
May she, where'er our footsteps stray,
Direct our paths, and clear the way!

Till, every scene of tumult past,

She bring us to repose at last,
Teach us to love that peaceful shore,
And roam through folly's wilds no more!

MOORISH LITERATURE

SCIENCE AND HISTORY AMONG THE MOORS

"The religion sacred to philosophers is to study that which is, for the most sublime worship one can render to God is the recognition and knowledge of his works."

—AVERROES.

267

MOORISH LITERATURE

SCIENCE AND HISTORY

(INTRODUCTION)

THE name "Moor" is used loosely to describe all those peoples who sprang from the mingling of the Berber, or Hamitic, stock of North Africa, with the Arabs or Semitic stock who swept over the region in the Mohammedan conquest. The chief achievement of this mixed or Moorish race was the establishment of their brilliant kingdom and independent caliphate in Spain. Under the most powerful of these Spanish caliphs, Ahderrahman III. (A.D. 912-961), their capital Cordova had six hundred mosques, including its still celebrated chief mosque, the most beautiful building of that age in Europe. The Moorish kingdom of Spain had then seventeen universities and over seventy large libraries. It was the most cultured land of Europe, the goal of scholars from less peaceful and less learned Christendom.

The Moorish kingdom in the course of the twelfth century broke up into many tiny States. These soon fought among themselves and plunged each other into a common ruin. African Moors, of far more ignorant and fanatic type, came to aid their Spanish brethren; and under the pressure of these barbarians, culture rapidly declined. The universities were broken up. The great scholar Averroes, who had been the pride of his nation, was accused of heresy. His teachings were found not sufficiently subservient to the

Koran; and finally, in 1195, he was driven into exile. This event, or Averroes' death soon afterward, may be reckoned as marking the downfall of the Moorish leadership in science and philosophy.

In our volume we give some of Averroes' most celebrated commentaries, as typifying the culmination of Moorish culture. We give also, as its opening note, the speech with which Tarik, the first conqueror of Spain, in the year A.D. 711 led his army to cross the Straits of Gibraltar and began the attack upon the earlier Christian inhabitants. This speech does not, however, preserve the actual words of Tarik; it only presents the tradition of them as preserved by the Moorish historian Al Maggari, who wrote in Africa long after the last of the Moors had been driven out of Spain. In Al Maggari's day the older Arabic traditions of exact service had quite faded. The Moors had become poets and dreamers instead of scientists and critical historians. The very name of Al Maggari's history may be accepted as typifying its character. He called it "Breath of Perfumes."

SCIENCE AND HISTORY

PHILOSOPHIC THOUGHTS

(By Averroes)

The first to preach the resurrection were the prophets of Israel after Moses, then the Evangelical Christians, then the Sabians, whose religion has been called by Ibn-Hazm the oldest in the world. The reason so many founders of religion established this dogma was because they supposed this belief would moralize men and induce them to be virtuous in their own interests. I do not quarrel with Al Ghazali or Motecallemin for saying that the soul is immortal, but I object to the idea that the soul is a mere accident, and that a man can take again the body which has fallen into decay. No, he may take another, similar to the first, but that which has been dead can not return to life. These two bodies are only one, viewed as a species, but they are two in number. Aristotle has said in the last lines of his "Generation and Corruption": "A body once corrupted can never become the same again; it can never return as an individual whole, but it can return to the specific variety of which it is a part. When air separates from water or water separates from air, each of these substances can not become again the thing it was, but must return to its own species."

How have we come to adopt these tales of the creation? Through habit. Just as a man inured to poison can take it with impunity, so a man used to them from childhood can accept the most unbelievable opinions. Therefore the

270

opinions of the masses are only formed through habit. The people believe that which they hear incessantly repeated. And that is why the power of religion is so much stronger than that of philosophy, for it is not accustomed to hearing the opposite of its belief, a thing which happens very often to philosophy: So one sees frequently, nowadays, men who, having entered suddenly into the study of the speculative sciences, lose the religious beliefs which they have only held through habit, and become *zendihs* (infidels).

The religion sacred to philosophers is to study that which *is*, for the most sublime worship one can render to God is the recognition and knowledge of his works, which leads us to know him, himself, in all his *reality*. In the eyes of God that is the noblest action, while the vilest action is to tax with error and presumption those who practise this worship, higher than any other, who adore him by this religion, the best of all religions.

Among the most dangerous of these fictions concerning a future life are those which counsel virtue as a means of arriving at happiness. In that case virtue is no longer worth anything, since one only abstains from voluptuousness in the hope of being doubly repaid in the future. The brave will only seek death to evade a worse evil. The good will only respect the belongings of others in order to acquire twice as much.

Wine is forbidden because it excites wickedness and quarrels; but I am preserved from those excesses by wisdom: I take it only to sharpen my wits.[52]

That renegade philosopher, Al Ghazali, has gathered up all he learned from the writings of the philosophers, and has turned against them the arms he borrowed from them.

As for us, the philosophers, at the risk of exposing

271

ourselves to the rage of the persecutors of philosophy, which was our mother, we will, when the time is ripe, uncover the poison hidden in Al Ghazali's book.

—————————

Our social state does not bring out all the resources and possibilities there are in women; it would seem that they are only destined to bear and rear children, and this state of servitude has destroyed in them the capability for larger things. That is why one never sees, with us, a woman possessed of the moral virtues—their lives pass like those of flowers, and they are a burden upon their husbands. From this comes also the misery which devours our cities, for there are twice as many women there as men, but the former are not permitted to work for their own support.

—————————

My father aided in rescuing from prison Ibn Badja, who was accused of heresy. My father does not understand that his own son will one day be regarded as a far worse heretic.

God alone knows if I am one; but it is absolutely certain that it was only the intrigues of my enemies which led to my condemnation. I thought only of editing Aristotle and establishing accord between religion and philosophy.

TARIK'S ADDRESS TO HIS SOLDIERS

(FROM THE HISTORY OF AL MAGGARI)

When Tarik had been informed of the approach of the enemy, he rose in the midst of his companions and, after having glorified God in the highest, he spoke to his soldiers thus:

"Oh my warriors, whither would you flee? Behind you is the sea, before you, the enemy. You have left now only the hope of your courage and your constancy. Remember that in this country you are more unfortunate than the orphan seated at the table of the avaricious master. Your enemy is before you, protected by an innumerable army; he has men in abundance, but you, as your only aid, have your own swords, and, as your only chance for life, such chance as you can snatch from the hands of your enemy. If the absolute want to which you are reduced is prolonged ever so little, if you delay to seize immediate success, your good fortune will vanish, and your enemies, whom your very presence has filled with fear, will take courage. Put far from you the disgrace from which you flee in dreams, and attack this monarch who has left his strongly fortified city to meet you. Here is a splendid opportunity to defeat him, if you will consent to expose yourselves freely to death. Do not believe that I desire to incite you to face dangers which I shall refuse to share with you. In the attack I myself will be in the fore, where the chance of life is always least.

"Remember that if you suffer a few moments in patience, you will afterward enjoy supreme delight. Do not imagine that your fate can be separated from mine, and rest assured that if you fall, I shall perish with you, or avenge you. You have heard that in this country there are a large number of ravishingly beautiful Greek maidens, their graceful forms are draped in sumptuous gowns on which gleam pearls, coral, and purest gold, and they live in the palaces of royal kings. The Commander of True Believers, Alwalid, son of Abdalmelik, has chosen you for this attack from among all his Arab warriors; and he promises that you shall become his comrades and shall hold the rank of kings in this country. Such is his confidence in your intrepidity. The one fruit which he desires to obtain from your bravery is that the word of God shall be exalted in this country, and that the true religion shall be established here. The spoils will

273

belong to yourselves.

"Remember that I place myself in the front of this glorious charge which I exhort you to make. At the moment when the two armies meet hand to hand, you will see me, never doubt it, seeking out this Roderick, tyrant of his people, challenging him to combat, if God is willing. If I perish after this, I will have had at least the satisfaction of delivering you, and you will easily find among you an experienced hero, to whom you can confidently give the task of directing you. But should I fall before I reach to Roderick, redouble your ardor, force yourselves to the attack and achieve the conquest of this country, in depriving him of life. With him dead, his soldiers will no longer defy you."

———————————————————

MOORISH LITERATURE

POETRY OF THE SPANISH MOORS

"Fortune, that whilom owned my sway,
And bowed obsequious to my nod,
Now sees me destined to obey,
And bend beneath oppression's rod."
PRINCE MOHAMMED BEN ABAD.

POETRY OF THE SPANISH MOORS

(INTRODUCTION)

WHILE the scientific leadership of the Moors faded with the breaking of their military unity in the twelfth century, they still retained in some of their smaller kingdoms, and especially in that of Granada, a high degree of culture. The love of beauty and the spirit of romance were strong among all the Spanish Moors; and so their poetry continued long after science failed them. Poetry indeed became their main expression. Granada, the last of all their Spanish kingdoms, did not fall before the advancing Christians until 1492. Then, as our histories have so often told, Ferdinand and Isabella, the Christian rulers of Spain, conducted a holy war for the destruction of Granada. Its last fortress surrendered, and its people withdrew to Africa. There, according to a characteristically dreamy legend, they still retain the keys of their mansions in Granada, treasuring them up for the day of their triumphant return.

Of the Moorish poetry which survived the fall of Granada, much was preserved by the Spaniards themselves and in the Spanish language. The victors knew how to value the spirit of the vanquished; and ballads of Moorish origin, telling of Moorish loves, long remained popular in Spain. The authors of most of these have been forgotten. The text of some of the best known of them is given here.

MOORISH POETRY

VERSES TO MY DAUGHTERS[53]

(By Prince Mohammed ben Abad)

With jocund heart and cheerful brow
  I used to hail the festal morn —
How must Mohammed greet it now? —
  A prisoner helpless and forlorn.

While these dear maids in beauty's bloom,
  With want opprest, with rags o'erspread,
By sordid labors at the loom
  Must earn a poor, precarious bread.

Those feet that never touched the ground,
  Till musk or camphor strewed the way,
Now bare and swoll'n with many a wound,
  Must struggle through the miry clay.

Those radiant cheeks are veiled in woe,
  A shower descends from every eye,
And not a starting tear can flow,
  That wakes not an attending sigh.

Fortune, that whilom owned my sway,
  And bowed obsequious to my nod,
Now sees me destined to obey,
  And bend beneath oppression's rod.

Ye mortals with success elate,
  Who bask in hope's delusive beam,
Attentive view Mohammed's fate,
  And own that bliss is but a dream.

SERENADE TO MY SLEEPING MISTRESS[54]

(By Ali ben Abad)

Sure Harut's[55] potent spells were breathed
Upon that magic sword, thine eye;
For if it wounds us thus while sheathed,

277

When drawn, 'tis vain its edge to fly.

How canst thou doom me, cruel fair,
Plunged in the hell[56] of scorn to groan?
No idol e'er this heart could share,
This heart has worshiped thee alone.

THE INCONSISTENT[57]

When I sent you my melons, you cried out with scorn,
  They ought to be heavy and wrinkled and yellow;
When I offered myself, whom those graces adorn,
  You flouted, and called me an ugly old fellow.

THE BULLFIGHT OF GAZUL[58]

King Almanzor of Granada, he hath bid the trumpet
      sound,
He hath summoned all the Moorish lords, from the hills
      and plains around;
From *vega* and *sierra*, from Betis and Xenil,
They have come with helm and cuirass of gold and
      twisted steel.

'Tis the holy Baptist's feast they hold in royalty and state,
And they have closed the spacious lists beside the
      Alhambra's gate;
In gowns of black and silver laced, within the tented ring,
Eight Moors to fight the bull are placed in presence of the
      King.

Eight Moorish lords of valor tried, with stalwart arm and
      true,
The onset of the beasts abide, as they come rushing
      through;
The deeds they've done, the spoils they've won, fill all
      with hope and trust,
Yet ere high in heaven appears the sun they all have bit

the dust.

Then sounds the trumpet clearly, then clangs the loud
    tambour,
Make room, make room for Gazul—throw wide, throw
    wide the door;
Blow, blow the trumpet clearer still, more loudly strike the
    drum,
The *Alcaydé* of Algava to fight the bull doth come.

And first before the King he passed, with reverence
    stooping low,
And next he bowed him to the Queen, and the *Infantas* all
    a-row;
Then to his lady's grace he turned, and she to him did
    throw
A scarf from out her balcony, 'twas whiter than the snow.

With the life-blood of the slaughtered lords all slippery is
    the sand,
Yet proudly in the center hath Gazul ta'en his stand;
And ladies look with heaving breast, and lords with
    anxious eye,
But firmly he extends his arm—his look is calm and high.

Three bulls against the knight are loosed, and two come
    roaring on,
He rises high in stirrup, forth stretching his *rejón*;
Each furious beast upon the breast he deals him such a
    blow
He blindly totters and gives back, across the sand to go.

"Turn, Gazul, turn!" the people cry—the third comes up
    behind,
Low to the sand his head holds he, his nostrils snuff the
    wind;

279

The mountaineers that lead the steers, without stand
      whispering low,
"Now thinks this proud *alcaydé* to stun Harpado so?"

From Guadiana comes he not, he comes not from Xenil,
From Gaudalarif of the plain, or Barves of the hill;
But where from out the forest burst Xarama's waters clear,
Beneath the oak-trees was he nursed, this proud and
      stately steer.

Dark is his hide on either side, but the blood within doth
      boil,
And the dun hide glows, as if on fire, as he paws to the
      turmoil.
His eyes are jet, and they are set in crystal rings of snow;
But now they stare with one red glare of brass upon the
      foe.

Upon the forehead of the bull the horns stand close and
      near,
From out the broad and wrinkled skull, like daggers they
      appear;
His neck is massy, like the trunk of some old knotted tree,
Whereon the monster's shaggy mane, like billows curled,
      ye see.

His legs are short, his hams are thick, his hoofs are black
      as night,
Like a strong flail he holds his tail in fierceness of his
      might;
Like something molten out of iron, or hewn from forth
      the rock,
Harpado of Xarama stands, to bide the *alcaydé's* shock.

Now stops the drum—close, close they come—thrice meet,
      and thrice give back;

The white foam of Harpado lies on the charger's breast of
      black—
The white foam of the charger on Harpado's front of dun
      —
Once more advance upon his lance—once more, thou
      fearless one!

Once more, once more;—in dust and gore to ruin must
      thou reel—
In vain, in vain thou tearest the sand with furious heel—
In vain, in vain, thou noble beast, I see, I see thee stagger,
Now keen and cold thy neck must hold the stern *alcaydé's*
      dagger!

They have slipped a noose around his feet, six horses are
      brought in,
And away they drag Harpado with a loud and joyful din.
Now stoop thee, lady, from thy stand, and the ring of
      price bestow
Upon Gazul of Algava, that hath laid Harpado low.

THE ZEGRI'S BRIDE[59]

Of all the blood of Zegri, the chief is Lisaro,
To wield *rejón* like him is none, or javelin to throw;
From the place of his dominion, he ere the dawn doth go,
From Alcala de Henares, he rides in weed of woe.

He rides not now as he was wont, when ye have seen him
      speed
To the field of gay Toledo, to fling his lusty reed;
No gambeson of silk is on, nor rich embroidery
Of gold-wrought robe or turban—nor jeweled *tahali*.

No amethyst nor garnet is shining on his brow,
No crimson sleeve, which damsels weave at Tunis, decks
      him now;

The belt is black, the hilt is dim, but the sheathed blade is
     bright;
They have housened his barb in a murky garb, but yet
     her hoofs are light.

Four horsemen good, of the Zegri blood, with Lisaro go
     out;
No flashing spear may tell them near, but yet their shafts
     are stout;
In darkness and in swiftness rides every armed knight—
The foam on the rein ye may see it plain, but nothing else
     is white.

Young Lisaro, as on they go, his bonnet doffeth he,
Between its folds a sprig it holds of a dark and glossy tree;
That sprig of bay, were it away, right heavy heart had he
—
Fair Zayda to her Zegri gave that token privily.

And ever as they rode, he looked upon his lady's boon.
"God knows," quoth he, "what fate may be—I may be
     slaughtered soon;
Thou still art mine, though scarce the sign of hope that
     bloomed whilere,
But in my grave I yet shall have my Zayda's token dear."

Young Lisaro was musing so, when onward on the path,
He well could see them riding slow; then pricked he in his
     wrath.
The raging sire, the kinsmen of Zayda's hateful house,
Fought well that day, yet in the fray the Zegri won his
     spouse.

ZARA'S EARRINGS

"My earrings! my earrings! they've dropped into the well,
And what to say to Muça, I can not, can not tell."

'Twas thus, Granada's fountain by, spoke Albuharez'
     daughter
"The well is deep, far down they lie, beneath the cold blue
     water—
To me did Muça give them, when he spake his sad
     farewell,
And what to say when he comes back, alas! I can not tell.

"My earrings! my earrings! they were pearls in silver set,
That when my Moor was far away, I ne'er should him
     forget,
That I ne'er to other tongue should list, nor smile on
     other's tale,
But remember he my lips had kissed, pure as those
     earrings pale—
When he comes back, and hears that I have dropped them
     in the well,
Oh, what will Muça think of me, I can not, can not tell.

"My earrings! my earrings! he'll say they should have
     been,
Not of pearl and of silver, but of gold and glittering sheen,
Of jasper and of onyx, and of diamond shining clear,
Changing to the changing light, with radiance insincere
     —
That changeful mind unchanging gems are not befitting
     well—
Thus will he think—and what to say, alas! I can not tell.

"He'll think when I to market went, I loitered by the way;
He'll think a willing ear I lent to all the lads might say;
He'll think some other lover's hand, among my tresses
     noosed,
From the ears where he had placed them, my rings of
     pearl unloosed;
He'll think, when I was sporting so beside this marble

well,
My pearls fell in—and what to say, alas! I can not tell.

"He'll say, I am a woman, and we are all the same;
He'll say I loved when he was here to whisper of his flame
   —
But when he went to Tunis my virgin troth had broken,
And thought no more of Muça, and care not for his
      token.
My earrings! my earrings! O luckless, luckless well,
For what to say to Muça, alas! I can not tell.

"I'll tell the truth to Muça, and I hope he will believe—
That I thought of him at morning, and thought of him at
      eve;
That, musing on my lover, when down the sun was gone,
His earrings in my hand I held, by the fountain all alone;
And that my mind was o'er the sea, when from my hand
      they fell,
And that deep his love lies in my heart, as they lie in the
      well."

THE LAMENTATION FOR CELIN

At the gate of old Granada, when all its bolts are barred,
At twilight at the Vega gate there is a trampling heard;
There is a trampling heard, as of horses treading slow,
And a weeping voice of women, and a heavy sound of
      woe.
"What tower is fallen, what star is set, what chief come
      these bewailing?"
"A tower is fallen, a star is set. Alas! alas for Celin!"
Three times they knock, three times they cry, and wide the
      doors they throw;
Dejectedly they enter, and mournfully they go;
In gloomy lines they mustering stand beneath the hollow
      porch,

Each horseman grasping in his hand a black and flaming
    torch;
Wet is each eye as they go by, and all around is wailing,
For all have heard the misery. "Alas! alas for Celin!"—

Him yesterday a Moor did slay, of Bencerraje's blood,
'Twas at the solemn jousting, around the nobles stood;
The nobles of the land were by, and ladies bright and fair
Looked from their latticed windows, the haughty sight to
    share;
But now the nobles all lament, the ladies are bewailing,
For he was Granada's darling knight. "Alas! alas for
    Celin!"

Before him ride his vassals, in order two by two,
With ashes on their turbans spread, most pitiful to view;
Behind him his four sisters, each wrapped in sable veil,
Between the tambour's dismal strokes take up their
    doleful tale;
When stops the muffled drum, ye hear their brotherless
    bewailing,
And all the people, far and near, cry—"Alas! alas for
    Celin!"

Oh! lovely lies he on the bier, above the purple pall,
The flower of all Granada's youth, the loveliest of them
    all;
His dark, dark eyes are closed, his rosy lip is pale,
The crust of blood lies black and dim upon his burnished
    mail,
And evermore the hoarse tambour breaks in upon their
    wailing,
Its sound is like no earthly sound—"Alas! alas for Celin!"
The Moorish maid at the lattice stands, the Moor stands
    at his door,
One maid is wringing of her hands, and one is weeping

sore—
Down to the dust men bow their heads, and ashes black
     they strew
Upon their broidered garments of crimson, green, and
     blue—
Before each gate the bier stands still, then bursts the loud
     bewailing,
From door and lattice, high and low—"Alas! alas for
     Celin!"

An old, old woman cometh forth, when she hears the
     people cry;
Her hair is white as silver, like horn her glazed eye.
'Twas she that nursed him at her breast, that nursed him
     long ago;
She knows not whom they all lament, but soon she well
     shall know.
With one deep shriek she through doth break, when her
     ears receive their wailing—
"Let me kiss my Celin ere I die—Alas! alas for Celin!"

TURKISH LITERATURE

LEGEND AND POETRY AMONG THE TURKS

"Once upon a time."

THE OLD, OLD BEGINNING.

While still I live, 'tis well that I should mirth and glee enjoy."

SULTAN MURAD II.

LEGEND AND POETRY AMONG THE TURKS

(INTRODUCTION)

TURKISH literature, as pointed out in our general introduction, is of a less advanced character than that of most of the Semitic literatures from which it is sprung. An epigrammatic summary of the Turkish character has said that every fourth word of Turkish is Arabic, every third idea Persian, and every second impulse Mohammedan. This, while not seeming to leave much of the original Turk, is perhaps not an unfair estimate of the extent of the Turks' indebtedness to the earlier races and religion upon which their civilization is built.

The Ottoman Turks, that is, the Turks who founded the present Turkish Empire, were a Tartar or Turanian tribe from Central Asia who adopted the Mohammedan faith and began their conquest of the Mohammedan world about the year 1300. They then possessed legends or childish tales of their own which still survive; and these are still told among the mass of the people with simple faith. One or two of these are given here, to show the natural human character of the race.

The Turks next turned, in literature, to poetry. Persian Mohammedan poetry was then at its best; and the Turks imitated, but scarcely improved upon, its forms. So great, indeed, became the Turkish admiration for poetry that almost every Turkish Sultan, from the year fourteen hundred down to the present, has written poetry. Our book gives a series, by themselves, of the best of these royal poems.

Turkish poetry has chiefly followed the Arabic fashion of expending itself upon language rather than upon thought. We are told that when the first Turkish epic poet Ahmedi presented to Sultan Bajazet's son his long epic history of Alexander the Great, the prince rebuked the poet's years of labor, saying that one tiny, perfectly polished poem would have been worth more than all the epic. Hence it is chiefly to the polishing of tiny poems that the poetic genius of the Turks has been applied. They have a favorite form called the "gazel," which might be likened to our English sonnet, except that the gazel is by far more intricate. It is, in fact, compared by the Turks to a flower with its petals constantly overlapping, forming a circle, and ending at the point where they began. In rhyme, for instance, the gazel opens with a rhyming couplet, and then through the whole poem the second line of each couplet repeats this opening rhyme.

We have tried to give the chief Turkish poets in somewhat chronological order, beginning with their first poet Ashiq, who died in 1332 and whose very name is forgotten, since *ashiq* means merely "the lover." In other words, Turkish poetry begins with the passion of an unknown lover, not apparently for woman, but for life and God. The collected poems of Ashiq are called a *divan*, the usual Persian and Turkish word for such collections; but very little of the *divan* of Ashiq has survived.

Among Turkish epic poets, the earliest is Ahmedi (died 1412), who wrote the Book of Alexander the Great. The first romantic song is that of Sheykhi (1426) on the loves of the maiden Shirin. The first religious epic is that of Yaziji-Oglu (1449), called the "Book of Mohammed." These, then, were the early singers. Of poets accounted of the highest rank, the earliest was Nejati (1508). Lamii was the scholar poet, a dervish or monk who delved into the older Persian literature and drew his themes perhaps from ancient

Zoroastrian tales. He is usually named as the second greatest of Turkish poets. Gazali, Fuzuli, and Nabi were also noted singers of the sixteenth century, which was the great age of the Turkish Empire, both in literature and in military glory.

Of the two poetesses on our list, Mihri has been called the Turkish Sappho. Yet as the life of a Turkish woman of rank is carefully secluded, no scandal ever attached to her personal life. Her poems are mere dreams of fancy. Zeyneb was equally honored, a lady of high rank and a student of the Persian and Arabic poets.

All other singers, however, are accounted by the Turks inferior to the great lyric poet Baqi (1526-1600). Baqi was at first a saddler, but he studied law and rose to the highest legal position of the empire. Poetry was the avocation of the great lawyer's leisure, and it won him the admiring friendship of the four successive Sultans who reigned during his life. The very name Baqi means "that which lasts," or "the enduring," so it has been frequently punned upon. The poet himself used a seal with a Persian couplet,
"Fleeting is the world, and without faith
God alone endures (or, Baqi alone is god); all else is
      fleeting"

OLD TURKISH TALES

THE QUEEN OF NIGHT

Once upon a time there was an old man who had three daughters. All of them were beautiful, but the youngest, whose name was Rosa, was not only more lovely, but also more amiable and more intelligent than the others. Jealous and envious exceedingly were the two sisters when they found that the fame of Rosa's beauty was greater than the fame of theirs. They, however, refused to believe that Rosa was really more lovely than they were, and they resolved to ask the Sun's opinion on the subject.

So, one day at dawn, the sisters stood at their open window and cried, "Sun, shining Sun, who wanderest all over the world, say who is the most beautiful among our father's daughters?"

The Sun replied, "I am beautiful, and you are both beautiful; but your youngest sister is the most beautiful of all."

When the two girls heard this, they were beside themselves with anger and spite, and determined to get rid of the sister who so outshone them. Saying nothing to her of what the Sun had told them, they on the following day invited Rosa to accompany them to the wood to gather a salad of wild herbs for their father's dinner. The unsuspecting Rosa at once complied, took her basket, and set out with her sisters, who led her to a spot she had never before visited, a long way from her father's house, and surrounded on all sides by forest. When they were arrived, the eldest sister said,

"Do thou, Rosa, gather all the herbs that are here; we will go a little farther on, and when we have filled our baskets we will return."

The wicked girls, however, went straight home, abandoning Rosa to her fate. When some hours had passed, and she found that they did not return, she feared that she might, while seeking for the herbs, have wandered from the spot where her sisters had left her. Too innocent to suspect them of the wicked treachery of which they had been guilty, she only blamed herself for her carelessness, and wept bitterly at the thought of remaining all night alone in the wild and lonely wood.

After a time the sun set, the twilight came and passed, and darkness fell. The birds ceased their songs, and the silence of the forest was broken only by the flutter of a bat or great gray moth, the melancholy hoot of an owl, and the faint little rustle made by the other flying and creeping things that come forth with the stars. Seated on a great tree-trunk, Rosa wept more and more bitterly as the darkness deepened, and no one came to her aid. Hours passed, the air grew chilly; and faint with hunger and cold, she was about to lay herself down to die, when suddenly a brilliant light, like the sparkling of many stars, shot through the wood and advanced toward the spot where she sat. It was the Queen of Night, who, attended by all her court, was returning to her palace after her usual journey, for it was now near dawn. Rosa, dazzled and frightened, covered her face with her hands, and wept more bitterly than ever. Attracted by the sound of her sobbing, the Radiant Lady approached the weeping girl, and in a kind and gentle voice asked how she came to be there. Rosa looked up, and, reassured by the benign countenance of the Queen of Night, told her story.

"Come then and live with me, dear girl; I will be your mother, and you shall be my daughter," said the Queen, who knew perfectly well how it had all happened.

Gladly the poor girl accompanied the Queen to her palace, and being, as we know, as amiable and intelligent as she was beautiful, her protectress soon became very fond of her, and did everything in her power to make her adopted daughter happy. She gave Rosa the keys of all her treasures, made her the mistress of her palace, and let her do whatever she pleased.

But let us now leave this lucky girl with the Queen of Night for a little while, and return to her sisters. Though they fully believed she must either have perished of hunger or been devoured by wild beasts, they after a time, to make quite certain, went again to their window and cried,

"Sun, shining Sun, who wanderest all over the world, tell us who is the most beautiful of our father's daughters?"

The Sun replied as before, "I am beautiful, and you are both beautiful; but your youngest sister is the most beautiful of all."

"But Rosa has long been dead!"

"No," replied the Sun, "Rosa still lives, and she is in the palace of the Queen of Night."

When the sisters heard this, their rage and spite knew no bounds. Long they consulted together as to the best means of bringing about her death; and finally these wicked girls decided to obtain from a witch of their acquaintance an enchanted kerchief which would make the person wearing it appear to be dead.

Well, they set out, and presently arrived at the palace at an hour when they knew that the Queen of Night would be absent and they might find their sister alone. Rosa was delighted to see them, for though they had often been unkind to her, she loved her sisters very dearly, and welcoming them warmly, she offered them everything she had, and pressed them to remain. They, on their part, pretended to be overjoyed at finding again the sister they had mourned as lost, and congratulated her on her good fortune. When they had eaten and drunk of the good things she set before them, and were about to take their departure, the eldest sister produced from her basket the enchanted kerchief.

"Here, dear Rosa," said she, "is a little present which we should like you to wear for our sakes. Let me pin it round your shoulders. Good-bye, dear!" she added, kissing her affectionately on both cheeks, "we will come and see you again before long and bring our father with us."

"Do, dear sisters, and tell my dear father that I will go to see him as soon as my kind protectress may give me leave."

Rosa watched her sisters from the window till they were out of sight, and then turned to the embroidery-frame which she had laid aside on their arrival. She had not, however, made many stitches, before a feeling of faintness came over her; and letting her work slip from her hands, she fell back on the sofa and lost consciousness. When the Queen of Night came home, she went first, as was her wont, to the chamber of her dear adopted daughter, and finding her thus, she said, as she bent over the maiden and kissed her beautiful mouth, "She has tired herself, poor child, over that embroidery-frame; she is so industrious."

THE QUEEN OF THE NIGHT.

But the beautiful lips were cold and white, and the maiden neither breathed nor stirred. Distracted with grief, the Queen of Night began to unfasten Rosa's dress in order to ascertain whether her death had been caused by the bite of some poisonous reptile, and while doing so, she observed that the kerchief on her shoulders was not one that her daughter was in the habit of wearing. When she had unpinned and taken it off, Rosa heaved a deep sigh, opened her eyes, and seeing the Queen bending over her, smiled and stretched out her arms to her dear mother, saying,

"I must have slept a long time! Oh, I remember!" she added, "I was feeling faint and giddy and lay down, and, I suppose, fell asleep immediately, for I don't recollect anything else."

"But where did you get this?" asked the Queen, picking up the kerchief from the floor. "I don't remember having given it to you."

"Oh, I have not told you that I had a great pleasure yesterday. My sisters, who had thought me forever lost, found out where I was and came to see me, bringing this kerchief as a present. Is it not pretty?"

These words told the Queen of Night the secret of the whole matter; but, not wishing to distress her daughter by acquainting her with her sisters' cruel perfidy, she only replied, "Yes, very pretty. Will you give it to me, Rosa? I should like to have it for myself."

Rosa was naturally only too pleased to be able to give her kind protectress something in return for all her favors; and she also promised her, though not without tears, never again to receive any visitors, not even her sisters, when she was left by herself in the palace.

These wicked creatures in a little while again stood at their window and cried, "Sun, shining Sun, who wanderest the world over, say, is there now any one more beautiful than we are?"

But the Sun only replied as before, "I am beautiful; you, too, are beautiful; but Rosa is the most beautiful of all!"

The sisters looked at each other in dismay. "The kerchief has then failed," said the elder to the younger. "We must try some other method of getting rid of her."

So the wretches went to the same old witch who had given them the magic kerchief, and got from her an enchanted sugar-plum. When at nightfall they again knocked at the door of the palace, the porter informed them that his mistress was absent, and had given orders that the palace-gates were not to be opened until her return. They, however, saw Rosa at her window, and pretending to be greatly distressed at their exclusion, asked her at least to accept from them the delicious sugar-plum which they had brought for her.

"Let down a basket," said the eldest; "I will put the sugar-plum inside, and you can draw it up."

Rosa did so, and drew up the sweetmeat.

"Taste it at once," cried the second sister, "and if you like it, we will bring you more of the same kind."

The poor girl, suspecting no evil, put the sugar-plum into her mouth; but scarcely had she tasted it, than she fell back as if dead; and her sisters, seeing this, hurried away home.

When the Queen returned and again found her favorite lifeless, she was both grieved and angry. All her servants, however, when questioned, assured her that no one had entered the palace during her absence, and that Rosa's sisters had only been allowed to speak to her from a distance as she stood at her high window. In the hope of bringing her to life again, as on the previous occasion, the Queen of Night searched every fold of the maiden's dress, but in vain; she could not discover the fatal charm.

"Perhaps," said she to herself, as she sat and gazed on the

lifeless features of her adopted daughter, "what I can not discover, chance may, and I could never bring myself to bury her, dead though she seems to be."

So the grieving Queen sent for a cunning workman, who made at her orders a coffer of silver; and after dressing Rosa in her most beautiful clothes and jewels, she laid her in it, closed the lid, fastened the coffer on the back of a splendid horse, and let him loose to wander at will.

The horse, following his fancy, carried his fair burden in a few hours' time into a neighboring country, the ruler of which was the handsomest man of his time; and this King, being that day out hunting with his court, happened to catch sight of the horse. Attracted by its beauty and fleetness, and by the strange shining burden it bore on its saddle, he approached, and seeing the animal to be masterless, he bade his people seize and lead it to the palace. The silver coffer the King caused to be carried into his bedchamber, and there he opened it. Imagine, if you can, his surprise on seeing within the form of a beautiful maiden. Though apparently lifeless, she was more lovely than any living woman he had ever beheld, and his heart became filled with such ardent love for her that he would sit for hours together gazing upon her beautiful features, neglecting duties and pleasures alike; and when his ministers came and prayed him to accompany them to the council chamber, he only said,

"Go, I pray you, and do justice in my name."

Days passed, his gentlemen tried to tempt him out hunting, but again he only replied,

"Do you go without me."

The royal cooks vied with one another in preparing the most delicious dishes for his table; but these he hardly tasted, nor did he even appear to notice what he was eating. When this state of things had continued for some days the ministers became alarmed, and sent a messenger to inform the Queen-Mother, who was away at her country palace. She came with all speed, and was much distressed to find her son so dispirited and melancholy. To all her anxious inquiries, however, he only replied that he was quite well, but preferred to remain alone in his bed-chamber. The Queen had, of course, already heard from the courtiers the story of the riderless horse and the silver chest; and she rightly guessed that her son had been bewitched by what he had found in it, and determined to discover what this might be.

So the very next day, while the King was at dinner with his vizier, his mother went to his chamber—for she had a master-key that would open all the doors in the palace—and there, extended on the divan, she saw the silver chest. Going hastily up to it, she raised the lid which the King had closed before leaving. At first she could only gaze in astonishment at the wonderful beauty of the maiden lying within; but her admiration presently changed to anger when she thought of her son; and seizing poor Rosa by her long hair, she dragged her out of the coffer and shook her violently, saying,

"You wicked dead thing! Why are you not decently buried instead of wandering about casting spells on Princes?" But as the Queen shook her the enchanted sugar-plum was jerked out of Rosa's mouth, and she immediately came to life again, and gazed around her in bewilderment. And as she opened her large, lovely eyes, the Queen's anger passed away, and she embraced and kissed Rosa tenderly, weeping with delight the while. The poor girl was so astonished by the strangeness of everything around her, that it was some minutes before she could ask:

"Where am I, noble lady, and where is my dear mother?"

"I know not, my child, but I will be your mother. For you shall marry my son, the King, who is dying for love of you."

As she spoke, footsteps were heard at the door, and the King entered. Imagine, if you can, his amazement and joy at finding, seated on the divan by his mother's side, the maiden he loved so dearly, restored to life, and twenty times lovelier than before. Not to make too long a story of it, the King took her by the hand, and asked her to be his wife. And when Rosa heard of his love for her, and saw how handsome and noble he was, she could not but love him in return. So they were married with great splendor, and there were feasts for the poor, and fountains running honey and wine, and rejoicings for everybody.

Well, the King and Rosa lived very happily together for some time; but her troubles were not over, for her wicked sisters had not yet done their worst to her. They had for long feared to go near the palace again, and nearly a year passed before they learned what had been the result of their last visit. One day, however, in order to make quite sure that Rosa was dead, they once more stood at their window, and cried,

"Sun, shining Sun, who wanderest all over the earth, tell us if thou hast, since our youngest sister died, seen any maiden fairer than we?"

But the Sun only replied as before, "I am beautiful; you, too, are both beautiful; but your youngest sister is the fairest of all."

"But Rosa is dead!"

"No, Rosa lives, and she is the wife of the King of the

neighboring country."

Well, if these wicked women could not bear that their sister should be considered fairer than they, still less could they allow her to be a Queen. So, disguised as two old women, they set off at once for Rosa's palace. When they arrived in the royal city, great rejoicings were going on because a baby prince had just been born.

"That is good news," said the elder to the younger when she heard this, "for now we will be the nurses." So they went to the Queen-Mother and gave themselves out to be wonderfully clever nurses from the neighboring country who had nursed the princes there; and the Queen-Mother, deceived by their story, put them in charge of her daughter-in-law and the baby. On the pretext of keeping the young Queen and her child free from evil spells, the make-believe nurses sent away all the other attendants from her apartments; and when they were left alone with their sister, they stuck into her head an enchanted pin.

She was immediately changed into a bird, and flew away out of the window; and her eldest sister laid herself down on her bed in her place.

When the King came in to see his wife, he could hardly believe his eyes. This could not be his wife. The false Queen, guessing his thoughts, said,

"You find me changed, dear husband? It is because I have been so ill."

The King, however, pretended not to have observed anything, but his heart froze within him as he looked on the object of this pretended transformation.

It was his custom to breakfast alone every day in the garden; and one day while he was sadly musing there, a

301

pretty bird flew down, perched on a branch overhead, and said, "Tell me, my lord, have the King, and the Queen-Mother, and the little Prince slept well?"

The King smiled and nodded, and the bird continued, "May they ever sleep sweetly. But may she whom they call the young Queen sleep the sleep that knows no waking, and may all things over which I fly wither away!"

This said, the bird spread its wings, and wherever it passed, the grass and flowers withered, and the place became a desert. The gardeners, in despair, asked the King if they might not kill the bird which caused the mischief; but he forbade them, on pain of death, to do it any injury.

Afterward the bird came every day while he was at breakfast in the garden; and the kind voice of the Prince soon made it so tame and fearless that it would perch on his knee and eat from his hand. This familiarity enabled the Prince to observe the bird's plumage more closely, and one day he caught sight of the pin in its head. Surprised at this, he ventured to withdraw it, when the bird disappeared, and his own dear wife stood again by his side. When he had recovered a little from the joy and surprise caused by this strange event, and had welcomed his wife back, he asked her to tell how it had all happened. And Rosa, whose eyes were now fully opened to the malice and wickedness of her sisters, told him all she knew of her own adventures.

When the Prince had learned the evil deeds of his sisters-in-law, he bade his guards bring these wretches before him, and condemned them both to a death suitable to their crimes. In vain did Rosa entreat him to pardon them. The King was inexorable. But when, at sunset, the criminals were being led away to execution, the Queen of Night appeared on the scene, followed by all her train; and touched by the distress of her adopted daughter, she prevailed upon the King to change the sentence he had pronounced. The two evil-doers were then offered the choice of dying a violent death, or living to witness their sister's happiness while deprived of the power of ever again being able to injure her.

They chose the latter fate; and it was not long before they both died of spite and jealousy.

THE DIVAN OF THE LOVER
THE EARLIEST TURKISH POEM

All the universe, one mighty sign, is shown;
God hath myriads of creative acts unknown:
None hath seen them, of the races jinn and men,
None hath news brought from that realm far off from
     ken.
Never shall thy mind or reason reach that strand,
Nor can tongue the King's name utter of that land.
Since 'tis his each nothingness with life to vest,
Trouble is there ne'er at all to his behest.
Eighteen thousand worlds, from end to end,
Do not with him one atom's worth transcend.

THE BOOK OF ALEXANDER THE GREAT

(By Ahmedi)

Up and sing! O 'anga-natured nightingale!
High in every business doth thy worth prevail:
Sing! for good the words are that from thee proceed;
Whatsoever thou dost say is prized indeed.
Then, since words to utter thee so well doth suit,
Pity were it surely if thy tongue were mute.
Blow a blast in utt'rance that the Trusted One,
When he hears, ten thousand times may cry: "Well done!"
Up and sing! O bird most holy! up and sing!
Unto us a story fair and beauteous bring.
Let not opportunity slip by, silent there;
Unto us the beauty of each word declare.
Seldom opportunities like this with thee lie;
Sing then, for th' occasion now is thine, so hie!
Lose not opportunities that thy hand doth find,
For some day full suddenly Death thy tongue shall bind.
Of how many singers, eloquent of words,
Bound have Death and Doom the tongues fast in their
      cords!
Lose not, then, th' occasion, but to joy look now,
For one day thy station 'neath earth seek must thou.
While the tongue yet floweth, now thy words collect;
Them as Meaning's taper 'midst the feast erect,
That thy words, remaining long time after thee,
To the listeners' hearing shall thy record be.
Thy mementoes lustrous biding here behind,
Through them they'll recall thee, O my soul, to mind.
Those who've left mementoes ne'er have died in truth;
Those who've left no traces ne'er have lived in sooth.
Surely with this object didst thou come to earth,
That to mind should ever be recalled thy worth.

305

"May I die not!" say'st thou, one of noble race?
Strive, then, that thou leavest here a name of grace.

———————————

Once unto his Vizier quoth the crowned King:
"Thou, who in my world-realm knowest everything!
With my sword I've conquered many and many a shore;
Still I sigh right sorely: 'Ah! to conquer more!'
Great desire is with me realms to overthrow;
Through this cause I comfort ne'er a moment know.
Is there yet a country whither we may wend,
Where as yet our mighty sway doth not extend,
That we may it conquer, conquer it outright?
Ours shall be the whole earth—ours it shall be quite."
Then, when heard the Vizier what the King did say,
Quoth he: "Realm-o'erthrowing Monarch, live for aye!
May the Mighty Ruler set thy crown on high,
That thy throne may ever all assaults defy!
May thy life's rose-garden never fade away!
May thy glory's orchard never see decay!
Thou'st the Peopled Quarter ta'en from end to end;
All of its inhabitants slaves before thee bend.
There's on earth no city, neither any land,
That is not, O Monarch, under thy command.
In the Peopled Quarter Seven Climes are known,
And o'er all of these thy sway extends alone!"

THE LOVES OF SHIRIN

(By Sheykhi)

The spot at which did King Khusrev Perviz light
Was e'en the ruined dwelling of that moon bright.
Whilst wand'ring on, he comes upon that parterre,
As on he strolls, it opes before his eyes fair.
Among the trees a night-hued courser stands bound
(On Heaven's charger's breast were envy's scars found).

As softly moved he, sudden on his sight gleamed
A moon that in the water shining bright beamed.
O what a moon! a sun o'er earth that light rains—
Triumphant, happy, blest he who her shade gains.
She'd made the pool a casket for her frame fair,
And all about that casket spread her dark hair.
Her hand did yonder curling serpents back throw—
The dawn 'tis, and thereof we never tired grow.
He saw the water round about her ear play;
In rings upon her shoulders her dark locks lay.
When yon heart-winning moon before the King beamed,
The King became the sun—in him Love's fire gleamed.
The tears e'en like to water from his eyes rolled;
Was't strange, when did a Watery Sign the Moon hold?
No power was left him, neither sport nor pleasure;
He bit his finger, wildered beyond measure.
Unconscious of his gaze, the jasmine-breasted—
The hyacinths o'er the narcissi rested.
When shone her day-face, from that musky cloud bare,
Her eyes oped Shirin and beheld the King there.
Within that fountain, through dismay and shamed fright,
She trembled as on water doth the moonlight.
Than this no other refuge could yon moon find
That she should round about her her own locks bind.
The moon yet beameth through the hair, the dark night,
With tresses how could be concealed the sun bright!
To hide her from him, round her she her hair flung,
And thus as veil her night before her day hung.

————————————————

When Ferhad bound to fair Shirin his heart's core,
From out his breast Love many a bitter wail tore.
On tablet of his life graved, shown was Shirin;
Of all else emptied, filled alone with Shirin.
As loathed he the companionship of mankind,

In wild beasts 'midst the hills did he his friends find.
His guide was Pain; his boon companion, Grief's throe;
His comrade, Sorrow; and his closest friend, Woe.
Thus wand'ring on, he knew not day from dark night;
For many days he onward strayed in sad plight.
Although before his face a wall of stone rise,
Until he strikes against it, blind his two eyes.
Through yearning for his love he from the world fled;
From out his soul into his body Death sped.
Because he knew that when the earthly frame goes,
Eternal, Everlasting Being love shows,
He fervent longed to be from fleshly bonds free,
That then his life in very truth might Life see.
In sooth, till dies the body, Life is ne'er found,
Nor with the love of life the Loved One e'er found.

THE BOOK OF MOHAMMED

(BY YAZIJI-OGLU)

THE CREATION OF PARADISE

Hither come, O seeker after Truth! if joy thou wouldest
    share,
Enter on the Mystic Pathway, follow it, then joy thou'lt
    share.
Harken now what God (exalted high his name!) from
    naught hath formed.
Eden's bower he hath created; Light, its lamp, he did
    prepare;
Loftiest its sites, and best and fairest are its blest abodes;
Midst of each a hall of pearls—not ivory nor teak-wood
    rare.
Each pavilion he from seventy ruddy rubies raised aloft—
Dwellings these in which the dwellers sit secure from fear
    or care.
Bound within each courtyard seventy splendid houses he
    hath ranged,
Formed of emeralds green—houses these no fault of form
    that bear.
There, within each house, are seventy pearl and gem-
    incrusted thrones;
He upon each throne hath stretched out seventy couches
    broidered fair;
Sits on every couch a maiden of the bourne of loveliness:
Moons their foreheads, days their faces, each a jeweled
    crown doth wear;
Wine their rubies, soft their eyes, their eyebrows
    troublous, causing woe:
All-enchanting, Paradise pays tribute to their witching
    air.

Sudden did they see the faces of those damsels dark of eye,
Blinded sun and moon were, and Life's Stream grew bitter
     then and there.
Thou wouldst deem that each was formed of rubies,
     corals, and of pearls;
Question there is none, for God thus in the Koran doth
     declare.
Tables seventy, fraught with bounties, he in every house
     hath placed,
And on every tray hath spread out seventy sorts of varied
     fare.
All these glories, all these honors, all these blessings of
     delight,
All these wondrous mercies surely for his sake he did
     prepare:
Through his love unto Mohammed, he the universe hath
     framed;
Happy, for his sake, the naked and the hungry enter
     there.
   O Thou Perfectness of Potence! O Thou God of Awful
   Might!
   O Thou Majesty of Glory! O Thou King of Perfect
   Eight!

Since he Eden's heaven created, all is there complete and
     whole,
So that naught is lacking; nothing he created needs
     repair.
Yonder, for his righteous servants, things so fair hath he
     devised,
That no eye hath e'er beheld them; ope thy soul's eye, on
     them stare.
Never have his servants heard them, neither can their
     hearts conceive;
Reach unto their comprehension shall this understanding

ne'er.

There that God a station lofty, of the loftiest, hath reared,

That unclouded station he the name Vesila caused to bear,

That to his Belovèd yonder station a dear home may be,

Thence ordained is Heaven's order free from every grief
and care.

In its courtyard's riven center, planted he the Tuba-Tree;

That a tree which hangeth downward, high aloft its roots
are there:

Thus its radiance all the Heavens lighteth up from end to
end,

Flooding every tent and palace, every lane and every
square.

Such a tree the Tuba, that the Gracious One hath in its
sap

Hidden whatsoe'er there be of gifts and presents good and
fair;

Forth therefrom crowns, thrones, and jewels, yea, and
steeds and coursers come,

Golden leaves and clearest crystals, wines most pure
beyond compare.

For his sake there into being hath he called the Tuba-Tree,

That from Ebu-Qasim's hand might every one receive his
share.

POEMS BY TURKISH RULERS

RUBA'I

Cupbearer, bring, bring here again my yester even's wine;
My harp and rebec bring, them bid address this heart of
      mine:
While still I live, 'tis meet that I should mirth and glee
      enjoy;
The day shall come when none may e'en my resting-place
divine.—*Sultan Murad II.* (reigned 1421-1451).

GAZEL

Souls are fluttered when the morning breezes through
      thy tresses stray;
Waving cypresses are wildered when thy motions they
      survey.
Since with witchcraft thou hast whetted keen the lancet of
      thy glance,
All my veins are bleeding inward through my longing
      and dismay.
"Why across thy cheek disordered float thy tresses?" asked
      I her.
"It is Rum-Eyli; there high-starred heroes gallop," did she
      say.
Thought I, though I spake not: "In thy quarter, through
      thy tint and scent,
Wretched and head-giddy, wand'ring, those who hope
      hope not for stray."
"Whence the anger in thy glances, O sweet love?" I said;
      then she:
"Silence! surely if I shed blood, I the ensigns should
      display."
Even as thou sighest, 'Avni, shower thine eyes tears fast
      as rain,

312

Like as follow hard the thunder-roll the floods in dread
    array.
        —*Sultan Mohammed II.* (1451-1481).

FRAGMENT OF GAZEL

Torn and pierced my heart has been by thy scorn and
    tyranny's blade;
Rent by the scissors of grief for thee is the robe that my
    patience arrayed.
Like the *mihrab* of the Kaaba, as shrine where in worship
    to turn,
Thy ward would an angel take, if thy footprint there he
    surveyed.
They are pearls, O mine eye! thou sheddest her day-bright
    face before;
Not a tear is left—these all are dried by the beams by her
    cheek displayed.
        —*Mohammed II.*

GAZEL

To obey, Eight hard for Allah, is my aim and my desire;
'Tis but zeal for Faith, for Islam, that my ardor doth
    inspire.
Through the grace of Allah, and th' assistance of the Band
    Unseen,
Is my earnest hope the Infidels to crush with ruin dire.
On the Saints and on the Prophets surely doth my trust
    repose;
Through the love of God, to triumph and to conquest I
    aspire.
What if I with soul and gold strive here to wage the Holy
    War?
Praise is God's! ten thousand sighs for battle in my breast
    suspire.
O Mohammed! through the chosen Ahmed Mukhtar's

313

glorious aid,
Hope I that my might may triumph over Islam's foes
    acquire!
> —*Mohammed II.*

GAZEL

Ah, thine eyes lay waste the heart, they 'gainst the soul
    bare
daggers dread;
See how sanguinary gleam they—blood aye upon blood
    they
shed.
Come, the picture of thy down bear unto this my
    scorched
breast—
It is customary fresh greens over the broiled flesh to
    spread.
Said I: "O Life! since thy lip is life, to me vouchsafe a
kiss."
Smiling rose-like, "Surely, surely, by my life," she
    answered.
As I weep sore, of my stained eyebrow and my tears of
blood,
"'Tis the rainbow o'er the shower stretched," were by all
    beholders
said.
While within my heart thine eye's shaft, send not to my
breast despair;
Idol mine! guest after guest must not to one same house
    be
led.
Through its grieving for thy hyacinth down, thus feeble
grown
Is the basil, that the gardeners nightly o'er it water shed.
Quoth I: "O Life! do not shun Jem, he a pilgrim here

hath come";
"Though a pilgrim, yet his life doth on a child's face
      hang,"
she said.

          —*Prince Jem* (1481).

FRAGMENT

Lo! there the torrent, dashing 'gainst the rocks, doth
      wildly roll;
The whole wide realm of Space and Being ruth hath on
      my soul.
Through bitterness of grief and woe the morn hath rent
      its robe;
See! O in dawning's place, the sky weeps blood, without
      control!
Tears shedding, o'er the mountain-tops the clouds of
      heaven pass;
Hear, deep the bursting thunder sobs and moans through
      stress of dole.

          —*Prince Jem.*

GAZEL

From Istambol's throne a mighty host to Iran guided I;
Sunken deep in blood of shame I made the Golden Heads
      to lie.
Glad the Slave, my resolution, lord of Egypt's realm
      became:
Thus I raised my royal banner e'en as the Nine Heavens
      high.
From the kingdom fair of 'Iraq to Hijaz these tidings sped,
When I played the harp of Heavenly Aid at feast of
      victory.
Through my saber Transoxania drowned was in a sea of
      blood;
Emptied I of kuhl of Isfahan the adversary's eye.

Flowed adown a River Amu from each foeman's every
      hair—
Rolled the sweat of terror's fever—if I happed him to espy.
Bishop-mated was the King of India by my Queenly
      troops,
When I played the Chess of empire on the Board of
      sov'reignty.
O Selimi, in thy name was struck the coinage of the
      world,
When in crucible of Love Divine, like gold, that melted I.
      —Sultan Selim I. (1512-1520).

GAZEL

My pain for thee balm in my sight resembles;
Thy face's beam the clear moonlight resembles.
Thy black hair spread across thy cheeks, the roses,
O Liege, the garden's basil quite resembles.
Beside thy lip oped wide its mouth, the rosebud;
For shame it blushed, it blood outright resembles.
Thy mouth, a casket fair of pearls and rubies,
Thy teeth, pearls, thy lip coral bright resembles.
Their diver I, each morning and each even;
My weeping, Liege, the ocean's might resembles.
Lest he seduce thee, this my dread and terror,
That rival who Iblis in spite resembles.
Around the taper bright, thy cheek, Muhibbi
Turns, and the moth in his sad plight resembles.
      —Sultan Soleiman, the Magnificent (1520-
1566).

GAZEL

If 'tis state thou seekest like the world-adorning sun's
      array,
Lowly e'en as water rub thy face in earth's dust every day.
Fair to see, but short enduring is this picture bright, the

world;
'Tis a proverb: Fleeting like the realm of dreams is earth's
display.
Through the needle of its eyelash never hath the heart's
thread past;
Like unto the Lord Messiah bide I half-road on the way.
Athlete of the Universe through self-reliance grows the
Heart,
With the ball, the Sphere—Time, Fortune—like an apple
doth it play.
Mukhlisi, thy frame was formed from but one drop, yet,
wonder great!
When thou verses sing'st, thy spirit like the ocean swells,
they say.

—*Prince Mustafa.*

GAZEL

Ta'en my sense and soul have those thy Leyli locks, thy
glance's spell,
Me, their Mejnun, 'midst of love's wild dreary desert they
impel,
Since mine eyes have seen the beauty of the Joseph of thy
grace,
Sense and heart have fall'n and lingered in thy chin's
sweet dimple-well.
Heart and soul of mine are broken through my passion
for thy lips;
From the hand of patience struck they honor's glass, to
earth it fen.
The mirage, thy lips, O sweetheart, that doth like to water
show;
For, through longing, making thirsty, vainly they my life
dispel.
Since Selimi hath the pearls, thy teeth, been praising,
sense and heart

Have his head and soul abandoned, plunging 'neath
    love's ocean-swell.
        —*Sultan Selim II.* (1566-1574).

GAZEL

Thy veil raise, shake from cheeks those locks of thine
    then;
Unclouded beauty's sun and moon bid shine then.
But one glance from those soft and drooping eyes throw,
The heart through joy to drunkenness consign then.
Were I thy lip to suck, 'twould heal the sick heart;
Be kind, an answer give, Physician mine, then.
Beware lest evil glance thy beauty's rose smite,
From ill-eyed rival careful it confine then.
O heart, this is Life's Water 'midst of darkness,
In night's gloom hidden, drink the ruby wine then.
My love's down grows upon her rosy-hued cheek,
A book write on the woes it does enshrine then.
Thy wine-hued lip, O love, grant to Selimi—
And by thy parting's shaft my tears make wine then.
        —*Sultan Selim II.*

GAZEL

Soon as I beheld thee, mazed and wildered grew my sad
    heart;
How shall I my love disclose to thee who tyrant dread
    art?
How shall I hold straight upon my road, when yonder
    Torment
Smitten hath my breast with deadly wounds by her
    eyelash dart?
Face, a rose; and mouth, a rosebud; form, a slender
    sapling—
How shall I not be the slave of Princess such as thou art?
Ne'er hath heart a beauty seen like her of graceful figure;

Joyous would I for yon charmer's eyebrow with my life
    part.
Farisi, what can I do but love that peerless beauty?
Ah! this aged Sphere hath made me lover of yon
    sweetheart.
                —*Sultan Osman II.* (1617-1623).

TO SULTAN MURAD IV.

Round us foes throng, host to aid us here in sad plight, is
    there none?
In the cause of God to combat, chief of tried might, is
    there none?
None who will checkmate the foe, Castle to Castle, face to
    face
In the battle who will Queen-like guide the brave Knight,
    is there none?
Midst a fearful whirlpool we are fallen helpless, send us
    aid!
Us to rescue, a strong swimmer in our friends' sight, is
    there none?
Midst the fight to be our comrade, head to give or heads
    to take,
On the field of earth a hero of renown bright, is there
    none?
Know we not wherefore in turning off our woes ye thus
    delay;
Day of Reckoning, aye, and question of the poor's plight,
    is there none?
With us 'midst the foeman's flaming streams of scorching
    fire to plunge,
Salamander with experience of Fate dight, is there none?
This our letter, to the court of Sultan Murad, quick to
    bear,
Pigeon, rapid as the storm-wind in its swift flight, is there
    none?

—Hafiz Pacha.

IN REPLY TO THE PRECEDING

To relieve Bagdad, O Hafiz, man of tried might, is there
      none?
Aid from us thou seek'st, then with thee host of fame
      bright, is there none?
"I'm the Queen the foe who'll checkmate," thus it was that
      thou didst say;
Room for action now against him with the brave Knight,
      is there none?
Though we know thou hast no rival in vainglorious,
      empty boasts,
Yet to take dread vengeance on thee, say, a Judge right, is
      there none?
While thou layest claim to manhood, whence this
      cowardice of thine?
Thou art frightened, yet beside thee fearing no fight, is
      there none?
Heedless of thy duty thou, the Rafizis have ta'en Bagdad;
Shall not God thy foe be? Day of Reckoning, sure, right,
      is there none?
They have wrecked Ebu-Hanifa's city through thy lack of
      care;
Oh, in thee of Islam's and the Prophet's zeal, light, is there
      none?
God, who favored us, whilst yet we knew not, with the
      Sultanate,
Shall again accord Bagdad, decreed of God's might, is
      there none?
Thou hast brought on Islam's army direful ruin with thy
      bribes;
Have we not heard how thou say'st, "Word of this foul
      blight, is there none?"
With the aid of God, fell vengeance on the enemy to take,

By me skilled and aged, vizier, pious, zeal-dight, is there
    none?
Now shall I appoint commander a vizier of high emprise,
Will not Khizar and the Prophet aid him? guide right, is
    there none?
Is it that thou dost the whole world void and empty now
    conceive?
Of the Seven Climes, Muradi, King of high might, is there
    none?
            —Sultan Murad IV. (1623-1640).

LUGAZ

There's an o'erhanging castle in which there flows a main,
And there within that castle a fish its home hath ta'en;
The fish within its mouth doth hold a shining gem,
Which wastes the fish as long as it therein doth remain.
This puzzle to the poets is offered by Murad;
Let him reply who office or place desires to gain.
            —Sultan Murad IV.

MUNAJAT

Allah! Lord who liv'st for aye! O Sole! O King of Glory's
    Bay!
Monarch who ne'er shalt pass away! show thou to us thy
    bounties fair.
In early morning shall our cry, our wail, mount to thy
    Throne on high:
"Error and sin our wont," we sigh: show thou to us thy
    bounties fair.
If cometh not from thee thy grace, evil shall all our works
    deface;
O Lord of Being and of Space! show thou to us thy
    bounties fair.
Creator of security! to thy Beloved greetings be!
These fair words are in sincerity: show thou to us thy

bounties fair

Iqbali sinnèd hath indeed, yet unto him thy grace
    concede;

Eternal, Answerer in need! show thou to us thy bounties
    fair.

                    —*Sultan Mustafa II.* (1695-1703).

322

TURKISH POETESSES

A GAZEL BY ZEYNEB

Cast off thy veil, and heaven and earth in dazzling light
      array!
As radiant Paradise, this poor demented world display!
Move thou thy lips, make play the ripples light of Kevser's
      pool!
Let loose thy scented locks, and odors sweet through
      earth convey!
A musky warrant by thy down was traced, and zephyr
      charged:
"Speed, with this scent subdue the realms of China and
      Cathay!"
O heart! should not thy portion be the Water bright of
      Life,
A thousand times mayst thou pursue Iskender's darksome
      way.
O Zeyneb, woman's love of earthly show leave thou
      behind;
Go manly forth, with single heart, forsake adornment
      gay!

A GAZEL BY MIHRI

Once from sleep I oped my eyes, I raised my head, when
      full in sight
There before me stood a moon-faced beauty, lovely,
      shining, bright.
Thought I: "In th' ascendant's now my star, or I my fate
      have reached,
For within my chamber sure is risen Jupiter this night."
Radiance from his beauty streaming saw I, though to
      outward view
(While himself a Moslem) he in garb of infidel is dight.

323

Though I oped my eyes or closed them, still the form was
　　　ever there;
Thus I fancied to myself: "A fairy this or angel bright?"
Till the Resurrection ne'er shall Mihri gain the Stream of
　　　Life;
Yet in Night's deep gloom Iskender gleamed before her
　　　wond'ring sight.

A GAZEL BY MIHRI

Faithful and kind a friend I hoped that thou wouldst
　　　prove to me;
Who would have thought so cruel and fierce a tyrant in
　　　thee to see?
Thou who the newly oped rose art of the Garden of
　　　Paradise,
That every thorn and thistle thou lov'st—how can it
　　　fitting be?
I curse thee not, but of God Most High, Our Lord, I make
　　　this prayer—
That thou may'st love a pitiless one in tyranny like to
　　　thee.
In such a plight am I now, alack! that the curser saith to
　　　his foe:
"Be thy fortune dark and thy portion black, even as those
　　　of Mihri!"

POEMS OF NEJATI

FROM HIS SPRING QASIDA

The early springtide now hath made earth smiling bright
     again,
E'en as doth union with his mistress soothe the lover's
     pain.
They say: "'Tis now the goblet's turn, the time of mirth
     'tis now";
Beware that to the winds thou castest not this hour in
     vain.
Theriaca within their ruby pots the tulips lay:
See in the mead the running streamlet's glistening, snake-
     like train.
Onward, beneath some cypress-tree's loved foot its face to
     rub,
With turn and turn, and singing sweet, the brook goes
     through the plain.
Lord! may this happy union of felicity and earth,
Like turn of sun of Love, or Jesu's life, standfast remain!
May glee and mirth, e'en as desired, continuous abide
Like to a mighty Key-Khusrev's, or Jemshid's, glorious
     reign!

Sultan Mohammed! Murad's son! the Pride of Princes all;
He, the Darius, who to all earth's kings doth crowns
     ordain!
Monarch of stars! whose flag's the sun, whose stirrup is
     the moon!
Prince dread as Doom, and strong as Fate, and bounteous
     as main!

FROM HIS QASIDA ON THE ACCESSION OF SULTAN

BAYEZID II.

One eve, when had the Sun before her radiant beauty
    bright
Let down the veil of ambergris, the musky locks of night;
(Off had the royal hawk, the Sun, flown from the Orient's
    hand,
And lighted in the West; flocked after him the crows in
    flight;)
To catch the gloomy raven, Night, the fowler skilled, the
    Sphere,
Had shaped the new-moon like the claw of eagle, sharp to
    smite;
In pity at the doleful sight of sunset's crimson blood,
Its veil across the heaven's eye had drawn the dusky
    Night.

Sultan of Rome! Khusrev of the Horizons! Bayezid!
King of the Epoch! Sovereign! and Center of all Eight!
The tablet of his heart doth all th' affairs of earth disclose;
And eloquent as page of book the words he doth indite.
O Shah! I'm he who, 'midst th' assembly where thy praise
    is sung,
Will, rebec-like, a thousand notes upon one cord recite.
'Tis meet perfection through thy name to my poor words
    should come,
As to rose-water perfume sweet is brought by sunbeam's
    light.

GAZEL

Truth this: a lasting home hath yielded ne'er earth's
    spreading plain;
Scarce e'en an inn where may the caravan for rest remain.
Though every leaf of every tree is verily a book,
For those who understanding lack doth earth no leaf

326

contain.

E'en though the Loved One be from thee as far as East
      from West,

"Bagdad to lovers is not far," O heart, then strive and
      strain.

One moment opened were her ebriate, strife-causing eyne,

By us as scimitars, not merely daggers, were they ta'en.

Yearneth Nejati for the court of thy fair Paradise,

Though this a wish which he while here on earth can
      ne'er attain.

RUBA'IS

O Handkerchief! I send thee—off to yonder maid of grace;

Around thee I my eyelashes will make the fringe of lace;

I will the black point of my eye ruh up to paint therewith;

To yon coquettish beauty go—go look thou in her face.

O Handkerchief! the loved one's hand take, kiss her lip so
      sweet,

Her chin, which mocks at apple and at orange, kissing
      greet;

If sudden any dust should light upon her blessed heart,

Fall down before her, kiss her sandal's sole, beneath her
      feet.

A sample of my tears of blood thou, Handkerchief, wilt
      show,

Through these within a moment would a thousand
      crimson grow;

Thou'lt be in company with her, while I am sad with
      grief;

To me no longer life may be, if things continue so.

POEMS OF LAMI'I

ON AUTUMN

O sad heart, come, distraction's hour is now high,
The air's cool, 'midst the elds to sit the time nigh.
The Sun hath to the Balance, Joseph-like, past,
The year's Zuleykha hath her gold hoard wide cast.
By winds bronzed, like the Sun, the quince's face glows;
Its Pleiads-clusters, hanging forth, the vine shows.
In saffron flow'rets have the meads themselves dight;
The trees, all scorched, to gold have turned, and shine
      bright.
The gilded leaves in showers falling to earth gleam;
With goldfish filled doth glisten brightly each stream.
Ablaze each tree, and blent are all in one glare,
And therefore charged with glistening fire the still air.
Amidst the yellow foliage perched the black crows—
As tulip, saffron-hued, that spotted cup shows.
A yellow-plumaged bird now every tree stands,
Which shakes itself and feathers sheds on all hands.
Each vine-leaf paints its face, bride-like, with gold ink;
The brook doth silver anklets round the vine link.
The plane-tree hath its hands, with henna, red-dyed,
And stands there of the parterre's court the fair bride.
The erst green tree now like the starry sky shows,
And hurling meteors at the fiend, Earth, stones throws.

ON SPRING

From the pleasure, joy, and rapture of this hour,
In its frame to hold its soul earth scarce hath power.
Pent its collar, like the dawning, hath the rose;
From its heart the nightingale sighs forth its woes.
Dance the juniper and cypress like the sphere;
Filled with melody through joy all lands appear.

Gently sing the running brooks in murmurs soft;
While the birds with tuneful voices soar aloft.
Play the green and tender branches with delight,
And they shed with one accord gold, silver, bright.
Like to couriers fleet, the zephyrs speed away,
Resting ne'er a moment either night or day.
In that raid the rosebud filled with gold its hoard,
And the tulip with fresh musk its casket stored.
There the moon a purse of silver coin did seize;
Filled with ambergris its skirt the morning breeze;
Won the sun a golden disk of ruby dye,
And with glistening pearls its pocket filled the sky:
Those who poor were fruit and foliage attained;
All the people of the land some trophy gained.

ROSE TIME

O heart, come, wail, as nightingale thy woes show;
'Tis Pleasure's moment this, come, then, as rose blow.
In burning notes make thou thy tuneful song rise;
These iron hearts soft render with thy sad sighs.
Within thy soul place not, like tulip, dark brand;
When opportunity doth come, then firm stand.
From earth take justice ere yet are these times left,
And ere yet from the soul's harp is breath's song reft.
They call thee—view the joys that sense would yield thee;
But, ere thou canst say "Hie!" the bird is flown, see.
Give ear, rose-like, because in truth the night-bird
From break of dawn its bitter wail hath made heard.
Their chorus all around the gleeful birds raise;
The streamlets sing, the nightingale the flute plays.
The jasmines with their fresh leaves tambourines ply;
The streams, hard pressed, raise up their glistening foam
       high
Of junipers and cypresses two ranks 'tween,
The zephyr sports and dances o'er the flower-green.

The streamlets 'midst the vineyard hide-and-seek play
The flowerlets with, among the verdant leaves gay.
Away the morning's breeze the jasmine's crown tears,
As pearls most costly scatters it the plucked hairs.
The leader of the play's the breeze of swift pace;
Like children, each the other all the flowers chase.
With green leaves dressed, the trees each other's hands
            take;
The flowers and nightingales each other's robes shake.
Like pigeon, there, before the gale that soft blows,
Doth turn in many a somersault the young rose.
As blaze up with gay flowerlets all the red plains,
The wind each passes, and the vineyard next gains.
The clouds, pearl-raining, from the meteors sparks seize;
And flowers are all around strewn by the dawn-breeze.
The waters, eddying, in circles bright play,
Like shining swords the green leaves toss about they.
With bated breath the Judas-trees there stand by;
And each for other running brook and breeze sigh.
The gales tag with the basil play in high glee;
To dance with cypress gives its hand the plane-tree.
The soft winds have adorned the wanton bough fair,
The leader of the frolics 'midst the parterre.
The narcisse toward the almond-tree its glance throws;
With vineyard-love the pink upbraids the dog-rose.
The water's mirror clear doth as the Sphere gleam;
Its stars, the flowers, reflected, fair and bright beam.
The meads are skies; their stars, the drops of dew, glow;
The jasmine is the moon; the stream, the halo.
In short, each spot as resurrection-plane seems;
None who beholds of everlasting pain dreams.
Those who it view, and ponder well with thought's eye,
It's strange, if they be mazed and wildered thereby?
Up! breeze-like, Lami'i, thy hermitage leave!
The roses' days in sooth no time for fasts give!

POEMS OF GAZALI

FROM AN ELEGY ON ISKENDER CHELEBI

High honored once was the noble Iskender;
O heart, from his destiny warning obtain.
Ah! do thou see what at length hath befall'n him!
What all this glory and panoply gain!
Drinking the poison of doom, ne'er a remnant
Of sweetness's taste in his mouth did remain.
Retrograde, sank down his star, erst ascendant,
From perfect conjunction, alas, did it wane.
Dust on the face of his honor aye stainless
Strewn hath the blast of betrayal profane.
The Lofty Decree for his high exaltation
Did Equity's Court, all unlooked for, ordain;
Forthwith to the Regions of Eden they bore him,
They raised him from earth's abject baseness and stain.
Circling and soaring, he went on his journey,
From the land of his exile to Home back again.
Neck-bounden he stood as a slave at the palace,
Freed is he now from affliction's hard chain.
Joyous he flew on his journey to Heaven,
Rescued forever from earth gross and vain.
In life or in death from him never, ay, never
Was honor most lofty, most glorious, ta'en!

FRAGMENT

Come is the autumn of my life, alas, it thus should pass
away!
I have not reached the dawn of joy, to sorrow's night
there is no day.
Time after time the image of her cheek falls on my tear-
filled eye;
Ah! no pretension to esteem can shadows in the water

333

lay!
Oh! whither will these winds of Fate impel the frail bark
      of the heart?
Nor bound nor shore confining girds Time's dreary ocean
      of dismay!

POEMS OF FUZULI

GAZEL

O breeze, thou'rt kind, of balm to those whom pangs
      affright, thou news hast brought,
To wounded frame of life, to life of life's delight thou news
      hast brought.
Thou'st seen the mourning nightingale's despair in
      sorrow's autumn drear,
Like springtide days, of smiling roseleaf fresh and bright,
      thou news hast brought.
If I should say thy words are heaven-inspired, in truth,
      blaspheme I not;
Of Faith, whilst unbelief doth earth hold fast and tight,
      thou news hast brought.
They say the loved one comes to soothe the hearts of all
      her lovers true;
If that the case, to yon fair maid of lovers' plight thou
      news hast brought.
Of rebel demon thou hast cut the hope Suleiman's throne
      to gain;
That in the sea secure doth lie his Ring of might, thou
      news hast brought.
Fuzuli, through the parting night, alas, how dark my
      fortune grew!
Like zephyr of the dawn, of shining sun's fair light thou
      news hast brought.

GAZEL

O thou Perfect Being, Source whence wisdom's mysteries
      arise;
Things, the issue of thine essence, show wherein thy
      nature lies.
Manifester of all wisdom, thou art he whose pen of might

Hath with rays of stars illumined yonder gleaming page,
the skies.
That a happy star, indeed, the essence clear of whose
bright self
Truly knoweth how the blessings from thy word that
flow to prize.
But a jewel flawed am faulty I: alas, forever stands
Blank the page of my heart's journal from thought of thy
writing wise.
In the journal of my actions Evil's lines are black indeed;
When I think of Day of Gathering's terrors, blood flows
from my eyes.
Gathering of my tears will form a torrent on the
Reckoning Day,
If the pearls, my tears, rejecting, he but view them to
despise:
Pearls my tears are, O Fuzuli, from the ocean deep of love;
But they're pearls these, oh! most surely, that the Love of
Allah buys!

GAZEL

Is't strange if beauties' hearts turn blood through envy of
thy cheek most fair?
For that which stone to ruby turns is but the radiant
sunlight's glare.
Or strange is't if thine eyelash conquer all the stony-
hearted ones?
For meet an ebon shaft like that a barb of adamant should
bear!
Thy cheek's sun-love hath on the hard, hard hearts of
fairy beauties fall'n,
And many a steely-eyed one hath received thy bright
reflection fair.
The casket, thy sweet mouth, doth hold spellbound the
huri-faced ones all;

The virtue of Suleiman's Ring was that fays thereto fealty
sware.

Is't strange if, seeing thee, they rub their faces lowly midst
the dust?

That down to Adam bowed the angel throng doth the
Koran declare!

On many and many a heart of stone have fall'n the pangs
of love for thee!

A fire that lies in stone concealed is thy heart-burning
love's dread glare!

Within her ward, with garments rent, on all sides rosy-
cheeked ones stray;

Fuzuli, through those radiant hues, that quarter beams a
garden fair.

GAZEL

From the turning of the Sphere my luck hath seen reverse
and woe;

Blood I've drunk, for from my banquet wine arose and
forth did go.

With the flame, my burning sighs, I've lit the wand'ring
wildered heart;

I'm a fire, doth not all that which turns about me roasted
glow?

With thy rubies wine contended—oh! how it hath lost its
wits!

Need 'tis yon ill-mannered wretch's company that we
forego.

Yonder moon saw not my burning's flame upon the
parting day—

How can e'er the sun about the taper all night burning
know?

Every eye that all around tears scatters, thinking of thy
shaft,

Is an oyster-shell that causeth rain-drops into pearls to

grow.

Forms my sighing's smoke a cloud that veils the bright
cheek of the moon;

Ah! that yon fair moon will ne'er the veil from off her
beauty throw!

Ne'er hath ceased the rival e'en within her ward to vex me
sore;

How say they, Fuzuli, "There's in Paradise nor grief nor
woe"?

MUSEDDES

A stately Cypress yesterday her shade threw o'er my head;

Her form was heart-ensnaring, heart-delighting her light
tread;

When speaking, sudden opened she her smiling rubies
red,

There a pistachio I beheld that drops of candy shed.

  "This casket can it be a mouth? Ah! deign!" I said; said
she:

  "Nay, nay, 'tis balm to cure thy hidden smart; aye, truly
thine!"

Down o'er her crescents she had pressed the turban she
did wear,

By which, from many broken hearts, sighs raised she of
despair;

She loosed her tresses—hid within the cloud her moon so
fair,

And o'er her visage I beheld the curls of her black hair.

  "Those curling locks, say, are they then a chain?" I said;
said she:

  "That round my cheek, a noose to take thy heart; aye,
truly thine!"

The taper bright, her cheek, illumined day's lamp in the
sky;

The rose's branch was bent before her figure, cypress-
    high;
She, cypress-like, her foot set down upon the fount, my
    eye,
But many a thorn did pierce her foot she suffered pain
    thereby.
  "What thorn unto the roseleaf-foot gives pain?" I said;
    said she:
  "The lash of thy wet eye doth it impart; aye, truly
    thine!"
Promenading, to the garden did that jasmine-cheeked one
    go;
With many a bright adornment in the early springtide's
    glow;
The hyacinths their musky locks did o'er the roses throw;
That Picture had tattooed her lovely feet rose-red to show.
  "The tulip's hue whence doth the dog-rose gain?" I said;
    said she:
  "From Hood of thine shed 'neath my glance's dart; aye,
    truly thine!"

To earth within her ward my tears in torrents rolled
    apace;
The accents of her ruby lips my soul crazed by their grace;
My heart was taken in the snare her musky locks did
    trace,
That very moment when my eyes fell on her curls and
    face.
  "Doth Scorpio the bright Moon's House contain?" I
    said; said she:
  "Fear! threatening this Conjunction dread, thy part;
    aye, truly thine!"

Her hair with ambergris perfumed was waving o'er her
    cheek,

On many grieving, passioned souls it cruel woe did
      wreak;
Her graceful form and many charms my wildered heart
      made weak;
The eye beheld her figure fair, then heart and soul did
      seek.
  "Ah! what bright thing this cypress of the plain?" I said;
      said she:
  "'Tis that which thy fixed gaze beholds apart; aye, truly
      thine!"

When their veil her tulip and dog-rose had let down
      yesterday,
The morning breeze tore off that screen which o'er these
      flow'rets lay;
Came forth that Envy of the sun in garden fair to stray,
Like lustrous pearls the dewdrops shone, a bright and
      glistening spray.
  "Pearls, say, are these, aye pearls from 'Aden's main?" I
      said; said she:
  "Tears, these, of poor Fuzuli, sad of heart; aye, truly
      thine!"

MUKHAMMES

Attar within vase of crystal, such thy fair form silken-
      gowned;
And thy breast is gleaming water, where the bubbles clear
      abound;
Thou so bright none who may gaze upon thee on the
      earth is found;
Bold wert thou to cast the veil off, standing forth with
      garland crowned:
  Not a doubt but woe and ruin all the wide world must
      confound!

Lures the heart thy gilded palace, points it to thy lips the

way;
Eagerly the ear doth listen for the words thy rubies say;
Near thy hair the comb remaineth, I despairing far away;
Bites the comb, each curling ringlet, when it through thy
     locks doth stray:
  Jealous at its sight, my heart's thread agonized goes
     curling round.

Ah! her face the rose, her shift rose-hued, her trousers red
     their shade;
With its flame burns us the fiery garb in which thou are
     arrayed.
Ne'er was born of Adam's children one like thee, O cruel
     maid!
Moon and Sun, in beauty's circle, at thy fairness stand
     dismayed:
  Seems it thou the Sun for mother and the Moon for sire
     hast owned.

Captive bound in thy red fillet, grieve I through thy
     musky hair;
Prone I 'neath those golden anklets which thy silvern
     limbs do wear;
Think not I am like thy fillet, empty of thy grace, O fair!
Rather to the golden chain, which hangs thy cheek
     round, me compare:
  In my sad heart pangs a thousand from thy glance's
     shafts are found.

Eyes with antimony darkened, hands with henna
     crimson dyed;
Through these beauties vain and wanton like to thee was
     ne'er a bride.
Bows of poplar green, thy painted brows; thy glances
     shafts provide.
Poor Fuzuli for thine eyes and eyebrows aye hath longing

341

cried:

That the bird from bow and arrow flees not, well may
all astound.

FROM LEYLI AND MEJNUN

Yield not the soul to pang of Love, for Love's the soul's
fierce glow;

That Love's the torment of the soul doth all the wide
world know.

Seek not for gain from fancy wild of pang of Love at all;

For all that comes from fancy wild of Love's pang is griefs
throe.

Each curving eyebrow is a blood-stained saber thee to
slay;

Each dusky curl, a deadly venomed snake to work thee
woe.

Lovely, indeed, the forms of moon-like maidens are to see
—

Lovely to see, but ah! the end doth bitter anguish show.

From this I know full well that torment dire in love
abides,

That all who lovers are, engrossed with sighs, rove to and
fro.

Call not to mind the pupils of the black-eyed damsels
bright,

With thought, "I'm man"; be not deceived, 'tis blood they
drink, I trow.

E'en if Fuzuli should declare, "In fair ones there is troth,"

Be not deceived—"A poet's words are falsehoods all men
know."

MEJNUN ADDRESSES NEVFIL

Quoth Mejnun: "O sole friend of true plight!
With counsel many have tried me to guide right;
Many with wisdom gifted have advice shown,

342

But yet this fiend hath been by no one o'erthrown;
Much gold has on the earth been strewn round,
But yet this Stone of Alchemist by none's found.
Collyrium I know that doth increase light,
What use though is it if the eye doth lack sight?
I know that greatest kindliness in thee lies,
What use, though, when my fate doth ever dark rise?
Upon my gloomy fortune I no faith lay,
Impossible my hope appeareth alway.
Ah! though in this thou shouldest ever hard toil,
The end at length will surely all thy plans foil.
No kindliness to me my closest friends show;
Who is a friend to him whom he doth deem foe?
I know my fortune evil is and woe-fraught;
The search for solace is to me, save pain, naught.
There is a gazel that doth well my lot show,
Which constant I repeat where'er my steps go."

MEJNUN'S GAZEL

From whomsoe'er I've sought for troth but bitterest
    disdain I've seen;
Whome'er within this faithless world I've trusted, all most
    vain I've seen.
To whomsoe'er I've told my woes, in hope to find some
    balm therefor,
Than e'en myself o'erwhelmed and sunk in deeper, sadder
    pain I've seen.
From out mine aching heart no one hath driven cruel
    grief away,
That those my friends of pleasure's hour affection did but
    feign I've seen.
Although I've clutched its mantle, life hath turned away
    its face from me;
And though I faith from mirror hoped, there persecuted
    swain I've seen.

At gate of hope I set my foot, bewilderment held forth its
   hand,
Alas! whene'er hope's thread I've seized, in hand the
   serpent's train I've seen.
A hundred times the Sphere hath shown to me my
   darksome fortune's star;
Whene'er my horoscope I've cast, but blackest, deepest
   stain I've seen.
Fuzuli, blush not then, should I from mankind turn my
   face away;
For why? From all to whom I've looked, but reason sad
   too plain I've seen.

ZEYD'S VISION

His grief and mourning Zeyd renewed alway,
From bitter wailing ceased he not, he wept aye.
That faithful, loving, ever-constant friend dear.
One night, when was the rise of the True Dawn near,
Feeling that in his wasted frame no strength stayed,
Had gone, and down upon that grave himself laid.
There, in his sleep, he saw a wondrous fair sight,
A lovely garden, and two beauties, moon-bright;
Through transport rapturous, their cheeks with light
   glow;
Far distant now, all fear of anguish, pain, woe;
With happiness and ecstasy and joy blest,
From rivals' persecutions these have found rest;
A thousand angel-forms to each fair beauty,
With single heart, perform the servant's duty.
He, wondering, question made: "What Moons so bright
   these?
What lofty, honored Sovereigns of might these?
What garden, most exalted, is this parterre?
What throng so bright and beautiful, the throng there?"
They answer gave: "Lo! Eden's shining bowers these;

That radiant throng, the Heaven-born Youths and
     Houris;
These two resplendent forms, bright as the fair moon,
These are the ever-faithful—Leyli, Mejnun!
Since pure within the vale of love they sojourned,
And kept that purity till they to dust turned,
Are Eden's everlasting bowers their home now,
To them the Houris and the Youths as slaves bow:
Since these, while on the earth, all woe resigned met,
And patience aye before them in each grief set,
When forth they fled from this false, faithless world's
     bound,
From all those pangs and sorrows they release found!"

POEMS OF NABI

MUKHAMMES

Alas! nor dew nor smiling rose within this mead is mine;
Within this market-place nor trade nor coin for need is
      mine;
Nor more nor less; nor power nor strength for act or deed
      is mine;
Nor might nor eminence; nor balm the cure to speed is
      mine.
  Oh, that I knew what here I am, that which indeed is
      mine!

Being's the bounty of the Lord; and Life, the gift Divine;
The Breath, the present of his love; and Speech his Grace's
      sign;
The Body is the pile of God; the Soul, his Breath benign;
The Powers thereof, his Glory's trust; the Senses, his
      design.
  Oh, that I knew what here I am, that which indeed is
      mine!

No work, no business of my own within this mart have I;
All Being is of him alone—no life apart have I;
No choice of entering this world, or hence of start have I;
To cry, "I am! I am!" in truth, no power of heart have I.
  Oh, that I knew what here I am, that which indeed is
      mine!

The Earth the carpet is of Power; the Sphere, the tent of
      Might;
The Stars, both fixed and wandering, are Glory's lamps of
      light;
The World's the issue of the grace of Mercy's treasures

bright;
With forms of beings is the page of Wisdom's volume
dight.
    Oh, that I knew what here I am, that which indeed is
mine!

Being is but a loan to us, and Life in trust we hold:
In slaves a claim to Power's pretension arrogant and bold;
The servant's part is by submission and obedience told;
Should He, "My slave," address to me, 'twere favors
manifold.
    Oh, that I knew what here I am, that which indeed is
mine!

I'm poor and empty-handed, but grace free is of the Lord;
Nonentity's my attribute: to Be is of the Lord;
For Being or Non-being's rise, decree is of the Lord;
The surging of the Seen and Unseen's sea is of the Lord.
    Oh, that I knew what here I am, that which indeed is
mine!

Of gifts from table of his Bounty is my daily bread;
My breath is from the Breath of God's benignant Mercy
fed;
My portion from the favors of Almighty Power is shed;
And my provision is from Providence's kitchen spread.
    Oh, that I knew what here I am, that which indeed is
mine!

I can not, unallotted, take my share from wet or dry;
From land or from the ocean, from earth or from the sky;
The silver or the gold will come, by Providence laid by;
I can not grasp aught other than my fortune doth supply.
    Oh, that I knew what here I am, that which indeed is
mine!

Creation's Pen the lines of billows of events hath traced;
Th' illumined scroll of the Two Worlds, Creation's Pencil
     graced;
Their garments upon earth and sky, Creation's woof hath
     placed;
Men's forms are pictures in Creation's great Shah-Nama
     traced.
    Oh, that I knew what here I am, that which indeed is
      mine!

I can not make the morning eve, or the dark night the
     day;
I can not turn the air to fire, or dust to water's spray;
I can not bid the Sphere stand still, or mountain region
     stray;
I can not Autumn turn by will of mine to lovely May.
    Oh, that I knew what here I am, that which indeed is
      mine!
From out of Nothingness his mighty Power made me
     appear;
Whilst in the womb I lay, saw he to all I need for here;
With kindness concealed and manifest did he me rear;
With me he drew a curtain o'er Distinction's beauty dear.
    Oh, that I knew what here I am, that which indeed is
      mine!

God's Revelation is Discernment's Eye, if't oped remain;
The picturings of worlds are all things changing aye
     amain;
The showing of the Hidden Treasure is this raging main,
This work, this business of the Lord, this Majesty made
     plain.
    Oh, that I knew what here I am, that which indeed is
      mine!

Now void, now full, are Possibility's storehouses vast;

348

This glass-lined world's the mirror where Lights Twain
    their phases cast;
The blinded thing — in scattering strange fruits its hours
    are past;
Ruined hath this old Vineyard been by autumn's sullen
    blast.
  Oh, that I knew what here I am, that which indeed is
    mine!

GAZEL

Ne'er a corner for the plaintive bulbul's nest remaineth
    now;
Ne'er a palm-tree 'neath whose kindly shade is rest
    remaineth now.
Day and night some balm I've sought for, to relieve my
    wounded heart;
Ne'er a cure within the heavens' turquoise chest
    remaineth now.
From its source, through every country, searched have I,
    but all in vain —
Ne'er a single drop, in mercy's fountain blest, remaineth
    now.
Empty earthen pots are reckoned one with jewels rich and
    rare;
Ne'er a scale in value's mart the worth to test remaineth
    now.
'Neath the earth may now the needy hide themselves,
    Nabi, away;
Ne'er a turret on the fort of interest remaineth now.

POEMS OF BAQI

A QAISDA ON SULTAN SULEIMAN

One night when all the battlements Heaven's castle doth
   display,
Illumed and decked were, with the shining lamps, the
   stars' array,
Amidst the host of gleaming stars the Moon lit up his
   torch;
Athwart the field of Heaven with radiance beamed the
   Milky Way.
The Secretary of the Spheres had ta'en his meteor-pen,
That writer of his signature whom men and jinns obey.
There, at the banquet of the sky, had Venus struck her
   lyre,
In mirth and happiness, delighted, joyed and smiling gay.
Taking the keynote for her tune 'neath in the vaulted
   sphere,
The tambourinist Sun her visage bright had hid away.
Armed with a brand of gleaming gold had leapt into the
   plain
The Swordsman of the sky's expanse, of heaven's field of
   fray.
To give direction to the weighty matters of the earth
Had Jupiter, the wise, lit up reflection's taper's ray.
There raised aloft old Saturn high upon the Seventh
   Sphere
Sitting like Indian elephant-conductor on did stray.
"What means this decking of the universe?" I wond'ring
   said;
When, lo! with meditation's gaze e'en whilst I it survey,
Casting its beams on every side, o'er all earth rose the
   Sun,
O'er the horizons, e'en as Seal of Suleiman's display.

The eye of understanding looked upon this wondrous
      sight;
At length the soul's ear learned the secret hid in this
      which lay:
What is it that hath decked earth's hall with splendors
      such as this,
Saving the might and fortune of the King who earth doth
      sway?
He who sits high upon the throne above all crowned
      kings,
The Hero of the battlefield of dread Keyani fray,
Jemshid of happiness and joy, Darius of the fight,
Khusrev of right and clemency, Iskender of his day!

Lord of the East and West! King whom the kings of earth
      obey!
Prince of the Epoch! Sultan Suleiman! Triumphant Aye!

Meet 'tis before the steed of yonder Monarch of the realms
Of right and equity, should march earth's rulers' bright
      array.
Rebelled one 'gainst his word, secure he'd bind him in his
      bonds,
E'en like the dappled pard, the sky, chained with the
      Milky Way.
Lord of the land of graciousness and bounty, on whose
      board
Of favors, spread is all the wealth that sea and mine
      display;
Longs the perfumer, Early Spring, for th' odor of his
      grace;
Need hath the merchant, Autumn, of his bounteous hand
      alway.
Through tyrant's hard oppression no one groaneth in his
      reign,

And though may wail the flute and lute, the law they
      disobey.
Beside thy justice, tyranny's the code of Key-Qubad;
Beside thy wrath, but mildness Qahraman's most deadly
      fray.
Thy scimitar's the gleaming guide empires to overthrow,
No foe of Islam can abide before thy saber's ray.
Saw it thy wrath, through dread of thee would trembling
      seize the pine;
The falling stars a chain around the heaven's neck would
      lay.
Amidst thy sea-like armies vast, thy flags and standards
      fair,
The sails are which the ship of splendid triumph doth
      display.
Thrust it its beak into the Sphere, 'twould seize it as a
      grain,
The 'anqa strong, thy power, to which 'twere but a seed-
      like prey.
In past eternity the hand, thy might, it struck with bat,
That time is this time, for the Sky's Ball spins upon its
      way.
Within the rosy garden of thy praise the bird, the heart,
Singeth this soul-bestowing, smooth-as-water-running
      lay.

If yonder mouth be not the soul, O heart-enslaver gay,
Then wherefore is it like the soul, hid from our eyes
      away?
Since in the casket of our mind thy ruby's picture lies,
The mine is now no fitting home for gem of lustrous ray.
Thy tresses fall across thy cheek in many a twisting curl,
"To dance to Hijaz have the Shamis tucked their skirts,"
      we'd say.
Let both the youthful pine and cypress view thy motions

fair;
The gardener now to rear the willow need no more assay.
The dark and cloudy-brained of men thine eyebrows black
        depict,
While those of keen, discerning wit thy glistening teeth
        portray.
Before thy cheek the rose and jasmine bowed in *sujud*,
The cypress to thy figure in *qiyam* did homage pay.
The heart's throne is the seat of that great monarch, love
        for thee;
The soul, the secret court, where doth thy ruby's picture
        stay.
The radiance of thy beauty bright hath filled earth like the
        sun,
The hall, "Be! and it is," resounds with love of thee for
        aye.
The cries of those on plain of earth have risen to the skies,
The shouts of those who dwell above have found to earth
        their way.
Nor can the nightingale with songs as sweet as Baqi's
        sing,
Nor happy as thy star can beam the garden's bright array.
The mead, the world, blooms through thy beauty's rose,
        like Irem's bower;
On every side are nightingales of sweet, melodious lay.
Now let us pray at Allah's court: "May this for aye
        endure,
The might and glory of this prospered King's resplendent
        sway;
Until the lamp, the world-illuming sun, at break of dawn,
A silver candelabrum on the circling skies display,
Oh! may the Ruler of the world with skirt of aid and grace
Protect the taper of his life from blast of doom, we pray!"
Glory's the comrade; Fortune, the cup-bearer at our feast;
The beaker is the Sphere; the bowl, the Steel of gold-inlay!

GAZEL

'Tis love's wild sea, my sighs' fierce wind doth lash those
    waves my tears uprear;
My head, the bark of sad despite; mine eyebrows twain,
    the anchors here.
Mine unkempt hair, the den of yonder tiger dread, the fair
    one's love;
My head, dismay and sorrow's realm's deserted mountain
    region drear.
At whatsoever feast I drain the cup thy rubies' mem'ry to,
Amidst all those who grace that feast, except the dregs,
    I've no friend near.
Thou know'st, O Light of my poor eyes, with *tutya* mixed
    are gems full bright,
What then if weep on thy path's dust mine eyes that
    scatter pearls most clear!
The Sphere, old hag, with witchcraft's spell hath parted
    me from my fond love,
O Baqi, see, by God, how vile a trick yon jade hath played
    me here!

GAZEL

Years trodden under foot have I lain on that path of thine;
Thy musky locks are noose-like cast, around my feet to
    twine.
O Princess mine! boast not thyself through loveliness of
    face,
For that, alas, is but a sun which must full soon decline!
The loved one's stature tall, her form as fair as juniper,
Bright 'midst the rosy bowers of grace a slender tree doth
    shine.
Her figure, fair-proportioned as my poesy sublime,
Her slender waist is like its subtle thought—hard to
    divine.
Then yearn not, Baqi, for the load of love's misfortune

dire;
For that to bear mayhap thy soul no power doth
      enshrine.

GAZEL

With her graceful-moving form, a Cypress jasmine-faced is
      she?
Or in Eden's bower a branch upon the Lote or Tuba-tree?
That thy blood-stained shaft which rankles in my
      wounded breast, my love,
In the rosebud hid a lovely rose-leaf, sweetheart, can it be?
To the dead of pain of anguish doth its draught fresh life
      impart;
O cupbearer, is the red wine Jesu's breath? tell, tell to me!
Are they teeth those in thy mouth, or on the rosebud
      drops of dew?
Are they sparkling stars, or are they gleaming pearls, that
      there I see?
Through the many woes thou wreakest upon Baqi, sick
      of heart,
Is't thy will to slay him, or is it but sweet disdain in thee?

GAZEL

Before thy form, the box-tree's lissom figure dwarfed
      would show;
Those locks of thine the pride of ambergris would
      overthrow.
Who, seeing thy cheek's glow, recalls the ruby is deceived;
He who hath drunken deep of wine inebriate doth grow.
Should she move forth with figure like the juniper in
      grace,
The garden's cypress to the loved one's form must bend
      right low.
Beware, give not the mirror bright to yonder paynim
      maid,

Lest she idolater become, when there her face doth show.
Baqi, doth he not drink the wine of obligation's grape,
Who drunken with A-lestu's cup's overwhelming
        draught doth go?

GAZEL

Thy cheek, like limpid water, clear doth gleam;
Thy pouting mouth a bubble round doth seem.
The radiance of thy cheek's sun on the heart
Like moonlight on the water's face doth beam.
The heart's page, through the tracings of thy down,
A volume all illumined one would deem.
That fair Moon's sunny love the earth have burned,
It warm as rays of summer sun doth stream.
At woful sorrow's feast my bloodshot eyes,
Two beakers of red wine would one esteem.
Baqi, her mole dark-hued like ambergris,
A fragrant musk-pod all the world would deem.

GAZEL

All sick the heart with love for her, sad at the feast of woe;
Bent form, the harp; low wail, the flute; heart's blood for
        wine doth flow.
Prone lies the frame her path's dust 'neath, in union's
        stream the eye,
In air the mind, the soul 'midst separation's fiery glow.
Oh, ever shall it be my lot, zone-like, thy waist to clasp!
'Twixt us, O love, the dagger blade of severance doth
        show!
Thou art the Queen of earth, thy cheeks are Towers of
        might, this day,
Before thy Horse, like Pawns, the Kings of grace and
        beauty go.
Him hinder not, beside thee let him creep, O Shade-like
        stay!

Baqi, thy servant, O my Queen, before thee lieth low.

ON AUTUMN

Lo, ne'er a trace or sign of springtide's beauty doth
     remain;
Fall'n 'midst the garden lie the leaves, now all their glory
     vain.
Bleak stand the orchard trees, all clad in tattered dervish
     rags;
Dark Autumn's blast hath torn away the hands from off
     the plane.
From each hill-side they come and cast their gold low at
     the feet,
Of garden trees, as hoped the streams from these some
     boon to gain.
Stay not within the parterre, let it tremble with its shame:
Bare every shrub, this day doth naught of leaf or fruit
     retain.
Baqi, within the garden lies full many a fallen leaf;
Low lying there, it seems they 'gainst the winds of Fate
     complain.

GAZEL

Tulip-cheeked ones over rosy field and plain stray all
     around;
Mead and garden cross they, looking wistful each way, all
     around.
These the lovers true of radiant faces, aye, but who the
     fair?
Lissom Cypress, thou it is whom eager seek they all
     around.
Band on band Woe's legions camped before the City of the
     Heart,
There, together league, sat Sorrow, Pain, Strife, Dismay,
     all around.

From my weeping flows the river of my tears on every
      side,
Like an ocean 'tis again, a sea that casts spray all around.
Forth through all the Seven Climates have the words of
      Baqi gone;
This refulgent verse recited shall be alway, all around.

GAZEL

From thine own beauty's radiant sun doth light flow;
How lustrously doth now the crystal glass show!
Thy friend's the beaker, and the cup's thy comrade;
Like to the dregs why dost thou me aside throw?
Hearts longing for thy beauty can resist not;
Hold, none can bear the dazzling vision's bright glow!
United now the lover, and now parted;
This world is sometimes pleasure and sometimes woe.
Bound in the spell of thy locks' chain is Baqi,
Mad he, my Liege, and to the mad they grace show.

GAZEL

The goblet as affliction's Khusrev's bright Keyani crown
      doth shine;
And surely doth the wine-jar love's King's Khusrevani
      hoard enshrine.
Whene'er the feast recalls Jemshid, down from its eyes the
      red blood rolls;
The rosy-tinted wine its tears, the beakers its blood-
      weeping eyne.
At parting's banquet should the cup, the heart, with
      blood brim o'er were't strange?
A bowl that, to the fair we'll drain, a goblet filled full high
      with wine.
O Moon, if by thy door one day the foe should sudden me
      o'ertake—
A woe by Heaven decreed, a fate to which I must myself

resign!
The fume of beauty's and of grace's censer is thy cheek's
      sweet mole,
The smoke thereof thy musky locks that spreading
      fragrant curl and twine;
Thy cheek rose-hued doth light its taper at the moon that
      shines most bright,
Its candlestick at grace's feast is yonder collar fair of thine.
Of love and passion is the lustrous sheen of Baqi's verse
      the cause;
As Life's Stream brightly this doth shine; but that, th'
      Eternal Life Divine.

THE ANCIENT CHURCH OF ST. SOPHIA.

*The former Christian Cathedral of Ancient Constantinople, now
converted into the chief Mohammedan Mosque.*

© UNDERWOOD & UNDERWOOD, N.Y.

GAZEL

When the sheets have yonder Torment to their bosom
    ta'en to rest,
Think I, "Hides the night-adorning Moon within the
    cloudlet's breast."
In the dawning, O thou turtle, mourn not with those

360

senseless plaints;

In the bosom of some stately cypress thou'rt a nightly
    guest.

Why thou weepest from the heavens, never can I think, O
    dew;

Every night some lovely rose's bosom fair thou enterest.

Hath the pearl seen in the story of thy teeth its tale of
    shame,

Since the sea hath hid the album of the shell within its
    breast?

Longing for thy cheeks, hath Baqi all his bosom marked
    with scars,

Like as though he'd cast of rose-leaves fresh a handful o'er
    his chest.

ELEGY ON SULTAN SULEIMAN I.

O thou! foot-bounden in the mesh of fame and glory's
    snare!

Till when shall last the lust of faithless earth's pursuits
    and care?

At that first moment, which of life's fair springtide is the
    last,

'Tis need the tulip cheek the tint of autumn leaf should
    wear;

'Tis need that thy last home should be, e'en like the dregs',
    the dust;

'Tis need the stone from hand of Fate should be joy's
    beaker's share.

He is a man indeed whose heart is as a mirror clear;

Man art thou? why then doth thy breast the tiger's
    fierceness bear?

In understanding's eye how long shall heedless slumber
    bide?

Will not war's Lion-Monarch's fate suffice to make thee
    ware?

He, Prince of Fortune's Cavaliers! he to whose charger
      bold,
Whene'er he caracoled or pranced, cramped was earth's
      tourney square!
He, to the luster of whose sword the Magyar bowed his
      head!
He, the dread gleaming of whose brand the Frank can
      well declare!
  Like tender rose-leaf, gently laid he in the dust his face,
  And Earth, the Treasurer, him placed like jewel in his
      case.

In truth, he was the radiance of rank high and glory
      great,
A Shah, Iskender-diademed, of Dara's armied state;
Before the dust beneath his feet the Sphere bent low its
      head;
Earth's shrine of adoration was his royal pavilion's gate.
The smallest of his gifts the meanest beggar made a prince;
Exceeding bounteous, exceeding kind a Potentate!
The court of glory of his kingly majesty most high
Was aye the center where would hopes of sage and poet
      wait.
Although he yielded to Eternal Destiny's command,
A King was he in might as Doom and puissant as Fate!
Weary and worn by this sad, changeful Sphere, deem not
      thou him:
Near God to be, did he his rank and glory abdicate.
What wonder if our eyes no more life and the world
      behold!
His beauty fair, as sun and moon, did earth irradiate!
  If folk upon the bright sun look, with tears are filled
      their eyes;
    For seeing it, doth yon moon-face before their minds
      arise!

Now let the cloud blood drop on drop weep, and its form
      bend low!
And let the Judas-tree anew in blossoms gore-hued blow!
With this sad anguish let the stars' eyes rain down bitter
      tears!
And let the smoke from hearts on fire the heavens all
      darkened show!
Their azure garments let the skies change into deepest
      black!
Let the whole world attire itself in robes of princely woe!
In breasts of fairies and of men still let the flame burn on

     —

Of parting from the blest King Suleiman the fiery glow!
His home above the highest heaven's ramparts he hath
      made;
This world was all unworthy of his majesty, I trow.
The bird, his soul, hath, *huma*-like, aloft flown to the
      skies,
And naught remaineth save a few bones on the earth
      below.
The speeding Horseman of the plain of Time and Space
      was he;
Fortune and Fame aye as his friends and bridle-guides did
      go.
   The wayward courser, cruel Fate, was wild and fierce of
      pace,
   And fell to earth the Shade of God the Lord's benignant
      Grace.

Through grief for thee, bereft of rest and tearful e'en as I,
Sore weeping let the cloud of spring go wand'ring
      through the sky!
And let the wailing of the birds of dawn the whole world
      fill!
Be roses torn! and let the nightingale distressful cry!

Their hyacinths as weeds of woe displaying, let them weep
Down o'er their skirts their flowing tears let pour—the
    mountains high!
The odor of thy kindliness recalling, tulip-like,
Within the Tartar musk-deer's heart let fire of anguish lie!
Through yearning for thee let the rose its ear lay on the
    path,
And, narcisse-like, till the last day the watchman's calling
    ply!
Although the pearl-diffusing eye to oceans turned the
    world,
Ne'er into being should there come a pearl with thee to
    vie!
O heart! this hour 'tis thou that sympathizer art with me;
Come, let us like the flute bewail, and moan, and plaintive
    sigh!
    The notes of mourning and of dole aloud let us
        rehearse;
    And let all those who grieve be moved by this our
        seven-fold verse.

Will earth's King ne'er awake from sleep?—broke hath the
    dawn of day:
Will ne'er he move forth from his tent, adorned as
    heaven's display?
Long have our eyes dwelt on the road, and yet no news
    hath come
From yonder land, the threshold of his majesty's array:
The color of his cheek hath paled, dry-lipped he lieth
    there,
E'en like that rose which from the vase of flowers hath
    fall'n away.
Goes now the Khusrev of the skies behind the cloudy veil,
For shame, remembering thy love and kindness, one
    would say.

My prayer is ever, "May the babes, his tears, go 'neath the
  sod,
Or old or young be he who weeps not thee in sad
  dismay."
With flame of parting from thee let the sun burn and
  consume;
And o'er the wastes through grief let darkness of the
  clouds hold sway.
Thy talents and thy feats let it recall and weep in blood,
Yea, let thy saber from its sheath plunge in the darksome
  clay.
  Its collar, through its grief and anguish, let the reed-pen
    tear!
  And let the earth its vestment rend through sorrow
    and despair!

Thy saber made the foe the anguish dire of wounds to
  drain;
Their tongues are silenced, none who dares to gainsay
  doth remain.
The youthful cypress, head-exalted, looked upon thy
  lance,
And ne'er its lissom twigs their haughty airs displayed
  again.
Where'er thy stately charger placed his hoof, from far and
  near
Flocked nobles, all upon thy path their lives to offer fain.
In desert of mortality the bird, desire, rests ne'er;
Thy sword in cause of God did lives as sacrifice ordain.
As sweeps a scimitar, across earth's face on every side,
Of iron-girded heroes of the world thou threw'st a chain.
Thou took'st a thousand idol temples, turnèdst all to
  mosques;
Where jangled bells thou mad'st be sung the Call to
  Prayers' strain.

365

At length is struck the signal drum, and thou hast
     journeyed hence;
Lo! thy first resting-place is Eden's flowery, verdant plain.
  Praise is to God! for he in the Two Worlds hath blessed
     thee,
  And caused thy glorious name, Hero and Martyr both
     to be.

Baqi, the beauty of the King, the heart's delight, behold!
The mirror of the work of God, the Lord of Eight, behold!
The dear old man hath passed away from th' Egypt sad,
     the world;
The youthful Prince, alert and fair as Joseph bright,
     behold!
The Sun hath risen, and the Dawning gray hath touched
     its bourne;
The lovely face of yon Khusrev, whose soul is light,
     behold!
This chase now to the grave hath sent the Behram of the
     Age;
Go, at his threshold serve, King Erdeshir aright, behold!
The blast of Fate to all the winds hath blown Suleiman's
     throne;
Sultan Selim Khan on Iskender's couch of might, behold!
The Tiger of the mount of war to rest in sleep hath gone;
The Lion who doth now keep watch on glory's height,
     behold!
The Peacock fair of Eden's mead hath soared to Heaven's
     parterre;
The luster of the *huma* of high, happy flight, behold!
  Eternal may the glory of the heaven-high Khusrev
     dwell!
  Blessings be on the Monarch's soul and spirit — and
     farewell!

367

TURKISH LITERATURE

THE MIRROR OF COUNTRIES
OR
THE ADVENTURES OF SIDI ALI REIS

"We roam the waters far and wide,
  And bring confusion to our enemies;
  Revenge and hatred is our motto."
            TURKISH SEA SONG OF SIDI.

THE MIRROR OF COUNTRIES

(Introduction by Professor Arminius Vambery)

The book of the Turkish Admiral Sidi Ali Reis, entitled *"Mirat ul Memalik"* (the Mirror of Countries), is in many ways interesting. In the first place, on account of the personality of the author, in whom we see a man of many varied accomplishments; a genuine type of the Islamitic culture of his time, and a representative of that class of official and military dignitaries to whose influence it is chiefly due that the Ottoman Empire, extending over three continents, attained to that eminent height of culture which it occupied during the reign of Suleiman the Great. Sidi Ali is the descendant of an illustrious family connected with the arsenal at Galata, in whom love for the sea seems to have been hereditary, and hence, as the Turkish publisher points out in his preface, Sidi Ali, being thoroughly acquainted with the nautical science of his day, excels as author on maritime subjects.

As a man of general culture, he was in harmony with the prevailing notions of his time, as mathematician, astronomer, and geographer; and also as poet, theologian, and in all branches of general literature; sometimes wielding his pen in writing lyrical or occasional verses, at other times entering into keen controversial disputes upon certain Koran theses or burning schismatic questions.

Besides all this he was a warrior, proving himself as undaunted in fighting the elements as in close combat with the Portuguese, who in point of accoutrement had far the advantage over him. But what stands out above all these accomplishments is his glowing patriotism and his unwavering faith in the power and the greatness of the

369

Ottoman Empire. He boasts that he never ceases to hope to see Gujarat and Ormuz joined to the Ottoman realm; his one desire is to see his Padishah ruler of the world, and wherever he goes and whatever he sees, Rum (Turkey) always remains in his eyes the most beautiful, the richest, and the most cultured land of the whole world. The Turkish Admiral has, moreover, a singularly happy way of expressing himself on this subject of his preference for his own Padishah and his native land; and this required no small amount of courage and tact where he had to face proud Humayun or Thamasp, no less conceited than the former.

With regard to the things which he saw and heard in non-Mussulman circles and districts in India, his accounts are poor compared with the descriptions of Ibn Batuta and other Moslem travelers. Sidi Ali has had hardly any intercourse with Hindus, and his route lay almost entirely through districts where the ruling caste, with whom he principally had to deal, were adherents to the Mohammedan faith. It does appear somewhat strange that he had such unbounded reverence for the Sultan of Turkey, and upheld him as the legitimate Caliph, although the caliphate had only fallen into the hands of the Ottoman rulers a few years previously with the overthrow of Tuman Bey by Selim II; and this seems the more strange, as Asia is so tenaciously conservative that even to this day the Turkish claim to the caliphate is a disputed point.

The authoritative and executive power of Turkey, formerly the terror of the Christian world, could not fail to exercise its influence upon the Moslem lands of Asia and their unstable governments, torn and harassed as they were by internal strife and petty wars, while the sultans of Turkey basked, not only in the glory of spiritual preferment, but also in that of temporal superiority. The picture which our author draws of the government of India and the East is certainly a very sad one. Civil wars and mutinies against the rulers of the land are every-day occurrences; the roads swarm with highwaymen, and even during the reign of the much-extolled Humayun, all intercourse with other lands was fraught with every imaginable kind of danger. Their rulers all suffer from a peculiar form of conceit, like the ruler of Bokhara, "who asked me, pointing to a ragged, motley crowd of ruffians, whether the army of the Sultan of Turkey were not exactly like this." Humayun, Thamasp, and even Borak Khan of Bokhara, all delighted in drawing parallels between themselves and Sultan Suleiman.

One thing, however, in the account of the Turkish Admiral is certainly surprising, namely the few facts by which he illustrates the Sultan's policy in Moslem Asia. We have always been under the impression that the Turks, during the era of their supreme power and universal sway, directed their attention more toward the Christian lands of the West, than toward the Moslem lands of the East, and that as a matter of fact their campaigns were nothing short of marauding raids, and empty conquests, while they might have utilized the many means at their disposal and the high prestige in which they stood toward the consolidation of their power in Asia, which would have been comparatively easy. This reproach is neither unfounded nor unmerited, for although the finest of the Ottoman rulers, Sultan Selim, did direct his attention chiefly toward the East, as proved by his campaigns against Persia and Egypt, most of his predecessors and successors have occupied themselves solely in making war in the West. Asia, which offered little to tempt the mercenary janissaries, was meanwhile left pretty well to its own devices, without any fixed form or plan of government. But, as in this narrative the threads of the policy pursued by those sultans, one by one, come to light,

371

we are struck with the fact that, after all, they were not quite so short-sighted as we gave them credit for, and that now and again they have given a thought to the bringing about of a better state of things.

THE MIRROR OF COUNTRIES
OR
THE ADVENTURES OF SIDI ALI REIS

I

When Sultan Suleiman had taken up his winter residence in Aleppo, I, the author of these pages, was appointed to the Admiralship of the Egyptian fleet, and received instructions to fetch back to Egypt the ships (15 galleys), which some time ago had been sent to Basrah on the Persian Gulf. But, "Man proposes, God disposes." I was unable to carry out my mission, and as I realized the impossibility of returning by water, I resolved to go back to Turkey by the overland route, accompanied by a few tried and faithful Egyptian soldiers. I traveled through Gujarat, Hind, Sind, Balkh, Zabulistan, Bedakhshan, Khotlan, Turan, and Iran, i.e., through Transoxania, Khorassan, Kharezm, and Deskti-Kiptchak; and as I could not proceed any farther in that direction, I went by Meshed and the two Iraks, Kazwin and Hamadan, on to Bagdad.

Our travels ended, my companions and fellow-adventurers persuaded me to write down our experiences, and the dangers through which we had passed, an accurate account of which it is almost impossible to give; also to tell of the cities and the many wonderful sights we had seen, and of the holy shrines we had visited. And so this little book sees the light; in it I have tried to relate, in simple and plain language, the troubles and difficulties, the suffering and the distress which beset our path, up to the time that we reached Constantinople. Considering the matter it contains this book ought to have been entitled, "A tale of woe," but with a view to the scene of action I have called it

373

"Mirror of Countries," and as such I commend it to the reader's kind attention.

II
THE BEGINNING OF THE STORY

When the illustrious Padishah was holding his court at Aleppo, in Ramazan of the year 960 (1552), I was commanded to join the army.

I celebrated Ramzam-Bairam in attendance on his Majesty, later on, however, I went to Sidi-Ghazi, made a pilgrimage in Konia to the tomb of Molla-i-Rumi, and visited the shrines of the Sultan ul-Ulema, and Shemsi Tebrizi, and of the Sheik Sadr-ed-din-Koniavi; at Kassarie I made a pilgrimage to the graves of the Sheiks Awhad-ed-din Kirmani, Burham-ed-din, Baha-ed-din Zade, Ibrahim Akserayi, and Davud Kaissari. Returned to Haleb (Aleppo), I visited the graves of Daud, Zakeriah, and Balkiah, as also those of Saad and Said, companions of the Prophet. The Kurban-Bairam I spent again in attendance on the Sultan.

I must here mention that Piri Bey, the late Admiral of the Egyptian fleet, had, some time previous to this, been dispatched with about 30 ships (galleys and galleons) from Suez, through the Red Sea, touching Jedda and Yemen, and through the straits of Bab-i-Mandeb, past Aden and along the coast of Shahar.[60] Through fogs and foul weather his fleet became dispersed, some ships were lost, and with the remainder he proceeded from Oman to Muscat, took the fortress and made all the inhabitants prisoners; he also made an incursion into the islands of Ormuz and Barkhat, after which he returned to Muscat. There he learned from the captive infidel captain that the Christian (Portuguese) fleet was on its way, that therefore any further delay was inadvisable, as in case it arrived he would not be able to leave the harbor at all. As a matter of fact it was already too late to save all the ships; he therefore took only three, and with these just managed to make his escape before the arrival of the Portuguese. One of his galleys was wrecked near Bahrein, so he brought only two vessels back to Egypt. As for the remainder of the fleet at Basrah, Kubad Pasha had offered the command of it to the Chief Officer, but he had declined, and returned to Egypt by land.

When this became known in Constantinople the command of the fleet had been given to Murad Bey, formerly Sanjakbey of Catif, then residing in Basrah. He was ordered to leave two ships, five galleys, and one galleon at Basrah, and with the rest, i.e., 15 galleys (one galley had been burned in Basrah) and two boats, he was to return to Egypt. Murad Bey did start as arranged, but opposite Ormuz he came upon the infidel (Portuguese) fleet, a terrible battle followed in which Suleiman Reis, Rejeb Reis, and several of the men, died a martyr's death. Many more were wounded and the ships terribly battered by the cannon-balls. At last, night put a stop to the fight. One boat was wrecked off the Persian coast, part of the crew escaped, the rest were taken prisoners by the infidels, and the boat itself captured.

When all this sad news reached the capital, toward the end of Zilhija of the said year 960 (1552), the author of these pages was appointed Admiral of the Egyptian fleet.

I, humble Sidi Ali bin Husein, also known as Kiatibi-Rumi (the writer of the West, i.e., of Turkey), most gladly accepted the post. I had always been very fond of the sea, had taken part in the expedition against Rhodes under the Sultan (Suleiman), and had since had a share in almost all engagements, both by land and by sea. I had fought under Khaireddin Pasha, Sinan Pasha, and other captains, and had cruised about on the Western (Mediterranean) sea, so that I knew every nook and corner of it. I had written several books on astronomy, nautical science, and other matters bearing upon navigation. My father and grandfather, since the conquest of Constantinople, had had charge of the arsenal[61] at Galata; they had both been eminent in their profession, and their skill had come down to me as an heirloom.

The post now entrusted to me was much to my taste, and I started from Aleppo for Basrah, on the first of Moharram of the year 961 (7 Dec. 1553). I crossed the Euphrates at Biredjik and when in Reka (*i.e.*, Orfah), I undertook a pilgrimage to the tomb of Abraham, having visited on the way between Nisebin and Mossul the holy graves of the prophets Yunis and Djerdjis and of the sheiks Mohammed Garabili, Feth Mosuli, and Kazib-elban-Mosuli. On the way to Bagdad I made a little detour from Tekrit to Samira, and visited the graves of Iman Ali-el-Hadi and Iman Haman Askeri, after which I came past the towns of Ashik[62] and Maashuk, and through Harbi, past the castle of Semke, on to Bagdad. We crossed the Tigris near Djisr and, after visiting the graves of the saints there, I continued my journey past the fortress of Teir, to Bire, and crossing the Euphrates near the little town of Masib, I reached Kerbela (Azwie), where I made a pilgrimage to the graves of the martyrs Hasan and Husein. Turning into the steppe near Shefata, I reached Nedjef (Haira) on the second day, and visited the graves of Adam, Noah, Shimun, and Ali, and from there proceeded to Kufa, where I saw the mosque with the pulpit under which the prophets of the house of Ali are buried, and the tombs of Kamber and Duldul. Arrived at the fortress of Hasinia, I visited the grave of the prophet Zilkefl, the son of Aaron, and in Hilla I made pilgrimages to the graves of Iman Mohammed Mehdi and Iman Akil, brother of Ali, and also visited there the mosque of Shem. Again crossing the Euphrates (this time by a bridge), I resumed my journey to Bagdad and went from there by ship to Basrah. On the way we touched Medain, saw the grave of Selmas Faris, admired Tak Kesri and the castle of Shah Zenan, and went past Imare Bugazi, on the road of Vasit to Zekya, past the strongholds of Adjul and Misra to Sadi-es Sueiba and on to Basrah, where I arrived toward the end of Safar of the said year (beginning of February, 1554).

III
ABOUT WHAT HAPPENED IN BASRAH

On the day after my arrival I had an interview with Mustafa Pasha, who, after seeing my credentials, made over to me the 15 galleys which were needing a great deal of repair. As far as could be, they were put in order, calked and provided with guns, which, however, were not to be had in sufficient quantity either from the stores there or from Urmuz. A water-supply had also to be arranged for, and as it was yet five months before the time of the monsoon,[63] I had plenty of leisure to visit the mosque of Ali and the graves of Hasan Basri, Talha, Zobeir, Uns-bin-Malik, Abdurrahman-bin-Anf, and several martyrs and companions of the Prophet. One night I dreamed that I lost my sword, and as I remembered that a similar thing had happened to Sheik Muhieddin and had resulted in a defeat, I became greatly alarmed, and, just as I was about to pray to the Almighty for the victory of the Islam arms, I awoke. I kept this dream a secret, but it troubled me for a long time, and when later on Mustafa Pasha sent a detachment of soldiers to take the island of Huweiza (in which expedition I took part with five of my galleys), and the undertaking resulted in our losing about a hundred men all through the fickleness of the Egyptian troops, I fully believed this to be

377

the fulfilment of my dream. But alas! there was more to follow—for:

What is decreed must come to pass,

No matter, whether you are joyful or anxious.

When at last the time of the monsoon came, the Pasha sent a trusty sailor with a frigate to Ormuz, to explore the neighborhood. After cruising about for a month he returned with the news that, except for four boats, there was no sign of any ships of the infidels in those waters. The troops therefore embarked and we started for Egypt.

IV

WHAT TOOK PLACE IN THE SEA OF ORMUZ

On the first of Shawal we left the harbor of Basrah, accompanied, as far as Ormuz, by the frigate of Sherifi Pasha. We visited on the way from Mehzari the grave of Khidr, and proceeding along the coast of Duspul (Dizful), and Shushter in Charik, I made pilgrimages to the graves of Imam Mohammed, Hanifi, and other saints.

From the harbor in the province of Shiraz we visited Rishehr (Bushir) and after reconnoitering the coasts and unable to get any clue as to the whereabouts of the enemy by means of the *Tshekleva*,[64] I proceeded to Katif, situated near Lahsa[65] and Hadjar on the Arabian coast. Unable to learn anything there, I went on to Bahrein, where I interviewed the commander of the place, Reis Murad. But neither could he give me any information about the fleet of the infidels. There is a curious custom at Bahrein. The sailors, provided with a leather sack, dive down into the sea and bring the fresh water from the bottom for Reis Murad's use. This water is particularly pleasant and cold in the spring time, and Reis Murad gave me some. God's power is boundless! This custom is the origin of the proverb: "*Maradj ul bahreia jaltakian*," and hence also the name "Bahrein."

378

Next we came to Kis, *i.e.*, old Ormuz, and Barhata, and several other small islands in the Green Sea, *i.e.*, the waters of Ormuz, but nowhere could we get any news of the fleet. So we dismissed the vessel, which Mustafa Pasha had sent as an escort, with the message that Ormuz was safely passed. We proceeded by the coasts of Djilgar and Djadi, past the towns of Keimzar or Leime, and forty days after our departure, *i.e.*, on the tenth of Ramazan, in the forenoon, we suddenly saw coming toward us the Christian fleet, consisting of four large ships, three galleons, six Portuguese guard ships, and twelve galleys (*Kalita*), 25 vessels in all. I immediately ordered the canopy to be taken down, the anchor weighed, the guns put in readiness, and then, trusting to the help of the Almighty, we fastened the *filandra*[66] to the mainmast, the flags were unfurled, and, full of courage and calling upon Allah, we commenced to fight. The volley from the guns and cannon was tremendous, and with God's help we sank and utterly destroyed one of the enemy's galleons.

Never before within the annals of history has such a battle been fought, and words fail me to describe it.

The battle continued till sunset, and only then the Admiral of the infidel fleet began to show some signs of fear. He ordered the signal-gun to fire a retreat, and the fleet turned in the direction of Ormuz.

With the help of Allah, and under the lucky star of the Padishah, the enemies of Islam had been defeated. Night came at last; we were becalmed for awhile, then the wind rose, the sails were set and as the shore was near ... until daybreak. The next day we continued our previous course. On the day after we passed Khorfakan,[67] where we took in water, and soon after reached Oman, or rather Sohar.[68] Thus we cruised about for nearly 17 days. When on the

379

sixth of Ramazan, *i.e.*, the day of Kadr-Ghedjesi, a night in the month of Ramazan, we arrived in the vicinity of Maskat and Kalhat,[69] we saw in the morning, issuing from the harbor of Maskat, 12 large boats and 22 *gurabs*, 34 vessels in all, commanded by Captain Kuya,[70] the son of the Governor. They carried a large number of troops.

The boats and galleons obscured the horizon with their mizzen sails (*Magistra*)[71] and *Peneta* (small sails) all set; the guard-ships spread their round sails (*Chember-yelken*), and, gay with hunting, they advanced toward us. Full of confidence in God's protection we awaited them. Their boats attacked our galleys; the battle raged, cannon and guns, arrows and swords made terrible slaughter on both sides. The *Badjoalushka* penetrated the boats and the *Shaikas*[72] and tore large holes in their hulls, while our galleys were riddled through by the javelins (*Darda*)[73] thrown down upon us from the enemy's turrets, which gave them the appearance of bristling porcupines; and they showered down upon us....

The stones which they threw at us created quite a whirlpool as they fell into the sea.

One of our galleys was set on fire by a bomb, but strange to say the boat from which it issued shared the like fate. God is merciful! Five of our galleys and as many of the enemy's boats were sunk and utterly wrecked, one of theirs went to the bottom with all sails set. In a word, there was great loss on both sides; our rowers were now insufficient in number to manage the oars, while running against the current, and to fire the cannon. We were compelled to drop anchor (at the stern) and to continue to fight as best we might. The boats had also to be abandoned.

Alemshah Reis, Kara Mustafa, and Kalfat Memi, captains

of some of the foundered ships, and Derzi Mustafa Bey, the Serdar of the volunteers, with the remainder of the Egyptian soldiers and 200 carpenters, had landed on the Arabian shore, and as the rowers were Arabs they had been hospitably treated by the Arabs of Nedjd.

The ships (*gurabs*) of the infidel fleet had likewise taken on board the crews of their sunken vessels, and as there were Arabs amongst them, they also had found shelter on the Arabian coast. God is our witness. Even in the war between Khaiveddin Pasha and Andreas Doria no such naval action as this has ever taken place.

When night came, and we were approaching the bay of Ormuz, the wind began to rise. The boats had already cast two *Lenguvurta, i.e.,* large anchors,[74] the *Lushtas* were tightly secured, and, towing the conquered *gurabs* along, we neared the shore while the galleys, dragging their anchors, followed. However, we were not allowed to touch the shore, and had to set sail again. During that night we drifted away from the Arabian coast into the open sea, and finally reached the coasts of Djash,[75] in the province of Kerman. This is a long coast, but we could find no harbor, and we roamed about for two days before we came to Kichi Mekran.[76]

As the evening was far advanced we could not land immediately, but had to spend another night at sea. In the morning a dry wind carried off many of the crew, and at last, after unheard-of troubles and difficulties, we approached the harbor of Sheba.[77]

Here we came upon a *Notak, i.e.,* a brigantine (pirate-ship), laden with spoils, and when the watchman sighted us they hailed us. We told them that we were Mussulmans, whereupon their captain came on board our vessel; he

381

kindly supplied us with water, for we had not a drop left, and thus our exhausted soldiers were invigorated. This was on Bairam day, and for us, as we had now got water, a double feast-day. Escorted by the said captain we entered the harbor of Guador.[78] The people there were Beluchistanis and their chief was Malik Djelaleddin, the son of Malik Dinar. The Governor of Guador came on board our ship and assured us of his unalterable devotion to our glorious Padishah. He promised that henceforth, if at any time our fleet should come to Ormuz, he would undertake to send 50 or 60 boats to supply us with provisions, and in every possible way to be of service to us. We wrote a letter to the native Prince Djelaleddin to ask for a pilot, upon which a first-class pilot was sent us, with the assurance that he was thoroughly trustworthy and entirely devoted to the interests of our Padishah.

V
WHAT WE SUFFERED IN THE INDIAN OCEAN

God is merciful! With a favorable wind we left the port of Guador and again steered for Yemen. We had been at sea for several days, and had arrived nearly opposite to Zofar[79] and Shar, when suddenly from the west arose a great storm known as *fil Tofani*.[80] We were driven back, but were unable to set the sails, not even the *trinquetla* (stormsail). The tempest raged with increasing fury. As compared to these awful tempests the foul weather in the western seas is mere child's play, and their towering billows are as drops of water compared to those of the Indian sea. Night and day were both alike, and because of the frailty of our craft all ballast had to be thrown overboard. In this frightful predicament our only consolation was our unwavering trust in the power of the Almighty. For ten days the storm raged continuously and the rain came down in torrents. We never once saw the blue sky.

I did all I could to encourage and cheer my companions, and advised them above all things to be brave, and never to doubt but that all would end well. A welcome diversion occurred in the appearance of a fish about the size of two galley lengths, or more perhaps, which the pilot declared to be a good omen.

The tide being very strong here and the ebb slow, we had an opportunity of seeing many sea-monsters in the neighborhood of the bay of Djugd, sea-horses, large sea-serpents, turtles in great quantities, and eels.

The color of the water suddenly changed to pure white, and at sight of it the pilot broke forth into loud lamentations; he declared we were approaching whirlpools and eddies. These are no myth here; it is generally believed that they are only found on the coasts of Abyssinia and in the neighborhood of Sind in the bay of Djugd, and hardly ever a ship has been known to escape their fury. So, at least, we are told in nautical books. We took frequent soundings, and when we struck a depth of five Kuladj (arm-lengths) the mizzensails (*Orta Yelken*) were set, the bowspreat[81] ... and ... heeling over to the left side, and flying the commander's flag, we drifted about all night and all day until at last, in God's mercy, the water rose, the storm somewhat abated, and the ship veered right round.

The next morning we slackened speed and drew in the sails. A stalwart cabin boy (or sailor) was tied to the *Djondu*, whereby the post at the foot of the mizzenmast was weighted down, and the sailrope slightly raised. Taking a survey of our surroundings we caught sight of an idol-temple on the coast of Djamber. The sails were drawn in a little more; we passed Formyan and Menglir,[82] and directing our course toward Somenat,[83] we passed by that place also. Finally we came to Div,[84] but for fear of the unbelievers which dwell there we further drew in our sails and continued on our course with *serderma*.

Meanwhile, the wind had risen again, and as the men had no control over the rudder, large handles had to be affixed with long double ropes fastened to them. Each rope was taken hold of by four men, and so with great exertion they managed to control the rudder.

No one could keep on his feet on deck, so of course it was impossible to walk across. The noise of the ... and the ... was deafening; we could not hear our own voices. The only means of communication with the sailors was by inarticulate words, and neither captain nor boatswain could for a single instant leave his post. The ammunition was secured in the storeroom, and after cutting the ... from the ... we continued our way.

It was truly a terrible day, but at last we reached Gujarat in India, which part of it, however, we knew not, when the pilot suddenly exclaimed: "On your guard! a whirlpool in front!" Quickly the anchors were lowered, but the ship was dragged down with great force and nearly submerged. The rowers had left their seats, the panic-stricken crew threw off their clothes, and, clinging some to casks and some to jacks, had taken leave of one another. I also stripped entirely, gave my slaves their liberty, and vowed to give 100 florins to the poor of Mecca.

Presently one of the anchors broke from its crook and another at the *podjuz*; two more were lost, the ship gave a terrible jerk—and in another instant we were clear of the breakers. The pilot declared that had we been wrecked off Fisht-Kidsur, a place between Diu and Daman;[85] nothing

384

could have saved us. Once more the sails were set, and we decided to make for the infidel coast; but after duly taking note of tide and current, and having made a careful study of the chart, I came to the conclusion that we could not be very far off the mainland. I consulted the horoscope in the Koran, and this also counseled patience. So we commenced to examine the hold of the ship and found that the storeroom was submerged, in some places up to the walls, in some places higher still. We had shipped much water, and all hands set to work at once to bale it out. In one or two places the bottom had to be ripped up to find the outlet so as to reduce the water.

Toward afternoon the weather had cleared a little, and we found ourselves about two miles off the port of Daman, in Gujarat in India. The other ships had already arrived, but some of the galleys were waterlogged not far from the shore, and they had thrown overboard oars, boats, and casks, all of which wreckage eventually was borne ashore by the rapidly rising tide. We were obliged to lie to for another five days and five nights, exposed to a strong spring-tide, accompanied by floods of rain; for we were now in the Badzad,[86] or rainy season of India, and there was nothing for it but to submit to our fate. During all this time we never once saw the sun by day, nor the stars by night; we could neither use our clock nor our compass, and all on board anticipated the worst. It seems a miracle that of the three ships lying there, thrown on their sides, the whole crew eventually got safely to land.

VI
WHAT HAPPENED IN THE PROVINCE OF GUJARAT

After five days, in God's mercy, the wind somewhat abated. All that was saved of the wreckage, cannon and other armament we left with the Governor of Daman, Malik

Esed, who, since the time of Sultan Ahmed, the ruler of Gujarat, had held office there. In the harbor were some *Djonk's*[87] i.e., monsoon ships belonging to Samiri, the ruler of Calcutta. The captains came on board our ship and assured us of the devotion of their chief to the Padishah. They brought us a letter which said that Samiri was waging war day and night against the Portuguese infidels, and that he was expecting the arrival of an Imperial fleet from Egypt under the guidance of the pilot Ali, which was to put the Portuguese to flight. Malik Esed, the Governor, gave me to understand that the fleet of the infidels was on its way, that it behooved us to avoid it and, if possible, to reach the fortress of Surat. This news frightened the crew. Some of them immediately took service under Melik Esed, and some went ashore in the boats and proceeded by land to Surat.

I remained on board with a few faithful of the men, and after procuring a *Dindjuy,*[88] or pilot-boat, for each vessel, we set out for the harbor of Surat. After great difficulties we reached the open. Presently the Kutwal,[89] Aga Hamsa, hailed us with a letter from Umad-el-mulk, the Grand Vizier of Sultan Ahmed, who informed us that there were large numbers of infidels about, and that Daman being a free port we had better be careful. He would allow us to come to Surat if we liked, as we were now in most perilous waters. This was exactly what we wanted to do, so we struggled on for five days longer, sailing at the flow, riding at anchor at the ebb of the tide, until at last we reached the harbor of Surat, fully three months after our departure from Basrah.

Great was the joy of the Mohammedans at Surat when they saw us come; they hailed us as their deliverers (*Khidr*), and said: "You have come to Gujarat in troublous times; never since the days of Noah has there been a flood like unto this last, but neither is it within the memory of man

386

that a ship from Rum (Turkey) has landed on these coasts. We fervently hoped that God in his mercy would soon send an Ottoman fleet to Gujarat, to save this land for the Ottoman Empire and to deliver us from the Indian unbelievers."

The cause of the disturbances was this: After the death of Sultan Bahadur, the ruler of Gujarat, one of his relatives, a youth of twelve years old, had succeeded to the throne. The army had acknowledged him, but one of the nobles, Nasir-ul-Mulk, had refused to take the oath of allegiance, and had raised the banner of sovereignty on his own behalf.[90] He had many adherents, took the stronghold of Burudj,[91] left a sufficient garrison to keep it, proceeded himself to another town, and then called in the aid of the Governor of the infidels (Portuguese) at Goa, promising that in return for his services the harbors on the coast of Gujarat, viz., Daman, Surat, Burudj, Ketbaye, Sumenat, Minghir, and Furmcyan, should be thrown open to the Portuguese, while he would retire to the land of the interior.

Sultan Ahmed had immediately collected an army to go to Burudj, and when informed of our arrival he took from our troops 200 gunners and other men, and advanced toward Burudj.

On the third day we who were left behind were attacked by the infidel captains of Goa, Diu, Shiyul, Besai, and the Provador;[92] five in all, commanding 7 large galleons and 80 gurabs. We went ashore, pitched our tents, and threw up entrenchments; for two whole months we were busy preparing for battle. But the tyrant Nasir-ul-Mulk, who had joined with the infidels, had hired murderers to kill me; they were, however, discovered by the guard and fled. Again another time he tried to poison my food, but, being warned by the Kutwal of Surat, this attempt to take my life also

387

failed. Meanwhile Sultan Ahmed had taken the stronghold of Burudj and sent two of his officers, Khudavend and Djihanghir, with elephants and troops to Surat, while he proceeded to Ahmedabad, where a youth, called Ahmed, a relation of Sultan Ahmed, had in the meantime raised a revolt. A battle followed, in which the usurper was wounded, Hasan Khan, one of his adherents, killed, and his army put to flight. Sultan Ahmed reascended his throne, and, as Nasir-ul-Mulk died of vexation over his misfortunes, peace was once more restored in Gujarat.

When the infidels heard of this they sent an envoy to Khudavend Khan to say that they did not mind so much about Surat, but that their hostility was chiefly directed toward the Admiral of Egypt, *viz.*, my humble person. They demanded that I should be given up to them, but were refused; and my soldiers would have killed the envoy, but I reminded them that we were on foreign soil and must commit no rash deeds.

It so happened that a runaway infidel gunner from one of my ships had enlisted on the ship of the envoy, and, knowing a good deal about our affairs, he had undertaken to prevent our departure after the holiday of Kurban. No sooner had this come to the knowledge of my men, than they attacked the envoy's ship and captured the infidel, who was executed on the spot, greatly to the alarm of the envoy.

There is in Gujarat a tree of the palm tribe, called *tari agadji* (millet-tree). From its branches cups are suspended, and when the cut end of a branch is placed into one of these vessels a sweet liquid, something of the nature of arrack, flows out in a continuous stream; and this fluid, by exposure to the heat of the sun, presently changes into a most wonderful wine. Therefore at the foot of all such trees drinking-booths have been placed, which are a great attraction to the soldiers.

Some of my men, having indulged in the forbidden drink, determined to kill their Serdar. One of these profligates, Yagmur by name, one evening after sunset surprised Hussain Aga, the Serdar of the Circassians. A few comrades rushed to his assistance, there was some fighting and two young men were wounded, and one, Hadji Memi, was killed. Then the soldiers pressed round, and implored me to punish the evil-doers, but I again reminded them that we were on foreign soil, in the land of a foreign Padishah, and that our laws had no force here. "What," they cried, "the laws of our Padishah hold good everywhere. You are our Admiral, judge according to our law, and we will be the executioners!" Thereupon I pronounced judgment according to the law of the Koran, which says: "Eye for eye, life for life, nose for nose, ear for ear," etc.

The man was executed, and peace restored. When the nobles of the Begs heard of the occurrence they took the lesson to heart, and the envoy immediately hired a conveyance and went to Sultan Ahmed.

But my troops were getting dissatisfied. In Surat, Khudavend Khan had been paying them from 50 to 60 paras per day, and in Burudj, Adil Khan had done the same. At last their pent-up feelings burst forth and they argued as follows: "It is now nearly two years since we have received any pay, our goods are lost, and the ships dismantled; the hulks are old, and our return to Egypt is practically made impossible." The end was that the greater part of them took service in Gujarat.

The deserted ships, with all their tools and implements, were given over to Khudavend Khan, under condition that he should immediately remit to the Sublime Porte the price agreed upon for the sale.

After receiving a confirmatory note to this effect, both from Khudavend Khan and Adil Khan, I started on my journey to Ahmedabad[93] in the beginning of Muharram of the year 962 (end of November 1552), accompanied by Mustafa Aga, the Ketkhuda (chief officer) of the Egyptian Janissaries, and Ali Aga, the captain of the gunners (both of which had remained faithful to their Padishah), and with about 50 men.

A few days took us from Burudj to Belodra,[94] and from there we proceeded to Champanir.[95]

On our way we saw some very curious trees, whose crowns reached up to the sky, and the branches swarmed with bats of such extraordinary size that their wings on the stretch measured 40 inches across. The most curious part about the trees, however, was that the roots hung down from the branches and, when touching the ground, planted themselves and produced new trees. Thus from one tree, from ten to twenty new ones sprung up. The name of this tree is the Tobi tree,[96] and more than a thousand people can find shelter under its shade. Besides these we saw several *Zokum* trees.[97] Parrots were very plentiful, and as for the monkeys, thousands of them made their appearance in our camp every evening. They carried their young in their arms, made the most ridiculous grimaces, and strongly brought to our minds the stories of Djihan Shah, according to whom these animals live in a community but acknowledge no head among them. At nightfall they always retired to their own place.

After a great many vicissitudes we at last arrived in Mahmudabad,[98] and after a journey of 50 days in Ahmedabad the capital of Gujarat. There I visited the Sultan, his Grand Vizier Imad-ul-Mulk, and other dignitaries. The Sultan, to whom I presented my credentials,

390

was pleased to receive me most graciously and he assured me of his devotion to our glorious Padishah. He gave me a horse, a team of camels,[99] and money for the journey.

At Cherkes, in the vicinity of Ahmedabad, is the grave of Sheik Ahmed Magrebi, which I visited. One day, being at the house of Imad-ul-Mulk, I met the infidel envoy, and our host addressed him in this way, "We have need of the Sultan of Turkey. Our ships touch the ports of his Empire, and if we were not free to do so, it would be bad for us. Moreover, he is the Padishah of the Islamitic world, and it is not seemly that we should be expected to deliver up his Admiral to you." I became very angry at this speech and cried: "Hold, thou cursed tongue! Thou foundest me with a shattered fleet, but I swear by God Almighty thou shalt see ere long not only Ormuz, but Goa itself, yield before the victorious arms of the great Padishah!"[100] To which the unbeliever made the following answer: "Henceforth not so much as a bird will be able to leave the ports of India." I replied: "One need not necessarily go by water, there is a land route also." He was silent after that, and the subject was dropped.

A few days after this Sultan Ahmed offered me the command of the Province of Burudj, with a very large income, but I refused, saying that I would not stay if he gave me the whole of the land. One night in my dream I saw the Khalifa Murteza Ali. I had a piece of paper before me with Ali's seal upon it. With this seal, the seal of God to help me, away with all fear, for in its strength all foreign waters were mine to command.

Next morning I told my dream to my companions and all were glad with me. I asked for permission to depart, and the ruler granted my request out of respect for our Padishah.

Amongst the learned[101] of this land of Banians[102] there is a tribe which they call the "Bats," whose business it is to escort merchants or travelers from one land into another, and for a very small remuneration they guarantee their perfect safety. Should the Rajputs,[103] *i.e.,* the mounted troops of the land, attack the caravan, the Bats point their daggers at their own breast, and threaten to kill themselves if they should presume to do the slightest harm to the travelers entrusted to their care. And out of respect for the Bats, the Rajputs generally desist from their evil purpose, and the travelers proceed on their way unmolested. Occasionally, however, the Bats carry out their threat, otherwise it would have no force. But if such a thing does happen, if a caravan is attacked and the suicide of the Bats becomes necessary, this is considered a terrible calamity, and the superstition of the people demands that the offenders be put to death, and not only the offenders themselves but the chief of the Rajputs deems it necessary to kill their sons and daughters also; in fact, to exterminate the whole of their race. The Mohammedans of Ahmedabad had given us two such Bats as an escort, and so, about the middle of Safar of the said year, we started on our overland journey to Turkey.

In five days we reached Patna,[104] traveling in carriages, and visited the grave of Sheik Nizam the *Pir* (spiritual chief) of Patna. Here Shir Khan and his brother Musa Khan had collected an army, to fight Behluj Khan, the ruler of Radanpoor.[105] For fear of our siding with their enemies, the people tried to retain us, and would not allow us to proceed on our journey until the battle should be over. We showed them, however, that we had not come to render either party any assistance, but that we only wanted to continue our journey in peace, and had a pass from their ruler to that effect. Then at last they let us go, and after five days we came to Radanpoor, where I was presented to Mahmud Khan, but he treated me very rudely, and insisted on forcibly detaining three of my companions before he would consent to our departure.

On the way we met some friendly Rajputs; their Beg was of great service to us, and gave me a letter of protection (free pass). The camels were hired, and after dismissing the Bats which the people of Ahmedabad had sent with us, we continued our journey.

VII
WHAT BEFELL US IN THE PROVINCE OF SIND

Leaving on the first of Rebiul-Evvel we came, after a ten days' journey, to Parker,[106] a town of the Rajputs. Here we were surprised by the infidels, but thanks to the letter of protection and a few presents, we were let free; quite anticipating further dangers, however, we were on our guard when next day a band of hostile Rajputs commenced a free fight with us. Immediately I ordered all the camels to be let down on their knees so as to form a ring round us, and then the firing began on all sides. The infidels, not prepared for this, sent us word that "they had not come to fight, but to exact the passage money," to which I made reply: "We are not merchants and carry nothing but medicines and Mohurs[107] on which we have already paid duty; but if there be anything further to pay we are quite prepared to do so." This had the desired effect; they let us pass, and for about ten days we wandered through deserts and sandy places, until we reached Wanga,[108] the frontier town of Sind. Here we hired fresh camels, and in five days we came to Djoona[109] and Baghi-Feth. The throne of Sind was then occupied by Shah Husein Mirza. He had reigned for 40 years, but during the last 5 years he had become invalided and unable to mount his horse, so now he only went about on board his ship in the river Sihun.[110]

At that time Isa Terkhan, the commander of the capital of Sind, called Tata,[111] had put to death a number of able officers belonging to Shah Husein, after which he had captured the treasure, stored in the fortress of Nasrabad, and divided it amongst his men, and then proclaimed himself as Humayun Shah. (It says literally that he had this title inserted in the Friday-prayers and ordered the *Nakara*[112] to be played.) Thereupon Shah Husein had nominated his adopted brother Sultan Mahmud as commander of the land troops, and he himself with 400 ships had set out against the rebels. Hearing of my arrival he received me with great honor. It was then the beginning of the month of Rabia-al-Sani. He gave me festive apparel[113] and conferred upon us the title of a God-sent army;[114] he offered me, besides all this, the governorship of Bender-Lahuri or Duyuli-Sindi. Of course I refused this offer, but when I requested permission to continue my journey I was given to understand that I should not be allowed to do so until after the successful termination of the campaign. He also wrote a letter to our glorious Padishah, explaining matters; in a word he did not rest until he had quite cleared us from being mixed up in this war with Isa Khan. The Mohammedans pleaded in vain that our arms could bring no evil upon them,[115] for, said they, "Are we not all of one nation, and are not many of our sons and brethren in the rebel army?" And this was perfectly true. I had an interview with Sheik Abdul Vahab and received his blessing; I also visited the graves of the Sheiks Djemali and Miri.

The campaign lasted a month, earthworks were thrown up and cannon raised thereon, but as Tata lies on an island and their shot did not reach so far, the fortress could not be taken. Nevertheless there was great loss of life on both sides. At last a compromise was decided upon. Mir Isa relinquished his adherence to Humayun Padishah, returned

394

to his allegiance to Husein Mirza, and sent his son Mir Salih with presents of submission. On the other hand, Husein Mirza gave the remainder of the treasure, which Mir Isa had divided amongst his troops, to Mir Salih. Isa was reinstated in his former rank, and Mirza sent him a formal acceptance of his allegiance by the hand of the Vizier Molla Yari. He also sent him a Nakara by Tugbeghi, the chief standard-bearer, and released from prison the ten rebels from the tribes of Argun and Tarkhan,[116] which had sided with Mir Isa, from his side, had sent back the wife of Husein Shah, called Hadji Begum, and in the first days of Djemadi-ul-evvel, Sultan Mahmud returned by land, and Shah Husein by water, to the city of Bakar. On the tenth day after his wife had rejoined him, Shah Husein died, and it was supposed that she had poisoned him.

Directly after his father's death, Sultan Mahmud divided the property in three parts. One part was for the wife of the deceased, and another part he sent to Mir Isa by a Khodja. The body was taken to Tata; he lent me one of his own ships, and providing himself with horses, camels, and other necessaries, returned by land to Bakar. While the body of Mirza, with his wife and an escort of 50 ships, was on its way to Tata, the soldiers attacked the remaining vessels and plundered them. The sailors took flight, and we, the passengers, were compelled to take command of the ships. Beset on all sides by the Djagatais (Central Asians), we relinquished our firearms, and barely escaped with our lives. At last, after struggling for ten days against the stream, we made our way to Nasirpur.[117] This town had been plundered by the Rajah, i.e., the Bey of the Rajputs.

We were greeted with the news that Mir Isa, with 10,000 valiant soldiers, was pursuing Sultan Mahmud, and that his son, Mir Salih, with 80 ships, was close behind us. This was very perplexing but I decided at once to turn back. We prayed long together, and then started on our return to Tata. Three days later we passed Mir Salih in the river. I went on board his ship with a few small presents, and he asked me where we were going. I said, "We are going to your father," whereupon he told me to go back with him. I said, "We have no sailors on board," so he gave me fifteen of his crew; and thus compelled to turn back, we had another weary ten days to get through. One day I chanced upon Mir Isa in a small town of Sind. Here I also found the former partizans of the late Mirza, who were tired of fighting and desired peace. Isa received me with great honor, forgave me the past, and allowed me to remain a few days, saying that he intended shortly to send his son Mir Salih to Humayun Padishah, and that I might as well travel under his escort, for, he added, "Sultan Mahmud will never allow thee to pass Bakar; he is a son of Ferrukh Mirza and wants to become Padishah." This proposal, however, did not suit me, and I insisted upon continuing my journey forthwith, suggesting that he should give us back the ships lately taken from us, and also to send a messenger in advance, for with God's help he, Sultan Mahmud, would probably have to submit to the Padishah (Humayun), and thus peace be restored. Isa agreed to this, and gave me seven ships with their complement of sailors. He wrote to the Padishah to assure him of his unalterable loyalty, and so we went on our way. We were struck with the enormous size of the fish (alligators) sporting in the river, as also with the numbers of tigers on the banks. It was necessary to keep up a perpetual warfare with the people of Semtche and Matchi, through whose territory our course lay, and thus we reached Siyawan,[118] and shortly after we came to Bukkur by the way of Patri[119] and Dible. Here I fell in with Sultan Mahmud and his Vizier Molla Yari. I offered a small gift to the former, who thereupon expressed his willingness to submit himself to Humayun, and also to make peace with

Mir Isa.

I composed a chronogram on the death of Husein Mirza and presented Sultan Mahmud with two gazels,[120] after which I requested permission to continue my journey. This was granted, but as the route past Kandahar was made unsafe by the inroads[121] of Sultan Bahadur, a son of Sultan Haidar, the Ozbeg, and as the season of the Semum (hot winds) had now commenced, the Sultan offered to give me an escort by the way of Lahore, warning me to be on my guard against the Djats, a hostile tribe which had its abode there. But whichever route I chose I should have to wait a while yet, and as a matter of fact I waited for a whole month. One night in my dream I saw my mother, who told me that she had seen her highness Fatima in a dream, and had learned from her the glad news, that I should soon be coming home, safe and sound.

When next morning I told this dream to my companions they were full of good courage. Sultan Mahmud, when he heard of it, at once consented to my departure. He gave me a beautiful horse, a team of camels, a large and a small tent,[122] and money for the journey. He also provided me with a letter of recommendation to Humayun, and an escort of 250 mounted camel-drivers, from Sind. Thus we departed about the middle of Shaaban, and reached the fortress of May in five days, traveling by the way of Sultanpoor.[123] As the Djats were very troublesome, we did not take the route of Djenghelistan (the forest), but preferred to go through the steppe. On the second day we came to the spring, but found no water, and many of my companions nearly succumbed with heat and thirst. I gave them some *Teriak* (opium), of the very best quality, and on the second day they were recovered. After this experience we deemed it advisable to leave the desert and to return to May, for the proverb says truly, "A stranger is an ignorant man." In the steppe we saw ants as large as sparrows.

Our escort from Sind was afraid of the wood, and I had to inspire my own people with fresh courage. I placed 10 gunners in front, 10 in the center, and 10 in the rear of our caravan, and thus, trusting in God's protection, we commenced the journey. The people from Sind also took courage after this, and went with us.

Thus, after manifold dangers, we came after ten days to Utchi,[124] or Autchi, where I visited Sheik Ibrahim and received his blessing. I also made a pilgrimage to the graves of the Sheiks Djemali and Djelali. In the beginning of Ramazan we resumed our journey and came to the river Kara, or Kere,[125] which we crossed by means of a raft. The people of Sind gave us permission to proceed as far as the Machvara,[126] and this river was crossed by boats. On the other side we found 500 Djats awaiting us, but our firearms frightened them and they did not attack. We advanced unmolested, and reached the town of Multan on the fifteenth of Ramazan.

VIII
MY EXPERIENCES IN HINDUSTAN

In Multan I only visited the graves of the Sheiks Baha Bahaeddin, Zekeria, Rukneddin, and Sadreddin. I received a blessing from Sheik Mohammed Radjva, and, after receiving permission to continue my journey from Sultan Mirmiram Mirza Hasan, we proceeded toward Lahore. In Sadkere I visited Sheik Hamid, received his blessing, and in the first days of the Month Shawwal we came to Lahore. The political state of the country was as follows: After the death of Selim Shah a son of Shir Khan, the former Sovereign of Hindustan, Iskender Khan, had come to the throne. When the Padishah Humayun heard this he immediately left Kabul and marched his army to India, took Lahore, and fought Iskender Khan near Sahrand. He won the battle and took 400 elephants, besides several cannon and 400 chariots. Iskender Khan escaped to the fortress of Mankut, and Humayun sent Shah Abul-Maali with a detachment of soldiers after him. Humayun himself proceeded to his residence at Delhi and dispatched his officers to different places. The Ozbeg, Iskender Khan, he sent to Agra, and others to Firuzshah Senbel,[127] Bayana, and Karwitch. War raged on all sides, and when I arrived at Lahore the Governor, Mirza Shah, would not let me continue my journey until I had seen the Padishah (Humayun). After sending the latter word of my arrival, he received orders to send me forthwith to Delhi. Meanwhile a whole month had been wasted, but finally we were sent off with an escort. The river Sultanpoor was crossed in boats and after a journey of 20 days we arrived, toward the end of Dulkaada, by the route of Firuzshah[128] in the capital of India, called Delhi. As soon as Humayun heard of our arrival he sent the Khanikhanan[129] and other superior officers with 400 elephants and some thousand men to meet us, and, out of respect and regard for our glorious Padishah, we were accorded a brilliant reception. That same day the Khanikhanan prepared a great banquet in our honor; and as it is the custom in India to give audience in the evening, I was that night introduced with much pomp and ceremony into the Imperial hall. After my presentation I offered the Emperor a small gift, and a chronogram upon the conquest of India, also two gazels, all of which pleased the Padishah greatly. Forthwith I begged for permission to continue my journey, but this was not granted. Instead of that I was offered a *Kulur*[130] and the governorship over the district of Kharcha. I refused, and again begged to be allowed to go,

399

but for only answer I was told that I must at least remain for one year, to which I replied: "By special command of my glorious Padishah I went by sea to fight the miserable unbelievers. Caught in a terrible hurricane, I was wrecked off the coast of India; but it is now my plain duty to return to render an account to my Padishah, and it is to be hoped that Gujarat will soon be delivered out of the hands of the Unbelievers." Upon this Humayun suggested the sending of an envoy to Constantinople, to save my going, but this I could not agree to, for it would give the impression that I had purposely arranged it so. I persisted in my entreaties, and he finally consented, adding, however: "We are now close upon the three months of continuous *Birshegal*,[131] (*i.e.*, the rainy season). The roads are flooded[132] and impassable, remain therefore till the weather improves. Meanwhile calculate solar and lunar eclipses, their degree of latitude, and their exact date in the calendar. Assist our astrologers in studying the course of the sun, and instruct us concerning the points of the equator. When all this is done, and the weather should improve before the three months are over, then thou shalt go hence."

All this was said solemnly and decisively. I had no alternative, but must submit to my fate. I took no rest, however, but labored on night and day. At last I had accomplished the astronomical observations, and about the same time Agra fell into the hands of the Padishah. I immediately wrote a chronogram for the occasion, which found much favor. One day, during an audience, the conversation turned upon Sultan Mahmud of Bukkur, and I suggested that some official contract (*Ahdnameh*, *i.e.*, "agreement") should be made with him, to which Humayun agreed. The document was drawn up, and the Emperor dipping his fist in saffron pressed it upon the paper, this being the *Tughra*,[133] or Imperial signature. Thereupon the document was sent to Sultan Mahmud.

The Sultan was much pleased, and both he and his Vizier Molla Yari expressed their thanks for my intervention in a private letter, which I showed to his Majesty, who had entrusted me with the transaction.

This incident furnished the material for a gazel, with which the Sovereign was so delighted that he called me a second Mir Ali Shir.[134] I modestly declined the epithet, saying that it would be presumption on my part to accept such praise, that, on the contrary, I should consider myself fully rewarded to be allowed to gather up the gleanings after him. Whereupon the Sovereign remarked: "If for one more year thou perfectest thyself in this kind of poetry thou wilt altogether supplant Mir Ali Shir in the affections of the people of the Djagatais." In a word, Humayun loaded me with marks of his favor. One day I was talking to Khoshhal, the Imperial archer, and the Sovereign's special confidant; a superb youth. He used to take part in the poetical discussions, and provided me with material for two gazels, which soon became popular all over India and were in everybody's mouth. The same good fortune attended my acquaintance with the Afetabedji,[135] Abdurrahman Bey, a courtier who also rejoiced in the confidence and affection of the monarch, and was his constant companion in private life. He also entered the poetical contest, and I composed two gazels upon him.

In a word, poetical discussions were the order of the day, and I was constantly in the presence of the Emperor. One day he asked me whether Turkey was larger than India, and I said: "If by Turkey your Majesty means Rum proper, *i.e.*, the province of Siwas,[136] then India is decidedly the larger, but if by Turkey you mean all the lands subject to the ruler of Rum, India is not by a tenth part as large." "I mean the entire Empire," replied Humayun. "Then," I said, "it appears to me, your Majesty, that the seven regions over which Iskender (*i.e.,* Alexander the Great) had dominion, were identical with the present Empire of the Padishah of Turkey. History records the life and the reign of Iskender, but it is not reasonable to suppose that he actually visited and personally ruled these seven regions, for the inhabited world (the fourth part of the present inhabited world) is 180 degrees longitude and from the equator about 60 degrees latitude. Its area, according to astronomical calculations, covers 1,668,670 *fersahhes*. It is therefore an utter impossibility for any man to visit and govern all these lands in person. Perhaps he only owned a portion of each of these regions (*Iklim*), in the same way as the Padishah of Turkey does." "But has the ruler of Turkey possessions in all these regions?" asked Humayun. "Yes, certainly," I replied, "the first is Yemen, the second Mecca, the third Egypt, the fourth Aleppo, the fifth Constantinople, the sixth Kaffa, and the seventh Ofen and Vienna.[137] In each of these regions the Padishah of Turkey appoints his Beglerbeg and Kadi, who rule and govern in his name. Moreover, I was told in Gujarat, by the merchants Khodja Bashi and Kara Hasan (God alone knows whether their story is true), that when the Turkish merchants in China desired to insert the name of their Sovereign in the Bairam prayers on Bairamday, they brought the request before the Khakan of China, stating that their Sovereign was Padishah of Mecca, Medina, and the Kibla (Direction of the prayer), and therefore entitled to have his name inserted in the Bairam prayers. The Khakan, although an unbeliever, had insight enough to see the justice of their request, which he granted forthwith; he even went so far as to clothe the Khatib[138] in a robe of honor and to make him ride on an elephant through the city. Ever since that time the name of the Padishah of Turkey has been included in the Bairam prayers, and to whom, I ask, has such honor ever before been vouchsafed?" The Sovereign (Humayun), turning to his nobles, said: "Surely the only man worthy to bear the title of Padishah is the ruler of Turkey, he alone and no one else in all the world."

Another time we were talking about the Khan of the Crimea, and I remarked that he also held his office under the Padishah of Turkey. "But," said Humayun, "if that be so, how, then, has he the right of the *Khutbe*?" "It is a well-known fact," I replied, "that my Padishah alone has the power to grant the right of *Khutbe* and of coinage." This statement seemed to satisfy everybody and we prayed together for the welfare of my Sovereign.

One day the Emperor planned a little excursion on horseback to visit the graves of the holy Sheiks of Lahore, and I accompanied him. We visited the graves of Shah Kutbeddin, the Pir of Delhi, of Sheik Nizam Weli, Sheik Ferid Shekr-Ghendj, Mir Khosru Dehlevi, and Mir Husein Dehlevi. When the conversation turned upon the poetical works of Mir Khosru I quoted some of his best poems, and under their influence I conceived a most telling distich. I turned to the Emperor, saying, "It would be presumption on my part to measure my powers against those of Mir Khosru,[139] but he has inspired me, and I would fain recite my couplet before your Majesty." "Let us hear it," said Humayun, and I recited the following:

"Truly great is only he who can be content with his daily
    bread.
For happier is he than all the kings of the earth."
"By God," cried the monarch, "this is truly sublime!"

It is not so much my object here to make mention of my
poetic effusions, but rather to show up Humayun's
appreciation of poetry.

On another occasion I called upon Shahin Bey, the keeper
of the Imperial Seal, and asked him to use his influence to
obtain permission for me to depart. In order not to come
empty-handed I brought him two gazels, and begged him
urgently to intercede for me. Shahin Bey promised to do his
best, and one day he actually brought me the glad news
that my petition had been granted, but that I was expected
to offer my request formally in verse. The rainy season was
now at an end; I wrote to the monarch, enclosing two
gazels, which had the desired effect, for I received not only
permission to leave, but also presents and letters of safe
conduct.

All was ready for the start. Humayun had given audience
on Friday evening, when, upon leaving his castle of
pleasure, the Muezzin announced the Ezan just as he was
descending the staircase. It was his wont, wherever he heard
the summons, to bow the knee in holy reverence. He did so
now, but unfortunately fell down several steps, and received
great injuries to his head and arm. Truly the proverb rightly
says, "There is no guarding against fate."

Everything was confusion in the palace, but for two days
they kept the matter secret. It was announced to the outer
world that the Sovereign was in good health, and alms were
distributed amongst the poor. On the third day, however,
that was on the Monday, he died of his wounds.[140] Well
may the Koran say, "We come from God and to him do we

return."

His son Djelaleddin Ekber was at the time away on a journey to visit Shah Ebul Maali, accompanied by the Khanikhanan.[141] He was immediately informed of the sad event. Meanwhile the Khans and Sultans were in the greatest consternation; they did not know how to act. I tried to encourage them and told them how at the death of Sultan Selim the situation was saved by the wisdom of Piri Pasha, who managed to prevent the news of his death from being noised abroad. I suggested that, by taking similar measures, they might keep the Sovereign's death a secret until the Prince should return. This advice was followed. The divan (council of State) met as usual, the nobles were summoned, and a public announcement was made that the Emperor intended to visit his country-seat, and would go there on horseback. Soon after, however, it was announced that on account of the unfavorable weather the trip had to be abandoned. On the next day a public audience was announced, but as the astrologers did not prophesy favorably for it, this also had to be given up. All this, however, somewhat alarmed the army, and on the Tuesday it was thought advisable to give them a sight of their monarch. A man called Molla Bi, who bore a striking resemblance to the late Emperor, only somewhat slighter of stature, was arrayed in the imperial robes and placed on a throne specially erected for the purpose in the large entrance hall. His face and eyes were veiled. The Chamberlain Khoshhal Bey stood behind, and the first Secretary in front of him, while many officers and dignitaries, as well as the people from the riverside, on seeing their Sovereign, made joyful obeisance to the sound of festive music. The physicians were handsomely rewarded, and the recovery of the monarch was universally credited.

I took leave of all the grandees, and with the news of the

405

Emperor's recovery I reached Lahore about the middle of the month Rebiul Evvel. This was on a Thursday. Traveling by the way of Sani-Pata, Pani-Pata, Kirnat, and Tani Sera, I came to Samani,[142] where I communicated the news to the Governor that the Padishah (Humayun) was giving audiences, and that he was in good health.[143] From there I went by the road of Sahrandi to Matchuvara[144] and Bachuvara,[145] and crossing the Sultanpoor by boat I returned to Lahore by a forced march. Meanwhile Prince Djelaleddin Ekber had ascended the throne, and in Lahore and many other places his name was inserted in the Friday prayers. Mirza Shah, the Governor of Lahore, however, would not permit me to leave, for he professed to have received orders from the new Emperor that no one was to be allowed to go to Kabul and Kandahar. The only way therefore was to go back to the Emperor (Ekber), and accordingly I went as far as Kelnor, where I met Djelaleddin Ekber and the Khanikhanan just opposite the fortress of Mankit.[146]

I was informed through Molla Pir Mehemmed,[147] the Khodja of Bairam Khan, that during the interregnum I should remain where I was, and that in a short time he would appoint me to some post either in Hind or Sind, whichever I preferred. I hastened to produce my *ferman*, given to me by the late Padishah, presenting him at the same time with a chronogram on the death of his father. My verses pleased the Mirza and, after examining the *ferman* of his father, he gave me leave to continue my journey, stipulating, however, that I should travel in company with the four Begs, which he was about to send with troops to Kabul.

Ebul Maali,[148] who meanwhile had been taken prisoner, was confined in the castle of Lahore. In return for my chronogram I received a lakh for traveling expenses, and began to prepare for my journey with the four Begs.

Amongst the many strange and wonderful things I saw in India I must make mention of a few. The unbelievers are called in Gujarat "Banian," and in India "Hindu." They do not belong to the Ehli-Kitab,[149] and believe in fate (*kademi-alem*). When a man dies his body is burned by the riverside. If the deceased leaves a wife past child-bearing she is not burned; if, however, she is not past that age she is unconditionally burned. If a wife of her own free will offers herself to be burned, the relations celebrate the occasion with great rejoicings. Should the Mohammedans interfere and forcibly prevent the self-sacrifice, fate decrees that their king must die, and no other be raised. For this reason, officers of the Padishah are always present on such occasions, to prevent any act of violence.[150]

Another curious custom is the use of tame gazelles in hunting. A noose is lightly thrown over their antlers, and then they are driven to mix with the wild gazelles. Like seeks like, and the latter soon make up to their tame companions, bringing their heads in close proximity to those of the others. The noose which is round the antlers of the tame animal falls over the head of the other and pulls it down. The more it struggles the more it gets entangled, and can not possibly escape. This method is in use all over India.

Buffaloes are very plentiful in the steppes. They are hunted with elephants. Turrets are placed on the elephant's back, in which several men are hidden. Thus they traverse the plain, and as soon as the elephant comes up with the buffalo he attacks him with his teeth and holds him till the hunters get off his back and capture him. Wild oxen (*Gaukutas*)[151] are hunted in a similar manner, but they are much stronger than other animals of their kind, and their

407

tongue is supposed to have such force that they can kill a man with it. The Emperor Humayun once told me a story to the effect that one of these wild oxen, having overtaken a man, flayed him with his tongue from head to foot. The Emperor vouched for the truth of this story with an oath. The best *kutas* are found in the land of Bahr-itch, perhaps that accounts for their being called *Bahri-Kutas* (which means sea-*kutas*), although they belong unquestionably to the terrestrial animals. I might go on enumerating many more interesting and curious things to be seen in India, but it would keep me too long.

About the middle of Rebiul Evvel we left for Kabul. We crossed the River Lahore in ships, and came presently to another large stream, which had to be crossed. Finding no ships at hand, we built a raft of barrels and chairs and so managed to reach the other side. Next we came to Bahara, where another river had to be crossed, this time in ships. When I told the Governor (Khodja) of this place what Ekber had commanded, he exclaimed, "God be merciful! As the Padishah was dead we have not collected the taxes, the people still owe them. I will send round, collect the moneys and hand them over to you."[152] Mir Babu's and the other Begs who were of the company consulted together and decided that as Shah Abul Maali had escaped from his prison in Lahore, and might possibly have taken refuge with his brother Kihmerd Bey in Kabul, it would not be safe for them to delay, but they suggested that I should wait till the tribute-money was collected, and follow them as soon as I could.

But I argued that the roads were unsafe and dangerous and that it would be much better to keep all together. I acted on the principle that "The contented mind shall be satisfied and the covetous man shall be humbled." So I relinquished my claim upon the tribute-money and continued my journey with the others. After crossing the rivers Khoshab[153] and Nilab[154] in ships, I set foot upon the shore of Bakhtar.[155]

OUR EXPERIENCE IN BAKHTAR-ZEMIN (KABULISTAN)

In the beginning of the month Djemaziul-Evvel we left the river Nilab and turned toward Kabul. For fear of the Afghans under Adam Khan, we made a quick march through the night, and at daybreak we arrived at the foot of the mountain. So far the Afghans had not seen us, but by the time we had reached the top there were thousands of them gathered together. We seized our guns, and with God's help managed to get out of their way, and came to the town of Pershuer, *i.e.*, Peshawur. Soon after, we crossed the Khaiber Pass, and reached Djushai. In the mountains we saw two rhinoceroses (*Kerkedans*),[156] each the size of a small elephant; they have a horn on their nose about two inches long. In Abyssinia these animals are much more plentiful.

Presently we reached Laghman,[157] and after a very toilsome journey through Hezareland,[158] we entered Kabulistan and its capital Kabul. Here I visited the two sons of Humayun, Mehemmed Hekim Mirza and Perrukk Fal Mirza; I also saw Mun'im Khan, and, after presenting the *ferman* from Humayun, I was treated with much honor. Kabul itself is a beautiful city, surrounded by mountains covered with snow, and pleasure-gardens with running brooks. Pleasure and merriment prevailed everywhere, feasting and banqueting were the order of the day. In every corner were gaily dressed, slender *Lulis*[159] enticing one with music and song to join the merry crowd; the populace, in fact, seemed to have no thought for anything but for pleasure and enjoyment.

"Who would long for houris and the Paradise whose good fortune has brought him amongst the *Lulis* of Kabul?"

We, however, had no time for such frivolities, our only aim and object was to reach home as soon as possible. Mun'im Khan remarked that the roads were snowed up, that the Hindu Kush could not possibly be passed, and that it would be far better for us to wait a few days in Kabul; but I quickly replied that men could overcome mountains, if they had the mind to do so. Thereupon the Governor commanded Mir Nezri, the Chief of the Perashi and Peshai, to accompany me, and his men were to conduct our horses and goods safely across the mountain pass. We left accordingly in the beginning of Djemazi ul Evvel and came to Karabag,[160] and from there to Tcharikar and Pervane or Mervan.

This was Nezri's native country. He collected his men, and they took us across to the other side of the mountain. It was a very difficult passage, but we accomplished it that day, and spent the night in a village at the foot of the pass.

XII
THE CONDITION OF BADAKHSHAN AND KHATLAN

Early in the month of Redjeb we came to the city of Anderab, and journeyed from there through Badakhshan to Talikan, where I had an interview with Suleiman Shah[161] and his son Ibrahim Mirza. On the day of our arrival the Mirza had met us, and received me in his pleasure-garden; I offered him some presents and a gazel. The Mirza, who understood poetry, entered into a poetical competition with me, and introduced me next day to his father, to whom I also offered gifts and a gazel. The Sovereign also showed me much attention and loaded me with signs of his favor. There was hostility between Pir Mohammed Khan, the ruler of

410

Balkh, and Borak Khan, the ruler of Transoxania, and the roads were made unsafe, the more so as Pir Mohammed's younger brother had raised a revolt in Kunduz, Kavadian, and Termed, which districts were now in great tumult. They advised me therefore to travel by the way of Badakhshan and Khatlan,[162] and both Suleiman and his son presented me with horses and garments of honor, besides giving me a letter of recommendation to Djihanghir Ali, the ruler of Khatlan, who had married his younger sister; and so I journeyed to Kishm, the capital of Badakhshan.[163] I saw the Sovereign's pleasure-garden, and Humayun's garden Duabe, and proceeded from Kalai Zafar[164] to Rustak, and from there to Bender Semti.[165] I approached Dalli, in Khatlan, from the Kashgar (eastern) side, and made a pilgrimage to the grave of Seid Ali Hamadani, and from there I went to Kulaba,[166] where I met with Djihanghir Ali Khan, and after presenting my letter of recommendation he gave me an escort of 50 men to conduct me to Charsui, where I crossed the Pul-i-Senghin[167] (stone bridge), and dismissed the men who had escorted us.

XIII

EVENTS IN TURAN (TRANSOXANIA)

On the day that I crossed the bridge I first set foot on Transoxanian soil. After a day's rest I proceeded to Bazar No (New-Market), and from there to a little place called Tchiharshembe, where I visited the grave of the Khodja Yaakub Tcharkhi. Then on to Tchaganian, *i.e.*, Hissar-i-Shadman.[168] I visited Timur Sultan, the Kagalga[169] of the Ozbeg rulers, and passed Mount Senghirdek,[170] where it always rains and a considerable stream is formed at the foot of the mountain, and I marveled at the wonderful works of God. The next station was Sehri-Sebz, *i.e.*, Kesh, where I met Hashim Sultan, who gave me permission to continue my journey to Samarkand. With great difficulty we got across the mountain[171] situated between the two last-named places; we touched the little town of Mazar, and in the beginning of Shaaban we reached Samarkand, which is a perfect paradise. Here I saw Borak Khan[172] (more correctly called Noruz Ahmed), who, in return for my humble offerings, gave me a horse and garments of honor. It was this same Borak Khan to whom his Majesty the Padishah had sent cannon and guns by the hand of Sheiks Abdullatif and Dadash. At the time of my arrival Abdullatif Khan, the rider of Samarkand, was dead,[173] and Borak had taken his place. Pir Mohammed Khan, in Balkh, and Burhan Seid Khan,[174] in Bokhara, declared their independence, and Borak's first business was to settle this matter. He began by taking Samarkand and proceeded to Shehri-Sebz, where a great battle was fought, in which the Ketkhuda (overseer) of the Osman soldiers fell. He then took the stronghold and marched to Bokhara, which place he laid siege to. Seid Burhan, the ruler of Bokhara, made peace with Borak, relinquished the place to him, and retired to Karakul, where the brother of Pir Mohammed Khan then reigned. He, however, gave up the place to Seid Burhan. When Borak Khan entered Samarkand, the Aga of the Osmans[175] had just started with a few men on their way to Turkey, having taken the way of Tashkend and Turkestan. Ahmed Tchaush was also on the point of returning to Turkey by the way of Bokhara and Kharezm, for part of the Janissaries had enlisted under Seid Burhan, and the remainder joined his son. About 150 remained faithful to Borak Khan. When he had communicated all this to me, he added: "I am now as a liar before his Majesty the Sultan of Turkey, for I can do nothing, but if thou wilt help me, something may yet be done." He offered me the government of a Province, but I said that with such a small army nothing could be done, moreover that, without the consent of my Padishah, I could not stir in the matter. He thereupon proposed to send an envoy to the Sublime Porte to explain the situation. As a matter of fact he had already decided to send Sadr Alem, a descendant of Khodja Ahmed Jesewi,[176] and gave him a letter, in which he expressed his willingness in the future to satisfy every wish of the Sultan. He discharged me, however. During my stay in Samarkand I made a pilgrimage to the grave of the prophet Daniel, to the place of the Khidr (Elias), to the cloak and to the wooden shoes of the Prophet, and also to the Koran, written by Ali himself.[177] Besides these places I visited the graves of the following sheiks and sages: the author of Hidayet, Ebu Mansur Matridi; Shah-Zinde, Khodja Abdullah, Khodja Abdi-birun, Khodja Abdi-derum, the Tchopanata, and the Kazizade of Rum, and the grave of the 444,000 Transoxanian sages.

But to return to Borak Khan. One day, while talking together, he asked me which of all the cities I had visited pleased me most. I replied with the following stanza:
"Far from home no one longs for Paradise.
  For in his eyes his native town is superior even to
    Bagdad."
"Thou hast spoken well," said the Khan.

Now as regards the embassage to Constantinople, Sadr Alem proposed to go by Turkestan, but when he was told that the Nogai tribe of the Mangit committed violence upon travelers, and that the roads swarmed with robbers and highwaymen, who gave no quarter to Mussulmans,[178] but plundered and ill-treated any that came in their way, he decided to travel through Bokhara.

Unfortunately, just then the news came that Seid Burhan had again declared war with Borak Khan, and that the latter's son Kharezm Shah had been attacked. Borak Khan

413

advised me thereupon to remain at Ghidjduvan until the return of the envoy. If no hostilities took place we might travel by that way, but otherwise we were to wait until he sent some one to conduct us safely through Bokhara. To this I agreed. On the fifth of Ramazan we started, touched Kala and Kermineh, crossed the river of Samarkand[179] at Duabe, and so arrived at Ghidjduvan,[180] where I visited the grave of Khodja Abdul Khalik.

As the Mirza was not here, and no news concerning him could be obtained, we went on to Pul Rabat. Meanwhile the troops of Prince Kharezm Shah had prepared for battle. Suddenly Khan Ali Bey, the Prince's tutor, accosted us with the question whither we were going. When I replied: "To Bokhara," he said: "Seid Burhan, the ruler of Bokhara, threatens to attack Prince Kharezm Shah, and we pray thee to help us." "How now!" I cried, "we help no man; Borak Khan has not requested us to do so; on the contrary, he has charged us to go to Ghidjduvan, and there to await the return of the envoy." So we continued on our way. As we approached Minar (Spire) about 100 redcoats (*Ala tehapan*)[181] rushed down upon us, crying: "In the name of the Mirza, turn back," and at the same time they struck one of my companions. Immediately we prepared to fight, when a Seid sprang forward and commanded the Ozbegs to stop. Both sides held back, and the Seid announced that the Mirza sent us greeting and desired us not to proceed any farther, but to look on from a distance. So we were compelled to turn back. With ten of my companions I had an interview with the Mirza, who renewed his request that we should help him; but I refused again, whereupon ten guns were forcibly taken from us and we were commanded to remain mere spectators. The Prince's bearing was very haughty before he had sighted the enemy, for as the proverb says:

"Our own fist is always of iron,

Until we receive the first box on the ear."

But no sooner had Seid Burhan appeared in sight, from the opposite direction, than the Prince retreated across the bridge to the Rabat (Karvanserai). I went on with six companions, which I left behind me in the court of the kiosk. Seid Burhan advanced with 1,000 Kizil-Ayaks,[182] *i.e.,* young men from Bokhara, and 40 Turkish archers, therefore well equipped for war. In a moment he defeated the Prince, who, being wounded by a bullet, took flight, leaving his colors, musical and other military instruments behind him on the battle-field. Of my three companions which fled with the Prince, one was wounded by a lance and died soon after, and while the others retreated with the Ozbegs into the Rabat where they were attacked by Seid Burhan, I went on to meet the army to inquire after the Mirza, leaving my horse in charge of two men. I heard that he was quartered close to the Rabat, and asked to be conducted into his presence, and just as I was crossing the bridge, attended by a few men, some villain wounded me with an arrow. This was the signal for a general attack; swords were raised on all sides, and I was very near losing my life.

Fortunately the attack had been witnessed by the Osmans serving under the Khan; they had recognized me and came to my rescue, calling out: "This man is the guest of our Prince, what then is the meaning of this?" The Ozbeghi (commander of 10 men) immediately stopped the attack and apprized the Khan of what had taken place, whereupon the latter, a glorious youth, hastened to me, embraced me, and begged my forgiveness, for it was by accident, he said, that I had become mixed up in the battle and I had been attacked on the principle of the proverb which says: "Wet and dry burn together." He commissioned two officers to conduct us over the bridge, during which transport two more of my people were attacked and received sword wounds. I lost on this occasion a beautiful led-horse, all my cooking apparatus, one pack-horse, and 10 saddle-horses, which were stolen by the soldiers. With much difficulty I got across the bridge, and, while I was resting at a little distance, the Khan, to please me, ordered the Turkish soldiers stationed in the Rabat to hand the place over to me, as we were innocent and free from all reproach. As I approached the place I called out: "Stop fighting; I am here, and the Khan will pardon you for my sake." Thus the Rabat fell into my hands and with it some of the lost horses, but many of the firearms were irrevocably lost. My two men, who had been taken prisoner in the fight, had escaped, and so we proceeded to the town, which we reached that night. Seid Burhan spoke thus to me: "Be thou my guide in this and in the next world; this land shall henceforth belong to thy Padishah, thou shalt rule in Bokhara and I will retire to Karakol." "Not so," was my reply, "if thou gavedst me the whole land of Transoxania I could not stay here. Know, O Khan! that I shall report before the Sublime Porte the injustice which has been done to thee, and my glorious Padishah will be gracious unto thee, and possibly the government of these provinces will be entrusted to thy care." These words pleased the Khan; he gave a banquet in my honor and showed me much kindness, and during the fortnight which I spent in Bokhara he visited me every day in the pleasure-garden which served as my residence. I composed a gazel in his honor, which highly delighted him and led to many poetical discussions. When at last I desired permission to continue my journey, he demanded of me that I should give him our iron guns in exchange for his brass ones. He pressed me so hard that I was compelled to give in, and received 40 brass muskets in return for all the iron ones which we had left. I also had to exchange my led-horse for a gelding, besides giving him two precious books.

Meanwhile the envoy from Borak Khan had arrived, who apologized to me for his son (Kharezm Shah), and made peace with Seid Burhan through the mediation of the Ghidjduvani Abdul Sultan. Thus peace and security were once more restored.

I delayed in Bokhara to make pilgrimages to the graves of Bahaeddin Nakishbendi, Kazi Khan, Tchar Bekir, Khodja Ebn Hifz Kebir, Sadr esh Sheriat, Tadj esh Sheriat, Seid Mir Kelal (the spiritual head of Baha-eddin), Sultan Ismail the Samanide, Eyub and Sarakhsi, and after that I journeyed to Kharezm.

Our way led first to Karakol, then to Farab, where we crossed the Oxus in ships, and early in the month Shavval I touched Iranian soil, namely Khorassan. The first town I stopped at was Tchardjui,[183] where I visited the grave of Khodja Meshed, a brother of Imam Ali Musa.[184] Then we took the road through the wilderness[185] to Kharezm. By day and by night we had to wage war against lions;[186] it was not safe for one man to go alone to draw water; but at last, after ten days of unutterable weariness, we reached Hezaresp,[187] and from there in five days, Khiva, where I visited the grave of Pehlevan Mahmud Pir.

XIV

OUR EXPERIENCES IN KHAREZM AND DESHTI-KIPCHAK

Toward the end of Shavval we left Khiva, and in five days we came to Kharezm, where I made the acquaintance of Dost Mohammed Khan and his brother Esh-Sultan.[188] I visited the graves of Sheik Nedjmeddin Kubera, Sheik Ali Rametin, Sheik Khalweti Yan, Imam Mohammed Bari'i, Sahib Kuduri, Djar Ullah Ulama, Molla Husein Kharezmi (the expounder of the Koran), Seid Ata, and Hekim Ata.

When it was brought to my knowledge that the holy Sheik Abdullatif had died in the city of Vezir, I could not rest until I had made a pilgrimage to his grave in company with a few friends. As this saint had been, moreover, my spiritual adviser in Sufism, I recited the whole Koran over his grave, to insure for him everlasting peace and bliss in Paradise. We also cooked a *pilaf* (a rice dish) and I prepared a chronogram in commemoration of his death.

Having received letters of commendation to the Manghit chiefs, from Hadji Mohammed Sultan, Timur Sultan, and Mahmud Sultan, the three sons of Agatai Khan, I returned to Kharezm, where Sheik Sadr Alem, the envoy of Borak Khan, had meanwhile also arrived. Our party consisted besides ourselves of the wife of Sheik Husein of Kharezm (daughter of Makhdum Aazam), the Sheik's son, and a few Moslems; we traveled in carriages. Most of the company wore clothes of sheepskin and they wanted us to do the same, for they said, the Manghit[189] are worse even than the Ozbegs, and when they see strangers they invariably take them for Russians,[190] which is synonymous to saying, they attack them. Thus we were compelled to don the outlandish garb (sheepskin), for, as I said to encourage my people: "A wise man follows the ways of the world and makes no trouble of it."

Thus equipped we started in the first days of Zilkaada. For more than a month we wandered about in the Deshti Kipchak[191] (Kirghiz steppe). It was late in the autumn, and at that time of the year not a bird, not a wild ass (*Onagre*) can be seen, for there is not a vestige of verdure, not a drop of water to be found. It was one interminable wilderness; one desert steppe. At last we came to a place called Sham, and shortly after to Saraidjik,[192] where we met some Hadjis and three of the Moslems which had been discharged at

Samarkand. These latter were quite naked, and at sight of us they cried: "Whither go ye? Astrakhan is taken by the Russians, Ahmed Tchaush has fought in battle with them, and our Aga has been plundered by the troops of Arslan Mirza. The way is blocked, be warned and go back." In vain I quoted the lines:

"We are but poor beggars, what harm can befall us?
For ten armed men can not rob one who has nothing."

The rest of the company, especially the merchants, were not of my opinion; they proposed to delay a few days in Kharezm and await events, for:

"Speed is from the devil and patience is from God."

The envoy and the other Moslems were of the same mind, and so I reluctantly retraced my steps to Kharezm. The envoy returned to Samarkand, but all the rest remained in Kharezm, and when Dost Mohammed Khan, the ruler of Khiva, inquired of me by which route I now proposed to travel, I replied, "I will go by the way of Meshhed in Khorassan to Irak Adjemi, and from there to Bagdad." Thereupon the Khan said: "Remain here with us. In the spring the Manghits seek their pastures, possibly the Russians may also quit the land by that time, and, remember, the way to Bagdad is long."

But I could not agree to this, and in support of my argument I quoted the proverb: "To the lover Bagdad is not far distant"; so at last the Khan had to give in. He agreed to my departure, gave me a beautiful horse, and to my companions he gave the carriage in which we had traveled up to here.

As regards our route my first plan was to travel by the way of the Caspian Sea and Shirvan, but my companions did not like this, because the Mussulman army which had lately broken up from Kaffa[193] had become involved in a bloody war with Abdullah Khan, who would not permit any Turks to pass that way. Next we made inquiries about the roads of Circassia, past Demir-Kapu, but we heard that the Circassians had raised a revolt. There remained therefore only the way of Khorassan and Irak, and concerning these districts we learned that the Persian King was in perfect harmony with our glorious Padishah,[194] but that the Bey of Kizilbash (the Shiite officer) would probably prevent us from obtaining admittance to the Shah. I thought to myself, "Where God does not slay, man's attempts are but futile"; moreover, "they who fear death should not venture on travels"; so after duly consulting the horoscope,[195] and having made quite sure that there was no other way open to us, I decided to travel through Persia. The camels were hired and all was ready; I went to take leave of Dost Mohammed, the ruler of Khiva, who remarked casually that it was quite impossible for us to travel with firearms through the enemy's land. Thereupon we gave half of our arms to the Khan, and the other half to his younger brother Esh Sultan. We received a letter of commendation to Ali Sultan, a brother of Tin Sultan, and being well stocked with provisions and large skins for water, and trusting in God, we started on our journey to Kharezm in the beginning of the month Zilhidje.

XV

OUR FATE IN KHORASSAN

By divine grace we got safely across the Oxus[196] and encamped on the opposite shore, awaiting the arrival of the rest of our party. While there, the wife of Sheik Husein sent me a message to say that she had a dream in which she had seen her father, the holy Makhdum Aazam, who had come from Vezir to Kharezm in company with another holy sage. Arrived in the town he had thus addressed the people, who

420

welcomed him joyfully: "Mir Sidi Ali has read the Koran over my grave in Vezir, and he has supplicated for my patronage. I have therefore come to help him and to lead him safely through Khorassan." This message filled me with joy. I struck camp next morning and the day following we arrived in Dorum;[197] we passed through, unmolested by Mahmud Sultan, and proceeded to Bagwai,[198] which place we also passed, without being hindered by Pulad Sultan, and came to Nesa.[199] Here I found Ali Sultan, former Governor of Merw, and brother of Tin Sultan, to whom I offered my letter of commendation from Esh Sultan, and was allowed free passage, for everybody in these parts is devoted to his Majesty our Padishah. Thus we came to Bawerd (Abiwerd)[200] and Tus, where I visited the graves of Imam Mohammed Hanifi and of the poet Firdusi; and on the first of Muharram of the year 964 I reached Meshhed-i-Khorassan, where I immediately made a pilgrimage to the grave of Imam Ali Musa Riza, the prince of Khorassan.

When at sea, during the great storm some time ago, I had vowed to give a *Tumen* to the Imam; now I fulfilled my vow, and paid a *Tumen* to Mutawali (the overseer of the Mosque and Mausoleum) and I also paid a *Tumen* to the Seid. In Meshhed I found Ibrahim Mirza, the son of Behram Mirza, who occupied the throne there; also Suleiman Mirza, the son of Shah, and his Vekil (representative) called Kokche Khalipha, who entertained me at a banquet.

In the course of our conversation, these gentlemen naturally wished to draw me into an argument upon the succession and sanctity of the Caliphs Ali, Ebubekr, Omar, and Osman; but I acted upon the principle that silence is the best answer to give a fool, and I was silent. They pressed me, however, and I told them the story of Khodja Nasreddin, who was once asked to read the Koran in the Mosque, to

421

which he had replied, "this is not the place." "And now," I said, "I have not come hither to argue with you, and I refuse to be questioned." It was with great difficulty that I at last rid myself of them.[201]

One of the guests, unfortunately, was a miscreant, of the name of Ghazi Bey; he gave vent to his wrath in these words: "It is not seemly to send such people as these to the Shah. How do we know that they may not kill the men we give them as an escort, and then take flight? Very possibly they belong to the Ottomans that were sent to Borak Khan, or perhaps they are the bearers of a secret correspondence, and it might be advisable to search them."

The Mirza (Ibrahim) approved of this plan, and the next morning 200 men in armor (*kurdji*) surrounded the *kervanserai* and took us prisoners. As the proverb says: "Those who can not be caught by fair means will be by foul play."

We were each of us put in charge of one of the guards; I was taken to the apartment of the Kokehe Khalipha, with my two attendants. My horses were given in another man's charge, and my other effects were entrusted to Mutawali's keeping. They made us undress, and as it was winter we suffered much from the cold. The next day the Mirza took from me all my official papers and sundry letters which I had received from different princes, and had them all put into a bag and sealed.

When my companions saw this they trembled for their lives, but I comforted them with the sayings, "He who falls through no mistake of his will not shed tears," and "Since fate has not forgotten to bring thee into this world, it will not forget to take thee out of it," and further, "Patience is the key to the final goal."

So we calmly resigned ourselves to our fate. A little later on all were put in chains, except myself; but I was strictly guarded by five men. This action of the Mirza troubled me not a little, and although I tried to make light of it, my heart was very heavy. I wrote a gazel to comfort myself, and with the inspiring thoughts suggested by it fresh in mind, I fell asleep, and being in a semiconscious state, a divine inspiration in the form of a *Murabba*[202] was vouchsafed to me, which I sent to Mutawali. This composition caused great excitement among the nobility of the place. About the same time one of the attendants of the Imam declared (whether it was true or feigned I can not say) that in his dream he had seen the Caliph Ali, who had charged him to go and set Mir Sidi Ali free. The news of this dream spread rapidly through the town and stirred up the people, whose sympathies were now all turned in my favor.

Mutawali and Seid went to the Mirza and said: "This man came on a pilgrimage to visit the shrine of the Imam. He is under a vow and desires to go to the Shah. As the Shah is on friendly terms with the Padishah of Turkey it is not right that we should in any way trouble this pilgrim now in the Ashura[203] days. If the man be a traitor, it is sure to come to light, for as the Koran says, 'A traitor is known by his countenance,' and there need be no further question of suspicion." These words of the wise man and of Seid did not lose their effect upon the Mirza. From my side I pointed out to him the unreliableness of the information upon which he had acted, and in order further to enlist his sympathies in my favor I sent him three poems, after which, partly for fear of the Shah, and partly regretting his rash deed, he gave us our liberty on the tenth of Ashura. He loaded me with presents and gave another banquet in my honor. He also restored to us our horses and our clothes; but many of my other possessions I never recovered. Four valuable books were taken, and the whole of my correspondence was conveyed by his armour-bearer, Ali Bey, and a Yassaul to the Shah in a sealed bag, the transport being effected on a barrow about the middle of Muharram of the said year. Traveling in the same caravan with us was one of the wives of the Shah and one of the wives of Behram Mirza, who were both returning from a pilgrimage to the shrine of the Imam. I made their acquaintance, and they treated us kindly. By my advice my companions comported themselves with due courtesy and modesty toward the retinue of these ladies, mindful of the saying: "The peace of two worlds depends on two things only, courtesy to friends and flattery to foes."

Arrived in Mshabur I visited the graves of Imamzade Mohammed Mahruk, and of Sheik Attar (*ferideddin*). Here I also met with Aga Kemal, the Vekil of Khorassan, who, however, did not interfere with us. In Sebzevar we met with a little hostility, but acting on the principle that "Barking dogs bite not," we soon got free from these firebrands and continued on our way.

XVI
OUR VICISSITUDES IN IRAK-ADJEM

Arrived in the Province of Irak we skirted the Demavend range, traveling from Mazendran to Bestam, where we visited the graves of Mohammed Aftah, Sheik Bayazid Bestami, and Sheik Ebulhasan Harkani. The next day we reached Damgan.

That night one of our company called Ramazan the pious, and known as *Boluk Bashi*,[204] had a dream. Bayazid Bestami with 40 Dervishes had appeared unto him and had spoken thus: "Let us pray for the safe return of Mir Sidi Ali." The Sheik, moreover, had written a passport and sealed it, "that we might not be molested by the way."—This was his dream,

424

and when I heard of it I rejoiced greatly and thanked God for his mercy vouchsafed; for this message (from the dead) virtually saved my life. After visiting the grave of Imam Djafar in Damgan, we proceeded to Semnan, where we visited the grave of Sheik Ala-ed-Dowleh Semnani. In this place they tried to draw us into sectarian controversies, but I restrained my comrades, and reminded them of the Hadis, which says: "*Ustur zahbak, zahabek in mazhabak*," i.e., "hide thy gold, thine opinions, and thy faith"; and I argued with them, saying, "Not one of you has traveled more than I have, and experience has made me wise. A wise man does not heed the words of the vulgar and the ignorant."

They saw the wisdom of my words, and acted upon my advice.

Before long we came to Rei,[205] where I made pilgrimages to the graves of Imam Abdul Azim, and of Bibi Shehrbanu, the consort of Imam Husein. Here I also met Mohammed Khudabend, a son of the Shah's, and the *Kurdji-bashi*[206] Sevindek Aga. Their presence was accounted for in this way: Some time ago the Shah had sent Ismail Mirza from Kazvin to Herat, and had now recalled him to Kazvin. The reason of this was that certain things which had happened during his rule had come to light, and by command of the Shah one of the nobles of Kazvin had been executed, and in like manner, also by order of the Shah, some followers of Ismail had been put to death. After this the Shah commanded Prince Mohammed Khudabend to appear before him, and the *Kurdji-bashi* was sent to fetch him. I was very pleased to meet the Prince, who assured me of the unwavering devotion of the Shah to our glorious Padishah.

Journeying from Rei it took us a month and a half (to the end of Safar) before we reached Kazvin, the capital of Irak.[207]

Upon the Shah being told of our arrival we were none of us allowed to enter the city, but had to take up our quarters in Sebzeghiran, one of the neighboring villages, under the protection of Mohammed Bey, the *Divan Bey*[208] of the Great Vizier Maasum Bey. Presently the *Ishik Agasi*[209] arrived, who took down our names, and the number of our horses, and gave his people private instructions to watch us strictly at night, until further orders.

We were told that the Shah was very angry that we had been allowed to leave Meshhed without any further inquiry, and that in consequence of this Kokche Khalipha and Mir Munshi (first secretary) had been deprived of office. Following up this information, the Kapchadji, Ali Bey, came to us by order of Yassaul Pir Ali, and said: "The people here have evil intentions, if you have any ready money about you, give it to me to keep, and if Providence deliver you out of this plight, I will return it; if on the other hand evil should befall you it is better that your riches should fall in the hands of friends than of foes."

But I replied: "People who have wandered so long in foreign parts carry no cash about them, and they who fear death do not venture so far from home. I believe in the words of the Koran: 'He who is appointed to die can not delay the hour, and without God's permission no man can slay.'"

It so happened that the Shah had by this time examined the letters which had been conveyed to him in a sealed bag, and the ladies who had traveled with us bore witness that we were poor and harmless folk. Moreover, I had sent the Shah a quatrian which had found much favor, so he set us free. The Shah commanded his Vekil,[210] Maasum Bey, to offer me a banquet, after which he would himself entertain me. Maasum Bey was also commissioned to give me the glad

426

news, that I was free to go where I liked, and, as an envoy was shortly to be sent to the Sublime Porte, I might, if I liked, travel by the way of Azerbaidjan, *i.e.,* by Tebriz and Van. Thereupon I requested that my desire might be made known to the Shah. I said, "We are not prepared to meet the hardships of the Van road in the winter time, and we beg to be allowed to travel by the way of Bagdad"; which request he graciously granted.

On the second day we were invited by the Shah to a banquet, and I presented my humble offerings. During the feast we conversed upon poetical and other subjects, and the Shah remarked to his courtiers: "These men do not look like intriguers; they are only pilgrims and religious fanatics"— and on the strength of this verdict Kokche Khalipha and Mir Munshi were reinstated in their office. I received a horse and two changes of robes, a bale of silk, and several other things; the two Serdars received each two robes of honor, and my five traveling companions, each one. Altogether the Shah behaved handsomely to us and showed a marked respect for the person of his Majesty the Padishah.

One day I was invited to a banquet in the large music-hall, all the Beys of the royal family being present. To give some idea of the magnificence here displayed I will only mention that from five hundred to one thousand *Tumens*[211] had been spent on the decoration of the hall. There were some hundreds of velvet and silken brocaded carpets, painted and embroidered in figurative designs; quantities of luxurious cushions and exquisitely artistic tents, canopies, and sunshades.

Yuzbashi Hasan Bey, one of the Shah's confidants, turned to me and said: "Is not this indeed a treasure-house?" "It is," I replied, "yet the wealth of kings is not measured by their gold and silver but by their military power." This remark silenced him; he did not return to the subject.

As the envoy had already started for Tebriz I was detained for another month, during which time the Shah showed me much attention, and I spent a good deal of my time in his presence. One day he ventured the remark: "Why were those 300 Janissaries sent from Turkey to assist Borak Khan?" I answered that these had not been sent to strengthen Borak Khan's forces, but merely as an escort to the late Sheik Abdullatif, because it was a well-known fact that the Circassians[212] had killed Baba Sheik, a son of the holy Ahmed Jesewi, on the road from Astrakhan, and that that route was therefore made unsafe. If the Padishah had intended to send military help, not three hundred, but some thousands of Janissaries, would have gone to Bokhara.

Another time I was drawn into a religious dispute with Mir Ibrahim Sefevi, one of the Shah's relatives and a sage. The conversation ran as follows:

IBRAHIM: "Why do the learned men of Turkey call us unbelievers?"

I: "It is said that the followers of the Prophet have been insulted by your countrymen, and according to the statutes of our religion he who insults his superiors is an unbeliever."

IBRAHIM: "That is what Imam Aazam (Ebn Hanifa) says, but according to Imam Shafi this belongs to the pardonable offenses."

I: "I understand that it is customary with you to accuse Ayesha, the wife of the Prophet (may God have mercy upon her), of immorality, and as this throws a stigma on the Prophet's name, it is synonymous to blasphemy. The people who can do this are in a state of

428

apostasy, and their life is forfeited. Their goods can be confiscated and their men put in prison. Any one persisting in this unbelief is subject to imprisonment, but if they renounce they may, without their wives, with or without marriage...."

IBRAHIM: "I must contradict this. In our eyes also, any one who accuses Ayesha of immorality is an unbeliever and a blasphemer and contradicts the Koran; because in the Sacred Book God Almighty testifies to the virtue of Ayesha. But all the same we can not love her because she set herself against Ali."

I: "How do you explain it that although the Hadis declares that the Ulemas are on a level with the prophets of the people of Israel, it nevertheless frequently happens that offensive language is used against the former?"

IBRAHIM: "Does the name Ulema not include our Ulemas also?"

I: "In a facetious way it includes all Ulemas, but beyond this it is a well-known fact that it is said of them: 'The flesh of the Ulema is poisonous, their odor is sickening, and to eat them is death'; and if in spite of this men will insult them, they must pay the penalty both in this world and in the next."

To this he could make no reply, and I turned the conversation into another channel.

The Shah once said to me, "Tell me, since thou hast traveled so much, which of the cities thou hast visited pleases thee best." And I replied: "I have indeed seen most of the cities of this world, but I have found none to compare with Stamboul and Galata."

429

The Shah allowed this to pass, and continued: "At how many *Tumens* dost thou estimate the combined income of the Beys and Beylerbeys of Turkey?" to which I replied: "The Beys and Beylerbeys of Turkey receive payment according to their rank, but they enjoy besides this generally a private income. Other princes remunerate their officers in proportion to the pay of the regiment which they command, but if the pay of the Beys and other officers in the service of the Emperor of Turkey were to be based upon this foundation, it would run not into *Tumens*, nor yet Lakhs,[213] but into *Kulurs*. To give you an example: The payments made to the Beylerbeys of Rumelia, Anatolia, Egypt, Hungary (Budin, *i.e.*, Ofen), Diarbekir, Bagdad, Yemen, and Algiers, are, each in themselves, as much as any other prince would lay out on the whole of his army. This proportion holds good for all the other Beylerbeys also, and is in strict accordance with the superior standing of our government. Quite a different system is adopted for the troops under Khans and Sultans, for there is always an element of uncertainty there; but in Turkey the army belongs to the Padishah. All Beylerbeys and officers are his servants, and an Imperial command is law and can not be trifled with."[214]

On this same occasion some of the officers asked whether the documents which had been taken from me by Ibrahim Mirza in Meshhed had ever been placed before the Shah. This question was answered in the affirmative, but I did not like to pursue the subject, mindful of the saying: "When evil slumbers, cursed be he who arouses it"—and I turned the conversation into another channel.

I preferred to plead my cause with another gazel, which the Shah graciously accepted, and which finally led to the desired result. We received permission to leave. He wrote a letter expressive of his unalterable respect and devotion to his Majesty the Padishah, gave me more presents, and commanded Nazr Bey, a brother of Yuzbashi Hasan Bey, to accompany me on the journey.

While in Kazvin I made a pilgrimage to the grave of Imam Shahzade Husein, and in the beginning of Rebiul Evvel I started on my journey to Bagdad.

Near to Sultani, we passed Abhar, and I stopped to visit the grave of Pir Hasan, the son of Akhi Avran, then on to Kirkan, where I visited the grave of Mohammed Demtiz[215], a son of Khodja Ahmed Jesewi, and from there to Derghezin and Hamadan, in which latter place the graves of Ain-ul-Kuzat and Pir Ebulalay, the armor-bearers of the Prophet, were visited. At Saadabad, our next station, I was met by the governor, who treated me with marked attention.

Then we took our way by Mount Elvend and Nihavend (in Suristan) to Bisutun, where I visited the grave of Kiazim, and in the village Weis-ul-karn, the grave of the saint of that name. We then proceeded to Kasri-Shirin and through Kurdistan to the fortress Zendjir. While there we were much interested in watching a *Huma* bird[216] high up in the sky. This is supposed to be a good omen, and we were therefore well pleased. Some enlarged upon the good fortune presaged by his appearance, others spoke of the curious properties of the bird, of whom Sa'di sings:

431

"The *Huma* is distinguished from all other birds,

In that he lives on bones, yet is not a bird of prey."

It is a known fact that this bird feeds exclusively on bones. The legend says that the *Huma*, before demolishing a bone, carries it up high in the air, and then drops it, with the result that it breaks into many pieces. He then swoops down upon these, divides them into equal portions, and devours them. This is the origin of the saying, when Persian officials, through extortion, obtain more than they can well digest: "They should follow the example of the *Huma* bird and divide their spoils into smaller, equal portions."

Here, at Zendjir, I dismissed Nazr Bey, whom the Shah had given me as an escort, and after crossing the great river Tokuz Olum[217] we came to Ban (or Sheri Ban). Toward the end of the same month of Kebiul Sani we reached Bagdad, where we were most hospitably received by Khizr Pasha. We did not delay, however, but hurried on to Turkey.

XVII
THE REST OF OUR ADVENTURES

In the beginning of Djemazi-ul Evvel we crossed the Tigris in ships, and after revisiting the sacred graves there we journeyed on. Past Kasri, Semke, and Harbi we came to Tekrit and Mossul, and by the old road of Mossul and Djizre to Nisibin. From there by Diarbekir and Mardin we reached Amed, where I saw Iskender Pasha, who received me most graciously. In the course of conversation I told him some of our adventures, to which he listened with much interest, and exclaimed: "You have gone through more than even Tamum Dari has done, and as for all the marvelous things which you have seen, they are beyond the dreams of even Balkiah and Djihan Shah."

Questioned upon the different sovereigns and armies of

the countries I had visited, I said: "In all the world there is no country like Turkey, no sovereign like our Padishah, and no army like the Turkish. From East to West the fame of the Ottoman troops has spread. For victory follows their banner wherever they go. May God keep Turkey in wealth and prosperity until the last day shall dawn. May he preserve our Padishah in health and happiness and our troops ever victorious. Amen!"

When asked whether our name was known in those remote parts, I answered. "Certainly, more than you would think."

In the further course of conversation I learned that a report of my death had reached the Porte, and that therefore the post of Egyptian Admiral had been given to Kurdzade, the Sandjak-bey of Rhodus. I thought to myself: "Long live my Padishah, I shall easily obtain another office"; and I comforted myself with poetic effusions. Of course I trusted in God Almighty, nevertheless I was always thinking about the conquest of Ormuz and Gujarat, and I argued thus to myself: "These fantastic dreams have so filled thy brain, that thou art being drawn down to the earth by them; the spirit of wandering is so strong in thee that thou canst not give thy body rest until it shall return to dust."

I resumed my journey to Turkey, in the hope soon to set eyes again on Constantinople. Arrived in Arghini I visited the grave of the prophet Zilkefl; from there by Kharput to Malatia and the grave of Seid Ghazi Sultan, a native of that place, and shortly after I reached Siwas, the first station on Turkish territory. Ali Pasha received me there with marked distinction; I delayed a short time to visit the grave of Abdul Wahab Ghazi, and to call upon Ali Baba, who gave me his blessing.

After this I continued my journey to Stamboul, across the

plain of Ken to Kara Hissar Behram Shah, and through Bozauk to Hadji Bektash, where I made pilgrimages to the graves of the saints of that place, and to Balam Sultan; then on to Kirshehr and the graves of Hadji Avran and Aashik Pasha, past Ayas Varsak to Angora, crossing the Kizil Irmak (Halys) by the bridge of Chashneghir.[218] I visited the grave of Hadji Bairam Sultan and his children, and the Khidr, and had a friendly interview with Djenabi Pasha. From Beybazari we came to Boli, touched Modurn, and on to Kunik, where is the grave of Sheik Shemseddin; next we came to Tarakli Yenidje and Keive, with the bridge over the Sakaria river, past Agadj-Deniz, on to Sabandja and Iznikmid[219] and the grave of Nebi Khodja. From there our way led past Ghekivize and Skutari, where I crossed the Bosphorus, and reached Constantinople in safety.

God be praised, who led me safely through manifold dangers, and brought me back to this most beautiful country of all the earth. Four years have passed away; years of much sorrow and misery, of many privations and perplexities; but now in this year 964 (1556), in the beginning of Redjeb, I have once more returned to my own people, my relations, and my friends. Glory and praise be to God the Giver of all good things!

His Majesty the Padishah happened to be at Adrianople, and on the second day after my return I traveled thither, to pay him homage. I had the good fortune to be most graciously received by his Imperial Majesty. The high Viziers, and especially Vizier Rustem Pasha, loaded me with kindnesses. I was appointed to join the Corps of the *Muteferrika* (officers in attendance on the Sultan) with a daily income of sixty *aktche*. And the *Kethhuda* (intendant), who had accompanied me on my travels, had his salary increased with eight *aktche*, and was appointed Muteferrika for Egypt.

434

One of the Boluk-Bashi (*Chef d'Escadron*) received eight *aktche* and my other traveling companions each six *aktche* above their ordinary pay. One of these latter was nominated to the post of Egyptian *Tchaush*, and the others joined the volunteers. They received their pay for the four years they had been away, payment being made out of the Egyptian treasury.

Toward the end of Rajab his Majesty the Sultan returned to Constantinople, and on the day that he entered the Konak of Tchataldja I was appointed Defterdar of Diarbekir.[220] Thus in his gracious kindness his Majesty had pleased and satisfied us all.

He who wishes to profit by this narrative let him remember that not in vain aspirations after greatness, but in a quiet and contented mind lieth the secret of the true strength which perisheth not. But if in God's providence he should be driven from home, and forced to wander forth in the unknown, and perchance be caught in the turbulent waves of the sea of adversity, let him still always keep in mind that love for one's native land is next to one's faith. Let him never cease to long for the day that he shall see his native shores again, and always cling loyally to his Padishah.

He who doeth this shall not perish abroad; God will grant him his desire both in this world and in the next, and he shall rejoice in the esteem and affection of his fellow-countrymen.

I completed this narrative in Galata in the month Shaaban of the year 964 (1556), and the transcript of it was accomplished in the month Safar of the year 965 (1557).

BIBLIOGRAPHIES

MEDIEVAL ARABIC

Some of the general works recommended for the early Arabic history and literature are also of value for this volume. The general theme is covered by:

R. A. NICHOLSON, "A Literary History of the Arabs" (New York, Scribners, 1907).

F. F. ARBUTHNOT, "Arabic Authors" (London, 1890).

For the legends of Mohammed, read:

WILLIAM MUIR, "Life of Mahomet" (new edition, Edinburgh, 1912).

D. S. MARGOLIOUTH, "Mohammed and the Rise of Islam" (London, 1905).

STANLEY LANE-POOLE, "Speeches and Table-Talk of the Prophet Mohammed" (London, 1882).

A. N. MATTHEWS (translator), "Mishcat ul-Masabih, a Collection of Traditions Regarding Muhammed" (Calcutta, 1810).

WM. MURRAY, "Abulfeda's Life of Mohammed" (Elgin).

For history and biography, consult:

BARON MACGUCKIN DE SLANE, "Ibn Khallikan's Biographical Dictionary" (Paris, 1842-1871), four volumes.

PHILIP K. HITTI, "Al Baladhuri's History of the Mohammedan Conquest" (Columbia University, New York, 1916).

"Albiruni's Chronology."

For romance the list is almost endless. It includes:

E. W. LANE, "The Thousand and One Nights" (London), three volumes.

JOHN PAYNE, "The Book of the Thousand Nights and One Night" (London, 1884), nine volumes.

SIR RICHARD BURTON, "Plain and Literal Translation of the Thousand Nights" (London, 1885), ten volumes.

SIR RICHARD BURTON, "Supplementary Nights" (London, 1887), six volumes.

J. VON HAMMER, "New Arabian Nights" (London).

T. HAMILTON, "Antar, a Bedoueen Romance" (London, 1820), four volumes.

T. CHENERY and F. STEINGASS, "The Assemblies of Al-Hariri" (London, 1898), two volumes.

W. J. PRENDERGAST, "The Maquamat of Al-Hamadhani" (Madras, 1915).

C. FIELD, "Tales of the Caliphs" (New York, 1909).

For philosophic themes, consult:

T. J. DE BOER, "History of Philosophy in Islam" (London, 1903).

D. B. MACDONALD, "Development of Muslim Theology, Jurisprudence, etc." (Scribners, New York, 1903).

J. L. BURCKHARDT, "Arabic Proverbs" (London, 1830).

And most important of all for general information is the new and authoritative

"Encyclopædia of Islam," edited by Houtsma, Arnold, and Schaade.

TURKISH LITERATURE

For the general conditions and history of Turkey, read:

SIR EDWIN PEARS, "Turkey and Its People" (London, 1911).

L. C. GARNETT, "Turkish Life in Town and Country" (Putnam, New York, 1911).

SIR CHAS. ELIOT, "Turkey in Europe" (London, 2d edition, 1908).

R. P. DAVEY, "The Sultan and His Subjects" (London, revised edition, 1907).

S. LANE-POOLE, "The Story of Turkey" (New York, 1897).

S. LANE-POOLE, "The Mohammedan Dynasties" (London, 1903).

E. A. FREEMAN, "The Ottoman Power in Europe" (Macmillan).

H. A. GIBBONS, "Foundation of the Ottoman Empire" (New York, 1916).

For the literature itself, read:

J. W. REDHOUSE, "History, System, etc., of Turkish Poetry."

E. J. W. GIBB, "Ottoman Poems" (London, 1882).

E. J. W. GIBB, "History of Ottoman Poetry" (London, 1902).

CHAS. WELLS, "Turkish Chrestomathy" (London, 1891).

ALLAN RAMSAY, "Tales from Turkey" (London, 1914).

FOOTNOTES:

1 Abu Muslim had been the chief means of transferring the Caliphate from the Omeyyads to the family of Abbas.

2 "Father of a villain": a play upon the name Abu Muslim.

3 *Al Mahdi, i.e.,* "the rightly directed."

4 The Caliph's full name was Abu Jafar Al Mansur.

5 *I.e.,* descendant of Ali.

6 An underground dungeon.

7 Five.

8 Praise of God.

9 Koran, ii., 238.

10 A famous musician of the period.

11 *I.e.,* "There is nothing new under the sun."

12 In the Mosque of Omar.

13 A miracle ascribed to Mohammed.

14 This was the technical sign for freeing a slave.

15 In this Assembly Al Harith arrives in the town of San'a in Yemen, in great poverty; and, while seeking relief, encounters a crowd, which is gathered about a preacher. The discourse is a stern warning against self-indulgence, and an exhortation to repentance. Harith, wishing to learn who the preacher is, follows him to a cave, and there finds him enjoying himself with good food, and even with wine. He begins to rebuke him, but the preacher, throwing off disguise, extemporizes some lines, confessing that his preaching was only a device to obtain charity. Harith asks the attendant the name of the preacher, and is told that he is Abu Zayd, of Seruj.

16 In this Assembly the author displays more than his usual rhetorical subtlety, and while there is none more admired by

440

those whose taste has been formed on Eastern models, there is none which appears more extravagant to the European student. Alliterations, verbal caprices, far-fetched expressions, and the conceits which were usual among poets of the age, so abound, that we may almost imagine the author to be desirous of satirizing what he professes to imitate. The subject is as follows: Harith in his passion for the society of literary persons makes his way to Holwan, a town in Irak, on the mountains east of Bagdad, and a resort of the higher classes from the heat of the capital. Here he meets with Abu Zayd, who is pursuing his calling of improvisatore and mendicant under various disguises, and enjoys for a long time his company and literary guidance. Abu Zayd, however, disappears, and Harith returns to his native place, Basra, where after a time he again meets Abu Zayd in the public library, among a crowd of dilettanti who are discussing the beauties of the popular poets. The admiration of one is especially excited by a line in which the teeth of a lady are compared to pearls and hailstones, and the white petals of a flower; and Abu Zayd instantly produces a number of comparisons in the same style, which give him a high place in the esteem of those present, when they are assured that he is really the author of them. They reward him, and the Assembly concludes by his reciting to Harith, who had recognized him, some lines on the fickleness of fortune.

17 Harith is in a circle of scholars, when a lame man makes his appearance, and after saluting them describes his former affluence and present penury in a very poetical and figurative style. Harith, perceiving his genius, and pitying his distress, offers him a denar on condition that he will improvise some lines in praise of it. This the lame man at once does, and on Harith offering him another denar on condition of his blaming it, he recites another composition in dispraise of money. Harith then recognizes in the lame man Abu Zayd, and rebukes him for his imposture. Abu Zayd defends himself in some new verses. The opening address of Abu Zayd is in imitation of a style said to be common among the Arabs of the desert.

18 Harith is journeying in a caravan to Damietta, and during one of the night-halts he hears two men conversing on duty toward a neighbor. The younger being asked for his opinion,

replies in a spirit of charity and generosity, upon which the other rebukes him, and sets forth the fitting conduct of a man to his neighbor in accordance with the teachings of selfishness and worldly wisdom. These addresses, especially that of the elder man, are expressed in a highly rhetorical diction, which captivates the literary Harith, and the next morning he looks for them, and discovers them to be Abu Zayd and his son. He invites them to his own quarters, introduces them to his friends, and procures for them valuable presents. Abu Zayd then asks permission to go to a neighboring village and take a bath, promising to return speedily. They consent, and he goes off with his son. After waiting the greater part of the day they find that he has deceived them, and prepare to continue their journey; Harith, when making ready his camel, finds some lines written on the saddle, which allude to a precept in the Koran in favor of separating after a meal. The plays on words in this Assembly are exceedingly ingenious and elaborate, and the opening description has much poetical beauty.

19 The following Assembly, remarkable for the poetical beauty of its language, and the delicacy of its versification, describes an adventure in which Abu Zayd obtains a sum of money from a company of generous scholars. Harith is engaged with some friends in a night conversation at Kufa, one of the chief seats of Arabian learning, when a stranger knocks at the door, and addresses the inmates in verses describing his want and weariness, his excellent disposition, and his gratitude for the favors he may receive. Struck with his poetical powers the company admit him, and give him a supper. The lamp being brought, Harith discovers that the guest is Abu Zayd, and informs the company of his merits. They then ask him for a story, and he relates that he had that evening met with a long-lost son, whom he would be glad to take charge of, did not his poverty hinder him. As he had taken care to mention in the narrative that he was of the royal race of Ghassan, the company are moved by his misfortunes, and at once raise a large sum of money to enable him to support his boy. Abu Zayd delights them with his conversation, but as soon as daylight appears he calls away Harith, to assist him in cashing the checks or orders which he had received. The simple Harith, who had been delighted with

the verses which the father had put into the mouth of his son, desires to see so eloquent a youth; upon which Abu Zayd laughs heartily, tells his friend, in some exquisite verses, that such a desire is the following of a mirage, that he, Abu Zayd, had neither wife nor son, and that the story was only a trick to obtain money. He then departs, leaving Harith mortified at the adventure.

20 This Assembly is the first of a remarkable series of compositions which, though they may be set down by Europeans as merely examples of laborious trifling, are highly esteemed by the Orientals as works of ingenuity and scholarship, and have found in every succeeding age numerous imitators. The incident is that Harith, being once on a visit to Meraghah, in Azerbijan, the northwest province of the present Persian monarchy, found a number of literary men lamenting the decline of learning, and depreciating all contemporary authors in comparison with their predecessors. Sitting in a humble place in the outskirts of the company was an elderly man, who showed by his glances and scornful gestures that he did not value highly the opinions of these critics. When they paused in their fault-finding he took up the conversation, and declared that one person, at least, of the present age was capable of rivaling any who had gone before in scholarship and the arts of composition. He is asked who is this genius, and answers that it is himself. The company are skeptical, but as the stranger persists in asserting his great ability, they determine to test him, and one of them proposes to him a most difficult task. He tells the company that he is a professional writer attached to the Governor, who, though a man of generosity, had declared that he would help him no further, till he had composed an address in which the alternate words should consist entirely of pointed and unpointed letters; that is, that the first, third, fifth words, and so forth, should consist of letters without a point, while the second, fourth, sixth, and so forth, should have only pointed letters. He adds that he had been striving a whole year to produce such a composition, or to find some one who could produce it. The stranger, on hearing this, accepts the task with alacrity, and instantly dictates an address in praise of the Governor, fulfilling the conditions that had been imposed.

21 This Assembly is well known to students. Harith is at

Barka'id. The feast at the end of Ramadan is approaching, and being desirous of joining in this solemnity he goes to the public prayer in his best attire. When the congregation has formed itself into rows, after the manner of Moslem worship, he espies an old man with his eyes closed, accompanied by an old woman. The man takes out of a bag a number of papers curiously written or illuminated in variously colored inks; and the old woman, going through the rows, presents them to those whom she guesses from their appearance to be charitably disposed. One of them falls to the lot of Harith, who finds on it some strange verses full of alliterations and plays on words. He keeps it, and when the old woman, being disappointed in her appeal, returns to reclaim it, he offers her a dirhem on the condition that she will tell him the name of the author. She informs him that the old man had composed the verses, and that he was a native of Seruj. Harith then guesses that he must be Abu Zayd, and is much concerned to find that he has become blind. When the prayer is over he goes up to him and discovers that he is indeed Abu Zayd, whereupon he presents him with a garment and invites him to his house. No sooner are they in private than Abu Zayd opens his eyes, which are perfectly sound, and Harith discovers that his pretended blindness was a trick to excite pity.

22 This Assembly, like several others that will be met with in the course of the work, is so essentially Arabic as almost to forbid intelligible translation. Two suitors, an old man and a youth, appear before the Kadi of Ma'arrah. The former narrates to the Kadi that he had possessed a beautiful and attractive, yet obedient and active, slave girl; that the youth had borrowed her, treated her roughly, and then returned her in an infirm state. The youth admits the charge, but declares that he had offered sufficient compensation; and then complains that the old man detained as a pledge a male slave of his, who was of good origin and qualities, and highly serviceable to his master. The Kadi perceives from the style of these addresses that the language is enigmatical, and bids the litigants speak plainly. The youth then improvises some verses to explain that by a slave girl the old man meant a needle which the youth had borrowed, and the eye of which he had broken by accident as he was drawing the thread through it; the male slave which the old man detained was a pencil, or *stylus*, for

the application of *kohl*, the dark pigment with which Orientals anoint the eyelid to heighten by contrast the luster of the eye. The old man in his turn admits the truth of this, but pleads in mournful verse his poverty and his inability to bear the loss even of a needle. The chief feature in the composition is the enigmatical description of the needle and pencil, which depends on the double meanings of the words and phrases contained in it. Some of these are so subtle that even the native commentators are undecided about them; and we may assume that the *double-entente* of passages like this was among the lessons which Hariri is said to have taught to his pupils.

23 The meaning of this passage, when applied to a *kohl* pencil, is as follows: I had a *kohl* pencil, the same at both ends, tracing its origin to the cutler, free from rust and defect; often brought near the apple of the eye; it conferred beauty and produced admiration; it fed the pupil of the eye with ointment, but went not near the tongue; when it was blackened with the ointment it was liberal of it, when it marked the eye it beautified it; when it was supplied with ointment it supplied the eye with it, and when more was required it added more. It remained not always in its case, and seldom anointed except two eyes at a time; it gave plentifully of the *kohl* that was on it, and was lifted up to the eye for the purpose; it was constantly attached to the *kohl*-case, although the two might be of a different material (that is, the pencil might be of gold and the case of glass or silver); though it was used for adorning, it was not of a soft substance but of metal.

24 This is one of the two Assemblies of Hariri which have been translated and annotated by De Sacy in his Chrestomathy. Harith in his wanderings comes to Alexandria, and, in accordance with his custom, makes the acquaintance of the Kadi, who, as appears in the sequel, is a good-natured and benevolent man. One evening, in winter, the Kadi is distributing the public alms, when an ill-looking old man is brought in by a young and handsome woman who accuses him of having married her on false pretenses. She declares that he had deceived her father by giving out that he had an excellent trade as a pearl-merchant; that he had been incautiously accepted, and that now, when it was too late, she had discovered that he had no business at all. Moreover, he had taken all her dress and furniture, piece by piece, and sold it

445

to keep himself in idleness, leaving her and her child to starve. The Kadi is indignant, and threatens to send the husband to prison, unless he can clear himself of the charge. The defendant is in no way disconcerted, but at once improvises some elegant verses, in which he admits his poverty, and that he had sold his wife's effects, but denies that he had deceived her in calling himself a "pearl-stringer," for the pearls which he meant were the pearls of thought, by stringing which into elegant poems he had been accustomed to make a large income from the liberality of the rich and noble. Now, however, times were changed; war and trouble had come upon the earth, and a race of niggards had succeeded the generous patrons of the old days. The Kadi accepts the excuse, bids the woman submit herself to her husband, and gives them some of the alms-money; on receiving which the old man triumphantly carries off his wife.

<u>25</u> In this Assembly Abu Zayd is found making gain by his usual questionable arts. At Rahbah, on the Euphrates, Harith beholds a crowd following an elderly man who is dragging along a handsome youth. The former accuses the boy of having killed his son, and it is agreed to go before the Governor. The purpose of the elder, who proves in the end to be Abu Zayd, is simply to induce the Governor to buy off so handsome a youth from punishment, with the view of taking him into his own household. When they are in court the old man makes his charge, and as he has no witnesses the boy is allowed to clear himself by an oath. But the old man dictates an oath in which he enumerates all the beauties of the boy, and invokes destruction on them if truth be not spoken. The boy refuses to swear by such an oath; and the Governor, who desires to take him out of the power of the old man, then makes up a purse to satisfy the prosecutor. A hundred denars are promised; but as the whole can not be collected at once the old man says that he will not give up the boy, but will watch him all night. The Governor consents, and soon the two are left together in the courtyard. Harith then accosts Abu Zayd, and asks who is the boy. Abu Zayd replies, that he is his son, and his assistant in his tricks; and that they intend to make their escape early in the morning, and leave the Governor to his disappointment.

<u>26</u> This and the following Assembly are justly reckoned

446

among the masterpieces of the author. To pass suddenly from the most solemn subjects to pleasantry, to place in the mouth of a clever impostor the most serious warnings that can be addressed to mankind, may be morally objectionable; but in the Moslem world, where religion is mixed up with all the concerns of life, and pious discourse and phrases abound, it excites little repugnance. The design of the author in the present composition was to produce an elaborate sermon in rhymed prose and in verse, and his genius takes a higher flight than usual. The incident on which the Assembly is founded is simple. Harith, in a fit of religious zeal, betakes himself to the public burial-ground of the city of Saweh, for the purpose of contemplation. He finds a funeral in progress, and when it is over, an old man, with his face muffled in a cloak, takes his stand on a hillock, and pours forth a discourse on the certainty of death and judgment; rebuking his hearers for their worldly selfishness, and warning them that wealth and power are of little avail against the general leveler. He then rises into poetry and declaims a piece which is one of the noblest productions of Arabic literature. In lofty morality, in religious fervor, in beauty of language, in power and grace of meter, this magnificent hymn is unsurpassed.

27 Harith, being in affluence, crosses from Irak to Damascus to enjoy the luxury of that city. After he has had his fill of pleasure he bethinks himself of returning homeward, and joins a caravan that is about to cross the Semaweh, the desert which lies between Syria and the Euphrates. The travelers are ready to depart, but are delayed by their inability to find an escort, which they think indispensable for their protection against robbers. While they are consulting they are watched by a dervish, who at last announces to them that he has the means of keeping them safe from harm; and, on their inquiring further, tells them that his safeguard is a magic form of words revealed to him in a dream. They are at first incredulous, but at length consent to take him with them, and to use his incantation. He then repeats it, and it proves to be a prayer full of assonances and rhymes, beseeching the general protection of the Almighty. They all learn it by heart and then set forth, repeating it twice a day on their journey. As they are not molested on the road they judge the charm to have been successful; and when they come in sight of 'Anah, the first

town on the other side of the desert, they reward him richly with what he likes best, gold and jewels. When he has taken all he can get, he makes his escape, and the next thing they hear of him is that he is drinking in the taverns of 'Anah, a city celebrated for its wine. Harith, shocked at this enormity in a pious dervish, determines to seek him out, and soon finds him reveling amid wine and music in the guest-chamber of a wine-shop. He taxes him with his wickedness, and then the old man improvises a Bacchanalian chant, which is one of the finest pieces in Hariri's work. In form this poem resembles that which is introduced into the last Assembly, though the meter is more light and lively, as Hariri, no doubt, desired to display his genius by the contrast. This Assembly is one of the most admired productions of the author, who has lavished on it all the resources of his marvelous rhetoric.

28 Maisuna was a daughter of the tribe of Calab; a tribe, according to Abulfeda, remarkable both for the purity of dialect spoken in it, and for the number of poets it had produced. She was married, whilst very young, to the Caliph Mowiah. But this exalted situation by no means suited the disposition of Maisuna, and amidst all the pomp and splendor of Damascus, she languished for the simple pleasures of her native desert.

29 Yazid succeeded Mowiah in the Caliphate A.H. 60; and in most respects showed himself to be of a very different disposition from his predecessor. He was naturally cruel, avaricious, and debauched; but instead of concealing his vices from the eyes of his subjects, he seemed to make a parade of those actions which he knew no good Mussulman could look upon without horror; he drank wine in public, he caressed his dogs, and was waited upon by his eunuchs in sight of the whole court.

30 Shafay, the founder of one of the four orthodox sects into which the Mohammedans are divided, was a disciple of Malek Ben Ans, and master to Ahmed Ebn Hanbal; each of whom, like himself, founded a sect which is still denominated from the name of its author. The fourth sect is that of Abou Hanifah.

31 The author of this poem was a hermit of Syria, equally celebrated for his talents and piety. He was son to a prince of Khorassan, and born about the ninety-seventh year of the

448

Hegira. This poem was addressed to the Caliph upon his undertaking a pilgrimage to Mecca.

32 Isaac Al Mouseli is considered by the Orientals as the most celebrated musician that ever flourished in the world. He was born in Persia, but having resided almost entirely at Mousel, he is generally supposed to have been a native of that place.

33 The family of Barmec was one of the most illustrious in the East. They were descended from the ancient kings of Persia, and possessed immense property in various countries; they derived still more consequence from the favor which they enjoyed at the court of Bagdad, where, for many years, they filled the highest offices of the State with universal approbation.

34 Taher Ben Hosien was ambidexter and one-eyed and, strange to say, the most celebrated general of his time.

35 Abu Tammam is noted as the first collector of the works of earlier poets. He gathered these in a valuable anthology. He was born near Damascus A.D. 807, and educated in Egypt; but the principal part of his life was spent at Bagdad, under the patronage of the Abasside Caliphs.

36 Abu Al Salam was a poet more remarkable for abilities than morality. We may form an idea of the nature of his compositions from the nickname he acquired amongst his contemporaries of "Cock of the Evil Genii."

37 The three following songs were written by Mashdud, Rakeek, and Rais, three of the most celebrated improvisators in Bagdad, at an entertainment given by Abou Isy.

38 Ebn Alrumi is reckoned by the Arabian writers as one of the most excellent of all their poets. He was by birth a Syrian, and passed the greatest part of his time at Emessa.

39 Ali Ibn Ahmed distinguished himself in prose as well as poetry, and a historical work of considerable reputation, of which he was the author, is still extant. But he principally excelled in satire, and so fond was he of indulging this dangerous talent that no one escaped his lash; if he could only bring out a sarcasm, it was matter of indifference to him whether an enemy or a brother smarted under its severity. He

449

died at Bagdad A.D. 898.

40 The thought contained in these lines appears so natural and so obvious, that one wonders it did not occur to all who have attempted to write upon a birthday or a death.

41 Radhi Billah, son to Moctader, was the twentieth Caliph of the house of Abbas, and the last of these princes who possessed any substantial power.

42 History can show few princes so amiable and few so unfortunate as Shems Almaali Cabus. He is described as possessed of almost every virtue and every accomplishment: his piety, justice, generosity, and humanity are universally celebrated; nor was he less conspicuous for intellectual powers; his genius was at once penetrating, solid, and brilliant, and he distinguished himself equally as an orator, a philosopher, and a poet.

43 The wolf.

44 The occasion of the following composition is thus related by Abulfeda. Carawash, Sultan of Mousel, being one wintry evening engaged in a party of pleasure along with Barkaidy, Ebn Fahdi, Abou Jaber, and the improvisatore poet, Ebn Alramacram, resolved to divert himself at the expense of his companions. He therefore ordered the poet to give a specimen of his talents, which at the same time should convey a satire upon the three courtiers, and a compliment to himself. Ebn Alramacram took his subject from the stormy appearance of the night, and immediately produced these verses.

45 Ali ben Mohammed was a native of that part of Arabia called Hejaz; and was celebrated not only as a poet, but as a politician.

46 Tabataba deduced his pedigree from Ali Ben Abu Taleb, and Fatima, the daughter of Mohammed. He was born at Ispahan, but passed the principal part of his life in Egypt, where he was appointed chief of the sheriffs, *i.e.*, the descendants of the Prophet, a dignity held in the highest veneration by every Mussulman. He died in the year of the Hegira 418, with the reputation of being one of the most excellent poets of his time.

47 Ben Yusef for many years acted as vizier to Abu Nasser, Sultan of Diarbeker. His political talents are much praised, and

he is particularly celebrated for the address he displayed while upon an embassy to the Greek Emperor at Constantinople. Yusef's poetry must be looked upon merely as a *jeu d'esprit* suggested by the beauties of the vale of Bozaa, as he passed through it.

48 The life of this prince was checkered with various adventures; he was perpetually engaged in contests either with the neighboring sovereigns, or the princes of his own family. After many struggles he was obliged to submit to his brother, Abu Camel, who immediately ordered him to be seized, and conveyed to a place of security.

49 Abu Alola is esteemed as one of the most excellent of the Arabian poets. He was born blind, but this did not deter him from the pursuit of literature. Abu Alola died at Maara in the year 1049, aged eighty-six.

50 Written to Abu Alchair Selamu, an Egyptian physician. The author was a physician of Antioch.

51 Abu Ismael was a native of Ispahan. He devoted himself to the service of the Seljuk Sultans of Persia, and enjoyed the confidence of Malec Shah, and his son and grandson, Mohammed and Massoud, by the last of whom he was raised to the dignity of vizier. Massoud, however, was not long in a condition to afford Abu Ismael any protection, for, being attacked by his brother Mahmoud, he was defeated, and driven from Mousel, and upon the fall of his master the vizier was seized and thrown into prison, and at length sentenced to be put to death.

52 It is unfortunate that both the philosopher and his opponents should have advanced the same argument in defense of themselves—namely, their own wisdom. The Arab philosophers were, amongst their kind, something like the *libertins* of the seventeenth century in France. "Often," says Al Ghazali, "I have seen one read the Koran, assist at religious ceremonies and prayers, and praise religion aloud. When I

451

asked him, 'If you consider prophetism as false, why do you pray!' he responded, 'It is an exercise of the body, a custom of the country, a method of having your life saved.' Yet he did not cease from drinking wine, and delivering himself to all sorts of abominations and impieties."

53 Seville was one of those small sovereignties into which Spain had been divided after the extinction of the house of Ommiah. It did not long retain its independence, and the only prince who ever presided over it as a separate kingdom seems to have been Mohammed ben Abad, the author of these verses. For thirty-three years he reigned over Seville and the neighboring districts with considerable reputation, but being attacked by Joseph, son to the Emperor of Morocco, at the head of a numerous army of Africans, was defeated, taken prisoner, and thrown into a dungeon, where he died in the year A.D. 1087.

54 This author was by birth an African; but having passed over to Spain, he was much patronized by Mohammed, Sultan of Seville. After the fall of his master, Ben Abad returned to Africa, and died at Tangier, A.D. 1087.

55 A wicked angel who is permitted to tempt mankind by teaching them magic; see the legend respecting him in the Koran.

56 The poet here alludes to the punishments denounced in the Koran against those who worship a plurality of Gods: "Their couch shall be in hell, and over them shall be coverings of fire."

57 Written to a lady upon her refusal of a present of melons, and her rejection of the addresses of an admirer.

58 Gazul is the name of one of the Moorish heroes who figure in the "Historia de las Guerras Civiles de Granada." The ballad is one of very many in which the dexterity of the Moorish cavaliers in the bullfight is described. The reader will observe that the shape, activity, and resolution of the unhappy animal destined to furnish the amusement of the spectators are enlarged upon, just as the qualities of a modern race-horse might be among ourselves: nor is the bull without his name. The day of the Baptist is a festival among the Mussulmans, as well as among Christians.

452

59 The reader can not need to be reminded of the fatal effects which were produced by the feuds subsisting between the two great families, or rather races, of the Zegris and the Abencerrages of Granada. This ballad is also from the "*Guerras Civiles*."

60 Shahar is the name of the coast-line between Oman and Aden.

61 The word here used is the old and correct one, *Dar-es-sena* ("the house of technics"), from which word the present *Tersane, i.e.*, "Arsenal," has originated.

62 Ashik is now a ruin opposite Samira.

63 *Mowsim Zemani*, literally, "the time of the season." From the Arabic word *Mowsim* the English "monsoon" has originated.

64 A small vessel, worked by sails and oars, for the carrying of freights, also called *Sacoléve*.

65 Lahsa and Katif, islands in the Persian Gulf, which, together with Ormuz, Bahrein, and Kalhata, were famous in the Middle Ages, as staple-towns for the commerce between Persia and India.

66 *Filandra*, a small ensign hoisted on the top of the mainmast.

<u>67</u> Khorfakan, a place on the east coast of Oman, between Ras Dibba and Fedzna.

<u>68</u> Sohar, also on the east coast of Oman.

<u>69</u> This is the same as "Calatu," mentioned by Marco Polo, see "Travels of Marco Polo," by Col. H. Yule, Vol. II, p. 381.

<u>70</u> Kuya appears to be really the name of the town Goa, the headquarters of the Portuguese in India.

<u>71</u> According to Bianchi, "*voile d'artimon*." The following passage is owing partly to the defective text, partly to the strange naval technical expressions, unclear and unintelligible.

<u>72</u> *Shaika*, a Kirghiz boat.

<u>73</u> Compare the Hungarian *d'arda*, *i.e.*, "spear," "lance."

<u>74</u> Of this expression only the word *longa* (*lenga*) can be identified with the Italian.

<u>75</u> A harbor-town in Persia, in the vicinity of Beluchistan.

<u>76</u> *Rectius*: Kidj-Mekran (Marco Polo's Kesmacoran), as Yule rightly observes, situated on the coast of that part of Kerman, then belonging to India. See "Travels of Marco Polo."

<u>77</u> On our modern maps given as Shabar, which is the name of the bay as well as of the place.

<u>78</u> Guador, on the west coast of Beluchistan, belonging to the Indian Empire.

<u>79</u> Zofar, or Dhofar, to the east of Shar. In the Middle Ages there was a city of that name, as mentioned by Marco Polo and Ibn Batuta.

<u>80</u> Literally, "Elephant's flood."

<u>81</u> Here follow some nautical expressions which I do not understand.

<u>82</u> Perhaps meant for Manglaus, Menglaur, in the District of Sahranpur.

<u>83</u> Somenat Somnath, a town in the south of the peninsula of Kathiawar, also the name of the District.

<u>84</u> More correctly Diu, an island belonging to the

Portuguese in West India, separated from Kathiawar by a narrow stroke of land, with about 13,000 inhabitants, and politically under Goa. (See "Imperial Gazetteer of India," IV., p. 305.)

85 Daman, a Portuguese possession in the bay of Cambay, with about 50,000 inhabitants; was pillaged first in the year 1531, and retaken in 1553.

86 Compare the Persian *badzed*, "whirlwind," "tempest"; more correctly "gust of wind," from *Bad*, "wind," and *Zeden*, "to strike."

87 In the text *Djonk*, "a large ship," used principally in China. First mentioned by the Monk Odorico di Pordenone in 1331.

88 Compare "dingy," "dinghy." Literally, the name of a ship or large boat, on the coast of Mekran; the word is also known in English, but it originates from Beluchistan. Correctly speaking, it means a pilot-ship.

89 *Kotwal, kutwal,* "commander of a fortress," also "policeman". Of Turkish origin, from the word kut, "to guard," "to watch"; would be more correctly, *kuteol,* meaning "guardian."

90 *Cheter Kaldirmak* means, literally, "to raise the sunshade" (umbrella), this being the symbol of sovereignty in India.

91 More correctly Broatsh, a place northwest of Surat, in the province of Gujarat, on the right bank of the Nerbudda. This place has from time immemorial belonged to the Moslem rulers of Ahmedabad, and has twice been pillaged by the Portuguese (in 1536 and 1546).

92 In the text, *Provador*, meaning "Admiral."

93 Ahmedabad, the chief town of the Province of that name, 310 miles north of Bombay.

94 More correctly Balotra, a town in Jodpur (Radjhputana).

95 Champanir, a mountain fortress in Gujarat, in the Province of Pendj-Mahal, 250 miles northeast of Bombay.

96 Compare Tuba-tree, with the Sidra-trees of the Mohammedan paradise.

97 *Zokum*, a tree which, according to the Koran, grows only in hell. Its fruit resembles the plantain and serves as food for the condemned.

98 At present there is only a place of that name known in Oudh, but not in Gujarat.

99 *Bir Katar deve*, "a team of camels." *Katar*, "team," means "ten camels."

100 Very characteristic is the piece of poetry here introduced. It is probably a Turkish sea-song of that time. It says:
"We roam the waters far and wide,
And bring confusion upon our enemies;
Revenge and hatred is our motto,
For we are Khairreddin's troops."
(Khairreddin Pasha was Suleiman's renowned Admiral, known in Europe as Barbarossa.)

101 In the text *Bami* may possibly be a slip of the pen and intended for "Brahmin."

102 *Banians*, "Indian merchants," more especially from the Province of Gujarat, who from time immemorial have traded with the harbor-towns of Arabia.

103 *Rajput*, a warlike race, probably descended from the ural-Altaic race.

104 This can not be the town of that name in Bengal, as this lies more to the south and could not be reached from Ahmedabad in five days.

105 Radhanpur, the capital of the district of that name in the Presidency of Bombay.

106 More correctly Parkar or Nagar-Parkar, the name of a district and a place in the Presidency of Bombay.

107 *Muhre*, "a stone," which, so says the legend, is found in the head of the serpent and the dragon, and possesses miraculous power. Many Dervishes carry one of these stones in their girdle to trade upon the superstition of the ignorant people.

108 As a town, Wanga is unknown to me, unless it be

456

intended for Wanna, in the district of Cathiawar in the Presidency of Bombay.

109 More correctly Junaghar, the name of a Province and town in Cathiawar, Presidency of Bombay.

110 The Indus.

111 Tatta (Thats, or Nagar Thats), in the District of Karachi.

112 *Nakara*, "a band of music," was formerly considered in Central Asia as a sign of sovereignty.

113 *Serpay vermek*, "to distribute festive apparel," is a great mark of distinction in Central Asia, but as the expression is unknown in Turkey the author has had to circumscribe it.

114 "He gave us the name of: a mystic army,"

115 Literally, "there should be no dragonstone, *i.e.*, sorcery, in your guns."

116 Argun and Tarkhan are two Turkish tribes in Central Asia, direct descendants of the Transoxanian warriors, which came with Baber to India.

117 Now Nasirabad, the name of several places in Sind.

118 Perhaps meant for Sehivan in Naushar on the Indus.

119 Patri, now a station on the railway-line to Bombay, Baroda, and Central India; also the name of a small State belonging to Kathiawar.

120 Our author, according to the spirit of the age, was not only a brave warrior and sailor, but also a poet, using the East-Turkish Dialect (Djagatai). His muse has no special features, and with regard to his choice of words they betray a strong tendency toward the Osmanli dialect. It is nevertheless interesting to note in how short a time he mastered this dialect and that, more than 100 years after Baber, the Djagatai tongue maintained itself as the court-and-book-language in India. In our translation we necessarily omit these poetic effusions as irrelevant.

121 Literally, "wandering."

122 In the text *Kheime* we *shamiane*, the latter being more a kind of large sunshade.

457

123 As there are several places called Sultanpoor and Mav, the stations here mentioned are difficult to identify on the map.

124 Utch, a small place on the left bank of the Pendtjend, a tributary of the Indus.

125 On modern maps of India it is marked as Gharra, by which name the Sutlej is also known.

126 On the way from Utch to Multan there is a river called Trimba. But I have not anywhere come upon a river called Machvara.

127 Sambal, a place in the District of Muradabad, in the northeast of India.

128 Also called Firuzpoor, in Punjab.

129 *I.e.*, Khan of the Khans, like the Mirimiran of the Persians, and the Beglerbeghi of the Turks.

130 Correctly, *Kurur,* that is, 10,000,000 rupees, equivalent to about $5,000,000.

131 *Birshegal,* probably a Hindustani word.

132 In the text *Kish, i.e.,* "winter," also "bad weather," "rainy season." Compare *Kish Kiamet, i.e.,* "very foul weather."

133 Opinions differ as to the exact nature of the *Tughra* (signature of Turkish rulers: more correctly, *tora,* meaning "decree"). Some say that it is merely a flourish, others hold that it is the impression of the hand. In Central Asia, Turkish monarchs used to dip their hand in blood, hence the expression *al-tamga,* "red seal." The descendants of Baber first introduced into India the use of the yellow dye, saffron.

134 Mir Ali Shir, the greatest poet of the Turks in Central Asia, was born, according to Khondemir, in the year 844 (1440) and died in H. 906 (1500). He wrote under the name of *Newai.* His compositions, which are unquestionably superior to any other East Turkish productions, enjoy to this day great popularity amongst the Turks of the interior of Asia.

135 *Afetabe,* "water-basin," and *Afetabedji,* "he who holds the water-basin"; a high court dignity in Central Asia, and later on also among the Moguls in India. The former Khans of Khokand had received the title of Afetabedji from the Sultan of

458

Turkey.

136 Our author means by Siwas the old seat of the Osmans, but in India and in Central Asia, *Rum* is generally understood to stand for the West, and more particularly for the Ottoman Empire.

137 As the Turks never conquered Vienna, this is a mere boast on the part of the Turkish Admiral. Possibly, in the Far East the news of the conquest of Vienna may have found credence, for the campaigns of Suleiman against Vienna fall about this time.

138 Khatib is the name of the Mollah who on Fridays says the *Khutbe*, or Friday prayer, in which the names of the Caliph and of the local ruler are inserted.

139 Mir Khosru Dehlevi (*i.e.*, from Delhi), one of the greatest poets of India, born 1253, died 1324. He wrote in Persian, which language had been introduced into India with the spread of Islam.

140 Elphinstone in the "History of India" relates his death as follows: "He had been walking on the terrace of his library, and was descending the stairs (which in such situations are narrow steps on the outside of the building and only guarded by an ornamental parapet about a foot high). Hearing the call to prayers from the minarets, he stopped, as is usual on such occasions, repeated the creed, and sat down on the steps till the crier had done. He then endeavored to rise, supporting himself on his staff; the staff slipped on the polished marble of the steps, and the King fell headlong over the parapet. He was stunned at the time and, although he soon recovered his senses, the injury he had received was beyond cure. On the fourth day after his accident he expired in the forty-ninth year of his age and the twenty-sixth of his reign, including the 16 years of his banishment from his capital."

141 This is meant for Bairam Khan, the faithful follower of Humayun, and, later on, the Atabek (tutor) of Ekber.

142 On modern English maps of India, these names are given as Sonpat, Panipat, Karnal, Tanesar, and Samani, in the same order on the way from Delhi to Lahore.

143 Very striking is the want of reserve wherewith this lie is

459

spread to serve a political purpose.

144 Matchivara, a town in Punjab in Ludiana.

145 Perhaps Bachrewan, a town in the province of Oudh.

146 A stronghold built by Selim Shah on the boundary mountains of Sewalik, against the Sakkars.

147 Elphinstone, "History of India," calls this man Pir Mohammed, the teacher or tutor of Ekber, while our author calls him Khodja Bairam Khan.

148 Ebul Maali, a Said from Kashgar, who had entered the service of Humayun in 1551. He had rebelled against Ekber and had taken possession of Kabul, where he was afterward defeated and imprisoned in Lahore. He died in 1563.

149 Literally, "Believers in the Book"; these, therefore, have none of the four Sacred Books, viz., Koran, Tevrat, Gospels, and Psalms. Consequently they are heathen.

150 The burning of widows (Suttee) has in recent times been put a stop to by the English, and it is very characteristic that the Moguls had, long before that time, endeavored to check the custom.

151 Also called *khutaz* and *kudaz*, a kind of horned cattle. Their tail is used as an ornament to hang round the horse's neck.

152 It appears from this passage that the Emperor's guests only received the gifts allotted to them when on their return journey; had, in fact, to collect them from the authorities of the districts through which they passed.

153 Khoshab, the name of a town in Punjab, situated on the river Djehlam, and not the name of the river itself, as our author states.

154 Nilab, "blue water," can not possibly be the river Kabul.

155 Bakhtar-Zemin, or Bakhtarland, *i.e.*, Bactria.

156 Generally translated by "rhinoceros." Baber (1356) makes mention of this animal under the name of *gherek*, and he describes it as being about the size of a buffalo.

157 Perhaps more correctly Lughman, east of Kabul.

460

<u>158</u> Hezare is the name of the mountainous region, northeast of Peshawur; also the name of an Iranian Mongol tribe, dwelling between Herat and Kabul.

<u>159</u> *Luli* is, in Central Asia, the name given to the Gipsies, to which tribe the dancing and singing damsels and the prostitutes generally belonged. This used also to be the case in Turkey; compare *Tchenghi*, "musician," "dancing girl," and *Tchingane*, "Gipsy."

<u>160</u> Kara-bag (black garden), marked on the maps merely as Bag (garden). Tcliarikar lies north of Kabul, and Pervane lies in the same direction as the pass of that name at the foot of the Hindu Kush. Our author did not take the route now generally used, across the Dendanshiken (tooth-breaker), but the other, which lies more to the east, and which was the one followed by Baber. This is one of the Pervan passes, which, starting from the place of that same name, leads to Badjgah, and from there into the valley of Enderab.

<u>161</u> Suleiman Shah was the son of Khan Mirza the Wise, a cousin of Baber's. He had usurped the throne of Bedakhshan in 1508, and was afterward established by Humayun as ruler over the whole of the Upper-Oxus territory.

<u>162</u> From the political condition already referred to, it is quite evident why our author chose this very difficult, roundabout route past Badakhshan, the same route which was taken by Sheibani Khan, Baber's adversary, during his campaign against Khosru Shah. Part of ancient Khatlan, also called Khotl, is now included in the Province of Kulab.

<u>163</u> Feizabad is now the capital of Badakhshan. It was Suleiman Shah, who made Kishm his residence.

<u>164</u> Kalai Zafar (castle of victory) is situated on the Kotchke, a tributary of the Oxus.

<u>165</u> Now Semti, on the left side of the Pendje.

<u>166</u> Now Kulab (1,810 feet above the sea), situated on a tributary of the Oxus.

<u>167</u> Neither Charsui nor Pul-i-Senghin are to be found on any modern map, but as the author identifies Hissar with Chaganian, *i.e.*, places the former in the dominion of the latter

461

province, we may take it that the Kafirnihan river was then the boundary-line of Transoxania.

168 Hissar, situated at the confluence of the Ilek and the Khanka-Derya, formerly known as Hissar-i-Shadman.

169 Probably an ancient title, which, in its present form, is not mentioned in any lexicons or vocabularies.

170 Senghirdek is mentioned on the modern maps of Central Asia, between Sehri-Sebz and Sari-Asiya (Yellow Mill), as the name of a stream and of a place, but not as the name of a mountain. *Sengghirdek* means "a stone tent."

171 This must be Mount Karatepe (Black Hill), (5181 feet).

172 Borak Khan, a son of Mahmud Khan, who was defeated by Sheibani. He was a native of the steppes in the northeast of Transoxania, and, favored by the bad government of Burhan Khan, he and his horsemen, consisting of Kirghises and Kalmuks, invaded the land, and took possession of the capital, Samarkand. He died in the year 1555. The incidents connected with his reign, which our author mentions, are the more valuable to us as we find no mention of them anywhere else.

173 He died in the year 1551.

174 Called by abbreviation Burhan Khan, an uncle of Obeidullah. He reigned only a short time, and died in 1556.

175 Aga of the Osmans was the title of a commander of the Janissaries which Sultan Suleiman had sent from Constantinople to Samarkand to support the authority of the Eastern Turks. Our author, therefore, came here unexpectedly in contact with his countrymen.

176 Khodja Ahmed Jesewi, the patron saint of Turkestan, whose grave in Aulia Ata is to this day eagerly visited by pilgrims.

177 When in Samarkand I could learn nothing about the cloak and the *Naalin* (wooden shoes) of the Prophet, but the copy of the Koran here referred to was extant in the Mausoleum of Timur. This latter, however, although a very old manuscript in Kufi letters, has not descended from Caliph Ali, nor yet from Caliph Osman; it has been brought to Turkestan by the descendants of Khodja Ahrar, and from

462

Samarkand the Russians took it to St. Petersburg.

178 Consequently they belonged at that time still to the Shaman faith, an interesting fact and easily explained when we consider that, at the time of Timur, both Kirghizes and Turkomans are described as heathen.

179 Its name is Zerefshan, or Kohik.

180 Ghidjduvan, the most northerly town of the Khanate on the Wafkend river.

181 May stand for colored coat, and merely indicates the distinguishing color of the regiment.

182 Literally, "Red feet," meaning people that go barefoot, hence the expressions, "vagabond," and "vagrant."

183 Tchardjui (more correctly Tchihar-djui, meaning "four brooks," after four tributaries of the Oxus which are there) was at that time Persian territory, and came only to be reckoned to Bokhara after the seizure of Abdullah Khan.

184 Name of the Shiite saint in Meshed.

185 Consequently the left side of the river.

186 Curious it seems that 300 years ago lions were so plentiful in those parts, while in modern times there has been no sign of them in the steppes of Turkestan.

187 In the text called Hezarus, by mistake.

188 Dost Mohammed Khan, or simply Dost, who was then the ruler of Kharezm, and his brother Esh-Sultan, were both sons of Budjuga Khan. Their rival to the throne was Hadjim Khan, who conquered both in turn and put them to death.

189 The tribe of the Manghit, now belonging to the settled population of Khiwa, seems at that time still to have led a nomadic life, inhabiting the steppe between the Aral and the Caspian Sea, now the home of the Kirghizes.

190 The Nomads of Central Asia feared the Russians, for three years before that time (1554) Czar Ivan Wassilyewich had conquered Astrakhan.

191 By Deshti-Kipchak, *i.e.*, the steppe of the Kipchaks, Oriental writers understand the steppe situated between Kharezm and the Volga territory. Ibn Batuta likewise accomplished the distance between Kharezm (now Urghendj) and Saraidjik in 30 days.

192 Saraidjik, small palace on the bank of the Ural, about one hour's distance from the Caspian Sea. Jenkinson in 1558 found the place still intact, but Pallas in the past century found only extensive ruins to indicate the place.

193 Ancient Theodosia in the Crimea.

194 At that time the King of Persia was Thamasp Shah, and it so happened that he was on friendly terms with Sultan Suleiman, for about this time a gorgeous ambassy was sent by the ruler of the Ottoman Empire to Kazvin, as recorded by Rauzat es Sefa in the Seventh Book.

195 *Istikhare*, "horoscope," is consulted by opening the Koran at hazard and the passage at which it opens gives the answer. Another way is by the throwing of dice, or by seizing the rosary (*Tesbih*) at hazard, when the even or uneven number of the beads decides the question.

196 This passage is of special geographical interest. As our author came from Kharezm, on the left shore of the Oxus, and crossed the river on his way to Khorassan, he refers here undoubtedly to the old course of this river, mentioned by Abulgazi. As the Oxus, in its course down-stream from Tchardjui, reveals several old river-beds, the direction here indicated by Sidi Ali must be one of the two courses which ran either from Hezaresp or from Khanka in southwesterly direction into the Caspian Sea. Most likely it was the latter branch, as it was at that time the more important of the two, and, according to Abulgazi, culture had reached a considerable height along its shores.

197 This is Derum, frequently mentioned by Abulgazi, as situated on the old road from Kharezm to Khorassan.

198 Bagwai, on the same road, but is now no longer marked on the map.

199 Nesa, frequently mentioned in the Middle Ages,

situated in the north of Persia. Its ruins have been visited by many modern travelers in the neighborhood of Ashkabad.

200 Abiwerd is more correct; it is the modern Kahka, a station on the Trans-Caspian line.

201 Curiously enough, the same custom still prevails in Persia, for when I visited this land three hundred years later, disguised as an Osmanli, I had much to suffer from the indiscretion of the Shiite fanatics. By night and by day, on the march and at rest, it was always this same vexed question of the succession, which had to be discussed.

202 *Murabba*, "quatrain," a poem consisting of four-line verses.

203 Ashura days, the first ten days of the month Muharram, which, especially in the Shiite part of Persia, were kept as holy days.

204 *Boluk-Bashi*, a degree of rank amongst the Janissaries; literally, "captain of a division."

205 In the immediate vicinity of Teheran.

206 *Kurdji-bashi*, "chief armor-bearer."

207 This surely must mean a month and a half after entering Persia, for the distance from Rei (Teheran) to Kazvin can easily be accomplished in two or three days. Kazvin was at that time the capital of Persia.

208 *Divan Bey*, "first secretary."

209 *Ishik Agasi*, "chief porter," a sort of master of ceremonies.

210 Literally, "representative"; at the court of the Shah it is also the title of the overseer over the culinary department.

211 *Tumen* means "ducat" in Persian, but as the word is here used in the dative it would appear that something has been omitted.

212 The Circassians were at that time not yet Mohammedans, for they were converted later on by Ferrukh Pasha.

It appears from this passage that the Pilgrims' route from

Central Asia to Mecca led in those days past Astrakhan, *i.e.,* by Kharezm and the lower Volga, and from there across the Caucasus via Constantinople to Arabia, about the same as in modern times, when pilgrims travel by the Trans-Caspian line, via Batum Baku and Constantinople to Mecca.

213 Lakh, about $500,000, a sum only used in India.

214 Our author refers here to the Feudal system still in use in Central Asia at the time that I was there, and he rightly criticizes the limited power of the rulers, which is the necessary result of it. In Persia the relation between the Khans and the Shah was based upon this principle till quite within modern times. The Sultans of Turkey, when at the zenith of their power, were absolute sovereigns of their land. But at the commencement of the decline the same relationship was established there, as we see from the conduct of the Derebeys.

215 *Demtiz* means "some one possessing strong, *i.e.,* active or powerful *dem* or *nefes* (breath)."

216 *Huma,* name of a mythical bird, a kind of Phoenix, which, as the legend says, lives in the air and never touches the earth, and is held to be a good omen. Thus, for instance, any one who has been overshadowed by this bird is destined to be a ruler. Hence the word *Humayun, i.e.,* "Imperial," an epithet applied to royal persons.

217 *Tokuz Olum,* signifying "nine fords" (if *Olum* be taken for the Turkoman word of the same meaning), is not known as the name of a great river, because, besides the Tigris, there are no large rivers in the neighborhood of Bagdad.

218 *Chashneghir, i.e.,* "cup-bearer," probably the name of the builder.

219 Iznikmid, now Ismid, has better preserved the ancient Greek name.

220 *Timar Defterdarlighi, i.e.,* superintendent of the finances of the army.

www.ingramcontent.com/pod-product-compliance
Lightning Source LLC
Chambersburg PA
CBHW031048110726
47900CB00003B/845